DESDAEMONA

Writing as Chaz Brenchley

The Samaritan
The Refuge
The Garden
Mall Time
Paradise
Blood Waters
Dispossession
Shelter

THE BEN MACALLAN NOVELS
Dead of Light
Light Errant

THE BOOKS OF OUTREMER
Tower of the King's Daughter
Feast of the King's Shadow
Hand of the King's Evil

SELLING WATER BY THE RIVER
River of the World
Bridge of Dreams

PHANTOMS AT THE PHIL (*Editor*)
The First Proceedings
The Second Proceedings
The Third Proceedings

Writing as Daniel Fox

MOSHUI: THE BOOKS OF STONE AND WATER
Dragon in Chains
Jade Man's Skin
Hidden Cities

Writing as Carol Trent

Time Again

DESDAEMONA

Ben Macallan

SOLARIS

First published 2011 by Solaris
an imprint of Rebellion Publishing Ltd,
Riverside House, Osney Mead,
Oxford, OX1 0ES, UK

www.solarisbooks.com

ISBN: 978 1 907519 63 5

10 9 8 7 6 5 4 3 2 1

A CIP catalogue record for this book is available from the
British Library.

Designed & typeset by Rebellion Publishing

Printed in the US

For Karen.

When life handed me lemons,
she gave me a tree to hang them on.

CHAPTER ONE

I MIGHT NEVER have found Sarah in time, if it hadn't been for the banshee.

For once in my life I had a comfortable room with a lock on the door, I'd paid the rent, I wasn't looking to move on for a while. It was only habit that took me down to the bus station that night. If restlessness can be a habit. Another boy in another life might go clubbing, dancing, drinking with his mates; me, I want to run. If I won't let myself do that, I have to walk. Maybe to the edge of town, downriver if there is a river: pushing the boundaries, wondering what comes next, where I'm headed and how soon.

Often, one way or another, I'll wind up at the bus station. Just checking in, checking timetables. Keeping an eye out, an ear open.

That night, I could hear it from three streets away. If you've never heard a banshee wail – and you likely never have – it's like a wet finger on the rim of a glass, except that the finger's wet with blood and the glass has shattered. It cuts through you like a broken blade, as sharp as rust can make it. It starts low and then screeches higher and louder, seeking the resonance of pain. It makes you want to sob, to shriek back, to cover your ears and run away; it makes you want to collapse and huddle in on yourself, shivering against the cold, cruel truth of the thing; it makes you want to go to the toilet, right there and then.

Some people do.

And we're the lucky ones, those it isn't wailing at. What it's like to be the banshee's focus, the wailee – well, I wouldn't know. You have to be family, and I'm not.

I heard it that night, though, and knew what it was, straight off. There's nothing like it. I had my bag on my shoulder; I rummaged, found what I needed, started to run.

Towards the bus station, towards the banshee, into the heart of that cry.

I'm not especially brave, don't think that. Just experienced. I've been out there a long time, and mostly I know what to do. And I've always been small, I've always stood out, I've been an object of attention all my life; I hate bullies, even if it's not me they're picking on. I know what it's like to be afraid all the time, every hour of every day. Banshees trade on that, it's their life-blood.

You really do have to hate a banshee.

So I RAN, straight for it. If the people I passed thought anything about me at all, they would just have thought I was a kid with mad hair running for a bus. They wouldn't be hearing the banshee; most people don't. Only the one it's singing to, and all their family round about.

Their family and me, obviously. I'm special that way.

The bus station needed upgrading, badly. It needed shiny new stands and plate-glass waiting areas, bright lights, CCTV. Instead it had high walls and dark corners, mean little windows and no security. Beside the concourse was a garage tall enough to take the double-deckers, all closed up and quiet at this time of night; between the two was an alleyway of rough ground where nothing was lit up, nothing looked out. There was just enough moonlight shafting down to show you what was going on, if you didn't mind watching in black and white.

The girl was pressed up against the wall there, past screaming now, past running, past helping herself or looking for someone else to help her. The banshee stood at the head of the alley, gloating, rubbing her hands. Wailing.

Sometimes they're beautiful, banshees: truly gorgeous young women. Sometimes they're motherly and you'd want to trust them, go to them, depend on them, if it wasn't for that wicked, wicked voice.

This one was the third option, a crone, bent and haggard and wrapped in a greasy grey shroud. That made it easier.

She lifted her hands, her voice rising in a shrill crescendo that made my belly twist like there was a knife in it. I stepped up quickly, ripped that rotting shroud off her head, stuck the trumpet of an air-horn in her ear and blew her away.

* * *

I F THERE'S ONE thing banshees can't stand, it's being drowned out by something louder. Where's the fun if you can't hear yourself shriek, where's the point if your victim can't hear you either?

Sometimes they fight. The young have nails – dirty nails, usually – while the motherly have weight, and can be vicious with it. This crone might have had the wiry strength of the very old and the very mad, but she didn't have the courage to go with it. She glared, she cursed, she spat at me; I gave her another blast of the horn, and she slunk away.

People were looking, of course. You can't let an air-horn go in public and expect not to be stared at. All they'd see was a kid, though, apparently on his own in the mouth of an alley. Making a nuisance of himself, but hey, no damage done. Why get involved?

Me, I have to get involved. I walked into the shadows of that alley, to where the girl was sliding down the wall like her legs wouldn't hold her up any longer.

I thought they'd done amazingly well, holding her up as long as they had. She was tougher than she knew, this kid.

And scared too, more scared than she'd ever known she could be. I knew how that felt.

I gave her a bit of distance, dropping to my haunches the opposite side of the alley, a six-foot stretch away, not to loom over her. Put a smile in my voice and said, "Okay, then?"

Stupid question, deliberately. I wanted to get the measure of her, see if I got a stupid answer or a stroppy one.

Or neither. She only stared at me, wordless. Letting me see just how not-okay she was.

Fair enough. I said, "Do you want anything? No

need to move, I could fetch you coffee, a Coke. Or hot chocolate, warm and sweet, do you good..."

She shook her head urgently. "Please, no – don't leave me, not here..."

Her voice was hoarse, from screaming or from shock, but there was a hint of Irish under all the strain of it. No surprise there, then.

"You could come with."

"No!" That was sharper, a jagged little cry that must have hurt her throat.

"Come on. You know enough to be afraid of the dark; why stay where the shadows are?"

She was mute again, shaking her head. It's a natural thing, a human thing; even when it's creatures of the night you're running from, you still shrink from the light. Darkness is for hiding in. That's hard-wired, but sometimes it's just wrong.

Who's after you, then, little girl?

She wasn't ready to tell me yet; I just asked her name.

"Sarah."

"Sarah what – Kavanagh? O'Brien?"

Her little gasp was a giveaway.

"Relax, I'm not magic. I don't do mind-reading. There are only five families the banshees are let haunt. They stretch a point these days, when so many girls marry out of the clan, but chances were you'd have the family name. You did know that was a banshee, right?"

She nodded. Of course she did. Grandma's tales, children's games; maybe she'd even heard one for real, in the family home before Grandma died.

"You know what it means?"

This time she didn't nod. She told me, flat and final. Brave girl, she only looked about sixteen, and she said, "It means I'm going to die."

"Nah, that's what it wants you to think. Banshees are greedy, they jump the gun, they try to make it happen. Maybe they'll get lucky, scare you to death. See, nobody audits them, no one checks up. They're not always right. 'Specially nowadays, when the bloodlines are so thin. Sometimes they don't know, they're guessing or hoping or playing the odds."

"It's right about me," she said stubbornly. "I'm pure O'Brien, nothing thin in my blood."

"And what, then, you're going to die of pride, is that it?"

"No." She was talking to her knees now, where she hugged them to her chest. "It, it knows what I saw, what I did, what's coming after me."

"Oh? What's that, then?"

"You wouldn't..." I would, though, and I watched her realise it. Didn't I just scare a banshee off, and wasn't that just as unbelievable? Maybe I would believe her. But – "How come you knew about the banshee, how come you heard her?"

"Just lucky, I guess. Lucky that I knew what to do, too." I let that sink in, which one of us had actually been lucky tonight, and then I pressed her. "What happened, Sarah? What did you see, to start all this?"

"It was... nothing. I thought it was nothing, nothing that mattered. Just nasty, a pack of dogs savaging a cat in this bit of woodland back home."

"And what, you interfered?"

"Yes, of course. They were big dogs, but I had this can of pepper-spray, my uncle brought it back from America and he made me promise to keep it with me, it goes on my key-ring, see? So I gave them a faceful. I think the cat got a bit too, it squawled and shot straight up a tree; but the dogs were rolling and pawing at their faces and yelping, and I thought that was that, it was over..."

"And then?" I could have made it easy for her, I could guess what was coming, but it'd do her good to spell it out.

"And then, I started to walk away but I thought, I thought I could hear voices in all the noise they were making. So I looked back, and they, they weren't dogs any more. Not properly. Like men in dog-costumes, they were, and more like men every moment; and then one of them lifted its head and stared straight at me, and it was a human face for sure, and it howled at me like a, like a..."

"Like a wolf," I finished for her, just the one small act of kindness.

She nodded. "I thought they were dogs, see? That's all, just big dogs..."

Throwing pepper in a dog's face, it's a classic. So she pepper-sprayed a pack of werewolves at play, all unknowing, just to save a stray cat; and now –

"How long have they been hunting you?"

"Three days," she said in a small voice. "I've been taking buses all the time, off one and straight onto another, and they're still following. And I've got no money left, there's nowhere to go now. And the banshee found me, and..."

And she thought she was doomed, dead bones walking. Except that she wasn't walking any more, she was just going to sit there and wait for them to find her.

It wouldn't be long now. One thing wolves are good at, it's being relentless. Running down prey. Now that I knew to listen for it, I could hear a howling on the wind. She'd been hearing that for three days, except when the banshee drowned it out.

I said, "All right, sweetheart. Here" – a bottle of water and a Mars bar from my backpack – "get this inside yourself, you'll feel better. Trust me, I'm a teenager."

She squinted at me through the shadows, didn't reach to take what I was offering. "Are you? Really?"

"Really truly. Seventeen."

"That's what you look like, more or less. Only you sound older. A lot."

"Yeah, I know. I've been seventeen for a long time now."

"I don't understand."

"No," I said, "that's right. You don't." *You never will.* "Now take," and I shifted to sit next to her, took her wrist in mine, unfolded cold stiff fingers and pressed the Mars bar into them, "eat, this is my chocolate which is given to you."

She choked down a painful little giggle, and started to fumble at the wrapper. A moment later she looked startled at her own forgetfulness, shook her head at me, said, "You, you can't stay, they'll hurt you too..."

"Not them. Trust me." Again, although this was a bigger ask. "I'm stronger than I look."

Her eyes were sceptical, and quite right too; that was a lie, straight and simple. I was exactly what I looked like, small and slender and scared. Only, it wasn't werewolves I was scared of. Which was something else I hoped she'd never understand.

After that, we didn't talk much. She ate; we waited. An alley was as good as anywhere.

Other people must have heard the howling as they came, but I suppose they'd put it down to dogs, the wind, whatever. Kids messing around. You see what you expect to see; even Sarah had thought dogs, even while she was looking straight at them.

I saw wolves, three of them, although they came loping across the tarmac in human form: boys in tracksuits, trainers, sweat. I could well believe that they'd been running for three days. The alley steamed, it roiled with the sour reek of hot wet dogs.

Sarah had her pepper-spray in her hand, but it would do her no good now. It wasn't a cat these three were after killing.

I signed for her to stay still, where she was, against the wall. Me, I stood up and took a pace or two towards them.

Their eyes were yellow, rimmed with red. Pepper-spray burns for a long, long time. Where they met my gaze, they flinched and looked away. Dogs are still dogs, whatever their ancestry. *Three of them,* I thought, *and I can face them down, just glower them away, win the cheapest victory of my life...*

But then there was a growl behind me, from the alley's other end. I heard Sarah's low terrified moan, and realised I'd been outflanked. I should have asked, how many. When I glanced back I saw one more, low and massive, wolf-form, pacing forward on stiff legs. He must have listened to his mother as a pup: *eyes and teeth, dear, eyes and teeth.*

The moment that I turned my head, the other three came at me.

I only had a second, so I did the only thing I could. I held my hand up high where they could see it, and shrieked my true name into the dank and rancid air.

WOLVES CAN'T COUNT, but boys can. The three of them stopped dead, a metre short of tearing me apart. They looked to the other one, I guess he was pack leader, but my name had been enough for him.

He was already slinking out of the alley, away into the night.

"Go on, then," I said wearily. "Get after him. And leave the kid alone. She's with me."

That was another lie, but I was getting away with some of them tonight. Those lads ran, and didn't look back.

I dropped beside Sarah again, felt the weight of her gaze like a question; didn't respond until she put it into words, one word, "Jordan?"

"That's my name."

"Why did they run away?"

Because that's what people do, when you give them a reason good enough. Dogs too, apparently. I didn't say that aloud, but maybe something of it showed in my face. I could feel her inching away from me.

"You said you weren't magic."

"I'm not."

"So why did they run?" When I still didn't answer, she tried to work it out for herself: "Just, just your name, and your hand, something about your hand..."

Girls can't count, apparently, or not in moonlight. I showed her, up close.

"Six fingers on my left. Like Anne Boleyn. That and the name told them who I am."

"So who are you? Someone to be scared of?"

"Not really. Not yet." Although I could be, if I only got a little older. "It's not me," I said, "it's the people looking for me. They're much, much scarier than werewolves. They'd be angry, if those guys tore me up in pieces. On the other hand, they'll be really happy if I get turned in as I am." Safe and sound and stupid, giving myself away. Again. "That's what's happening now, the boys have run off to spread the news where it'll do them most good." Give the dog a bone. "Which means we've got to move, right now. Will you be all right to go home? They won't bother you again, I promise." Too busy with other stuff, bothering me.

She nodded, but, "I haven't got any money."

"That's all right, I'll buy your ticket. And your mum's got a mobile, yes? Give me the number, I'll tell her to meet you at the other end."

"Oh God, she'll be so..."

"*Relieved* is the word you're looking for." Though it'd probably show up as anger, at least to start with. "Keep schtum about the wolves, yeah? You can say about the banshee, say that's why you ran. Say you met a boy who scared it off with an airhorn." I thought she'd done better, driving off four werewolves with a pepper-spray, but it'd be best if her mother kept her close for a while.

Some things the mortal world is good for; there was a late coach that would take her all the way. I waited to see her aboard, although that half-hour was a price in terror that I struggled to keep hidden. I flashed her with my mobile as she climbed the steps, and again as she waved through the window; I watched the bus pull away, and then I phoned her mother.

"Mrs O'Brien? You don't know me, but I have news about your daughter... No, please don't worry, she's on a bus and she's coming home... Something frightened her, that's all, and she had to run. That's the way it happens sometimes. She's fine now, I promise." I told her when Sarah was due in, endured her rush of thanks and then, "I'm sorry, but did you offer a reward, for information...? Well, yes, I would... No, no, this isn't any kind of threat. I told you, she's on the bus already, on her way. There's nothing I can do to alter that. Look, I'm sending you a picture now to prove it."

Mobile phones make this all so much easier; kidnappers must love them. So do I. Once she had the photos, once she was reassured, I got back to business. "This is how I live, you see, Mrs O'Brien. I find missing people, and when I can, I send them home. Sometimes people are grateful, sometimes they pay me. There's no obligation, no contract, but – well, I've bought Sarah's ticket tonight, to fetch her back to you. And if you offered the reward already, and if you're truly glad to have your daughter safe..."

I gave her my PayPal account, and left it to her conscience. Come the morning, waking up to a house with Sarah in it rather than a house full of empty, I thought she'd pay something at least. Mothers usually do.

I hoped she would, because this night was costing me, more than just one ticket. Word spreads fast, when wolves are howling. Never mind the bedsit with its rent all paid, never mind the things left behind; I got on the next bus out. Everything I needed, I carried in my bag or in my pockets. Even the bag was simply handy, nothing crucial. It was the first lesson I'd learned on the road, on the run; anything outside my skin could be replaced.

Second lesson, anyone outside my skin couldn't be trusted, and I didn't trust myself that well. I'd been let down too often.

I sat and gazed at my reflection in the dark of the window, fiddling with my hair. I'd had it green for a month now, green and spiky; that'd have to go. I could take it darker, maroon or blue or all the way back to black. Better to shave it, though, and start again.

Start again. Slide down the ladder, all the way back to the beginning. New town, new streets, new dangers. I couldn't think how long I'd been doing this, I didn't dare let myself remember. I still had all the energy of seventeen, that's what kept me going; but I had the black moods too, the aching loneliness, the utter certainty that nothing was ever going to change for the better.

In my case, of course, that was absolutely true.

I tucked my bag against the window, my head against the bag, and fell asleep as the bus rolled on.

CHAPTER TWO

"HI."

She was tall, she was gorgeous, she was sitting opposite me.

New town, new troubles. That's a rule. Every now and then I get complacent; I start to think that I've been everywhere, seen it all, nothing's going to surprise me now. On my bad days, I can look out of a bus window and anticipate just what kind of trouble I'm coming into. It's not prophecy, there is no gift of foresight in my family. It's just the arrogance of experience. Once you start thinking that way, that you can see what's coming round the corner, you really are in trouble.

Every time I get that cocky, or that bored, something comes out of left field and bites me.

This particular day, I was in a seafront café, killing time. The last customer had left his paper on the table, so rather than sitting and staring out over the stony beach, watching the tide come in, I was struggling with that day's Sudoku. My plan was to read the paper cover to cover and solve all the puzzles before I even started the sitting-and-staring thing. With luck, that might last me from one tide to the next. I'm not very good at puzzles.

What I hadn't anticipated – well, why would I? – was this girl, swinging into an empty chair at my table, when she might have sat anywhere. Me, I was eking out a frugal filter coffee; she had a thimble-sized espresso that must have cost her twice as much, and a giant triple-choc muffin that would have fed me for a day. Living on the run, you spend a lot of time in public spaces, surrounded by treats you daren't afford. A muffin today could be fish and chips tomorrow, a drink the next day, drunk the day after. Next thing you know there's a good jacket on your back, new boots on your feet and you're begging in doorways because you've got nothing left. No money, no pride, no resistance.

If I do that, I'm dead. And not in a good way, not rest-in-peace and pushing up the daisies. I wouldn't mind that. I could push up daisies quite happily, from now till the sun turns nova. I like daisies. Even from underneath.

No, these people I'm avoiding – I call them people, I'm generous like that – they would make me very badly dead, and never let me lie down after. I need to stay on my feet, I need to stay sharp and sober; I need cash in my pocket and more in the bank, something for a rainy day. It rains a lot where I come from, more where I'm going.

So, no muffins for me. Usually no muffin-toting girls either, I'm scrupulous about that. I only talk to girls when they're in trouble already. They don't need my troubles coming after them.

This one had come to me, though, picked me out. I thought she was trouble from the start. I don't read minds and I can't see the future, but call it instinct or experience, something was prickling my spine.

You could call it something else, if you wanted: adolescence, hormones, lust. Being seventeen. That doesn't go away, however long you practise.

"Hullo," I said politely, warily.

She was long and slim and very neatly put together, dark hair tumbling over denim, old worn black jacket and jeans that somehow hadn't faded into grey. They probably didn't dare. Right from the start I saw a focus in her, a determination that must go all the way through, like the writing in a stick of Brighton rock. In another world, another lifetime, I thought she'd have raven-feathers in her hair, a bear's tooth on a thong around her neck, the smell of strange herbs about her. She'd be the village shaman, talking to spirits, and even the headman would be afraid of her, a little...

Seventeen. I told you. She was devastating to me, she was sitting at my table, and I couldn't afford her. Not for a minute.

If I'd stood up, if I'd left, if I'd run away...

Nah. She would just have come after me. Faster, fitter, and on longer legs. What chance did I ever have?

She picked a chocolate chip out of her muffin, nipped it delicately between sharp white teeth, then pushed the plate towards me.

"Go on, you know you want to."

I was used to offering help to strangers, people in need. Having it offered to me, that was new, and I wasn't sure I liked it.

"I'm sorry," I said, "I don't think I know you?"

"And you're far too nicely trained to take food from a stranger. Sure. My name's Desi. What should I call you?"

"Michael." Easy to remember, easy to forget; a name with no significance. I'd long since quit playing games with names. "Do you often offer to feed stray boys, Desi?"

"Only when they're sitting in a café surrounded by good things and looking as hungry as you do."

"That's got to include half the boys you ever see in cafés." Hunger goes with the territory; it's a genetic flaw. Young males need to be chewing.

"And when I want to talk to them anyway. It's a bribe. Eat it quick, before I change my mind."

She didn't mean that; she wasn't going anywhere. More's the pity.

I still wasn't biting. I said, "Why me?" If I'd been a regular lad about town, relaxed and easy and looking to play, she would still have been way out of my league. I couldn't match her physically, socially, any way you want to count. She knew that; we both did.

"Because I know who you are, and your name's not Michael. I've been waiting for you."

IT FELT LIKE falling off a ladder. That way time slows down all in a moment as you realise you're going, then the desperate casting around for something, anything to grab hold of, and at last some kind of acceptance, letting go of hope, almost giving yourself permission to fall in the split second before you do.

This was the moment I'd been running from so long, and I guess maybe I'd persuaded myself that it was never going to catch up. Now suddenly here it was, and this wasn't the way I'd imagined it at all, quietly in a café by the sea. I'd expected thunder, special effects, a voice rolling out of the clouds and fingers of fire reaching for me...

Well, no. I'd have liked that, maybe. If it had to come, it could do me that last little courtesy, a touch of drama to make it all seem worth while.

It had come in the shape of a deeply attractive girl instead, and I was desperate to get away from her, one last chance at running. She was smart, though, sitting between me and the door; I'd never get there. Even if my legs would carry me.

Once I'd stopped glancing from side to side for some impossible rescue that simply wasn't on its way, I dragged my eyes back to Desi's face. I wanted her to know just what she was doing to me, before she hauled me off to wherever her masters were waiting.

Besides, she really was very good to look at. Black brows, pale skin, cheekbones that could lay waste to a city. One last glimpse of a fierce beauty, something worth remembering. They say the image of a murderer is trapped forever in their victim's eyes; maybe it works the other way too, maybe the victim can spend eternity looking on the face of their betrayer. With this face, I didn't think I'd mind so much.

She wasn't gloating, or contemptuous, or even just mercenary-cold and practical. If anything, she looked puzzled.

Puzzled, but quick; she caught on before I did. I had an excuse, though. Bowel-loosening terror, that's excuse enough for me. No blame if I was thinking slowly.

"Oh," she said. "No," she said, "not that. I'm not here to hand you over. Who do you think I am?"

I ran my hand over my face, and found it slicked with a chilly sweat. Charming. "Lady," I croaked, losing my voice along with my dignity, my brains, almost everything I value, "you're the bright one. Why don't you tell me? I haven't a clue who you are."

"My name," she said again, "is Desi. And I've got a job for you. Wait there."

I suppose I could have made a dash for it, while she was at the counter. I wouldn't have fancied my chances, though. I did what she told me, waited there, struggling to recover. She came back with a tray.

For her, there was another jolt of espresso. For me there was fresh coffee, sandwiches, fruit.

"You weren't making much headway on that muffin," she said, "so...?"

I'd have got there, given time. Hell, I still would; I'd take it all, and gladly. Once I trusted her.

"I don't know who you think I am," I said, lying through my teeth, and pointlessly, "but tell me how you found me?"

"Statistical analysis," which was what, the third time she'd startled me. She smiled, when she saw that. "I do know who you are, because you wouldn't be here else. And you wouldn't have shaved your head, and you wouldn't be hiding your left hand in your lap that way. I've studied all the reports on you, all the rumours, all those places you turn up without warning. That's how I found you. You may have thought there wasn't a pattern, but of course there is. Nothing's ever truly random, Jordan, it all comes down to numbers in the end."

"Please don't use that name," I said.

"No?"

"No." It was a bad habit to get into, because you could never tell who might be listening, tomorrow if not today, there if not here.

"All right, then. So long as you stop pretending it isn't you."

I shrugged. "You were talking about patterns, numbers?"

"Yup. Bus routes, mostly. Don't worry, I don't think anyone else has figured it out yet. Probably nobody else has put a computer onto you." And she tapped the bag at her side, just the size and shape to carry a laptop. "But mine has been tracking you for months, and... Why are you laughing?"

I couldn't tell her that. It wasn't funny at all, but: "I can't believe it. That's how you found me, with a computer? You're a geek, is what you're telling me?"

"You should be glad, I seem to be the only one."

She was right, of course. The others had the habits of centuries to slow them down, they still depended on signs and scents and whispers. They were more likely to cast runes and argue over omens than they were to code software.

"Okay," I said, "I'll try to be glad. Meanwhile, tell me about this job." I had to know what had driven her to hunt me down, when people so very much older than her had been trying for so very long.

"I want you to find my sister," she said.

"Oh." Such a shame, all that clever computer-work for nothing. "Lady –"

"Desi."

"Desi, I'm sorry, but you really have got the wrong guy. I'm not a detective."

"No, but that's what you do, isn't it? You find lost people?"

"I guess. But I do it the other way around. I start with someone who's lost, find out who they are and what happened, point them back home if I can. I don't go looking for particular people, absolutely not."

"Why not?"

"For my own safety. I can't rent an office, hang a sign up on the door..."

"You don't have to. I found you anyway."

Ouch. I was busily trying not to think about that. "Look, it's just not what I do, okay?"

"Maybe it's time you did. You can't go on living the way you are. What you need to do is break the pattern. Deliberately start doing something else, acting differently. Looking for my sister."

She was pleased with that, and it showed; her smile hit me like an arc-light in the darkness, like a length of two-by-four.

That wasn't fair, she was taking advantage. And she knew it. I chewed my way through a BLT, trying to summon up killer arguments to match, failing entirely. I could just go on saying *no*, and eventually she'd have to give up and go away – wouldn't she? – but it felt weak.

Besides, she might take the sandwiches with her.

"I'm not saying yes," I told her firmly, "but – well, tell me about her, okay? How you lost her, why she went..." *You talk, while I eat*.

Desi nodded. "I'll talk," she said, "while you eat. Good plan."

I glowered at her, ducking another of those lethal smiles. If God was on the side of the big battalions, I might as well surrender now; I was out-thought, outgunned, outmanoeuvred, comprehensively outclassed here. There was only the one of her, but I even felt outnumbered.

She said, "My sister's not like me – what?"

Oh, hell. I'd been thinking *that's a relief*, there was only the one of her; I must have mumbled it aloud. That can get to be a habit, when you spend too much time alone. At least she hadn't heard it clearly, around a mouthful of bread. I shook my head, swallowed, said, "Nothing. Sorry. Go on about your sister."

She was magnificent even when she frowned, this dark fearsome beauty. I basked in her displeasure, for what little time it lasted; then she shrugged and went on. "She gets scared when she's out of her depth, she can't deal. So she runs away." All too obviously, Desi couldn't imagine that quality of fear, but she wasn't being judgmental. She didn't judge her sister, she wasn't judging me.

"She's done this before?"

"All her life."

"Where does she go, then? When she runs?"

"It depends. Wherever she feels safe. Sometimes that means people, long-time friends; sometimes it means places, old haunts, where she was happy."

"Okay, you know what she does, you know what she looks for; you know her better than I ever will. I'm sorry, Desi, but I'm still not getting this. Why do you think you need me?"

"Because I have looked in all those places," she said, with the exaggerated patience of somebody who was running very short of temper, "and I have talked to all those people, and she is not there. Trust me, I'm not wasting my time. I'm good at this – I found you, didn't I? – but I can't find her. Which is why I've spent months tracking you down, because I think maybe you can. I know about looking, how to search; what you know about is hiding, how to avoid a search. You know more about that than anyone else I can think of."

I didn't know enough, obviously. I hadn't avoided her. She could see the irony, as easily as I could.

There was something magnificent in the way we both ignored it.

"What happens if I say no? Do you blackmail me, threaten to hand me over...?" That was the tradition in fiction. I should know, I think sometimes I've read it all. Public libraries are better than bus stations for hanging out in when you have long empty days to fill, and I was irresistibly drawn to books about kids on the run.

"No," she said, still in that extremity of patience, making a great exhibition of her self-control. "I don't do that. I get up and walk out and think of something else. It just won't be as good as this."

"Perhaps you'd better do that, then. If I go around with you, asking questions, making myself visible – well, it's not exactly hiding, is it?"

"Hiding in plain sight, there's nothing better. You'll be all right, I promise. I've got your back."

I just looked at her. She was tall for a girl, taller than I am; fit, yes, whatever you want the word to mean; competent, clearly. And strong-minded, not intimidated, ready to take on the world to find her sister.

And none of that, nothing on that long list of qualities amounted to a solitary bean, against the troubles I faced if I ever came out of the shadows. She ought to know that.

Tall for a girl, fit and ready for anything, she still was a girl: slender-shouldered and lightly muscled, a match for me but not for stronger men. Against the people I was hiding from, she'd have as much chance as a match in a hurricane.

Ashamed of my own fear and mourning the loss of her already, I turned my head away. Silence could speak for me, the opposite of consent. She was smart, she'd understand. That didn't mean she'd forgive – people like her have no time for cowardice, it's the one thing they can't get their head around – but she'd get the message, that at least.

I stared out through condensation at a dull flat leaden sea that more or less reflected my own feelings, my own take on the future, grey and depressing and eternal.

She said, "Jordan."

The name snapped me back into the moment, snapped my head around again to glare at her, "I told you, don't call –"

Oof. One more time, she startled me past reason, past response. Just for a moment, between one eyeblink and the next, she took on her Aspect and showed herself to me.

She didn't move, she didn't change. She didn't grow horns or wings or fur and fangs, she didn't drop to all fours and start howling. She didn't need to. She just sat there like a teenage boy's high fantasy, eye-candy for the gods, and she let me see her other self. Just a glimpse: all I needed, all I could take without warning.

Dark hair, determined eyes, long and elegant fingers; none of that was altered, but briefly, everything was different. In the silence I could hear the clamour of a distant war, I could smell the copper taste of blood in the air, but that was incidental. She was the focus, she was the source. Her shadow overhung me, the café, the whole damn town. She could stretch out her hand and crush it, if she chose.

She didn't choose to do that, not today. She drew it all back into herself instead, like a warrior disarming; then she smiled at me, shatteringly.

"I told you, Jordan. I've got your back."

It still wasn't enough, and she must know that. Even she, even this new she, couldn't stand against what I had ranged against me.

Even so, I was sweating, shaken, almost afraid of her again. I said, "You're a daemon."

"Yes," she said. "What did you think the name was short for?"

Desi: I'd assumed Désirée, or something equally in need of shortening. Just that little hint, though, and, "Oh, right – Desdaemona. Clever. Do you scatter handkerchiefs in your wake, for jealous boys to upset themselves?"

I was talking for its own sake, buying myself time. I think she knew that, but she played along. "I don't use handkerchiefs."

"Oh. Right." I was starting to sound like a looped sample. "No, I don't suppose you do." Daemons are still human – supposedly – but you wouldn't expect to catch one with a cold.

Thing is, the gap between us and them, between human and supernatural, it's not the unbridgeable river that most people want to think. That's a metaphor that breaks down both ways; it's certainly not unbridgeable, and it's not much like a river. More of a marsh, maybe, with solid ground on both sides and a lot of squidgy stuff between. Shifting tracks and stepping-stones that may or may not take your weight, dark pools and bogs in wait for a mis-step, teasing treacherous lights to draw you in, voices that whisper like the wind in the reeds to make promises they might keep, maybe, one day...

Some things are really no good in metaphor. You just have to say what you mean, and let it go. What I'm saying, most people are born human and die human and never come within touching-distance of any other choice. They might rub up against non-humans or not-quite-humans, no-longer-humans, every day of their lives, but absolutely nothing will rub off. Not a trace of magic, not a flicker of an uncanny moment.

The other end of the scale, that's where you find the immortals, the Powers that Be, and many of *them* were never born at all. The gods and goddesses and their closest hangers-on, angels and demons and demi-gods and such. They're mostly pure originals, untouched by any human gene-flow.

Between the two, though, between hundred-per-cent human and hundred-per-cent other, it's not a gulf at all, it's a graduation. Not a bell curve, the difference is exponential: like Mount Olympus, gods at the top and most aspirants struggling on the lower slopes, getting stuck. Falling off. But you can climb it, partway at least. You can change your luck, pick up some gene therapy, supersede your nature.

Some people get promoted. That's in the gift of the gods – or in the lap of the gods, which is worse – but any major Power can elevate a human. Give them just a lick of something extra, or raise them all the way to godhood: it's a whim thing, you can't depend on it, and it doesn't always work out for the best.

Some people manage their own promotion. Through study, achievement, recklessness, luck, any or all of those, it is possible to acquire powers that you weren't born with. Again, it's not always a good idea, but there's a lot out there who want it.

Some people start as victims and end up somewhere else, if they survive. Bullied kids grow up to be bullies in their turn. Like gangsters, vampires are made, for the most part; werewolves also start off by being bitten.

Then there are a few people, a very few – well, one, that I can think of – who will fight to stay human, not to take the least little step off into wonder. It is kind of eccentric, but it makes sense to me.

Some are born great; some achieve greatness; some have greatness thrust upon them. If you're cynical, for *great* just read *magic* throughout. But remember that those at the top really do think they're great, better than the rest of us. That's important.

Daemons, now: daemons are born human, and then they volunteer. They're mercenaries. They sign up to serve some more or less powerful being, for a specified period of time, and if they don't get ripped off or ripped up, if they survive, they leave that service with something more than they took in.

They may not be immortal, but they can be very, very long-lived. They may not bleed ichor, but some of them probably don't bleed at all. What they come away with depends on who they served and how, how long for, how well. I suppose you could sign up to do a god's paperwork, maybe data-entry in this day and age, and come away a super-clerk; mostly, they were soldiers then and they're super-soldiers now. Which makes them super-scary once they're back in the world, out on the streets and looking for work. Think 'Nam vets to the nth degree, damaged and dangerous.

Desi didn't look damaged, in her human aspect or otherwise. I'd looked her all over, more than once; I did it again now, and still couldn't see the harm. Dangerous, sure, I'd never doubted that. Even before she flashed her other self at me.

Nor did she really look old enough to have been through a Power's service. Daemons age very slowly, so she was probably older than she looked – hell, she'd have to be – but she must have volunteered unusually young. Stupidly young, though I wouldn't dare say so.

One startlingly attractive teenage girl, signing the best years of her life away: okay, there could be reasons for that. Young people can be rash. I should know. Why her master or mistress would have accepted her, that was another issue. And what she did for them, exactly, the nature of her service: that was something else again, that I was not – quite – rash enough to ask. There was a glint in her eyes and a set look to her smile that suggested she was tracking my thoughts closely, she knew where they were leading and I'd really better not go there.

Fine. Save it for later. Except that there wasn't going to be any later, because I was still going to turn her down. A daemon would be dead handy for seeing off stray werewolves and such, but that wasn't what she was offering. If she came up against the people who were hunting me, she'd just be dead, and I'd be no better off. Worse off, indeed, dead and doing...

I opened my mouth to say so, to say *no*, flat and final; and before I could make a sound, she slid a photo across the table.

This was her sister, you could see it instantly, an absolute likeness. At the same time, you could never confuse the two. Everything Desi had that made her beautiful, they shared: the hair, the skin, the bone structure. The body I had to take on trust, this was just a head-and-shoulders shot; but I'd trust her for all of that, the height and the grace and the figure that was lean without being at all boyish.

But whatever it was that Desi had to make her so magnetic, the sister was missing it. It wasn't just that I was looking at a photograph, against the reality of flesh. The girl in the picture was softer and more vulnerable; she lacked her sister's confident edge, and that electric sense of danger brewing, the whiff of ozone before the storm breaks.

Put it another way, she wasn't a daemon. Just a girl, unusually pretty perhaps but normal else, except that she looked haunted. The kind of girl you might actually make a move on, if you were a normal boy. If you could work up the courage, if she didn't run away before you got there.

"What's her name?" I asked, when all this time I'd been so utterly determined not to.

"Fay."

It suited her: dark and uncertain and full of promise. I wondered what Desi had been called before – daemons tend to choose their own names, after their release – but again decided it was wiser not to ask.

"Younger, older?"

"It depends how you want to count."

Forwards, from zero, but I knew what she meant. Desi had stepped almost out of time, being in service to a Power; the years no longer touched her as they used to. Fay must have been ageing year on year, while Desi kept all her teenage bloom. To all appearances they could have swapped entirely, younger sister suddenly seeming older by a distance.

"How old is this photo?"

"Three years. It's the last we have."

That wasn't as bad as it might have been, by an order of magnitude. Fay must have gone missing while her sister was away, but daemon-contracts tended to be counted in decades, with centuries not unheard-of. Sign away your soul for a hundred years, risk your life and more, sometimes your afterlife; if you survive, here's a vestige of immortality, another few hundred years of youth and strength. There were men and women enough who found such an offer attractive.

Just not many teenage girls.

Still, she couldn't be a centenarian, if her sister had been a teenager three years ago. She might be hopelessly out of my class, but I was relieved not to be thinking of her as a crone in biker-chic drag.

One more question, then, another that I knew I shouldn't ask:

"What's she running away from?"

A hesitation, the first I'd caught in Desi; then, "The world's a cruel place, and she found a cruel corner of it," and that was an evasion, and no use to either one of us.

She knew it, too. I only had to glance up from the photo. She shrugged an apology and said, "She fell in love. Same old, same old, right?"

"Right. I suppose it was the wrong boy?"

"Absolutely it was." And we might be effortfully flippant about it, but this was serious, this was the real thing. Her words skated casually over the surface of the story, but her voice was ploughing the depths, and it was dark down there. "He loved her too, of course, and his parents wouldn't have it, naturally. So they scared her off; I told you, she was easily scared. So she ran for home."

"And he came after her?"

"No, not that. She found she was pregnant."

Ouch. "And?"

"And she got rid of it; but he found out, and then so did his parents."

"And what?" Suddenly I was lost. "Were they Catholic or something?" A lot of people disapprove of abortion; but if they disapproved of the girl anyway, to the point of chasing her away, I didn't think they had a moral leg to stand on.

"Jordan." One more time, my true name, with a weight of impatience behind it. "Are you always this slow? The boy was an immortal; both his parents are Powers."

Oh, hell. In a very literal sense, very likely. *Some are born great:* the baby would have had some touch of the supernatural, at least. With a pureblood father, it might have had a great deal more. They don't breed true; it's impossible to predict, but sometimes immortal blood can overwhelm the mortal and make a Power in a human womb.

They might have been parent, grandparents to a demigod, a major player in the world; and scared little Fay had destroyed it, cast it out.

"Now I understand why you came to me."

"Finally!" But she wasn't really teasing. Her fingertips touched mine, across the table. I have no idea what she felt, but I felt like a lightning-conductor doing my job, taking the full charge all through me. It can be like that, when merely human skin meets something more potent.

Of course, it can also be like that when a boy is blessed – or tormented – by the touch of a girl he doesn't dare fancy.

"You've spent a long time," she said, "hiding. You're really good at it. My sister's barely started, but I guess she's got talent too, or they'd have found her. They are looking."

I was sure that they were looking. A human doesn't often kill a more-than-human being. For a girl to abort an immortal's child, sooner than carry it to term – that was unheard of. Retribution would be unbounded, unimaginable.

"Maybe you should just let her run," I suggested. "If you found her –"

"We," she said, taking me for granted in a way that sent a warm glow pouring through me, like liquid honey.

"If *we* found her, that might just expose her. She could be safer where she is, out of everyone's sight, yours included."

Desi shook her head. "She'll make a mistake, sooner or later, and they'll track her down. I found you."

I was probably more visible than one vulnerable girl, I probably made more noise; when I needed to, I shouted my name to the four winds. And then got the hell out of there, but it was all data for her triangulations.

"If they know you're her sister, they could be watching you. You might lead them straight to her."

"Not me. The last creep that tried to eyeball me, he's still looking for his eyeballs."

Eww.

"Look," she said, "are you busy tonight?"

I might have laughed, but I kept it down to a wry smile. "My social calendar is remarkably empty just now. What did you have in mind?"

"A dry run. A practice bout. See how we shake down as a team, learn to work together. Like that. I came across this, while I was waiting for you to show up."

She took back the photograph of Fay, and exchanged it for a sheet of folded paper.

"What is it?"

"You'll see," and her hand closed over mine as I went to unfold it. "Read it when I've gone, and meet me outside at sunset. Just give me your phone for a second."

She had my right hand trapped; I fished awkwardly left-handed into a right-hand pocket, endured her grin and handed her the phone. She punched in a string of numbers. After a moment, there was a chime from her bag.

"Now I've got your number, and you've got mine. Sunset. See you then."

And she stood up and walked out of there, leaving me bereft. I had nothing left to look at except my phone, where it lay on my open palm: still slightly warmed by the impact of her fingers, undetectably oiled by the touch of her skin.

I know this is sad, I know it is; and no, I didn't sniff the phone. I didn't want to lick it or frame it or fetishise it any other way. Just, for the little minute that I sat there, before I put it away, I thought it was maybe the most erotic thing I'd ever held in my hand.

Seventeen. Sometimes it just rises up and kicks you in the teeth.

CHAPTER THREE

She'd left me the sheet of paper, but it didn't tell me much. Except that we live in a sad and a random world, and I knew that much already.

It was one of those 'Missing' flyers that people run up and distribute by hand all around town, Arial typeface and upper case and a bad black-and-white print-out of what must have been a happy colour photo. Only most people do it when their dog runs off after a bitch in heat, or their cat hasn't been home for a week.

This was for a boy, a young man. I'd seen them for younger kids, when the authorities didn't seem to be doing enough; but Matthew Thomson was nineteen, well past the age of any consent, entitled to come and go as he chose. Authority just wouldn't be interested.

I wondered why Desi was, why she thought I should be. Mostly I was embarrassed for him; what reason could his parents have, to humiliate him this way? No wonder he'd fled, if they were this neurotic and smothering...

So why didn't he just leave home, like a normal nineteen-year-old? Go off to college or go round the world, call it a gap year and never bridge the gap? The flyer offered nothing but the bare facts, a description of him and his clothes, the date he'd not returned from the shops, two weeks ago. The gaps between the words, that was where the hurt lay, in all the guilt and doubt and speculation.

I was thinking about it all day, on and off. Matthew, Fay, myself: all gone missing, all being searched for. Maybe Matthew was another runaway. Or else he was deep in trouble somewhere, praying for rescue; or else he was dead already, or drugged into bewilderment, or dizzy in love and just not thinking. Two weeks was a long time not to think about what you'd left behind, but I'd known longer. One guy I knew, he hadn't phoned home once since he'd sneaked out of an open window, long years back. Not once. He didn't even have his parents' number.

SUNSET, SHE'D SAID. It made for a long day. I was there, though, on the esplanade outside the café just as the sun's rim touched the sea's horizon, in a far flare of light. I leaned on the railings above the beach and watched colours soak into a blotting-paper sky; and just as the last of the sun sank out of view, just as darkness closed like water overhead she was there at my elbow, smiling, pleased with herself or with me.

"So," she said, "any thoughts about Matthew?"

"Not enough data. He could be dead, he could be shooting up in a sewer somewhere; he could be on the other side of the world, waiting for that sun to rise over his tropical paradise island. I'd just be guessing, and that's no good to you. Or to him."

"Right. Although you don't really think he's on some tropical paradise island, do you?"

"Least likely option, maybe. Still an option."

"In your dreams. If paradise islands are an option, why are you still here? Listen, though. Last time I was here, this town was full of dossers. Runaways, addicts, surfer groupies; regular as swallows, here comes summer and here they came. You could find beggars or kids to rent on any corner. They bedded down in doorways, on benches, on the beach. This year? Nothing. The streets are empty."

"Good community policing," I suggested. "Council provision and zero tolerance, going hand in hand. They're either in hostels a nice hygienic distance from the centre, or they're in police cells, or they've just been scared away."

"Something scared them, that's for sure. What I heard, they showed up as usual, but then they disappeared, one by one. There are enough regulars – and let's face it, enough out-and-out weirdos – that you notice faces when they're not around."

"So what are you saying?" Actually I thought I knew, but it's always good to spell these things out.

"I'm saying they were preyed on, systematically. Word's out now, and the smart ones, the lucky ones, have got the hell away from here. That's why there's nobody left. Natural selection: it's the early worms that get picked off. Followed by the slow, the stubborn, the stupid. Survivors run."

Tell me about it. This I knew. "And that's why they took Matthew Thomson? Because the street-kids were gone too soon?"

"Right."

It's always a mistake, to start eating the locals. Sooner or later, it's going to cause a ruckus. When you're hungry, though, when food's been plentiful and is suddenly scarce, when you see a target of opportunity, a stray nineteen-year-old...

Desi was right, I do know how they think. And so does she.

"What's your guess?" I asked.

"Vampires. And I'm not guessing."

"What did you do?"

"Spent a couple of nights on a bench, under cardboard. Until this very pretty well-spoken boy came up with a mug of soup and a blanket, said he worked for a charity and if I'd rather sleep warm and eat in the morning I could always try his place, any time after sunset."

"You're sure he was a vamp?"

"I could smell it on him. They may shower and they don't sweat, but they have terrible bad breath. It's the unprocessed diet, I guess, very rich in bacteria. Flossing just doesn't cut it."

A vampire with halitosis and a business-card; she showed it to me in the street-light. *Headrest*, their charity was called. Bed and breakfast, free of charge. No questions asked, no preaching. No drugs on the premises, please, no knives.

Well, they wouldn't want their food tainted. Or fighting back.

The cattle that came to the slaughterhouse, by invitation only: oh, it was clever. One short summer, it must have seemed like one long harvest festival. Vampires are conservative, though, they don't like change. They were still working the same tired trick at the dog-end of the season, and one bright idea doesn't constitute a survival strategy.

She said, "I hate vampires. When I was in service, my master used to call them immigrants. Never mind how long they've been here, he said, they're not rooted in this land. Their blood will always make them strangers."

"And that's why you hate them?"

"No, that's why he hated them. He was kind of old-fashioned that way. Me, I don't care where they come from, Transylvania or Tunbridge Wells; they're still vermin. Leeches. Come on, let's go salt a few leeches."

SHE KNEW WHERE we were going, and the quickest way to get there. Something about that bothered me. I said, "You've scouted this."

"I was a daemon in service, but it's not all kick-ass guns and trumpets. Any army these days is intelligence-led. Know thine enemy, yes? Of course I scouted it."

I thought we were looking for a missing boy, I hadn't realised I was signing up with an army. And I still wanted to know why her master had taken on a teenage girl, what use he'd had for her. *Any army is intelligence-led*: there was an ominous ring to that. Right now, though, it wasn't the issue.

I said, "Desi, when did you do that?"

"These last few days. While I was waiting for you. Why?"

"Because your clever software couldn't tell you when I'd be turning up. You couldn't be sure I was coming at all."

"Right. I made an educated guess, and I was lucky. So?"

"So you were lucky twice. I did come, and you found me; and hey, look, there's a little local vampire difficulty I can help you out with, sort of a training exercise, how useful..."

She still wasn't getting it. I wanted to rage at her; instead I spelled it out, slow and simple. "I'm not a fighter, you know that. And you could have gone in there on your own, at any time. You're a daemon, this stuff is meat and drink to you. Any arguments so far?"

"No. What's your point?"

"My point," I said, "is that if you're right, they snatched Matthew two *weeks* ago. And you've done nothing all this time, just sat back and waited for me. How much longer were you going to wait?"

"As long as it took. Jordan, you're not thinking of this as a rescue mission, are you?"

We were going to have to settle on something she could call me, that we'd both be comfortable with. Later. I said, "If you'd gone in as soon as you figured it out —"

"It would still have been too late, he would have been cold bones for a week already. They've probably hunted again since then. But listen, I'm not a vigilante. It's not my job to keep the streets safe for our nation's children. I want to find my sister, that's all."

"So why are we doing this? Just to see if I freeze, if I pass out, if I run screaming at the sight of blood?" I was half inclined to walk away, right then; I did stop walking to make her turn and face me, sort this out.

"No," she said. "I know you better than that."

"Desi, you don't know me at all."

"I know the stories, which is why I knew you'd come tonight. Matthew's gone, but there could be some other kid down there: fresh meat, still alive, still worth saving. We might land lucky, if they've hunted tonight and fetched their dinner home. That's why you'll go in."

"And you?"

"Who, me?" She stretched long arms up towards the moon, clawing her fingers like a cat pleased with its own grace, confident in its concealed strength and oh, so malevolent in its intent. "You said it, I'm a daemon; mayhem is what I do best. And I just do so hate vamps."

THE PLACE SHE brought me to was an old brick warehouse on the edge of town, beyond a busy junction. If this was a vampires' nest, they could hardly have chosen better. The loading-bay doors were chained and rusted shut, leaving just the one way in and out: through an office, easy to control. High white-painted walls held no inconvenient windows. No risk of letting the sun in, all uninvited; no chance for passing strangers to see whatever went on inside.

Did no windows mean no watchers? I looked for cameras, and couldn't see any. Modern warehouses have their security all built in, but this was a hundred years old.

"No CCTV," I said, speaking softly even though we were in a gully on the far side of the junction, all the evening's traffic between us and them.

"See, I knew you'd be useful. I wouldn't have thought to look."

Daemon-thinking: it isn't really confidence, it's certainty. Confidence is still an act of faith, however well-grounded. Desi didn't need faith. She knew how good she was.

"How do you want to play this, then? Kick the door in, and see what's what?"

She chuckled. For a moment, I thought she wanted to reach over and rumple my hair for me, except that I'd shaved it all off. For that same moment, I was almost sorry.

"No," she said, "not that. Tempting, but let's be careful." *Daemons may be strong and fast and vicious*, she was saying, *but that doesn't make us dumb.* "I spy a flat roof, and some kind of structure up there, like it might be the head of a stairwell. How's about we look for a fire escape?"

A PEDESTRIAN UNDERPASS took us beneath the roadway. Say *underpass* and then say *vampires*, all my experience wants to say *run!* Places of reeking shadow, broken tiling and the gutters sticky with something dark and viscous and not quite dry – perhaps it never does quite dry down there – the walls stained and sprayed with graffiti that you can't quite make out, perhaps it's in another language but it's not one you'd ever like to learn. Just looking at the shapes of it can make your head spin and your stomach twist, you know you never want to hear it spoken. And then there's a sound, a whisper, and you don't know where it came from but it might have been behind you; except you're sure you heard the echo of a scratching, as it might be a fingernail picking at a tile just ahead...

Vamps shall not live by blood alone. They feed on threat, on fear, on the breath of corruption and the hollow sound of a footfall in the dark.

Eternal adolescents: I'm in no position to mock. But underpasses are the vamp equivalent of a shopping mall. They're the mall-rats, we're the shopping.

I went down there in trepidation, and in Desi's shadow; and even before we hit bottom I was feeling idiotic. And a little bewildered, unsure what was happening here, what we were coming into.

It was like no underpass I'd ever encountered. A smell did rise up to meet us, but nothing foul or dank: perfumed rather, as though they'd used a floral disinfectant. The steps had been scrubbed free of graffiti, chewing-gum, urine stains, whatever. It was like walking down into an architect's model, a city planner's dream, the world's most optimistic subway. All in white and brightly lit, not a dead bulb overhead or a puddle underfoot, it could have been a hospital corridor if only hospitals were kept this clean.

There was writing on the walls, but it wasn't graffiti. It was art, perhaps, unless it was psychotherapy: *Your Future This Way!* it told us, and *Give Yourself A Break*. Further on, where a ramp led us back into the real world again – so much darker and more threatening, only to underline how weird that subway was – the walls said *Onward and Upward*.

A smaller sign said *Headrest this way: good food, good beds, warm welcome*.

It was a honey-trap, all part of the service. Make the homeless feel at home, calm the anxious, bring them trooping in. In slaughterhouses they keep a Judas goat to do the same, to lead the flocks to the knife. It was wicked, it was clever, it was very unexpected; and it must have been a lot of work, setting all this up. Vampires aren't fond of work, as a rule. No wonder they didn't want to let it go too soon.

No wonder, in other words, they'd lingered on too late. They'd tempted fate, and here she came.

SHE LED ME up that ramp at a trot, alert in ways that I could never be, using senses that I couldn't even understand. I followed hunched and nervous, awkward in my own body where she looked so natural, so utterly in control of hers.

A well-lit pathway led directly to the factory door. There was a sign here too, an arrow pointing. *Headrest. It's What You Need.*

Even at my most desperate, I don't think I'd have taken that bright path. I never did trust an open invitation. The whole underpass was over the top, just too much altogether, with its clean white lines and its merry sloganising; paranoia is a survival trait.

We went over a fence at the ramp's head, out of the sodium haze of the street-lights and into the shadow of that high-sided, windowless building. Her black denim was perfect for night-time escapades, probably one reason why she wore it. Another, surely, was that she looked ultimately fabulous in black.

All my own clothes were neutral shades, the opposite of attention-grabbing. Attention-proof, almost. With my gaudy cockatoo crest, nobody saw anything but my hair; without it, shaven-headed, I could fade into any crowd, or melt into the night.

In Desi's wake, I melted.

As she'd predicted, there was a fire escape. Rusted and ramshackle, just an iron ladder bolted to the rear wall. I was glad not to be seeing it in daylight. A one-handed shake from Desi made it rattle and creak, all the way to the top. She said, "One at a time, I reckon. I'll go first."

Fine by me. In a regular flesh-and-blood kind of way, I probably outweighed her; she had those slender muscles that girls are gifted with, that boast some phenomenally unfair power-to-weight ratio. Just let her take on her Aspect, though – if an unwise vampire poked his head over the edge, say, to see what all the iron banging was about – and I thought she'd rip that ladder right off the wall. Same mass, just suddenly much, much heavier.

Either way, it made sense for her to lead. Besides, if there was any risk of a curious vampire waiting at the top, I wanted her to meet it.

So, of course, did she. She went up that fire escape like – well, no. Not at all like a rat up a drainpipe. Much more like a fit, lithe girl up a ladder, but so swiftly, I barely had a chance to enjoy it. Black on black, there wasn't much to see in any case: a fall of hair, the outline of an elbow, the thrust of a leg. An abiding sense of elegance and rush, grace in a hurry – or no, that's not right either. She wasn't in a hurry. When you're that confident, you probably don't ever need to hurry. She was just moving fast tonight. Grace at a canter, perhaps.

I stood and watched, till her silhouette flowed liquidly over the hard line of the parapet. A short time later her soft whistle came down to call me, but by then I was already climbing, willing as an old dog who knows just how bad things could get, but goes regardless. In a dog it's obedience and loyalty; Desi had another, stronger hold on me.

Hormones have a lot to answer for.

She helped me over the parapet, and I could have howled with pleasure. It wasn't fair. I'd spent so long avoiding female company, not to be tempted, not to draw them into my danger; and now here she came hunting me, and she was so concentrated, pure essence of *girl*. Was it any wonder that I was dragging after her like a lovelorn mooncalf?

She said, "No guards, one door, stairs going down. Come on."

"Hang on a sec." I couldn't believe we hadn't

talked about this yet. "Desi, what are we actually going to do down there?"

"We're going to put an end to this. A spiky end for preference, although I might just rip a few heads off, that works too. You must have a stake or two in that useful bag of yours?"

I nodded. Stake, mallet, always. You meet vampires all over. But, "I really don't do action scenes."

"I know, sweet. You do survival, though, you do that very well. You just stay behind me and stay alive."

I nodded, reluctantly. "Okay, Desi. I've got your back."

She chuckled, and turned towards the stairwell. I watched her for a moment – that back, those legs – before I got a grip, shook my head, followed after.

A trace of her perfume hung in the air where she'd walked. I could have tracked her blindfold.

This must have been the original door, weathered and peeling, starting to rot at the hinges. A couple of good shoulder-charges, I thought, I could break that in.

Desi just gripped the handle and pushed.

For a moment there she seemed to be glowing, if you can glow darkly. It was like she was in focus, and everything else was blurred; like she was made of more solid stuff, more real than the world around her. She made me feel kind of blurred myself.

The door opened, with no obvious resistance. I was dimly aware of accompanying noises, tearing wood and groaning iron, but mostly – like everything, like the peering street-lights and the cars that paused on the road below, like the breathless wind and the greedy, sucking stars – I was aware of her.

CHAPTER FOUR

"Oops. I THINK it was meant to open outwards."

Broken hinges, a frame wrenched half loose from the brickwork; I thought she was right. And she'd forced it inward with one hand, no effort. I'd always known that daemons were heavy artillery, but I'd never been this close to the damage.

It almost made me feel better about standing on that roof in the dark, with the stink of corruption wafting up from an unenticing stairwell. Almost.

Then Desi started down.

No drama: no whispered instructions, synchronised watches, nothing. She just went without a backward glance, assuming that I'd go with.

Assuming? Knowing, more like. I was right there at her heels, slipping the bag off my shoulders and fumbling inside for the comfort of a stake while my feet felt their way through the gloom, stumbling to keep up with Little Miss Eyebright who could no doubt see in the dark.

Somehow, in the unhurried urgency of that moment, I forgot about being scared. She just didn't give me the time, I guess. There was a palpable sense of menace rising up the stairwell, on the back of a foetid odour and the suggestion of light down below. I really didn't want to see it any more clearly – the phrase *corpse-candle* had bubbled up into my head, all unwelcome – but Desi was heading straight for it and I was behind her and that was just the way things were. Being terrified could wait.

Besides, they were only vampires. I'd faced vamps before.

Well, not faced, exactly. Fled, more like. I keep saying, don't have me down as a hero. I was in this for the long run, survival; heroics were a luxury I couldn't afford.

DOWN ONE FLOOR and here was a corridor, long and dimly lit, just enough to show us rooms opening to either side, their doors ajar or broken or missing altogether. Could be dormitories these days, vampires are heedless of where and how they sleep; if it's not Transylvania, who cares?

But if Headrest was a charity, I didn't think anyone had been along recently to check up on it. If it was a council-sponsored project – well, maybe. Dodgy deals are the backbone of local government, and vampires are good at sniffing out friends in high places. They have so much to offer – sex, wealth, power-games, status – and that's before they even get to the threats, let alone the extra little twist they have within their gift, *we can make you one of us*. Anywhere you find an infestation of vampires, it's always worth looking at the town council. And the police, of course; and the local business association, the school board, anyone with influence or authority. Masons are a favourite, so are the Soroptimists, the Rotarians, any high-minded self-selecting élite. Where two or three are gathered together, you will so often find a vampire among them. Or a whole clan of vampires.

Oh, and the clergy, of course. Vicars and deans. There's at least one bishop I know of, who's never seen out and about in daylight. Crucifixes and holy water, the paraphernalia of religion only trouble believers; there are few of those left among the undead. The rest do so like the theatre of church life, the dressing up, all those high Gothic arches by candlelight. And the way the helpless, the homeless, the utterly lost come knocking at their doors after dark.

DOWN ANOTHER FLOOR, and now we were coming into the candle-light. My fist was clenched tight around the rough wood of the stake, my lungs had clenched tighter yet and I was trying not to stir the air that I slithered through.

The wooden staircase turned into an open iron spiral, descending into what had once been a single vast space. There was no obvious clue as to what they used to warehouse here; it might have been anything from cotton to carboys to cast-iron engineering, anything that needed a lot of room a hundred years ago.

These days, it smelled like they were warehousing carrion, unrefrigerated meat.

I've never been to a slaughterhouse, never want to go, but I fancy they must smell like that. Only cleaner, probably. Not so foul.

The space below had been remade to look like what it was meant to be, a shelter for the homeless. That great open floor was divided now into dining-room and dormitories and private cells, all with hardboard and two-by-four. They hadn't troubled with cables and fittings and bulbs; there were candles all over, to light all those separate chambers. They hadn't troubled with ceilings either, so that from our vantage we were looking down into an array of lidless boxes.

Anyone who wanted to, they could look up and see us, just as easily.

What did we see? A happy party, largely: a dozen vamps all clustered around one table in the dining-room. There's something about vampires, even from a distance, a sort of instinctive revulsion. The way they were packed together, half-naked and swarming over each other, so intense – I wasn't fit to break it up myself, but I was very keen to see Desi do it.

That little orgy, and another handful in singles and pairs elsewhere. They were busy, or else they were sleeping, not looking up; but vampires do have very good hearing. The small, greedy noises they were making wouldn't have covered for us, if we'd been loud.

If I'd been loud, I mean. Even swift and forthright as she was, even in her boots on iron rungs, Desi made no more noise than she wanted to, which meant none at all.

DOWN AND AROUND, down and around again; and we were finally, thankfully out of immediate view, our feet on the ground and partition-walls risen all around us.

From above, the space had looked almost like

one of those laboratory mazes, white-walled rat-runs with rewards for smart behaviour. Now we were down among the rats, white walls too high for leaping. I gulped; Desi lifted one hand to hush me, to hold me still.

The stairs had brought us down at a T-junction, short corridors to either side and a long one ahead. The width of the building, and the length of it. Right now there was no one moving in any direction, but I still thought it would be a really good idea not to stay standing there. Happily, so did Desi.

Her hearing must be at least as good as a vampire's. Two doors off each short corridor; she pointed to them one by one, with her fingers making the count. *Two in there, one in there; none there* – a closed fist, no fingers; I may not be brave nor strong, nor a daemon, but at least I could manage not to be stupid – *and one in the last.* That must be the office, where an outer door opened to the world; that room *did* have a ceiling to it, and the partition-wall looked a lot older and more solid.

Desi headed that way: remove a danger, secure an exit. Both at once, in one swift action. I couldn't fault her.

I couldn't even catch up with her, she was that swift. At the door before I understood; inside before I could think to follow.

I listened for a challenge, for a scream, for anything. All I heard was a stifled grunt, a noise that sounded like green wood snapping, and then a slow, wet, ripping sound.

By the time I reached the doorway, Desi had her bag open on the desk and was rummaging through it, entirely ignoring the vampire dead on the floor at her feet.

I've seen this before, but not often, and it does make repulsively compelling viewing.

When a vampire is – finally! – killed, it doesn't go to dust in a neat implosion, the way the movies like it. When has death ever been so clean? What you get is a more biological reversion, anti-evolutionary, heading back towards primordial ooze as fast as it can slither. Flesh slumps on the bones, to hint at the skull beneath the skin; then it slides off, to give you a good look at the real thing. Then it deliquesces entirely, while you watch. It's a fast-forward kind of rot, where you need to step back quickly or you find yourself standing in a puddle of corpse-liquor. Ruins the carpets, and leaves you with a pile of yellowing bones that's really hard to explain away. Professionals break them up in a mortar, usually, or else they use a coffee-grinder. Sometimes they keep the canines, threaded on a necklace. Vampires do so treasure their superior, sophisticated image; there's no better way to stir them up than to wear their body-parts as a trophy.

I've never been interested in trophies, nor in provoking creatures demonstrably stronger and more malevolent than I am.

Daemonstrably, neither was Desi. She found what she was looking for in the bag, a plastic bottle which she tossed casually across to me. "Here," she said, "sprinkle this around, will you? Over by the front door especially."

The bottle said 'Dandelion and Burdock,' and I thought that might be the most dishonest act of labelling I'd ever seen. The liquid inside was clear, with an iridescent sheen where it caught the candlelight; I thought of genies and how very, very unwise it is to let them out, and how some idiot always, always does.

"What is it?"

"Geek fire," Desi said, stepping over the increasingly slimy body. A glistening, putrescent gel was dribbling out of its sodden sleeves now, pooling around its ivory knuckles.

I shook my head, dragged my gaze away. Said, "Unh?"

"Some friends put it together for me, in a laboratory. They started off with petrol, and ended up with this. It burns longer, hotter, nastier."

That's what I'd figured. But, "You're telling me it's flammable –"

"More or less," she said cheerfully. "Mostly more, to be honest."

"– and you want me to splash it about, in a room lit by candles?"

"Yes, please." She was halfway out of the door by now, talking to me over her shoulder. "I'd hold it at arm's length, if I were you. Be on the safe side. If it doesn't catch, toss a light at it – but it will catch. It always does."

"*Desi...!*" It's really hard to shout in a whisper, when there are creatures in earshot who'd be really pleased to kill you if they only knew you were there. I was quite proud of what I achieved, a scream at the volume of a hiss.

"What's up?"

"If I set a fire by the only exit –"

"– then the vamps have no way out. That's right. They'll probably try jumping through the flames; they usually do. It's a mistake. Live and learn. Or, in this case, not."

"What about us?" There'd be no easy retreat, back up to the roof and down the fire-escape and away; the only stairs were this end of the building, just where she wanted me to set the fire.

"Oh, don't worry so much. I'll get us out."

Don't worry, she said, and then she left me.

After a moment's staring at the empty doorway, I just decided to do what she'd asked. Very, very worriedly. She'd have cracked up laughing if she'd seen; but she wasn't there, and I was not going to fool around with this stuff.

I moved all the candles away from the heavy outer door before I uncapped the bottle. The liquid inside flowed thickly, more like shampoo than water, more like grease than shampoo. I squeezed a dribble onto the door-frame and felt my whole face twitch at the sharp, oily smell of it. For a moment that was welcome, as it cut through the rank stink of the decaying body behind me. Then my mind caught up with my nose.

Thing is, you never truly sense anything at a distance. What you detect is what comes to you: the giddy little photons that your brain interprets as light and colour, sight; the pressure-waves that constitute a sound; the vapours that you smell.

It's the vapours that catch fire, not the petrol. Vapours like these that I was smelling now, that were filling the room, where naked flames were burning at my back.

Suddenly I was working very much faster, smearing the stuff all around the door, squeezing it out in dollops and backing away as I squeezed.

At long last – well, that's what it felt like; in fact it wasn't really very much time at all – I lost my nerve altogether and just flung the bottle towards the outer door, sent a guttering candle after it and dived out of there, pulling the inner door shut behind me.

Just in time: it wasn't quite closed before the

flash and the soft *whumpf!* coupled with a sudden pressure-wave that slammed it for me.

The office door and office walls might be sturdier than the more recent partitions, but I wouldn't want to guess how long they could contain that fire. I had the feeling I'd just tossed a shovelful of Hell's furnace-coal into there. As soon as the outer door burned through or the window shattered, whichever came first, the flames could suck in all the fresh oxygen they wanted, a roomful in a single breath, and after that...

I FOUND DESI still being wise, cleaning up the other short corridor before she – we – tackled the main group. I saw her coming out of one room – vampires don't bleed, but she was shaking something off her hands, not wanting to get it on her clothes – and pausing at the door to the other, listening intently. Two in there, her fingers had said. I even remembered what they'd been doing to each other; I'd had a swift glance at it from above.

Maybe you get bored, after a few centuries of regular sex. Once you've run the gamut of all the flavours. I wouldn't know. One thing for sure, though: nothing could ever, ever drive me to what vamps do for fun. That thing about being so sophisticated, superior, élite – it's a mask, and they can only keep it up with their clothes on.

Two of them, deeply distracted, and even so Desi was being cautious. No blaming her for that. I once spent a long night with a couple of professionals. And moved on swiftly in the morning – bounty hunters aren't picky over what they hunt, who they turn in for cash – but I'd learned a lot, just listening to them. Maybe one of them could stake a single vampire before it could yell for help; two vampires, no chance. Even for Desi, it would be a challenge. And she wasn't even using stakes.

I hung back out of her way, hoping she could hurry, before my pent-up firestorm blew any possibility of silence or surprise.

Which is how come I saw the feet, coming softly down the spiral stairs between us.

There must have been one vamp at least on the upper floor, doing God knows what behind one of those ruined doorways. And now here it came – here *she* came, stocking'd legs and the briefest of skirts – and she obviously knew that something was going on down here, because she'd kicked her shoes off and was treading very lightly.

One half-turn of that spiral staircase would give her a direct view of me, where I stood dithering; another half would show her Desi. I could shout a warning, but that would give us both away and bring the whole nest boiling down on top of us. So I did the other thing, the only thing I could think of: I slithered rapidly through the other door on my short corridor, into the room that Desi's hand had marked off as empty.

Much relief, no surprise; she'd been right. It was a shadowy, stinking space with a darkly soiled bed, a broken nightstand, nothing more. Nothing moving. I stood behind the half-closed door with more than one reason to hold my breath, and counted seconds. Two for the vampire to see Desi and make a choice, fight or fly or shriek for help. No shriek; three more for her to keep coming, then, round one more turn of the stairs and so down to ground, directly behind Desi.

And one more second after that, all for me, to find the courage I needed. I did that, and then edged out again. There was the tableau, just as I'd pictured it: Desi entirely focused on that other door; vampire-girl edging forward, flexing her fingers and probably licking her fangs, entirely focused on Desi; me, sneaking up on the sneaker-upper, stake in hand.

Vampire, parasite, wickedness embodied. Also vampire intent on my new friend's blood and her life with it, and I didn't have so many friends that I could afford to be casual about any one of them. Either way, this girl's ass was mine.

Or her heart, for preference. The way to a girl's heart is between her ribs, with a good stout wooden stake.

Trouble was, she really was just a girl. Shorter than me and my sort of age, another eternal adolescent; pale and slender, with her bottle-blonde hair cropped short. I've always been vulnerable to the nape of a girl's neck.

Vulnerable was how she looked herself. From the back, she was just another underage endearing Goth-chick in ripped fishnets and leather accessories, her roots showing and her tour T-shirt only half tucked in.

If Desi had brought me along tonight as a test, right here was where I failed it.

I didn't, couldn't stake that girl. Not from behind. Instead, I took two quick steps and jabbed my stake just where it ought to go, only not hard enough by a distance, by about a finger's length. At the same time I put my hand around her neck: thumb on that sweet nape and the fingers closing one by one over her slender throat. One, two, three, four – *five...*

Vampire-girls can count, evidently. And think fast on their stocking'd feet. She stood very, very still. I worked the point in a little deeper, to encourage that sensible thinking. A regular human girl should've been leaking blood by now; she wasn't, but it was the finger-count that held her anyway. A vampire in her prime – and they all are – could have twisted away from point and grip, ripped my own throat open and drunk deeply before I'd so much as yelped. One thing the bounty hunters taught me, you never try to hold a vampire at stake-point. It's not something you can learn on the job; it's not the kind of job where you get to learn from your mistakes.

The stake was for me, to make me feel better; my fingers were enough to keep her quiet, spelling out my name. In mediaeval times, the deer belonged to the king and hunting them was a capital offence. The same holds true for me. My ass is claimed already. Once she knew who I was, the last thing she'd ever do was bite me.

Desi had opened that door at last and slipped inside, as quiet as we were and as lethally inclined. One bare-handed girl against two vampires; or put it the other way, one daemon against two distracted undead caught in all the mess and tangle of their physical play, and her only problem was to keep them from yelling out.

I don't know how she did that. I couldn't see, and I was distracted myself. Vampires don't breathe, but they need air for speaking; I'd have known if this girl was going to yell, I'd have felt her sucking it in. I was ready, or so I told myself; I didn't want to kill her but I could if I needed to, of course I could, one quick thrust...

Just occasionally, it's an advantage to come with a legend attached. She didn't make a sound, she didn't twitch a muscle. That was relief almost beyond measure, until Desi came back out, wiping her hands on a length of torn sheet.

Her first sight of me, of us, and she scowled monumentally.

"What are you playing around for?"

"I was watching your back," I countered, blushing even as I said it, realising just how it sounded: smart-ass, sullen, seventeen.

"Oh. Right." She was swift to catch on, as well as swift to kill. "Thanks, then. Even so – well, you're the one with the stake."

"I know, but I thought maybe she could tell us, you know, where..." My voice trailed away lamely.

"What you mean is, she's all sweet and sexy and you didn't want to stake her, right? Jay, we don't have time for this."

Before I could move, before the vampire could, Desi's right hand speared out flat-fingered, open-palmed; it looked like a jab to the ribs, a karate skill, something any wise teenager might have picked up at self-defence classes in the school gym.

I felt the shock of that impact, right through the vampire's body and into mine. I felt the cold, strong body stiffen and arch, and my hand closed tightly on her throat, just in case. That extra finger gives me really good grip.

There was a sucking, tearing sound, and I saw Desi's hand pull back. Saw what the fingers were hooked around, what she held in her palm.

She smiled tightly, straight into the vamp's eyes, and patted her pockets with her free hand. "I'm sure I've got a toothpick here somewhere – oh, but tell you what, Jay, you're the one with the stake," again, "and I guess you can let her go now. Here, catch..."

Then she lobbed it to me, high and slow. It was simple instinct, the love of the ball game; even knowing what that was, even though there was a bitter bile rising from my belly, I reached unthinkingly to snatch it out of the air.

Left-handed, of course, which did mean letting go the vampire's throat. Too late for her to do us any harm, she was far past screaming now; but bless her, she turned around to give me full sight of her face.

Vulnerable, did I call her? Endearing? Just goes to show, how little you can read from behind. She did still look young, and she did have one of those little-girl faces that can be so seductive when they're dressed in sin. But – oh, hell. Those baby-blue eyes must always have been clouded with an unholy hunger; the bee-stung lips might have pouted appealingly, but they could never have hidden either the teeth or the eagerness to bite.

And now, now the eyes were screaming, if the throat couldn't; now the mouth was stretched wide, those lips were drawn back to let the fangs scratch at air, the most that they could manage. And it wasn't terror that gripped her, and it wasn't pain. It was frustrated rage, no more. She wanted to kill, to go on killing; she'd had a long unlifetime of it and wasn't sated yet. That was all. It was a howling passion that she had, writ into her marrow: eyes and teeth, and the fingers as they clawed at nothing tangible, nothing she could reach.

Vampires don't die easily. They're undead already, which doesn't help; there's no true life in their bodies. No breath, no beat of blood. Tradition records the simpler ways to put them down: a stake through the heart, a swift beheading. Sunshine, fire. Sunshine we couldn't wait for, but fire was coming; I could feel it at my back.

An unkind man – or a woman, Desi in a less generous mood – might have left this girl to the fire and a slow death. Undead she might be, and very much not killed yet, but she wasn't going anywhere now. Even a vampire finds it hard to be actively wicked when her heart has been ripped wholesale, bare-handed from her chest. There was a hole, punched straight through T-shirt, flesh and bone. It wasn't pretty, but I didn't need to look. I knew already. I was holding her heart in my hand.

Not killed yet, but she was surely waiting to die. It couldn't be put back. Vampires have no circulation of blood, nothing to pump, but their heart is still imperative. Perhaps it's psychosomatic, the romance of it: *aargh! you have pierced me through the heart, how can I live?* They do go for romance and tragedy in that high Gothic, Byronic sort of way; I guess those who live by the gesture can die by the gesture.

I held her heart in my hand, stone-cold, stone-heavy, stone-still. No flicker of life in it now, as there hadn't been for however long, who knew? And she glowered at me, flailed at me, hated me with everything she had, and now it was easy. I could put my stake's tip to that chilly flab of unheeded muscle, slick with some liquor that was very, very far from honest blood; I could force old sharp wood into her abstracted heart; I could watch almost dispassionately as she seized up, as she crumpled, as the unlife leached out of her.

Then she was dead, truly and properly dead, and I hoped to mourn later for the girl she used to be, the loss of her. Right now Desi glanced at my stake and said, "Are you keeping that for a souvenir?"

God, no. It was rank already, sliming on its skewer like a crawling kebab. No need to touch it: just a sharp flick of the wrist and the heart slid off, to fall down onto the body which was already starting to glisten.

"Okay," I said softly, "I blew that, and I'm sorry."

"First time?"

"First time for live action, catch the girl and kill her, yes." I'd staked a couple in their sleep, where they lay with fresh blood on their lips, but that was different.

"Don't be sorry, then. You picked a hard one. After this it gets easier."

I didn't really want it to be easy, not ever; but her eyes had moved down the long corridor, to the door that led into the dining-room, where we knew that most of the nest was gathered.

"Desi, I'm not going to be much use to you in there." Unless a sacrificial victim could be useful. I could walk in waving my hand in the air, shouting my name, and they likely wouldn't kill me; or I could keep quiet, wave my stake around and die nobly for the cause. What cause, I wasn't certain.

"Oh, you'll be surprised," she said, unaccountably cheerful. And led the way, striding boldly down the corridor, not even thrusting me forward to be that brief distraction.

CHAPTER FIVE

THE SMELL OF smoke went with us, all the way. Luckily a vampire's sense of smell isn't as well-developed as their other senses. Just as well, given the way they choose to live, and what they have to live off. Spilled blood, dried blood, decaying blood, host to every bacterium that wants it: that's how they decorate their nests, and I'd sooner breathe carbon monoxide, thanks. I was grateful to be breathing honest smoke.

Trouble with smoke, though, it does make you cough. Me, at least, it makes me cough. Not Herself, she inhaled it like balsam fumes. Desi could smoke eighty a day without damage, if she didn't fuss so much about her clothes.

So she went swanning down the corridor, and did that oh-so-sensible waiting-and-listening thing at the door. And I scuttled after her, holding my breath as long as I could, not long enough. And gave up in a long whooping gasp for air, announcement enough on its own, *someone's out here and he's surely not a vampire, he's breathing*; and breathed more smoke than oxygen, and was suddenly hacking brutally as my lungs tried to turn themselves inside out and scrub each other clean.

Desi just... *looked* at me, with all the weary longsuffering, all the amused contempt that girls and immortals both have within their gift. Then she sighed, and shrugged, and kicked the door in.

Literally kicked it, literally in: ripped it right off its hinges and sent it hurtling into the space beyond, carrying with it both the vampires who'd been rushing up to investigate my coughing. That bought us a little space, a little time.

Not much of either. Two down, but not for long; and still, oh, a double handful, say ten more to go. Desi looked, she pointed; I looked, I saw overwhelming odds and followed orders. It couldn't make much difference, in the end. There were vamps all over, and all of them were interested in us. All bar one, at least, who spared us a glance, saw the odds the same way I did, and so turned his attention back to what lay on the table before him.

His attention, and his tongue.

This was the dining-room, after all; and it was a boy laid out on that table, a young man naked, bloody at neck and wrists and thighs. What else could have kept so many vamps so close, so eager, so intimate with each other? I'd thought them orgiastic, and they were. When you're a vampire, feeding and sex are so close, they're almost the same thing.

That one was greedy, or hungry, or just unperturbed. He went on lapping.

The others were coming at us, at me as much as Desi. I should have been terrified. Better, I should have been running. At best, of course, I shouldn't have been there at all. Too late for that, but running still ought to be an option.

With my eyes on that table, though, I couldn't do it. Nothing to do with shame, suddenly nothing even to do with Desi. This was a rescue mission after all; never mind why I'd come, I wasn't leaving without that boy.

If the majority in that room had their way, of course, I wouldn't be leaving at all. Just another course at dinner. Two surprises, Desi and me; two treats, perhaps, with unexpected flavours. Maybe we could give them indigestion, a pain in the gut, that at least...

I'd rather give them a far sharper, far more specific pain, just a handspan higher. I shifted the stake to my left hand for the added purchase of that extra finger, and set myself like a pikeman ready to receive cavalry.

I'm no fighter, but I must have fought most of the creatures you find on the street, one time or another, when running away was suddenly not an option. Not actually vampires hitherto, but I'd done my homework just in case. Legendarily, they're as arrogant and conservative in battle as they are in everything. They really do think of themselves as the cavalry, the officer class, innately superior.

The first that came at me, it came in fine form, leaning into its own speed like a sprinter. Its mentor should have been proud. Me, I was just muckily, mortally grateful. It was male, too, which helped again. I hadn't known until now that I had problems stabbing pretty girls.

This one wasn't even pretty; so many of them are Byronic in dress and attitude, it's easy to forget that they don't all look like romantic poets.

He must have been expecting me to scream, to turn, to run away. That's what we do, we mucky mortals. Instead, I ducked under his reaching hands, good and low, and let momentum do its work, carrying him helplessly forward above me. The undead are body-bound, and the conservation of energy still applies. They may be strong, but they're working with what used to be human muscles; they can't stop dead in mid-air.

So there he was, plunging over me, and I had that good solid stake in my good left hand. Generally, things in that hand go where I want them to go. The point ruined his velvet waistcoat, his silk shirt and his skin, all in a moment; then the heel of my right hand slammed up against the butt of the stake to drive it deep.

He screamed and then he died, going from undead to dead-dead; and his body pulled free of my stake as I pushed myself upright and started looking around for the next vampire, before the first had begun to rot.

From Biggles to Douglas Bader, every book about fighter pilots talks about how you can be tangled up in a hectic dogfight one moment and find the sky entirely empty the next.

This was like that. I'd seen vamps heading for me in a grand stampede, I'd fought the first of them – if you could call it a fight, just a duck-and-thrust, a fool's mate to kill a fool – and I'd stood up into vacancy, an absence where a mêlée ought to be. No one coming at me, no one between me and that table where their earlier victim lay, no one else in sight.

There was a lot of noise, but that was all behind me. I didn't need to look. That was Desi: Desi with her Aspect on, attracting all the attention that there was. It suited me. I didn't mind being a footnote in her adventure. I left it all to her, and headed straight for the table.

And discovered when I got there, just how wrong she'd been before. This had already turned out to be a rescue mission, despite her denials; more than that, though, it wasn't a nameless stranger needing rescue, a fresh victim plucked from park or pub or alleyway. His face was drawn and pale – *drained*, I suppose – but they'd kept him clean and fed, shaven even, in the interests of good husbandry. I knew him, just from the one bad black-and-white print-out on a flyer.

His name was Matthew Thomson, and they'd kept him alive in here for a full two weeks. They must have been feeding from him daily; scars and scabs and red raw punctures marked out his major veins and arteries, wherever blood rose close to the skin. He looked like a medical illustration, Harvey's first speculative chart of how the circulation might go.

He looked as close to death as anyone could be, who wasn't technically dead already. His body might have been cared for – who wants to eat from a dirty plate? – but they'd cared nothing for his mind. His eyes were dull and vacant, as if he really were the cattle they'd used him for.

"Matthew? Matthew, can you hear me?"

Nothing, no flicker of response. I thought it was only stubborn instinct that kept him breathing, kept his traitor heart pumping all that good blood to waste on vampire greed.

"Okay, never mind, you don't have to talk. Be good now, sit up for me, you can do that much. We'll get you out of here, but you have to help, I can't carry you by myself..."

Desi could, undoubtedly, but Desi was busy. I watched her in snatched glances, while I worked

Matthew up. She had one vamp by the neck, both hands; a twist and a tug, and – eww...

She let the body drop, hurled the head full-force at another vampire coming at her. The two skulls crunched together, the one undead and the other very thoroughly dead. Even a bonecrushing blow like that might not kill a vampire, but they still don't work so well with a shattered head. He fell over, and it would be a while before he got up again.

It might well be too late. Strange lights danced on the high ceiling; no one would need to smell the smoke any more, you could taste it, see it thickening the air. There would be no getting out through the office doorway now. That only left the stairs to the roof and the fire escape. Desi might get us through the flames, but we'd need to go soon. While the stairs were still there, basically.

Matthew was sitting up on the table, I'd got that far with him. I left him gripping the edge with both hands – first signs of some reviving spirit, I hoped – and waded into the mob of screaming vampires, to lend what assistance I could.

Too intent on Desi, they never saw me coming; they never heard me, making far too much noise themselves. I took two out from behind, with my trusty southpaw stake technique. No hesitation now, although one of them was a girl all dressed up in white lace with her long spine showing down to the cleft of her buttocks. That lace was freshly stained, streaked dark and wet, which did make it easier to strike.

Desi had her Aspect on, turned all the way up to eleven. It was hard not to watch her, not to feast my eyes on the smoky glory that was a daemon in full flow. Even with vampires all about me, any one of whom could have torn me apart with casual ease, it was still hard.

The hot stink of them was enough to keep me focused, just. There was one at my side, and I felt his startled fury as I staked him below the ribs. Then I felt the power of his grip on my windpipe, not for blood tonight, just to strangle. My chest heaved helplessly, my vision darkened; I worked the stake desperately in and up, until at last it scratched his heart.

It seemed to me that his fingers were the last thing to slacken, his chokehold on my throat his last intent, lost only reluctantly as he failed – barely! – to take me with him into death.

Even dead, he was a monster. His flesh sucked at my stake, and wouldn't let go. I'd worked so hard to get it in there, it wasn't coming out in any hurry. I kept a grip on the haft, but that only left me one-handed and disarmed, both at once, with another vampire just breaking free of Desi's glamour and bearing down on me...

Not just any vampire, either. They're hierarchical like whoa; there's always a king-pin. Akela, leader of the pack. This one oozed authority, and intelligence with it. I guess that's how he could turn away from Desi at her most magnetic, to deal with me.

And I guess that's why he paused on his very way to killing me, lifted his head, sniffed the air, gazed up at the fiery reflections overhead and understood.

And spat, and decided after all not to waste his precious time killing me, nor warning any of his weaker-minded brethren. He just sprang up onto one of those convenient dining-tables and upward from there again, to the top of the partition that divided this room from the next. Light-footed as a tightrope runner, he ran and jumped from one partition-top to another, and I scrambled up onto a table myself to watch him as he made his way into the smoke. He did – just – reach the staircase in time. He made a fine leap from partition-wall to spiral railing, swung himself over and onto the treads, and ran up out of sight the moment before the fire found the staircase, decided it was a chimney and lovingly enfolded it in flame.

No going up now, for us or for the vampires. If Desi had a Plan B, a withdrawal strategy, I hoped it involved drains and sewers and going down.

I checked Matthew, who was just where he had been, slouching on a table's edge; jumped down from my own table, and stooped to the dead vampire whose flesh was still holding on to my stake. A foot on his chest for purchase, left hand on the haft for grip; one slow, smooth motion, and I drew it out.

And turned back towards the mayhem, just in time. Desi kicked one vamp towards me, and I caught him staggering. Caught him on the point of my stake, indeed, and rammed it home sharp and savage.

Desi had this neat technique of backing off as they were coming at her, so they tended to reach her fastest-first, one or two at a time. By now she'd backed halfway round that big room, leaving a trail of broken furniture in her wake, along with all the broken bodies. She'd reverted to tradition now, no more messing around bare-handed; she held a snapped-off leg of table and wielded it as lightly as a rapier. I stumbled over carcases in an effort to catch up with her, and they looked like a piledriver had punched through their chests.

I did get one more, bravely in the back again. By that time, he was the last vampire standing.

Desi spun her table-leg from hand to hand like a sawn-off quarterstaff. "Time to go?"

"Please." That fire was eating through the building at our backs; I could feel the heat of it, baking the sweat dry on my skin. Matthew had actually got himself onto his feet and staggered a few paces away from the partition, where the paint was visibly starting to blister.

Still, he wasn't in any state to run or climb or even crawl to safety. I wasn't up for much of that myself, and I couldn't see how Desi thought she'd get us out of here. All very well for her to be confident, but she had a body that the rest of us mere mortals could only envy.

Well, envy and lust after, in my case, obviously.

She went calmly to where Matthew was swaying in the centre of the room, picked him up and carried him over to an outside wall.

"Can you hold him for a minute, Jay? I need to concentrate..."

Matthew was taller and heavier than me, but he was naked and trembling, on the very edge of collapse. No wonder, no blame to him for that. I propped him up willingly, my shoulder under his arm, while we both watched Desi.

It was just a plain brick wall she faced. The old loading-bay doors stood at the far end of this room; we'd seen how they were chained from the outside, and they'd been boarded up entirely in here. Even so, I'd have fancied my chances with an axe. Eventually. Not fast enough, with that fire licking at our backs. I might have fancied Desi's chances more, except that we didn't have an axe.

She preferred to outface brick. She did that, scowling as though she could glare a hole in it; it glared back in all its Edwardian solidity, a century of standing fast.

Then she leaned forward, set her palms against it, dropped her head between her arms so that her hair fell down in a dark cascade to hide her face.

Daemons don their Aspect like a coat, and shrug it off as easily. I've always known that. What I learned that day, it isn't just a toggle, on or off. The glimpse I'd had in the café had been nothing, just a twitch, a flutter. Fighting so many vampires together she'd been a dark star shining on an immeasurable wavelength, and I'd thought that was the peak of her, as far as she went, full volume.

Now she was like a black hole suddenly, drinking light, and I thought I'd never plumb the depths of her. I thought I wouldn't dare; once you sank into the heart of that darkness, you'd never find your way up and out into light and air again.

Lord, but it was tempting, though. Not only Matthew was shivering now. All my body was electric, alive with the charge of her, tingling and straining to be closer. It was an effort to stand where I was, to hold still, to stop my feet dragging towards her; it was an impossibility even to think of looking away. She drew all the light and heat there was; the pull of gravity and the strength of stone, all was hers. There was nothing in the world now, except Desi.

Desi and that wall. And she leaned against it, and there was no great swell of unexpected muscles under her jacket but something swelled like music in the air around her, like a rising wind; and then she pushed that wall down.

Well, not all of it. There was a lurch and a crumble, a cloud of mortar and dust, and suddenly a Desi-sized hole was revealed in a rush of incoming air.

"Quick," she snapped, pulling Matthew away

from me and lifting him like a child, "all that oxygen is going to –"

All that oxygen did. It found its way to the fire, fed it and overfed it. A flare of light gave us vicious shadows for a moment, and then a blast of heat. Desi was out through that hole already, with Matthew slung in her arms; it caught me following, framed within the brick, my face to the sweet fresh air and nothing but my back to aim at. I felt it like a hard hot shove to my spine, that only sent me staggering out faster.

Firelight blazed a path into the night. I stumbled a few paces over fallen brickwork, the rubble of Desi's exit, then found cool grass beyond. Grass and shadow, and Desi waiting; Desi saying, "Let's get out of here, there are sirens on the way."

I'd met a siren once, blonde and brassy and irresistible, trouble to the core. I was looking up apprehensively, listening for the beat of wings in the night, when I heard instead what she was hearing already, fire engines wailing on distant roads. There would be police on their way too, no doubt, and come morning they'd find bones in the ashes of the warehouse.

Emphatically, we didn't want to stick around.

"Where have you put Matthew?"

"Up against the fence there, in the light. They're what he needs now, sirens to take him to hospital, soon as they find him."

"If you think he's safe. He's the only survivor as far as they know, a witness with a tale to tell. The vamps must have had powerful friends in town –"

"Jay. The vamps are all dead. Who's to care what he says?"

"Not all; one of them got away, one at least."

Amazing, that she'd been too busy to notice. "Even if he legs it, those friends of his might still want to cover their backs."

The sirens were getting closer. She thought fast, nodded briefly. "You're right, he needs protection. Still got that 'Missing' flyer? Phone his parents. I'll call the press. With that kind of attention, nobody's going to disappear him a second time."

First, though, she took my hand and towed me away. Away from the road, the lights, the underpass, the building that we'd left ablaze. Traffic was starting to clog the junction as people slowed, stared, pulled up on the hard shoulder; there would be gawpers up here even before the sirens blasted their way through.

We took off over the fields, and she held my hand all the way. In the dark, in all the post-traumatic shudder and the blundering wonder of it all, I couldn't tell if she still wore her Aspect dialled down low, or if it was my own sorry hunger that kept me at her heels. In the end, I suppose it didn't matter. This was where she wanted me; this was where I was.

She stopped at last, on a headland overlooking the sea.

"Better make those calls," she said. "I don't suppose we'll get a signal from down there."

"Are we going down there?" I peered over and saw a long, steep scramble, with just a sliver of silver-lit beach below.

"Don't you want to?"

That wasn't fair. I'd go anywhere with her, and she knew it. This time I truly didn't know why, but again it didn't really matter.

I read the number for Matthew's parents by the dim reflected light of my phone-screen, and dialled.

They answered in a hurry, despite the time; no surprise there, the families of the missing always do.

I told them he'd been found, he was safe – I hoped! – and they should enquire for him at the local hospital. Then I hung up, without even asking about the reward that was spelled out on the flyer. I had little right to that, and less interest tonight.

Desi had called the local paper in the meantime, and the police too, just to let them know that people knew. If that didn't keep Matthew safe, nothing would. Nothing that we could do, at least, from a clifftop in the middle of nowhere, the middle of the night.

She seized my hand again – my left hand every time, the one that gives the better grip – and towed me down that cliff beside her. We slipped and skidded, yelled and jumped and somehow kept each other upright, more or less; and got to the bottom breathless and intact, and turned to each other, and –

AND THAT'S WHEN she drew her Aspect on again, which really wasn't fair. She could have done that at the top, and I'd have felt safe and secure all the way down, rather than human and all too vulnerable.

Or she could have left it off, then and now, and we could have been human and vulnerable together.

But she had to do it her way, this way, making sure. So she got me primed, fizzing with adrenalin and endorphins; she turned the big guns on, and what could I do? She pulled me close, and I went; she kissed me, and I stretched up – not too far, just an interesting little distance – into her kiss, leaned into her strength and was lost entirely.

She let me breathe in the end, because I needed to. Then she breathed herself, and shrugged her

Aspect off and was just a girl, firm and supple and astonishing, astonishingly tangled up with me. Her head dropped onto my shoulder, and for a moment I thought she was going to cry; I thought even the daemon was suffering some post-traumatic nerves.

But she raised her head again, and no, that wasn't tears in her eyes but something more demanding, more needy, unexpected and almost desperate, a hunger to match mine; and she said, "I'm sorry," and her voice was husky, thick with something very different from tears, "but I get so, so *horny* afterwards, I just have to –"

"Not this way, you don't," I said, "we'll do this naked." Meaning, *leave it off, we don't need your Aspect coming between us, we can manage just fine on our own.* And I worked one hand free to unzip her jacket, just to prove that I wasn't being entirely metaphorical here; and I guess some small part of my mind must have been thinking even then, even under the megawatt dazzle of what that girl could do to me; because it was my left hand that I'd freed, my clever hand, the one with the extra finger that could do so very much more than simply deal with a zipper or two, the odd button, whatever else it came across...

CHAPTER SIX

"Gods, but you needed that."

"I'm sorry? *I* needed that? I wasn't the one who threw herself at me, ripped my clothes off right there on the beach and still wasn't satisfied, had to drag me back to her digs and..."

"Oh yeah, like you needed dragging. Granted I had to spell it out for you, but that's par for the course, you're a boy. Otherwise – honestly, Jay, with me it's just post-traumatic lust, it's Pavlovian, I was trained this way. For you – well, that felt desperate. Which is not wholly erotic for me, and not wholly flattering either. How long has it been?"

Too long, but that was obvious. I said, "If you have to count, it's too long," and started counting, finger by finger, down the knuckles of her spine.

She squirmed pleasantly, chuckled rather less pleasantly and said, "Can you even remember her name?"

"Desi, I can't even remember her language." At least that sounded like a joke. And at least it skirted us away from more difficult territory, some of the things I'd done for money on the street. None of which had left me any the less desperate for this.

"Oh, we all speak the same language," she said, "lying down." Her hands spoke to me then, girl-talk, and the gist of what they said was, *Want to start again? Now that the rush is behind us?*

"Shift over."

"Whaffor? I'm comfy."

"So am I, mostwise."

"So?"

"So I just desperately need a pee, all right?"

"Y'know, I am so glad you said that."

"Why?"

"Two reasons. First, me too. Bags I go first."

"No chance. This is my room" – that we'd crept our way up to, leaving a trail of damp sand on the stairs – "that's my en-suite, and I'm bigger than you. What's second?"

"Second is, it proves you're still human."

"Oh, and what, you were doubting that, were you?"

"Just a bit. I don't know what they do to make you daemon, but –"

"You don't *want* to know, either. Trust me, you don't. But yes, I'm still human. I'm not the one with the freak hair and the mutant little finger. And the exotic family tree... Oh, I'm sorry. Sore point? Not the right thing to mention? ... I guess not, no. Quick on the uptake, me. I say something that propels a boy from one side of the bed to the other and into a fugue of silence, doesn't take me too long to figure out I've put my foot in it. Again. It's one of my human failings. Along with needing to pee. I'll go do that, and if you're still over there when I come back, I'll just –"

"Desi?"

"He moves. He speaks. What does he say?"

"Sorry. I'm a clown."

"Big feet, freak hair if you ever let it grow, slapstick manners and a secret sorrow – check. You're a clown. It's okay, I promise not to laugh. We've all got secret sorrows. We really ought to get up and go in search of mine. Shall I run a bath, while I'm in there?"

SHOWERS ARE GOOD for keeping clean, and that's pretty much all that I aspired to. I hadn't seen a bath for weeks. For dunking, the best I could usually manage was an hour at a municipal swimming pool, those times I felt secure enough to be near-naked and a long dash from my bag. Those rare times, when I was very new in town and not being immediately chased.

Here there was hot water, and it came up to my chin. It slopped over, indeed, when Desi slipped in to join me.

Then there was soap and a yellow plastic duck and such, but really it was all about the water. Splashing about is fun and I like to wash, but it's more than that. Deep as it gets and hot as it comes, I do just love to be in water. I think I must have been seafood in a former life. One of those weird modern discoveries, some bleached blind crustacean that hangs around on the ocean floor next to a thermal vent: hot, hot water.

The next life, I really don't care about so much. Just so long as I get one.

* * *

"DON'T YOU EVER take that off?"

"What?"

"You know what. That thong around your neck, with the amulet."

"Nope. Never do."

"Why not?"

"I'm a teenager, it's my thing. Some people wear black all the time."

"I take it all off for bed. And baths."

"I noticed."

"Keep your feet to yourself, and don't change the subject. What is it, some kind of charm?"

"Some kind, yes."

"Going to tell me?"

"No."

"You might as well, I'll find out eventually."

"Of course you will. I'll probably tell you myself, when I'm drunk sometime. That's my plan, to get you to get me drunk."

"Shouldn't be hard."

"Nah, I'm a cheap date. Half a pint of cider does for me. I don't get the practice, see. Don't get much of anything."

"You'll get less, if you're not careful."

"Mmm?"

"Feet!"

"Sorry."

"No, you're not. Turn around."

"Do what?"

"Turn *around*. Face the other way."

"What for?"

"First, so that I know where your feet are. Second, so I can shave your head for you."

"Oh – no, it's okay, I've got an electric –"

"I've got something better. Are you turning round, or getting out? Those would be your options."

I turned round, of course I did, and was not so much nestled as clamped between her thighs. She ran a thumb across my scalp, and hummed lightly.

"Mmm – last night it was sandpaper, but this morning it's velvet. Fine velvet. Hold still, and I'll make it silk."

Firm fingers soaped my head lingeringly, like a massage. Then I heard a snick and a click, and didn't really understand them until I felt the cold edge and the heavy blade of a classic cut-throat razor slide across my skin.

Do I need to tell you, I held very still indeed?

"Should I do your eyebrows too?"

Razor. Eyes. "*No!* Uh, no, thank you. I think the colour's good enough."

"Maybe – though you should really have your lashes tinted too, if you're trying to get away with colour."

She was probably right, but I couldn't afford it: neither the money nor the exposure. A boy with pure white lashes but not albino eyes, covering up his strangest, most attractive feature? The beauticians would talk for sure. I wore dark glasses a lot, and tried not to let anyone close enough to see what they were hiding.

Winds change. Tides turn. Moods are just as shifty.

We got dry, got dressed. Got on with the day.

I was feeling a little trepid as I went downstairs in her darkly magnificent wake. Landladies aren't famous for the welcome they extend to unexpected guests at breakfast. I've faced worse, but I do hate sour faces in the morning.

I wanted to slip a finger through a belt-loop on Desi's jeans, in a little-boy reach for reassurance. All right, actually I did slip a finger through Desi's belt-loop, but I unslipped it pretty quick, when she looked back at me over her shoulder. Just a glance, but speaking. Saying *I am not your girlfriend,* basically. Playtime was over; we'd had a long lascivious night of it, each of us with our separate needs, but one swallow – no, don't go there, but one night of hot, hard sex doesn't make a relationship. If she was anything to me, I suppose she was my employer. Certainly she was the one who'd be paying for breakfast, if I got any.

I put my hands in my pockets and walked small, as if I was embarrassed and eager to be gone. Not at all hungry. If I looked like a weak-tea-and-dry-toast kind of boy, no threat to the store-cupboard, I figured I'd have a better chance of being allowed to stay. Hell, I could actually fill up on dry toast and be grateful. Breakfast is a luxury.

Coffee's not, coffee is essential; my motor doesn't run on tea, weak or otherwise. If I couldn't even blag a coffee, I'd go down to that same seafront café and Desi could come and find me when she was done.

TEN MINUTES LATER we were sitting at a table in the window, sea-view the other side of the glass, big cafetière on this side, plus glasses of juice and bowls of cereal, with hefty fry-ups promised soonest.

Desi caught my expression. "What?"

"Oh, nothing."

"*What?*"

"Just, I've been running from daemons so long, and in all this time, it never occurred to me" – even after last night, which was slow of me, but I wasn't going to say so – "that you could use your Aspect not as a weapon of war, but just to charm someone. That's all."

"Charm," she said, "is a weapon of war. You should know that. Even so, I should probably be ashamed of myself. But, hell – you needed your breakfast, we've got a long day ahead, and I wasn't in the mood for a fight."

I nodded urgently around a mouthful. It's hard to be grateful in sign-language, harder still to say, *I wasn't criticising, honest.* By the time I'd swallowed, the moment had passed. I only said, "What sort of long day have we got ahead?"

She had her employer face on. "You're going to find my sister for me, remember?"

"I hadn't forgotten." Although I might vaguely have hoped for one quiet day of getting-to-know-you. I guess she thought we'd done enough of that. "Where do you want to start?"

A professional private eye would have started with fees and expenses, but I couldn't think of anything less appropriate. I had no idea what her resources were, except for Aspect-deep measurements of charm and strength, ferocity and determination. So long as she kept covering the costs – one way or another – I'd tag along.

"That's up to you," she said. "I've been everywhere I can think of."

"Okay. Let's start with her friends, then, yeah? The last place she lived, the people she hung out with…"

"Jay, I *told* you, I've already been there. All the obvious places, all her secret places. What I need from you is new ideas, where she might go when she can't go anywhere she knows."

"Yes, but this is where it starts. I need to know where she's been, who she was..."

"I can tell you all of that. We don't need to waste time going back over old ground."

"No. Everything you know leads to dead ends. Sorry, but you're the last person I need to listen to."

Oh, that hurt. It hurt me, just to say it; I watched it impact, and that hurt me worse.

She sat quiet for a minute, then nodded unexpectedly. "I'll take you to her last address. It's been three years, mind, and the room was only rented. Chances are, there'll be no one there who remembers her."

"What about her friends, then?"

"I don't know who she was friends with, when she disappeared."

"You weren't close?"

"I wasn't here." She was saying *I was already in service,* and her voice was sharp enough to cut herself. It really was not the time to ask any of the questions I had about that service: who her master was, what he asked of her. Why the period was so short, why she signed up so young. Why she left her sister vulnerable...

The moment I started articulating questions, they came in strings, like sausages. I needed answers to all of those and more, but chances were I'd have to winkle them out slyly. Desi could be almost as evasive as I was.

One thing for sure, she couldn't evade me in these next hours, if we were travelling together. We'd have time to get to know each other better; I'd have time to ask questions, up to a point. I didn't want to push it.

What I did want, I wanted to enjoy it. She might not be my girlfriend, but she was still the girl I'd spent the night with. Gratitude is ungraceful, but I could crush that decisively under what else I felt every time I looked at her: excited, horny, intrigued, hopeful, reborn. Scared. She scared me in the best way, and she made me scared for her; it had been such a long time since I'd felt that way about anyone outside myself, it was like a revelation.

My smart, self-aware, self-centred forebrain was struggling to remind me that I really needed to be scared on my own account, that being with her was dangerous for me. Poor thing, it just kept getting overruled by the dark pulsing mass that lurked behind it, that looked at Desi and remembered the night just gone and simply didn't care anymore.

I WANTED TO enjoy that journey, and I did – but not in any way that I'd imagined. No heart-to-heart with Desi, across a table on the train or side by side in coach seats; no sly glances at her immaculate profile, no shivering at the tactile intensity of her voice. Like chains swathed in silk, that voice was. Or like distant, muted horns, sweet and sensual and slow; and you know there's a clarion edge there too, only she's keeping it throttled back. I suppose that's her Aspect, lurking in the shadows, waiting to be drawn on.

I couldn't see her face, couldn't hear a word from her.

Well, you don't, riding pillion on a Harley.

OF COURSE DESI rode a Hog, what the hell did I expect? Freedom and power and an assertive, demanding kind of beauty, all in one loud, egotistical, look-at-me package. The black gleamed brighter than the chrome, the roar drowned out all traffic else. It idled like a tiger, silken and guttural and deadly; it revved like a chain whipped over corrugated iron, a deliberate insult to the soundscape. She rode it like a slap in the face of God.

And I hung on behind, breathless in the wind, helpless in its noise. Reminding myself constantly that she was my boss and not my girlfriend, even if my arms were wrapped around that warm, solid miracle of a waist, even if we did the bump-and-grind together every time she braked.

Reminding myself also that this crude physicality was only compensation, that I'd far rather be face to face with her in a train carriage, having a conversation, getting to know her better. Goodness, yes. Of course I would. Whoo, yeah...

LONDON? I BARELY know it. Bring me inside the M25 and I'm a stranger. Which is odd, because London is the classic place kids run to when they need to lose themselves. You'd think it would be my natural refuge.

But that same summoning works for other people too. Other peoples. There may be more supernaturals among us than your average human could ever imagine, but they're still spread thinly through the population. And they seek each other out, of course they do; they congregate. In other words, they come to London.

I keep away. Always have. I'm a small-town drifter, me.

*   *   *

YOU'RE NOT LOST, if you don't know where you're going. We were still somewhere south of the river, because we hadn't crossed a bridge; that was more or less all I knew.

One of those suburban high streets, that twenty years ago would have been a run of independent local traders. Now it was mostly charity shops and restaurants, with a supermarket on the corner to show what killed the trade. Desi turned off into shady tree-lined streets with big houses, broad empty forecourts, a dozen doorbells by every front door. Each house was subdivided into little flats and bedsits; front gardens had been paved over to provide parking, and the occupants were all off at distant jobs, so no wonder the whole neighbourhood was empty...

I'm exaggerating, of course. There were cars, on the road and parked up; there were pedestrians. Just not many of either. And, of course, nothing like us. Pensioners, women with buggies, youths in clumps: they all turned to look, and I could feel myself flinching, trying to shrink into her shadow as Desi drove blithely by. This was my nightmare, that sense of the whole city turning to look at me. It would only need one pair of eyes.

A random boy in a crash-hat, riding pillion behind a girl: on the bike, at least, I ought to be safe. I just didn't feel it.

Desi pulled off the road onto one of those spacious forecourts. She switched off her engine and the sudden silence, the sudden stillness, felt like a trap. She kicked the bike's stand down and pulled off her helmet; I thought the world was watching, and not to see that glorious dark fall of hair.

A glance back over her shoulder held the casual impatience of a girl not feeling any of this. *You can let go of my body now,* her eyes said, and, *I can't actually dismount until you do.*

Reluctantly, then, I did that. And lifted my own helmet away from my smooth shaved scalp, and she said, "God's sake, Jay, how did you ever keep ahead of the pack so long? You give yourself away every moment." With every nervous breath, she meant, and every sidelong glance, every tense little muscle in my face.

"Well," I muttered, "by not coming to London, among other things. This is where she was living, is it? When she disappeared?"

"That's right. One of the attic rooms. She'd been here three or four months, it was the last address she gave me; but when I came out of service, when I came to find her, she'd just gone. Left everything behind, and disappeared."

"Where are her things now?"

"Still here, maybe? I don't know. They wouldn't let me take anything away."

"I don't see how they could have stopped you." Legally, perhaps – but short acquaintance with Desi was enough to say she'd pay scant attention to the law.

"Well, no – but there wasn't anything useful. Just a bag of clothes and stuff, what she'd grabbed when she ran the first time. No notes to her big sister, no clue where she'd gone. And honestly, Jay, I don't think there's anything useful you can learn here. You've seen it now, and I hope that helps; but I talked to everyone in the house when she was freshly gone, and none of them could help me. I don't suppose there's anyone left here now who remembers Fay, even. These places turn over fast."

"Who owns it?"

"Someone in Dubai, I think. Sorry."

"No, actually, that's good news. An absentee landlord is bound to have somebody close, to keep an eye on the tenants and handle the maintenance."

"A caretaker, you mean?"

"Half caretaker, half manager, I guess I mean."

"Not here. Lose a room's rent? You've got to be kidding."

"Oh, not on site, maybe, but on call – and the tenants would have to know how to call him. There's got to be someone, Desi."

Her face twitched, and I felt an indecent surge of triumph. This wasn't really why she'd come to me – she'd asked me to think like a victim, like a runaway; playing detective was the other hand in the game – but it was somewhere to start. And it should be safe. Some random concierge out in the sticks, he wouldn't know me from a hole in the wall.

"Come on," I said, "let's see if anybody's home. Ask for the number, yeah?"

I'd already turned away and started walking. This must be hard for her; she was used to being better than other people. When she'd done everything daemonically possible, there should be nothing left for a mere human to pick up. But there was no point asking me to be her bloodhound if she didn't let me lead; and now I was challenging her on her own territory, asking questions that she should have asked herself.

I thought she could use a little space.

I also thought that I was dangerously close to enjoying this. On the road with a striking, intriguing girl was one thing, and should have been plenty. Using my brain for more than self-protection, that was something else, a whole new dimension. Living in 3-D at last. I liked it; I might even be good at it, if one bright idea shows a trend. I could see a whole career-path stretching ahead, Sherlock J and his beautiful assistant Desdaemona, finding what was lost and expunging vampire nests *en route*, defeating evil and bringing light to dark places...

You can still be a rank idiot at seventeen, even after however-many years of practice. I knew this, I was watching myself at it, and yet still feeling that bubble of excitement rise –

– AND I SEIZED a tree, a good-sized sapling growing to one side of the forecourt, and went to swing around it one-handed like a kid, just to give her the chance to laugh at me –

– AND I SHRIEKED and fell away, scrambling backwards into the shrubbery, because what my hand had seized and tried to spin around wasn't tree, whatever my eyes were telling me.

I'd used my good hand, the left, the clever one. Just by chance, because the tree was on that side of the forecourt, that side of me. I ought to learn to be left-handed, I suppose: more nasty surprises, maybe, but less chance of getting caught out by something fatal.

As it happens, this wasn't fatal. It was only the shock of it that made me shriek, let go, fall over. My hand had reached for slim trunk and dusty bark, and my fingers had closed on something else altogether. A normal human wouldn't have known, wouldn't have felt a thing different; but as humans go, I'm already abnormal. Just counting on my fingers, I can go all the way up to eleven.

I felt what was there for the world to feel, bark with grainy wood beneath; and I felt what was also there, a life besides tree-life, a personality, a purpose.

Shock and fear, I felt those too, like an echo of my own emotions in that bare moment before I let go, before I fell.

Movement came a beat later, while I was sprawled on my arse and staring, doing my backward crab-scuttle into the leaf-litter and muck of a city shrubbery.

There was a shiver that encompassed the whole tree, from high-flung leaves to slender trunk and further, deeper down. A lot of those leaves fell, though they shouldn't have been ready; worse, the earth was shifting suddenly beneath me.

Rippling, rising, breaking apart.

The tree dug itself up, in a handful of seconds. Ripped its own roots right out of the ground.

They weren't really so rootlike, now they were exposed. Just as there weren't as many branches as I'd thought, and the whole tree didn't reach as high as it had seemed to, and that trunk was actually bifurcated in a way I hadn't noticed, and...

And it was already a woman of sorts as she loped the ten metres to the house wall – in three simple strides: not that much of a woman yet – and then climbed it. Climbed it like a creeper, vegetatively. Reached her arms high and her twiggy fingers just attached to the brickwork; and her legs lifted one by one and her toes were long and flexible, spreading across the bricks and digging into the mortar and taking her weight as she stretched up and reached higher...

She was fast, so fast I could barely see her do it. It was like stop-motion photography in the real world and speeded up past bearing, a hundred years' worth of upward growth all in a couple of seconds.

Then she was onto the tiles and away, running up the pitch of the roof, almost human now that she needed more balance than cling. What had been bark might even pass for clothing, at a distance.

Me, I sat in the dirt and watched her go.

Desi didn't. Desi went by me – I would say in a blur, but she had her Aspect on full force; she was bright and clear and exact, it was the rest of the world that was blurred in comparison. She went up that wall just as fast as the shapeshifter had, only not at all creeperly.

The two of them vanished across the roofline, with a scurry of slipping slates. Me, I picked myself up, brushed off the worst of the muck and went to the house door.

The shapeshifter had been swift but silent going up that wall, making no more noise than a plant makes in its growing, the occasional creak but otherwise only the whisper of her passage. Desi was – well, something else. Graceful as ever, gorgeous to watch, darkly dynamic and lethally effective, but not silent. No. It's not a silent thing, ramming fingers into bricks, kicking them into brickdust.

Still, I saw no faces at windows, no one tumbling out of the door to see what was what. I rang all the doorbells anyway, a long column of buttons and lit names beside a keypad, but I was already certain that nobody was home.

Underneath all those buttons was a helpful notice: "In emergency, please call the janitor," with a mobile number appended.

I was just copying that into my phone when Desi came back, trotting briskly along the road. Just her, regular Desi, no Aspect now. She had a dead leaf in her hair, but she wasn't even sweating.

I picked the leaf out for her, and said there was no one in. I didn't ask what had happened to the shapeshifter.

"Just as well," she said. "Even so, we'd better get out of here. Come on."

"Why? I'm guessing that you caught up with –"

"Jordan, are you so certain that the dryad was the only one on watch? No other spies, no birds gone flapping off to find their master?"

Actually, it wasn't a dryad: they inhabit their trees, not become them. This wasn't the moment, though, for a discussion of parasitism versus cryptobiology. And no, of course I wasn't certain, now she came to mention it.

Also, the shapeshifter might have been here to look for Fay, but it was my touch that had triggered her flight. I was the one in danger here, if a second watcher carried word to where it would do them most good, me most ultimate harm. Desi knew it, too.

Even so, she'd said my name aloud.

Even so, "We can take five minutes," I said.

"For what?"

"To get inside, and find Fay's things. I know you've been through them, but there may be something you missed. Why else would they still be keeping watch here, after all this time? They think she's coming back – which means there must be something worth coming back for."

"No, it means they don't know Fay very well. When she cuts and runs, she just leaves it all behind. Nothing matters that much."

Not even her family, apparently; she'd abandoned her sister, along with everything else. Unless she felt that her sister had already abandoned her.

That was for later. For now, I turned back to the door. "Can you get us in here?"

I thought she'd just push it open, if she didn't push it off its hinges. Instead, she punched numbers on the keypad, the lock clicked, the door swung open.

"Smart," I said.

"Stupid," she said. "Three years, and they haven't changed it."

"Smart of you to try, I meant."

She shrugged. "Fay gave me the number. This was meant to be her refuge: new home, new name, new life. And big sister back from the wars, to look after her."

And it hadn't worked out that way, and she blamed herself; she didn't need to say so. I was still fumbling for some response when she shook her head, stepped into the hallway and said, "Your five minutes are wasting. It's not much, to search a house."

"You don't know where they would've put Fay's stuff?"

"No idea. It was still in her room, when I was here. They may not have kept it at all."

Even so, we still didn't need to search the house. Almost all of it was private flats, private rooms, other people's territory. Fay's stuff wouldn't be behind any of those locked and numbered doors.

Communal storage areas, then. Up in the attics? Probably not; Desi had said Fay had an attic room. If there'd been a box-room up there, it was likely doing service as a toilet or a shower now. Maybe an old scullery, by the back door – but cellars were a better bet. And right here in the hall was a door with a bolt on it, no number, no lock.

I slammed the bolt back, opened the door, saw a light-switch and steps going down. Desi grunted, behind me. I didn't know what that meant, and didn't stop to ask; I was taking her five-minute deadline seriously, for my own sake.

You learn to be cautious in my kind of life, but I went down those stairs like a man in a hurry, like I knew just what I'd find at the bottom. I've lived my life in boarding-houses, one sort or another. This was just a little grander, a lot more expensive.

Dim bulbs, no shades. Whitewash, peeling off damp brick walls. At the foot of the stairs, a passageway opening into three separate windowless spaces. One had a hatch high up, and must have been a coal-hole once.

There were bicycles that were clearly cared for and presumably used, when their owners could be bothered to drag them out. Another day, in other company, I might have taken one for myself; they were good bikes.

Otherwise, pretty much everything down there was junk. That kind of junk that accumulates in any busy house. Stuff that still works and is too good to throw away, it's just been superseded; stuff that you bought but never found a use for; stuff that people gave you, ditto ditto. All that stuff you're sure you'll find someone to pass it on to, or you'll post it on e-Bay or Freecycle sometime, or you're just hanging on to it for now in case the new one blows. It's kipple, it accumulates; it is the space-eater.

Do I sound superior? My life has no space, I can't accumulate; I've given up ownership. I'm not a missionary about it, but – like an ex-smoker, like a vegetarian, like anyone who's broken an addiction – I can't resist sounding smug sometimes. Making a conscious virtue out of a brutal necessity. I have my bag, the emergency kit, always with me; apart from that, I dress myself from charity shops, summer and winter, and leave last season's gear in exchange. If I have to run, I abandon whatever's not in the bag.

This cellar was the opposite of me, full of weight and excess. There were boxes empty and not empty, there were tea-chests broken and spilling their contents in corners. There was lumber. There was coal, actually in the coal-hole: one final spill of it left over from before the heating was converted, swept aside and ignored because what on earth can you do with half a sack of coal when you've switched your boiler onto gas and boarded up your fireplaces?

There were toasters and sandwich-toasters, Teasmaids and coffee machines, more kitchen gadgets that I didn't understand. There were extra bicycles, broken and abandoned. There was a lawnmower, although it must have been a long, long time since the house had ever had a lawn.

There was broken furniture, whose drawers were filled with tins of paint and turpentine and oil. There was –

There was a rucksack that Desi pointed at and said, "There. That was Fay's," just as I saw *Fay* embroidered in glittering thread on the red top flap.

It was hers, and it was full; it was what we'd been looking for. I dragged it out heedlessly from under a heap of pans all strung together, which fell with a very satisfying clatter.

"Anything else?" I asked.

"No, that'll be it. She was on the run, remember? When she came here, she was already running. Everything she brought with her would have fitted into that."

UP THE STAIRS, then, and out of there, back to the bike. I clamped the helmet on, swung my arms through the straps on Fay's rucksack – which made an uncomfortable fit with my own emergency kitbag, but I could live with it – and Desi drove us away. Nothing to be seen, no retribution coming for either of us, but she had her Aspect on, I could feel it like a bass thrum through my fingers to match the thrum of the bike between my legs.

It was only once we were moving that I realised I had no idea where we were going, where she would take me now.

CHAPTER SEVEN

NOT VERY FAR at all, as it turned out. Back up on the high street and a little way along, the bike turned suddenly into a parking-slot as though it were the one in charge here. I was a little bewildered – she'd been the one keenest to get moving – until she took off her helmet and shook back her hair, glanced at me over her shoulder and said, "Lunch. Coming?"

I'd had breakfast; I was fit until teatime. I could get used to this notion of regular meals, but I probably shouldn't.

Even so – well, I'm young, I'm male, I love to chew. Besides, she'd been switching her Aspect on and off all morning; that surely burns fuel. Not to mention playing rip-chase over the roofscape with a shapeshifter. She had a right to be hungry, and I had an obligation not to make her feel bad about it.

She'd found an Asian foodstore, squeezed in between an estate agent and a tapas bar: boxes of complex and obscure vegetables out on the pavement, the lure of spices within. I went to follow her inside, and she blocked me with a forearm.

"Helmet off, sunshine."

"Whaffor? We'll only be a minute..."

"So you don't look like a bank robber, idiot. They don't like it."

Young man in a full-face helmet, visor down: she was right, that had to look threatening. I really didn't want to show my face, but the art of obscurity is often about exposure. Hiding in full view: Desi had said it yesterday. And the alternative was to wait outside with the bike. On my own, in the open, where I might be sniffed out by any number of creatures that didn't need eyes to find me.

Helmet under my arm, then, I went with her into the shadowy aromatic welcome of the shop.

"FRESH SAMOSAS," DESI said, wielding tongs neatly, dropping fried-gold pastries into paper bags. "Bhajis, too. We'll get them heated up at the till. Just grab anything else you want. Drinks are in the fridge over there; get me a mango lassi, would you? Oh, and a bottle of Coke. Big one. Be quick."

I was right, she was hungry. By the time I came back with drinks there was barely room for them in her basket, alongside the heaped bags and the yoghurt, the chutney, the pickled chillies, the bright soft textures of the sweets...

We joined the queue at the till, and I kept myself occupied if not entertained by watching the CCTV monitor above. There must have been half a dozen cameras watching the shop, the frontage, the storerooms and the alley behind. The display kept shifting on an automatic loop from one to another, so that I could keep an eye all around and reassure Desi that the bike was safe, and myself that we weren't being crept up on, front or back.

Every minute or so, I ducked my head for ten seconds, so that the camera watching our queue wouldn't broadcast my face to the whole shop and wherever else a feed might run.

We shuffled forward slowly while the guy behind the till had animated Urdu conversations with his customers and his telephones and his staff, while his busy fingers rang through baskets of exotica. When we finally reached him, there was another delay while all Desi's samosas and bhajis went into a mini-oven to be warmed through; he passed the time by scolding her for not spending enough in his shop, which I thought was coming on a little strong in the circumstances.

She grinned sheepishly, hiding her face behind her hair and coming over all bashful and apologetic. This was no side of Desi that I'd seen or was prepared to believe in, but she did it very well.

At last, we had our arms full of hot food and were heading out of there, when we were suddenly pinned by a voice behind us, a single word, a question.

"Fay?"

I WAS IN front, but even so I felt it, when Desi took her Aspect on her.

Felt it? I was undone by it. This was the real thing, full-focus. It ripped my breath away.

It took an effort of will and body, just to turn around. I felt as though she'd sapped all my strength from me, to feed her own; as though it were a zero-sum game, one of us had to lose what the other gained.

Still, I made the turn, and caught her gaze for a moment. I guess looking into the eyes of the Gorgon would be worse, but not by much. Hers were dark and devouring, two black holes in a dreadful pale face. I couldn't recognise the girl I woke up with that morning; I would never have wanted to see this girl again.

Her turn to turn, and the poor guy behind her must have caught the full force of that look, plus all the power that backed it. The CCTV monitor fritzed suddenly and blanked out; in that singular slow moment, I thought nothing could save his life. Her locks weren't exactly writhing snakes, but even from the back, she looked deadly.

And she lifted her hand, and I'd have reached to stop her – whatever the cost – except that just in that same moment the young man said, "No," and saved himself.

Lord knows how he did it, where he found the words, but he said, "No," and she was already letting her hand fall, her Aspect slip a little; and he said, "No, I'm sorry, you're not –" and, "I thought you were –" and by then she was just herself again, unreinforced, no longer terminal. He caught his breath and added, "You do look just like her, from the back."

"My sister," she said.

"Really? Well, yes. I guess, kind of obvious, now you say it. Only, she never said she had a sister..."

"I've been away," Desi said neutrally. Try not to speculate. "You haven't seen Fay, have you? Or heard from her?"

"No, not for years. She used to walk our dogs for us, but then she was just gone, and no one knew... You haven't – ?"

"No. Sorry. I'm looking for her myself. She's the family mystery."

And with that, a flippant word and a casual shrug, Desi turned again and swept me up with a whole different category of glare. Didn't give me a moment to talk to this guy, to get his number for follow-up; one jerk of her head and we were both headed straight for the bike. She might not have had her Aspect on, but she could still manoeuvre me.

No TALKING, ON the bike. Which she knew, which might be why she took us further than she might have planned: far enough for all that hot food to get half cold again before we stopped by a park, found a patch of grass in sunlight, spread out a picnic that was already rancid with unasked questions.

I couldn't help myself, I had to ask them.

Easy one first, just to get her in the mood. "What did you do with the shapeshifter?"

"The – ? Oh, you mean the dryad?"

"Shapeshifter, but let's not bicker. What happened with her?"

"There are gardens, over the back of those houses. When she realised she wasn't going to get away, she sunk her feet in soil and turned halfway back to a tree again. Tried to hug me to death."

I could imagine it: living wood, *animated* wood, flexible and implacable, wrapping itself around her mortal body like a constrictor. I knew that body with a fresh intimacy and I'd never call it soft, even without her Aspect on her; but everything's comparative, and she was talking about wrestling with a *tree*...

"So what happened?" I said again.

"Oh, I uprooted her. So then she tried to smother me, creeper-like; she really didn't have any imagination. Couldn't think outside the box."

"Desi." One more time. "What *happened?*"

"I tore her apart. What do you think happened?"

That was more or less what I did think, but I had to check. "You didn't wait to ask her anything? Like, who she was working for, who she was trying to get to when she ran?"

"No, I didn't. It wasn't a good time for talking, she was trying to twine these very long fingers around my throat. Besides, I know who planted her there; that's enough."

"I don't. A powerful family of immortals is after your sister, you've told me that, but not who they are. And it wouldn't be them at any rate, running the search at this level. They'll have local agents in the field, to handle watchers."

"Of course, but we don't need to go after those."

"If we knew who they were, they might be easier to avoid." Which was true all the way up, and she really would have to give me some names. She didn't want to, that was clear, and I could understand her reluctance. The Powers have ways to eavesdrop on the world, and naming the one you most want to avoid is as good a way as any to bring them slamming down on top of you. All too literally, sometimes.

I'm always careful myself, for the same reason. I don't like to use my own name, and I try never to be too specific about the people who are chasing me. You'll have noticed.

"It's not us they're after," Desi said.

Whether that was true or not, I could best keep Desi cooperative by keeping her mind on her sister. I hoped. I said, "The more we know about who Fay's hiding from, the better chance we have of working out where she might have gone. And I don't just mean the people at the top; it's the people on the street who matter more, the ones who are actually looking for her. The ones who set that shapeshifter to watch."

She grunted, and filled her mouth with bhaji. That was tactics, and I could outwait her. I dunked a samosa into yoghurt and nibbled patiently, made sure that my patience was visible and all-enduring.

At last she swallowed and said, "I don't want them to know I'm looking for her. If they start keeping an eye on us, we could lead them directly to her."

Which I'd pointed out myself at our first encounter, but she'd overridden it. No more did I want them to know that we were looking, absolutely I did not; but, "We can't hope to find her if we don't ask questions. Is that why you wouldn't let me talk to the guy in the foodstore?"

"I wasn't stopping you –"

"Desi, you hustled us away from there like your pants were on fire."

"Well. I was hungry." Half a smile, and, "I get all sorts of hungry, after I've had my Aspect on. You've seen that. It's kind of urgent."

True, all true; and still she was wilfully distracting me, and I wasn't going to play along. "You could have left me with him."

"No. I brought you into this, you're my responsibility; and I'm not stupid, Jay, I do realise it was your touch that triggered things off this morning. I'm not leaving you exposed."

"You've got to let me do the job, or there's no point involving me in the first place."

"Well, but that man didn't have anything to tell us. He said so. Fay was his dog-walker, that was all."

"That was all he was prepared to tell her scary sister, chance-met in a shop. It's not all he knows."

"He hadn't seen her for years, since she disappeared."

"Maybe, maybe not. Did you ever wonder if she didn't run away, the way you think? Maybe something ordinary and mortal happened to her, the way it happens to other pretty teenage girls."

She shook her head violently, illogically. "No. I *know*. She's hiding up somewhere, that's all. Not dead yet."

"I still need to talk to those who knew her. People like him. If all he can tell me is where she used to take his dogs, that tells us something. Dog-walkers meet each other, form unpredictable friendships. Or you meet other people in parks. Runaways, homeless folk. It's a network, and we have to follow every thread we can find."

"All right. You've made your point. I don't think we ought to go back to the house, though. Or anywhere near it. They left a watcher there, they're bound to check up on her; if they left only that one, they'll still be ready for us next time. So there'd better not be a next time."

I didn't dispute that. I didn't tell her that I'd got the janitor's phone number, either. Just nodded and said, "No arguments here. Let's have a look through her things, then. See if there really is anything in there to tempt her back."

"Not here. We'll go back to my place, where we can be private."

It was the first mention that she had a place of her own. I just hadn't thought. Desi had been living so much my own rootless life while she hunted me, it hadn't crossed my mind that she would have a house somewhere, a roof and a door, a key and a fixed claim. Why wouldn't she, though? A free agent with a life to make for herself, like any young person newly released into the world, she'd made herself a home. Of course she had.

"Where's that, then?"

"Get aboard. You'll see."

FORTY MINUTES LATER, London was behind us and we were into territory I didn't know at all. I thought I'd been all over, but apparently not. I must've been subconsciously skirting the whole Thames Valley.

We passed Slough, we passed Maidenhead; we came to Henley-on-Thames, and didn't pass it by. What I knew about Henley I could count on my hands, I didn't need my fingers. They have a regatta on the river every year, and Dusty Springfield is buried somewhere in town. That was it, the sum of my knowledge. I would add one guess, though, that there would be a lot of money in Henley. Houses would be expensive.

Desi brought us down to a waterside property, a white-painted cottage with a balcony jutting out above the tow-path for that uninterrupted view of the regatta action. I blinked, and reassessed the worth of a daemon's service. Upwards.

"Your master must have paid you well," I said. A little snide, perhaps, but not half so snidy as the part I didn't say, *whatever you did to earn it.*

She glanced up at that balcony, and her smile had a lot of distance in it. "He was generous," she said.

Then she turned away from the cottage, crossed the towpath and jumped aboard a boat.

*   *   *

THERE WAS STILL no disputing it, her master had been generous indeed. Not riverbank-cottage generous, perhaps, but even so. This was no plastic toy boat for weekend chugging up and down the river; nor even my own sometime dream, a narrowboat fit for living in, the kind of home you carry with you.

This was a genuine Dutch barge, seventy foot of welded steel construction, wide of beam and high of headroom. She'd been fitted out like a New York loft inside, designed for very gracious living; on the outside, she could still have been a working vessel. She had bow and stern thrusters for ultimate manoeuvrability in awkward British waterways, a powerful diesel engine that could take her out to sea without a second thought.

Oh, she was a lovely craft. I knew about Dutch barges from library books and waiting-room magazines; I'd never imagined being aboard one. I went over her from stem to stern, above decks and below, while Desi mixed up a jug of something and laughed at me from the galley.

When she was bored of yelled questions about tonnage and beam and hydraulic drive, she just stopped talking. When I came to see why, she pressed a glass into my hand and said, "Drink that."

I sipped obediently. Clink of ice, a hint of fizz, rich fruity flavours with something dry to cut them, just a hint of alcoholic bite beneath: sip turned to swallow, swallow turned to gulp and I glanced over to make sure there was a refill waiting. "What is it?"

"A little something of my own. I call it the Silencer. Are you going to sit down?"

"Yeah, sure – hey, is this white oak, all this panelling?"

"Yes, it is. Fifty years' time, it'll look lovely. Sit *down*."

When Desi gets forceful, she doesn't really need anything extra. Just those eyes, that voice. I sat, quite abruptly, on a long sprung sofa that must surely unfold into a double bed. The boat's interior was all one long open space, except for the bathroom – the head, she called it – in the bows. If she had guests staying over, they'd need to be friends. Or just not body-shy. Well, I could be that. I could be both of those. I settled back – it really was startlingly comfortable for a shipboard sofabed, once I'd slipped my bag off my shoulder and set it next to Fay's, right by my feet there – and didn't move even when she went up on deck, even when the whole barge rocked a little to tell me that she'd jumped ashore.

A couple of minutes later she was back with the rest of my things and hers, from the bike's panniers. She dropped mine on the sofa beside me, while her own went on a broad futon at the further end of this long cabin. Fair enough. Boss, not girlfriend. Yes.

My things, her things: sorted. Any open questions about tonight's accommodations: closed. That left Fay's things, her rucksack: unopened, not yet sorted. Next order of business.

Desi unzipped the cover, decanted the contents onto a coffee-table right in front of me.

She tipped, I sorted. I don't know if it was the Silencer having its effect or something more potent, these physical reminders that a girl was lost out there, but neither of us spoke much for a while.

Clothes: I checked the pockets where there were any, then folded them into a neat pile, very aware that they were a girl's things, and a stranger's, and that her sister's eyes were on me. Handling them helped me to understand just how young Fay had been. This was her running-away gear and there was something irreducibly teenage about the choices she'd made, the things she couldn't bear to leave behind. Pretty blouses, shoes, scanty thongs. I was silent now, but if I'd watched her packing, I'd have been scornful.

Books: *Catcher in the Rye, Chocolat,* Jilly Cooper. Giveaways again. I might have chuckled, but just then Desi made a soft sound of her own, and I swallowed mine.

Toiletries I barely looked at, just to check for prescription drugs – none – or illegal drugs, ditto. Shampoos and sanitary towels I simply didn't care about.

Random items: an MP3 player, a phone, a diary. A teddy bear.

THAT WAS IT. I double-checked all the pockets, but there really was no more.

"It's nothing much to come back for," I muttered, turning it all over one more time.

"No. But then, she didn't come back, did she? They only thought she might."

"They must've had some reason for thinking so."

"Maybe. If so, this wasn't it. Maybe they were hoping to tempt her back with something else, some lie, some bait we didn't see or couldn't recognise. Maybe it's a honeytrap, some guy in one of the other rooms, an old flame. Whatever. There's nothing here."

She said that, but she said it with the teddy bear in her arms.

I forbore to point that out; I'm generous that way. Besides, she was my boss.

I said, "Maybe there's something she did leave behind, only they took it away. She wouldn't know that. A memento of the boy who made her pregnant?

A photo? She's a teenage girl, and there're no photos here. That's not right. Was she on Facebook?"

Desi shook her head. "Not her thing. She didn't have a lot of friends, and she wouldn't be interested in faking it."

Ouch. I'd tried social networks for a while, when I was sick of the hollow shell of my life, when I thought that any regular contact would be better than none at all. I was wrong. False name, false premise: I was faking it from the start.

"Okay. Never mind. This was a dead end," a wave towards the heaps of Fay's stuff, turned over and rejected.

Turned over and rejected...

"Wait a minute. This was what she grabbed when she ran away the first time, yes? She ran to London and took with her what she needed, what she thought she needed, which was this. Then that room wasn't safe any longer" – don't know why, but save that – "so she ran again. But she left all of this. Phone, clothes. Teddy bear. So what did she take this time? What's missing, what did she always have, that isn't here?"

Desi looked at the piles, looked through the piles, shook her head. "Nothing."

"Desi," one more time, "are you sure she ran? If everything she had is here, then..."

Then maybe Occam had got his razor out, and maybe she wasn't a mysteriously-vanished runaway after all. Maybe she was a body, rotting under leaves or underwater: just one more victim of one more random attack.

"No," Desi said. "She ran. It's what she does. She's a survivor."

Everyone's a survivor, until they meet the thing

they can't survive. I didn't say that aloud. Desi knew it, although she might be in denial.

Instead, "Okay – but it was either a very sudden decision, or wherever she went, she knew that she couldn't take stuff with her. Any stuff at all. Was she religious?"

Desi stared across that pitiful little heap of abandoned possessions, snorting with laughter. "Oh, what, you think she went to be a nun?"

"It's a classic. A closed order, anonymous behind walls and under a wimple; leave all the world behind, and just go." I could see the attraction.

"I don't think nunneries work like that anymore, Jay – and I'm damn sure they wouldn't have taken Fay, if they did."

Actually I was fairly sure that I could find a nunnery that did and would – but if Desi didn't know about it, after years of serving a Power, then likely neither would Fay.

Which brought us back to my growing suspicion, that in fact she hadn't run at all. Where do you go, with nothing? And how do you get there? "Did you think to check hospitals, at the time? Or later?"

"I wasn't around at the time," she reminded me. "Later, yes – but the only thing I found was that someone else had been there before me, asking the same questions. Getting the same answers. That's not what happened, Jay. If she'd been hurt, I'd know."

"Really?"

"Yes. Really."

"If she was dead?"

"The same."

"If she'd been caught, taken? Say she didn't see them coming, say she didn't get the chance to run before they caught up with her. Say they got her. This is exactly what we'd find: a sudden vanishment, with nothing taken. I'm sorry, but that makes a lot of sense to me."

"No. That's not what happened."

"And you know this how?"

"I just do."

I could perhaps be persuaded to believe in some kind of unreliable telepathy between twins, but: "Desi, you weren't that close. You can't have been. She was a teenager, you knew she was vulnerable, and you went off into service and left her..."

I was being deliberately provocative, in hopes of eliciting a furious confession; there was way too much that she didn't want to tell me.

She went very still, where she was sitting on the floor just across the table from me. I closed my eyes and waited to feel the slam of her Aspect, followed by the slam of her body. Not in a good way, but I hoped it wouldn't hurt too much. I hoped she wouldn't break anything, at least...

I waited, through that one long breathless moment – and something hit me stingingly on the nose. Something hard, that was cold and wet when it fell into my lap.

I opened my eyes, and it was an ice-cube from the jug. I looked at her, and she was grinning broadly.

"You'll have to do better than that," she said. "You can be as cynical as you like; she's my little sister, and I always did know when she was hurting, or when she needed rescue. That was my job, from way back."

"What about your parents, why wasn't it their job?"

"Because they're dead. They died young, both of them. Nothing sinister, nothing catastrophic: just ordinary everyday tragedy, two people meeting their mortality too soon. Mum had an embolism, Dad smoked himself to death. Fay and I pretty much brought each other up. I dealt with her troubles when she met them, she tried to stop me getting into troubles of my own. We work well together, Fay and I."

"So why didn't she come to you, when she needed help this time?"

"Because I was gone, and she didn't know where to find me. I'd made sure of that. I thought she was old enough to deal on her own, and I wanted space; I wanted my own life, and I took it."

"By selling yourself to an immortal?"

"I never said I was smart, did I? Together, we kept each other straight; apart – well, I signed my soul away, and she fell in love with Jacey. That's what we do. Opposite directions, hopelessly the wrong things."

I had more and more questions, and I really ought to be taking notes, getting organised, asking them in order; but here was something that came boiling up, erupting like a missile from deep blue water.

"Jacey? Not Jacey *Cathar*?"

"Mmm."

"He was the father of – ?"

"He would have been, yes."

She didn't need to say any more than that. No wonder she was trying so hard to find her sister; it wasn't simple guilt and anxiety that drove her. The guilt was clear, she made no effort to hide that. Delete 'anxiety', though, and substitute 'raw terror', you'd be closer to the mark.

Thing is, I talk blithely about Powers and immortals as if they were all one, all to be equally feared. That's not true at all. They are all to be feared, but some are much more fearful than others.

The Cathars, now: well, you can tell from the name. They keep that mediaeval moniker, despite – or because of – all its implications. Once they led a heretic sect, their own private fiefdom; after the crusade, after the massacres, they walked away. That's what immortals do, they leave the bodies where they lie and start again. A little wiser, a little meaner.

In this instance, with all that mediaeval meanery intact. Hierarchies endure, and so does the feudal outlook, and the Cathars have it in spades. They are the Cosa Nostra of the overworld, and they keep everything – all the power, all the secrets – strictly family. The bloodline means everything to them. Immortals don't have many children; that's the counterweight, what keeps us common folk from being overrun. Making a baby between themselves is so difficult and rare, they tend to breed outside the tribe, but even the most fertile of human lovers can turn barren in a Power's bed. What family they do contrive, that's their treasure and their trust.

Jacey is the youngest son of the Cathar line, their little prince, true-born child of two immortals. We'd never met, but the supernatural world is just as vulnerable to gossip about its gilded youth at play. I did know his reputation.

Which was spotless, actually, in an international-jetset-playboy kind of way. He might leave a trail of wreckage in his wake, but none of it was malicious. Mostly broken hearts – male and female both, the way I'd heard it – for all the bright young things who thought they could pin down a Power. He'd broken a few Ferraris too, and trashed the odd hotel room in a temper, but nothing your average rockstar doesn't do. There was no litter of corpses, is what I'm saying, at least none that rumour could attach.

And this paragon, this young lion, this golden apple of his parents' eyes had made Fay pregnant – not bothering with contraception, probably, not even thinking about it because babies just don't happen when you're young, when you're immortal – and by the time she found out she'd already been scared away by that whole Cathar family thing, terrorised into understanding that she was not a fit partner for their beautiful boy.

So she had an abortion, because she was young, because she didn't understand. I couldn't guess what the Cathars would be planning in retribution, as and when they caught up with her. It would be terrible beyond measure, beyond imagining. Beyond life.

Desi knew. She watched, she waited, she gave me the time I needed; then she said, "Now do you see?"

Oh, I saw. I said, "Why didn't you tell me before?"

"Because the basic facts were scaring you enough already. If I put names to them, I thought you might just run away, and I'd only have to find you again."

I could see that, too. I could see me getting up and walking off this boat right now, walking right away. I could even see her letting me go, at least a little way. She wouldn't want us fighting about it here; things might get broken, and promises would be the least of them.

Logically, it shouldn't make a difference which Powers were chasing Fay. She could only die once, after all. Even so, there are shades and degrees of dying, there are values of merciless where you really wouldn't want to go. Logic led inexorably to that closed door and whatever lay beyond it, whatever the Cathars had waiting for Fay when they caught her. Which they would, surely, if Desi and I didn't find her first; and even then...

"What are you going to do, if we catch up with Fay before they do?"

"*When* we catch up with her."

"If you like. How in hell do you imagine you can protect her from the Cathars?" Hope is a frail, wispy thing you can nourish on vagueness and ignorance, but that name just crushed it.

Desi shrugged. As a question it wasn't worth answering, because there was no answer; if she had an army at her back, she still wouldn't have an answer to the Cathars.

Instead she said, "It's not really about protection. I might help her run faster, hide deeper down. But really it's about being there. Not abandoning her. Not sitting here knowing who's after her and thinking, 'Okay, nothing I can do about that.' What do you want me to do, just leave her to do the best she can until they catch her?"

That's what people had done for me. The only people at my back were the ones hunting me down. But then, I'd never had a sister.

As nastily as I could, I said, "I see. It's about making you feel better."

Daemons can still blush, apparently. I hadn't known that. "No, Jay, it's not about making me feel better. It's about making her feel better. Not letting her go down into the dark alone. If it comes to that. Maybe it won't: not even the Cathars are omniscient. The two of us together, Fay and me, maybe we can drop right out under their radar and get clean away. You've kept hidden long enough."

"No. Not long enough." Never that. I touched the amulet at my throat, that sense of death in waiting, and said, "Never mind. Maybe you'll be lucky. Maybe not, but it doesn't matter either way unless we find Fay before the Cathars do. And whatever I say" – however right I was, and however anxious for her, however desperate not to see that dark splendour broken – "you're not going to stop looking, are you?"

"No, Jay. I'm not."

"No." So her mission was still my mission. As it always had been, really, since she first slid that photo of Fay across the table at me like a gently-guided missile. Vulnerability has always been my weakness, as terror has always been my strength. "Okay if I go ashore?"

"Of course," she said, as though I really didn't need to ask; and then, "What for?" as though she had every right to know.

"Thinking space. I just need to get my head around this."

"You can't do that here? I won't distract you, if you want to be quiet."

She'd distract me at the opposite end of a Trappist monastery, but that wasn't the point. "I think best when I'm walking."

Desi looked at me, I thought a little narrowly. When I slung my bag over my shoulder, her gaze tightened further, and a little frown-wrinkle appeared between her eyes. I wanted to reach out and smooth it away with my thumb, only I didn't fancy a broken thumb.

"Want some company?"

"I'm better on my own," I said.

"That's just habit," she said, "and you really ought to break it. Tell you what, though. As you're going," and she produced a money-clip and started peeling notes, "bring us back dinner, will you? Any kind of takeaway, I'm not fussy. Oh, and a couple of bottles of wine."

"You'll be lucky," I said. "Do I look eighteen to you?"

She considered. "No, you look about one day short."

"Yup. And I always get carded."

"Sweet boy, you can order fake cards off the internet these days."

"I know, but I don't want one." Alcohol is just one more temptation into ruin. I needed to stay solvent, and I needed to stay sharp; both of those made my youth a blessing.

"All right, buy chocolate, then. For afters. Anything you fancy. I've got wine on board. Just make sure there's plenty of takeaway. Extra rice and stuff. I'm hungry."

"Desi, you can't be! We had lunch..." Not that long ago, even. And she'd eaten most of it.

"And now this is dinner. Spend time with me, Jay, you'll have to get used to three meals a day. Or more."

Oh, I could do that, it wouldn't be a hardship. Neither half of that, the spending time or the getting used to food. It just wouldn't be wise. It couldn't last forever, it probably wouldn't last long at all; and then I'd be back on the streets, back on the run, short of friends and short of money. Hunger's like any kind of pain, you can get used to it so long as it's constant. Let it go, and when it comes back – and it will – it's a whole order of magnitude worse.

She gave me more than enough cash, as if we'd had a conversation: *we have to learn to trust each other sometime.* If I had meant to run, she was gifting me incentive, a contribution to the running expenses. Although I didn't mean to, she was still laying temptation in my path, testing my good faith as much as my courage. I hoped not to let her down. If I did, I hoped not to let her catch me.

*   *   *

I DIDN'T MEAN to run, I wasn't going to; I jumped ashore with barely a twinge of bad conscience. Which didn't seem enough, somehow, so I ramped it up by walking along the river towpath for a while: down to where the path became a wooden walkway across a weir, where I could pause and look back and see for certain that she wasn't following me.

Which she really wasn't, so then I did feel guilty for that imbalance of trust, one-way traffic on a two-way street. Even so, I stood on the walkway for five long minutes, watching; then I went on past the weir's noise.

Back on the bank, where I could keep an eye on the walkway to be doubly sure, I called the number I'd written down from Fay's doorway, for the building's janitor.

"YES, HULLO?"

The voice was broken in the strangest way, as if he had gravel in his crop. It drew me, rather. I'm comfortable with damage, signs of the world's harm; that's where I've lived most of my life, among the scarred and the disoriented, the dispossessed. I'd heard countless men, and women too, croak like ravens around oil-rag fires in the far dark, their voices as dirty and shiftless as their skins.

I said, "I think you look after a house in Croydon, is that right?"

"That's right, yes. What's the trouble?"

"Oh, no trouble, I'm not a tenant. I'm actually making enquiries about someone who used to live there, a girl called Fay. She moved out about three years ago. I was wondering if you knew anything about her?"

"I remember Fay," he said, and my heart sang.

"You don't happen to remember where she went, do you? She didn't leave a forwarding address, a phone number...?" Questions that expect the answer *no*, but I did still have to ask.

"Not her. She didn't move out, she disappeared. Didn't even take her things. I know, I had to pack 'em."

And I'd pinched 'em, but no need to confess to that...

At least, I'd pinched what he'd packed. If there'd been anything of value – something worth coming back for, say – it might have ended up in the janitor's flat rather than her backpack. Maybe that's unfair, maybe I've read too much cheap fiction and in fact the janitorial world is ruled by scruple and good order – but I suddenly had a second reason for wanting to talk to this man, maybe to track him to his own quarters, search his rooms while he was off janitising...

"Really? Isn't that unusual?"

"It is, yeah. People do flit, but usually there's a reason. It's not like she was behind with her rent or anything. And when they do a runner, they usually take their stuff with them. She only had a bagful, and she left it all behind."

"Well, I'm not asking to see her things" – really, I wasn't – "but I would like to come and talk to you, if you don't mind. It's quite important that I find her, and the more I hear, the more worried I get. Was her disappearance reported to the police, do you know?"

"No. Well, not by me, I had no reason; she was paid up for another two months. Grown woman –

well, she was a kid, but legal, y'know? – she can do what she wants."

"You didn't think maybe something had happened to her?"

"Yeah, maybe – but I've a daughter myself, and I've been to the police once or twice when I've been worried. I know what they're like. Over eighteen, they don't want to know."

Maybe that was sincere, or maybe he was just a jobsworth; down the phone, I couldn't tell. One more reason to meet him face to face.

I said, "Look, would it be possible to meet you somewhere? Doesn't have to be at the house" – *please not, or you'll want to show me her things* – "I could come to you..."

Rather to my surprise, he accepted that and gave me an address in Chiswick, a time the following day.

WHICH LEFT ME with the one overriding problem, how to drop Desi. She'd only want to come with if I told her, and I really thought I ought to go alone. She'd already hustled me hard away from one guy who'd known Fay, and was conspicuously reluctant to put me in touch with any others. Nothing sinister about it, I thought, we just had very different ideas of how to find her sister; but if she really wanted my help, she'd have to let me work my own way.

Or I'd have to sneak around behind her back, like now, and feel guilty about it. Guilty and frustrated, because I'd far rather ride pillion on her bike and have her at my side tomorrow, but I really didn't trust her. As we knew.

On my way back upriver, I first felt someone follow me. Nothing concrete, nothing I could point to: only a whisper on the wind, a stray current in the river, a shifting shadow that obscured the moon, something that touched my hair-trigger nerves to life.

I looked around and couldn't see her, but that was no surprise. It was getting dark and there were trees and buildings, shadows galore to lurk in, not to mention all the boats moored up along the bank. Besides, she'd be good at this. She'd hate it, if I spotted her.

Me, I liked it that she was out there somewhere, not trusting me. I didn't deserve her trust; it was not exactly a relief, but a happy irony to find that she didn't deserve mine either, that we were both of us suspicious and deceptive people.

In that happiness, then, as instructed, I went shopping.

SHE LEFT ME once she was sure, slipping back to the boat no doubt to be there innocently waiting when I returned. Either that, or I was better at losing a tail in the street-lights and the traffic. I'm used to small towns and quiet byways: quick of eye and quick of foot, always looking for the alley through to the car-park where there's a back door into the supermarket. It's a game I'd played for a long time, with my life as the stake; I played just as hard that night, and soon I didn't have the least impression of her, not a notion that I was still being followed.

I bought chocolate bars and juice, tea and coffee and milk; then – for once in my life, hoping not to regret it later – I let my nose and my curiosity guide me to a meal without thinking about the cost of it now or the cost of it later.

By the time I came back to the boat, there was a gangplank in place, no need to jump aboard. Just as well, with my arms full of shopping. Not that she'd done it on my behalf; her bike was stowed on the foredeck, held upright with hefty straps and chains. I thought that anyone trying to steal Desi's Hog would likely live – for a while – to regret it, but it's probably best to be pre-emptive, where the alternative is to be mayhem-ptive.

She must have heard me step aboard, unless she felt the boat shift under my weight. I'm not that heavy, but boats are sensitive. At any rate, her silhouette loomed below me, just as I reached the companionway. I passed the bags down one by one; she sniffed at the hot ones and said, "What have we got, then?"

You'd know, if you'd managed to keep up – but it's like Fight Club, part of the game is not to mention the game. She knew that I knew that she knew, and that was enough.

"Nepalese," I said casually, as though I'd eaten Nepalese nearly often enough to find it boring.

"Oh, fab. Did you get the pig's trotters?"

"Actually, I did. Those are for you." She looked at me, and I said, "You did say you were hungry."

"I did. I am. We'll share. Come and get a drink, while I lay this out."

I sipped wine and watched her set out dish after dish, waited for an explosive, "*How* much did you order?" – and waited in vain. Which was really frustrating. Which I guess she knew. It was her money and I'd gone way over the top with it, and she seemed entirely content, humming to herself, licking her fingers when she got scalding-hot sauce on them, fetching spoons and forks and plates, the very image of a happy housewife. Houseboatwife.

I didn't believe it for a moment, this was another

level of the game; so I played along, sat when she told me to sit, ate when she told me to eat.

Turns out Nepalese food is a lot like Indian, all curries, just that some of the ingredients are different. Like pig's trotters. Turns out those are mostly gristle, and what isn't is still not nice to chew. Which didn't stop Desi chewing her way through everything I didn't. After a while I gave up, sat back and watched in awe.

Eventually she noticed, and scowled, and said, "You're not eating enough. Eat more."

"I can't," I said. "You've eaten it all already."

"I have not – oh. I'm sorry. Did I do that again? You should've said. Or just snatched. It's your own fault" – rallying swiftly to her own defence – "you shouldn't be so careful all the time."

"Desi, I have to be careful."

"Not any more. I said, I've got your back."

I couldn't afford to believe that. I said, "How long for?"

"As long as it takes. Obviously."

"Yes, but then? Once I've found Fay? Say I do that, then the two of you go off together, and you don't have my back any more. Don't say I can come too; three can't hide, even as easily as two, they're just that much easier to spot. And we'd have twice as many people looking for us, mine as well as yours. It's no good, Desi, at some point I have to be on my own again. Which means not getting used to any of this." I gestured widely with my empty glass, at the whole package, food and boat and her together.

She made a face, and didn't argue. "At least have another glass of wine. You can afford that, can't you?"

"Not really." But I did, if only to give me nerve enough for the next bit. We were both of us evasive by nature, or else by training; I had to pin her down. I said, "Okay, look, we went back to Fay's last known address and that didn't help." Except for the janitor I wasn't telling her about, except for Fay's dog-owning buddy who Desi hadn't let me speak to. "Maybe we need to look back earlier, to her childhood friends – look for the places she might have run to, rather than the one we know she ran from."

"I told you, Jay, I've done that."

"And I told you, I have to do it again."

"No." And then, when I didn't respond, just sat there and outwaited her, she said, "You can't."

"Why can't I?" Asking very gently, giving her all the space she needed.

"Because her friends are scattered all over, the lucky ones. The ones who aren't dead already, or very, very hurt. Come to think of it, maybe it's the dead ones who are lucky. They don't have to be scared any more. The Cathars had the same idea: talk to her friends, see if they could find her. Don't take *no* for an answer. Like that."

CHAPTER EIGHT

WE WENT THROUGH Fay's diary nonetheless, because we had it now. The contacts section was blank. Desi said, "She used a separate address-book, cats on the cover, she'd had the same one forever. Since she went to big school at age eleven. I bought it for her. You know what those are like, by the time you get to be nineteen: half the pages are loose and coffee-stained, almost everyone in it's moved at least once so it's all scribbles and mad addenda squeezed in at any angle they'll fit, it's stuffed with random scraps of paper for all those contacts you don't have room to write in or haven't got around to yet. She kept it held together with rubber bands."

Actually, I didn't know what those are like. I'd never had an address book, nor been close to anyone who did. My only friends had been my parents' friends and their occasional children; hence, now, no friends at all. I bit that all back, though, not to sound pathetic or sorry for myself. Worse things happened,

in my life and in Desi's. In hers, the Cathars; in mine
– well, my parents, for a start. And their friends.

She sat turning through the pages of the diary,
reading the occasional scrawled note of her missing
sister's lost life. It was a private moment and I'd have
let her keep it so, but it went on too long. She'd got
stuck, I thought, in her mourning.

"At least you know how the Cathars found her
friends, then."

"Mmm?"

"If they've got her address-book. They didn't get
at them through you, you didn't lead them there."
Something in her voice when she told me, I was sure
she blamed herself. "It's not much, maybe, but it
must be some sort of comfort."

"Oh – yes, I suppose. There is always that." She
didn't sound comforted. I guess she didn't want to
think about her sister's friends, any more than I
wanted her to dwell so deeply on her sister. I had the
sense that I'd blown that one, so I did the only other
thing I could think of, reached out an arm for the
wine and topped up her glass.

She gave me half a smile, and, "Sorry, was I getting
morbid?"

"Not that." Maudlin, perhaps. "Far away,
perhaps. You're entitled, she's your sister –"

"But I need to stay focused. Right. What do you
want to do tomorrow?"

"Umm. How would you feel, if I said I wanted to
go off by myself?"

"Oh. Truly?"

"Truly."

"I think I'd feel disappointed."

"I will be looking for Fay. Just, I don't think I
should take you where I want to go."

"I didn't mean let down. I thought today was useful, that's all. We're good together."

That was odd: I thought we worked against each other, every step of the way. Every turn of the wheel. I was disappointed too, but not for professional reasons.

"Besides," she went on scowlingly, "who's got your back, if I'm not there? You go getting into trouble for my sake, Jay, I want to be there to get you out of it. There's nowhere in this world or any other where you can go safely but I can't."

That was probably true, if only because there was nowhere in this world – or any other – where I could go safely, full stop. She wasn't getting the point, why I wanted to leave her behind, and I certainly wasn't going to clarify it for her.

So I ducked it; I said, "Let's talk about it in the morning, okay?"

She glowered. "Don't think about sneaking off early, before I wake up. I have ears like a lark." And then she blinked, and grinned, and said, "Whatever. You know what I mean."

"No sneaking off," I promised. "If I'm up first, I'll wait. We can argue it out over the eggs and bacon."

"I haven't got eggs. Or bacon."

"I'll shop," I said. "If you'll trust me this time. I've still got your change."

Again with the frowning, and, "Jay, I trusted you last time. Did I ask for the change?"

"It's not about the change. You followed me, downriver."

"Did not. I thought about it, maybe, then decided against. You'd come back, or you wouldn't. I can't keep you here by force. I suppose I could steal your trousers, but..."

"Desi, I knew you were there."

"It wasn't me." She was staring now: not angry, just baffled.

My turn to stare. If not her, who...?

There were too many possible answers, and almost all of them were frightening. Some were frightening past measure.

Desi looked just as scared, for a moment, on my behalf. Then her Aspect cut in. Not by her choice, I think, it just seemed to happen. Like a turbocharger: hit the right revs, the right level of stress or adrenalin or whatever, and slam! There it was, willy-nilly.

Under the impact of that gaze, that stature, that simple *presence*, my panic ebbed away. She didn't really grow a foot in height, her shoulders a foot in breadth, it only seemed that way; just as she couldn't really protect me, but I felt safer none the less.

"What did you see, Jay?"

Nothing that I could describe to her; in honesty, nothing at all. I did my best to explain that hypersensitivity that comes from long years on the run, but even to my own ears it only sounded like paranoia.

I was ready for her to say so. Instead, she headed for the companionway. "Stay here, and bolt the hatch behind me. Not that it'll do much good against anyone who can get past me, but..."

"Where are you going?"

"To look. See if we're being watched."

"You mean you believe me?"

"I'd be a fool not to. Your instincts are why you're here."

I could have kissed her then, except – well. Boss, not girlfriend. And she was moving fast. And she had her Aspect on, and I really didn't want to confuse one thing with another.

My voice chased after her: "Don't go far..."

She paused on the stairs, and looked back over her shoulder. "That's why you should bolt the hatch. Anyone tries to come through that, I'll hear. I may not get back in time to save you, but I'll give your corpse a beautiful revenge."

And with that she blew me a kiss, the daemon in full fig, all dark energy and danger; and was gone, swiftly and completely.

I scuttled in her wake, to slam and seal that hatch. The bolts were unexpectedly sturdy, but that was small reassurance: the hatch was only wood. I'd seen Desi push her way clean through a very solid brick wall. The people I was most afraid to find on this boat, they'd walk towards it and that hatch would disintegrate before them, sooner than stand in their way.

Desi wouldn't hear that. I could always scream – but then she'd come, and all her cheerful bravado would be as meaningless as her strength. She could die too, but there'd be no coming back for her, and then who would be left to look for Fay?

No, if they came I'd be as silent as the hatch, as silent as the grave they'd not allow me. She'd come back and I'd be gone, and that was all the memorial I'd have, my sudden absence from her boat and from her life. It didn't seem enough.

So I left those bolts alone, threw back the hatch and went up on deck. I didn't want to cower like a rat in a trap; I'd rather run. I should be running now. But there was Desi, out there somewhere on my behalf, and I couldn't do it. I couldn't do anything except stand and wait in the open air, in the sounds of the river and the smells of the town, the occasional waft of curry that I hoped was on the breeze and not on me. If doom was coming – oh, hell, let it come. I was sick of running.

I waited, and someone came: like a shadow among shadows, a threat on the wind, making my hackles rise again. But this time it was only Desi, as I'd thought before.

Only, did I say? It was Desi at her extremes, fully stretched. Her physical – her *extremely* physical – body might be walking along the towpath in a normal human manner, if any normal human had ever been so lithe, so indefatigably alive; but her mind, her spirit, everything else she had was encompassing the night. I was sure her eyes could see in the dark, Iand thought she could hear conversations on the other side of town, but it was more than that. I could feel her on the breeze: sniffing, tasting, insinuating herself. Reaching.

And then she shook her head and shrugged off her Aspect, and there was that sudden shuddering sense of the world's attention drifting away; and she tilted an eyebrow at me and said, "What are you doing up on deck? I told you to stay below. And bolt the hatch."

She didn't sound angry. Just as well, as I had nothing to offer by way of an excuse, only a mute and useless shake of the head.

"You didn't even bring your bag up, did you?"

I actually hadn't realised, but she was right.

"If you're not going to do what I tell you," she said, all boss but not stroppy, more long-suffering, "it'll land us both in trouble, sooner or later. But not tonight. I can't find anyone out there. Well, there are people around, but so far as I can tell they're all legit."

"They don't have to be superhuman to be looking for me. Lots of plain regular folks would like the bounty too."

"I know that. But truly, Jay, I can't find anyone watching the boat. There are kids snogging in the park, but they've been drinking cider and they're out of their skulls. Otherwise it's just dog-walkers and boat-owners out for a stroll. If anyone was spying, I'd find them."

"Did you check all the trees?"

"*Yes*. They're trees, and they've all been there a long time. And that's my story, not yours: the dryad was watching my sister's house and not looking for you at all, and I scragged her anyway. But yes, I still checked the trees. Okay?"

"Scragged?"

"Scragged," she repeated menacingly, stepping one pace closer. "Should I demonstrate?"

"No, thanks. I'll take your word for it. Good word, scragged."

"Right. Now get below."

"I thought you'd just decided it was safe out here?"

"Can't be safe enough, and I don't want to be on alert all night. There's a price to be paid, if I keep my Aspect on. You know that."

I did; I had the soreness and the bruises to prove it. And the sweet, exhaustive, exhausting memories too, which would outlive all the signs of rough handling. She was no more gentle in bed than out – and she was stepping one pace closer still, with that slightly glazed look on her face and the hint of sweat somehow about her although I didn't think she ever actually sweated, and –

– AND SHE STEPPED back abruptly, shook her head hard, said, "Sorry. That's not fair. Last night was – extreme, but even so. You're not here to service my needs. Not like that. I shouldn't have let it happen."

"Are you saying you're sorry it did?"

"No, I'm not saying that. Only that it shouldn't have. It's not fair on you."

"Um, I really didn't mind..."

She laughed, but she had to toss it back over her shoulder; she was already heading down into the cabin. "Maybe not, but I do. I have my pride, and I have rules. You're here to do a job for me, and I shouldn't abuse that. Just because the Aspect always leaves me, oh..."

"Horny?" I supplied, tagging along behind.

Another laugh, which I regarded as a victory. A small one, in the face of loss. "I was going to say hot, but horny's probably more honest. So that, yes. But I shouldn't take it out on you. And another thing," a determined change of subject, "we should've taken dinner up on deck. Curry on shipboard, it's great, but you can smell it for a week," and she stormed around the cabin slamming open all the portholes. She was right, but again I really didn't mind.

I gathered up empty cartons and carrier bags, packed them into each other and offered to take them down the towpath to the bins.

"Don't you dare! That's a hundred metres –"

"– and you just said it was safe –"

"– and then I said we can't be safe enough. Leave the garbage up on deck – and *come back down*. I'm going to take a shower. A cold one."

...And she didn't want to be thinking about me, worrying about me while she was doing it. Right.

She disappeared into the head, bolting the door loudly at her back. I sighed, and started puzzling out how to turn the sofa into a bed. I'd rather be in the shower with Desi, cold or not, but she was probably right. Best to keep this professional. If I couldn't afford to get a head for wine, or a taste for regular meals, no way could I afford a girlfriend.

I poured myself another defiant glass of wine in lieu, before I began the search for bedclothes. If I drank enough to give myself a really bad hangover in the morning, maybe that'd help me not acquire the habit of it...

MEN HAVE PROBABLY deceived themselves with thoughts like that since alcohol was discovered and the hangover with it. And women have probably laughed at them since the morning after.

Desi laughed at me when I explained it, when she came out of the shower to find the bottle empty and the sofabed made up. I thought she'd just open another bottle, that seemed to be the way she met the world, the daemon thing to do; but instead she turned the lights out and told me to go to bed.

I DID THAT, because there was nothing else to do in the dark. I couldn't even sit up reading, knowing that my light would be disturbing her at the other end of the cabin.

I lay very still and listened for her breathing; she did still need to breathe, like she needed to eat and pee and such, those reassuringly human processes. I tried to match her breathing with my own, and found it remarkably easy; and after a little while tried to add one and one to get two people breathing in harmony where one of them was asleep and the other not, and the sum did not add up. She was doing what I was doing: lying wide awake and gazing into the dark. Listening, breathing.

It needed one of us to stir, to speak, but neither of us would. I guess we both knew that.

*   *   *

SO THERE WE were, caught in this stupidity, determinedly trapped and neither one of us even drunk enough to float away on a sea of alcohol. When I did at last start to drift, it was something else that lifted me: not sleep and not wine, but soft music like a cord to ensnare my thoughts, a light thread that twined and tangled all through my head, slow and sweet and running like cool spring water.

Unusually for a boy my age, I don't listen to a lot of music. Don't have download access, can't afford batteries, daren't risk the distraction. Anyone with earphones isn't listening for whatever might be coming up behind him.

Maybe that's why I get earwormed so easily, just because I don't get that much exposure. What I hear – what I overhear – is other people's music, as I pass; or else it's shopping-mall muzak, and even that can burrow deep into my subconscious and play itself over and over for days on end.

This was something utterly different, and – when I thought about it, brief flashes of awareness, of wonder and confusion – I couldn't figure out where it had come from, where I might have heard it before, to have it rise up and entrance me now.

Mostly, though, I wasn't thinking at all. It robbed me of thought, almost wholly. I didn't listen to it, I bathed in it, it encompassed me entirely; and was her song, our song, the song of the two of us together.

I didn't need to sing it back to her; she knew. And so she came to me, slipping through the open porthole like something woven from weed and water, alien and powerful and given in gift to me.

She sang me out of bed and to my feet, and I stood

there as naked as she was, unafraid, entranced; and she reached out a hand to take mine, to lead me out and away...

AND THAT WAS the mistake she made, just the one mistake and a small one, but it was enough. Because even spirits can be right-handed, apparently, and we were facing each other, so the hand that she reached for was my left.

I'm determinedly right-handed myself, I work to keep myself that way; but it's the left that saves my life, over and over. That extra finger connects me to the world in a wholly different way. Like a third eye that sees by other light, except that it's a finger, so of course it works by touch.

It touched her, and suddenly I wasn't drifting any more. I could still hear her singing, and it wasn't in my head at all. It was hers, her snare, insidious and relentless, and the touch of her hand in mine was cold and strong and clammy; and her song was like the river in sunlight, idle and glimmering and seductive, but the smell of her was like a dredge from the muddy bottom, dark and heavy with rot.

I screamed, I think. I know I tried to jerk away from her. But she held me fast, and I couldn't pull free; she threw her other arm around me and it was like being gripped by the river, or perhaps by reeds. She looked tolerably human in the dark of the cabin, or at least she'd taken human shape, but she'd kept the inexorable strength of water.

And I was just a boy and I could do nothing against her, while she held me pinned against her chill wet flank. I did yell, but her song absorbed my noise and scattered it, and Desi never stirred.

The undine dragged me over to the open porthole. Only then she had to let go of my hand, to tear a hole wide enough to squeeze me through it. She'd come in half-liquid like her song, oozing through whatever gap there was, but she couldn't make me do that, however strong her singing. Or her tug. She might have wrenched the better part of me through somehow, but it would've been way too broken to be of any use to the people who wanted me.

They wanted me whole, so she ripped out the porthole to oblige them; and in the slender moment that she needed to tear heavy brass hinges like paper, I clamped that good left hand of mine tight around her throat.

I've said already, that hand gives good grip: more than one small extra finger would normally warrant. I don't suppose Anne Boleyn could have crushed Henry's throat one-handed, however much reason he gave her.

I could have done that much, but I couldn't trouble the undine. She might have taken human shape; that didn't make her human. Her life was underwater, her body seemed to be made mostly of water, and if she came up it wasn't for the air.

Not to breathe, at any rate. She wouldn't suffocate, however hard I gripped; nor did she have veins and arteries, a jugular, carotids that I could usefully cut off.

What she did have, she must have built herself. Some kind of lungs-and-voicebox system, bellows and reeds, or she wouldn't have been able to sing. It's air in vibration, that's what the ear picks up. So she did need air after all, and delivery; and so she needed a mouth to feed it in and out, and between lungs and mouth was – ?

Yup. So I did crush her throat, and it didn't trouble

her breathing because she wasn't doing that at all, but it did entirely cut off her song.

Which wouldn't have mattered a little bit, if I'd been alone in that long cabin. She had me already, and I was what she came for. She disregarded my stranglehold entirely and hauled me towards the porthole, and I went with her because I could do no other, I was helpless in her grasp.

And then Desi hit us.

I felt her coming, and so surely must the undine; any daemon is a force of nature when they draw their Aspect on. Desi hit us like a hammer. She slammed all the breath out of me, and for a moment I thought she'd slammed all my ribs out with the spine still attached. Blessedly I had a soft landing, back on the bed again. I lay there – gagging rather than gasping, mouthing like a landed fish and utterly bereft of air, all the paralysis of a punch in the solar plexus – and the only thing I didn't let go of was the undine's throat.

The rest of her was in Desi's hands.

It was a strange and terrible battle, half-seen and half-felt, as though I were only half there where it mattered, where the focus was. The undine had a hint of light about her, like phosphorescence on the surface of the ocean. I saw Desi mostly, wrestling with a wet shadow, but it was by the dark light of that shadow that I saw her. And I still held one end of it, though there was nothing human left to the undine's shape by then; she shifted as they rolled, as they blatted each other back and forth across the bed, against the bulkheads, over the decking. I just lay back and held on grimly, some kind of anchor-point. There wasn't anything else I could do, but for sure I was not letting the undine get away.

Desi neither, Desi clung to her like Janet clung to

Tam Lin as he went through all the changes. She clung, and she did more than cling; she wrestled, and she ripped. She flung off bits, parts, wet portions that slapped against the hull and I couldn't see what happened to them after.

Even so, even ripped to ruin, the undine had the river's strength in her, the force of weirs and currents and ages of flow. That slow abiding met Desi's urgency, and fought back hard. It was no certain thing, which one would lose. I had nothing to offer, no way to help, except that I could hold the creature here; and even my iron grip was growing tired, before at last Desi wrapped arms and legs around the undine and just squeezed. Like a boa, like a bear.

She might be shifty, but the undine wasn't infinitely elastic; and she was a river creature, not from deep waters. This was pressure from all sides, inescapable, and she couldn't take it. Things broke.

She might have screamed, then, except that I still had her throat. Instead I could hear noises as of air bubbling through thick mud, down where her chest had been. Whatever kind of air-sac or lung she'd made for herself, to hold what she'd need to sing with, I guess it had burst.

She was slack in my grip then, and slack in Desi's. Desi was careful, though; no point checking for a pulse – how would we know what strange flows had sustained her? – but she went over that not-so-human body and broke everything that she could find to break.

Long before she was done, I was feeling no reaction, not a twitch of life, only the tugs of whatever Desi was doing. Still, I didn't ask her to stop. Nor did I release my own grip until there was a rush of foul water, a rising stink that made me gag abruptly, and nothing in my hand but slimy, gristly weed.

And then there was light, as Desi flicked on the cabin lamps; and there we both were, wet and naked and streaked with rank mud and barely registering that because we were both looking at what lay slumped across the bed, spewed half across the cabin.

In the dark and singing, she could have passed for human. So long as she kept the singing up she could keep up the illusion too, even to the touch. After that, when the singing stopped – no. It wasn't skin I'd held, nor muscles that fought back. It was a body she'd pieced together, apparently, from what she had available, all she could find in the river's murk. There were sticks and reeds and weeds and garbage, bucketsful of mud and water. Bones too, but not her own: rat-bones, dog-bones, I didn't want to look for worse. None of it could sustain life on its own account, not now. She must have invested it with hers, to the danger-point where damage to that ramshackle scarecrow corpse meant damage to her own self, to her spirit. The sticks and reeds were all in pieces. The bones were splintered, the weeds shredded, the garbage crushed and torn out of all recognition; and so she died, and the coherence with her, and so this... disintegration...

For a while, there just weren't any words. Desi let her Aspect slip away, gazed around at the wreckage, sniffed; and looked at the hole in her boat's hull where the porthole had been ripped out, and pushed wet dark hair back out of her eyes and sniffed again.

Me, I just watched Desi.

At last she looked at me. Her mouth twitched into a wry half-smile, and she did find something to say. "There should be enough hot water for a shower, just about. Just the one, though. We'd better share."

So we did that, squeezed into the awkward head

together. We washed each other's backs, because there wasn't room enough to wash our own; and got our elbows in each other's ribs, and soap in each other's eyes, and grumbled wetly at each other; and the hot water ran out too soon, so that we both tried to jump yelping out from under the chilly jet and ended sprawled in a tangle beneath the toilet, bumped and bruised and giggling. Lucky, she'd had a soft landing on top of me; other way around, she might not have found it so funny.

She was on top, so she had to get herself up first. She took her time, and was still too quick for me. By the time I'd scrambled up, she had towels in her hands. She handed me one and turned away, stepping back into the chaos of the cabin and rubbing at her own hair as she went, just that insightful moment before I could offer to do it for her.

I wanted distraction, contact, warmth. Out there was the other thing, a cold fear that hadn't died at all, for all that the undine lay in ruin on the floor. My feet wanted to run, and my head agreed with them. What held me back was indefinable, heart and hormones, some combination of the two. Not honour, for sure: I'd made promises before, and broken them blithely or blindly or whichever way I had to, whatever way first offered.

The difference this time was that the promises were made to Desi, and I'd keep them if I could. It was all very simple, really.

ROUGHLY DRY, I looked around for my jeans, and found them kicked aside and sodden. There'd been a lot of water slopping around by the end there. The boat was built for storms at sea and there were scuppers in every corner, so that had drained away, but this end of the cabin was soaked and stinking. I had spares in the rucksack, but as I started to unzip it Desi looked up from poking a desultory toe at riverweed and said, "What are you doing?"

"Getting dressed. If we tackle the clean-up naked, we'll just get all slimed-up again, and there's no more hot to wash in."

"And if you do it with your clean clothes on, you'll get those all slimed-up instead, and you'll still want to wash after, and there'll still be no more hot. Come to bed."

"Sorry?"

"You can't sleep in that," with a gesture towards the sofa-bed, streaked and soaked, "and there's no dry floor, and if there was I wouldn't let you have it. Come to *bed*, Jay, and we'll sort this out in the morning."

She looked so forlorn, standing there with her hair in rats'-tails, holding her hand out to me, naked in the ruin of her home: I didn't offer any of the very good reasons why we should deal with it now, before the mud dried hard and the reek embedded itself in all the fabrics. I just took her hand and let her lead me to her own bed, where she killed the lights and drew me in and we nestled in the shivery warmth of each other until we fell asleep.

AND WOKE IN the darkness, and talked a little:

"Where do you suppose she came from, Jay?"

"The river. Ouch!"

"I know, the river. She brought half of it in with her. But how did she find us, how did they know to send a naiad, how did they know we were on a boat...?"

"Oh – I know what you're thinking. Two

shapeshifty women in one day, they've got to be working together, right?"

"Yes, of course."

"Forget it. Just coincidence, that's all. The tree-creature this morning, she was on watch for Fay, or for you, maybe, or anyone interested in your sister. This one tonight was after me. That was my fault, if you like. I'm sorry."

"I don't like, and I don't believe in coincidence. That's too much."

"No, it's really not. People are looking for Fay, we know that, we're doing it too; and people are looking for me. We know that, you did it. You found me. Others do, sometimes. I was stupid, being down by the river so long and not thinking about the water. I even went and stood on that walkway over the weir, right above the flow of it. That's when she will have sensed me; she was probably in the weir, they love a scouring flow. Not a naiad, by the way, that was an undine. Ouch!"

"Don't keep correcting me, will you?"

"Then don't keep being wrong. And don't pinch me again, I can outpinch you. I've got more fingers. It's the song gave her away, that's undine all through. I'd have figured it out, maybe, if she'd tried singing me down from the river bank. But she was smart, she just watched, and followed me back upriver. She'll be what I felt, when I thought it was you on my tail. She must've thought she'd lost me when I went into the town, but even then she could trade on the news that she'd seen me, that's currency. Only she landed lucky, or she thought she did, when I came back to the water. She thought she could take me, hand me over her own self, that's riches. And she nearly did it, too. She'd have had me, if it hadn't been for you."

"I'm sure she would," Desi murmured, against my shoulder-blade. "But then you wouldn't have been anywhere near here, if it hadn't been for me."

"And your boat wouldn't have been wrecked, if it hadn't been for her coming after me. We could play that game forever, and never fix the blame where it belongs." Or the gratitude, either.

"Right. Go to sleep."

So WE DID that again, and in the morning we swept and scrubbed and hauled stuff up on deck to let it dry in sunlight, and broke for breakfast in a riverside café, and then went back to scrub some more. And when Desi started phoning boatyards to see about getting her porthole refitted, I made gestures to show her that we'd used all the cleaning materials she had, and the smell was still lingering, and I was going into town to shop for more.

And then I walked a hundred yards up from the river to the railway station, and jumped on the first train to London.

CHAPTER NINE

I DID SEND her a text, to let her know – *not run away, gone to see a man about Fay* – but I didn't send it until I was safely off the little local train that she might've chased down, onto the London express that I was fairly sure she couldn't catch even on the Harley. That was maybe an hour after I'd left, maybe time enough for her to be wondering where I'd got to. If she wasn't too distracted. Boat with a hole in it, after all; she might not have missed me all morning.

In all my sneaky planning, I'd forgotten to pick up anything to read, so I stared out of the window all the way to Paddington. And then had to spend good cash money on an A-Z, to find out how to get to Chiswick; and then – well, small-town boy with parsimonious habits, I chickened out of the Tube and set off to walk it. Quickly.

It's quite a long way, from Paddington to Chiswick. I was sweating before I got there, running my hand over the damp stubble on my scalp and wishing I'd run the shaver over it first, somewhere in the morning before I left.

At least the right house wasn't hard to find: behind an overgrown hedge, with boarded-up windows and the front door standing wide to welcome me. A builder's van was parked in the road, and builder's clutter had accumulated on the pavement and in the tiny front garden. There was a generator dumped on the scabby turf, guttering to itself; a coiling cable led through to an angle-grinder on the bare hall floor.

The whole set-up reeked of trap. But I have a paranoid turn of mind, and I was on a razor's edge after last night; it was hard to keep the two hunts separate in my head, the hunt for Fay and the hunt for me. I did need to be wary here in London, but I didn't need to see traps laid in settings that were not about me. I'd phoned a man who knew Fay, that was all. He had no idea who I was, and I'd given him a false name anyway. He was the janitor of her building; why wouldn't he do odd building work for other people? Or arrange to meet me where he happened to be working?

Even so, I did what I could to cover my back. It'd be stupid not to take precautions. Horror-movie stupid, kids walking alone into obviously haunted basements. That sort of thing.

With my precaution in my hand, then, and my hand securely in my pocket, I stood on the doorstep and called inside.

"Mr Tasker?"

"In here, come on through." But actually he came out from a back room, into the hallway to meet me. Following his voice, so that I had all the benefit of that gravelly croak first, before I saw the man that made it.

He looked near as rough as his voice was: one of

those gaunt hard-muscled men who get that way from sheer labour, not at all at the gym. His hair was clipped and greying, although nowhere near as short or white as mine; he might have been fifty, or five years either side. He was stripped to the waist, and his skin was grey with cement-dust not thick enough to hide the tattoos beneath. They looked crude, home-made, the kind you pick up at school or perhaps in prison, just broken outlines badly drawn; but he had them on his arms, on his chest, on his belly, on the backs of his hands.

He smiled with a glint of gold in the shadows, and lifted his hand as though to shake mine; and then I saw him check himself, the way adults do sometimes when they're not sure whether a teenager has been socialised as far as handshakes. He beckoned instead, and turned back into the room.

His back was crawling with the same tattoos, and it looked as though they went down below the waistband of his jeans. In the dim light and under the dust, I couldn't make out the pattern, but whatever it was, he was surely fond of it.

A man's tattoo habit wouldn't creep me out, after some of the things I've seen; but something in me always creeps a bit, walking into a strange house where a stranger's waiting. I kept my hand in my pocket and my finger poised on a hair-trigger.

Down the stripped hallway, stepping carefully over the angle-grinder; past the foot of the stairs – I could hear hammering up there and drew comfort from that, another presence in the house – and into the half-light of a kitchen with its window boarded over. Old tiles underfoot, cracked and filthy; all the cabinets ripped out and the sink gone too, and the cooker. Raw pipes showing.

He turned to face me, and his smile looked kind of raw too, as though he was still practising. In his voice like cracking rocks he said, "So you're going to tell me everything you know about little Fay, is that right?"

"Well, the other way round, actually; I was hoping for you to tell me..."

"I don't think so, lad. No time for that." His hand was quicker than I was, and I was poised to be quick; he had a sudden clamp around my left elbow, crushingly tight. The pain of it came burning down my forearm. My wrist cramped; I did just manage to work my finger, one little touch, before numbness seized my hand and left me helpless.

He'd lifted me onto tiptoe, effortlessly; I could swing my other arm at him, but that was pointless. So was swearing, but I did that anyway.

He clipped me casually across the side of the head, with a palm like rock; said, "So let's see what the kid is hiding, shall us?" and drew my frozen hand out of my pocket.

And saw that it held nothing more lethal than a mobile phone, and laughed, with a sound like an avalanche of pebbles; and slipped the phone mockingly back into my pocket again, all out of reach now with his gripping my arm that way, and called, "Billy!"

"Aye, guv?" The voice that came back from upstairs was young and cowed, and no comfort at all.

"Just bring us the angle-grinder from the hall. Look sharp, now."

A scurry of feet on the hollow stairs, looking sharp; a boy appeared in the doorway with the angle-grinder in his hands, the cable dragging after. Clipper-headed like his boss, stripped to the waist like his boss; even so, I thought he looked more like me. My age, anyway, and scrawny like me, scared like me. One thing for sure, I was right royally scared, and not of the angle-grinder.

Not *only* of the angle-grinder.

Sometimes I just hate it when I'm right.

The man was looking at my hand. The left one, naturally.

Almost musingly, if shale can muse, he said, "I was going to take a finger off, just to get you talking – but you wouldn't miss one, would you? I'd have to take two. And that head of yours, if you didn't shave it, you'd be your mummy's white-headed boy, I reckon. Billy, put that down and come here."

"Don't do it, Billy," I said urgently. "You get away from here, get help. Get the police, get anyone..."

Billy wasn't listening to me, and I didn't blame him. By the look of it, this man owned him, body and soul. There's more than one way to sell yourself, and Desi had had the best of it; this lad, I thought, was somewhere down the other end of the scale.

The man had some touch to him, more than human. No one is that strong by nature, nor by work. I simply couldn't shift his grip at all; he was massive, monumental, something utterly abnormal within a human-seeming skin.

And then his tattoos began to move.

They spelled out words, I thought, seeing them in close-up, though not in any language that I knew. Nor any that I cared to learn. There was something sick-making about the shapes they made beneath his skin, let alone the meanings they suggested in my head, even before they started marching.

The man reached out his other arm, and took a grip of Billy's neck where the boy had come obediently close. I thought obedience defined his life, because defiance would never dare to. He looked more than sick, utterly desperate.

And the tattoos slid and jerked their disarticulated way down the man's arm; they swarmed over his hand and passed out of my sight, and didn't I just know that they would reappear under the boy's skin, swarming across his shoulders?

While they did that, the man was murmuring to Billy, "I want you to go fetch the Green Man, run and fetch him, fast. You know where to find him..."

Which was when I stopped listening, because I knew the Green Man. He was a friend of my parents, and never ever any friend of mine. Besides, I was increasingly aware, through the pain, of what was happening to the man's hand and arm, where he was gripping me.

The skin had darkened, set and split. That same shadow was spreading over his shoulder, over his chest, over his scalp; as those dreadful tattooed words fled him and swarmed into his boy, so his abandoned body changed.

What I saw was mirrored in what I felt, as all sense of movement left him. He still had me locked in that unshiftable grip, and there was nothing human remaining in him now. He was massive in a whole new way, a monument of rock.

Just in time, the boy twisted away from the grip on his neck. A moment later, that hand too would have hardened, inexorably about his flesh; he'd have been as much a prisoner of stone as I was.

It was the words beneath his skin that compelled him. His terror was swamped, overridden. If I thought I could still see Billy in his eyes, in the little moment before he turned and ran off on his errand, then I was probably fooling myself. Trying to. In truth, I thought Billy was buried under a stony fall of words.

Whether he could recover, whether the words would march out again and leave him, Billy as he was before – well, maybe. I couldn't guess. Nor work out whether his fear had been blind, or dread of what was coming, or foreknowledge because he'd been through this already. Nor whether the words could return to reanimate this man who held me, or whether they only ever migrated onward, leaving statues in their wake.

I DIDN'T KNOW, and it couldn't make any difference. Not to me. I was alone in there, with a dead arm seized by lifeless rock; and one of the pitiless and terrifying creatures of my long acquaintance, one of those I'd been fleeing all this time, would soon be on his way.

I couldn't do a thing. Pulling and twisting my elbow only brought back the pain, even through the crushing numbness. Not even my left hand, my smart little finger could have picked that rock apart, and of course it was my left that was trapped anyway.

So I was helpless, held standing, my doom coming upon me at long last. The hunt had to catch up with me sooner or later, that had always been inevitable; I suppose it would always have felt too soon. It did that day, for sure. I was as melancholy as I was fearful, overswept with misery as much as dread. It was a hasty, patchy life I led, but it was my own, and it was going to be snatched from me, and I wasn't ready. However long Billy took to find the Green Man, it wouldn't be long enough.

It wasn't the dying that shrivelled me up inside, nor even the knowing whose hands they were that would kill me. It was the horror of what would come after, what would come and come and never find an ending...

WHAT CAME FIRST – after I'd been through all the panic, the useless tugging at a rock-hard grip, and had just about persuaded myself into a kind of dull resignation – was a roar in the street outside.

A roar that rose and fell, rose and fell again to a muted rumble, died to silence.

Then a crash, as it might be a door being kicked off its hinges.

Then the stomp of boots on bare boards, the loom of a shadow in the doorway.

Half a chuckle, half a sigh as she stepped through; I could hear both quite clearly through the helmet's mask, which meant that she was exaggerating them, just to be utterly certain that I did hear.

Now my panic was back, full force. Now I was fighting against the stone hand that held me, ripping skin off my elbow, greasing the grip with my blood, achieving nothing.

She lifted her helmet off and said, "Jay, it's okay, for crying out loud, this is me..."

Oh, I knew that; and no, it wasn't okay at all. She was here, and the Green Man was coming. Never mind all the questions that had to come; right now there was nothing in my head except to get her out of here, and maybe incidentally myself.

"Can you," I gasped, still writhing, "can you break me free of this? Quickly?"

"Slow down," she said, and put her hands on my

shoulders and just held me, a vision of misplaced patience until I was still. "That's better."

"It isn't. Really, Desi, it isn't. We've got to move..."

"More haste, less speed, you ever hear that? God knows what happened here, explain it to me later, but – no. This is what, volcanic? I can't break that."

"I thought, with your Aspect, you could maybe snap the fingers off...?"

"Not even that."

"Go, then. Get away. Quickly, someone's coming."

"I'd kind of figured that. And it's all right, I've got a Plan B. Wait there." She gifted me a grin broad enough to say that she knew just what she'd said, and she'd done it deliberately; and then she stooped, and hoisted the angle-grinder up off the floor.

I swallowed and said, "It'll, um, it'll be quicker if you go through my arm..." *Rather than his,* is what I meant: flesh and bone, sooner than solid basalt.

"Sweetheart, if there was that much hurry, I wouldn't bother with this thing. Just pull your arm clean off, the Aspect is plenty good enough for that. I'm still hoping to get you out of here whole. Hold still."

The angle-grinder screamed into life, and once again I held very still indeed.

SHE TOOK THE stone man's hand off at the wrist. I guess it was as close as she dared come, for fear of the blade skidding into me. I didn't think there was actually any risk of that; she'd put her Aspect on, just to hold the tool steady. Rock-steady was how she held it, like she was mechanical herself. Sparks flew, and clouds of choking, stinging dust; trust her though I did, I still sweated coldly from first to last, giving all that dust something to cling to.

At last the blade cut through, and my arm fell dead to my side, with the heavy hand still attached like some curious bondage elbow-cuff. I staggered, just a little, and it was the wall and not Desi that caught me; for a moment I wondered if she were a little weak-knee'd with relief herself, she was carrying herself so low.

Then she grunted with satisfaction and stepped, reached; I understood that she'd just been peering beneath the dust-cloud, looking for something specific.

Looking for a sledgehammer, as it happened.

I'd wondered already whether the dreadful letters would be passed back into this stone man and bring life to his limbs again, life to his body, voice and thought and action. Not if Desi had her way. She hefted the hammer, took casual aim and swung with all her grace and focus, power in motion, all the force of her Aspect: magnificent to watch even when your eyes were weeping and your legs were still unsteady.

The great head of the hammer struck that rock form in the midriff, with a dull booming note, and I felt not a scrap of pity for the man who might or might not still somehow be inside there –

– AND THE BASALT column of him barely shivered, and it was the shaft of the hammer that snapped.

And it was the head of the hammer that rebounded from the rock to come flying straight at me, and it would have killed me if that hadn't been the moment when the dust hit my lungs with a slapstick exactitude of timing, so that I doubled up coughing and it skimmed over my head and slammed into the wall that had been holding me up.

That was a supporting wall, solid brick, and the hammerhead was embedded in it deep enough that Desi pretty much had to use her nails to work it out.

I watched her do it – how could I not? She had her Aspect on, and she was Desi, and neither way could I take my eyes off her – and then said, "Can we go now? Please?"

"Yes," she said, somewhat to my surprise. "Right now, if you like. Are you fit to walk?"

I was, just about – it was my arm that was half-crushed, my legs were fine, if wobbly – and I would have asserted that loudly, if I hadn't been overtaken by another coughing-fit.

Desi took my good elbow and practically worked me like a puppet, upright and then forward to the hall doorway. There, she turned with a swift economy of movement and hurled the hammerhead.

This time, the full force of her Aspect hit me as hard – well, almost as hard – as the hammerhead hit the stone man. I only gasped. The stone man, the pillar of basalt shattered, as any rock might that had a thunderbolt hurled at it, Thor's hammer in all but name.

He wouldn't be worrying about any missing hand now. That was my worry and mine alone, if it came to life again. I barely had any worry left to spare for poor Billy, stuck with all those words.

No time for that; Desi dragged me out into blessedly fresh air, onto the kerb where the motorbike was ticking gently.

She looked up the road and down, and for a mad, crazy moment I thought she was more than anxious, almost as scared as myself.

All she said, though – when she was sure she'd seen nothing – was, "Can you manage the helmet by yourself?"

One-handed, that would have to be. I said, "Yeah, sure," but she maybe heard the doubt I wasn't prepared to admit to. My left arm was both numb and amazingly painful suddenly, which seemed unfair.

At any rate, she whipped out the spare helmet, clamped it on my head and did the strap up for me swiftly and unpityingly, giving me no time to fumble or object. Then her own went back on and we bestrode the bike and were away.

I only had the one fit arm to hold on by, so I really had no choice but to wrap it around her waist and huddle close against her back. No choice at all.

ON THE ROAD, she let her Aspect slip, so she must have thought we were safe. I didn't. This was London, and she didn't take us out of it. Not to the boat, which I suppose I'd expected and been hoping for; nor to any other retreat, near or distant.

She drove in towards the centre, rather, and found a place to park up near Tottenham Court Road. Even without knowing London, I knew that: bookshops fading into electronic tat, Centre Point, first glimpse of theatres.

The first coffee house we came to, walking, she tried to steer me into it and seemed genuinely startled by my resistance.

"What's up? I need coffee. I need to sit and drink coffee, while I explain to you just what a braindead autonomic numbfuck you really are. Probably with jabby fingers, to make myself clear."

I was expecting the tirade, I even thought I'd earned it, but, "I don't want to go in there."

"Why not? We'll sit where we can see out of all the

windows, and I'll sense trouble coming anyway, get sharp away before it finds us..."

"Desi, I've got a dead man's stone hand hanging off my elbow." I thought we could safely agree that he was dead. One way or another. "It's probably quite conspicuous."

"Oh. Yes." I'd been hiding it, best I could, by folding my arms and cupping the right hand around it. That meant I could support my whole left arm as well, which was still multitasking, massively painful at the same time as being utterly dead.

Desi was on my right, with her own arm through mine; she was so focused on steering me in her direction of choice, she perhaps hadn't noticed how much she was supporting me.

"Tell you what," she said, "I'll just get take-out. Then we can find somewhere a bit more discreet. Will you be okay for two minutes out here? Come in if you like, but..."

But I didn't like, that was the point. On the street, you can hide an oddness – an extra finger, say, or a hand of rock clamped around your elbow – more easily than you can in a building. It's a privacy thing; once you're sharing a space, people assume the right to look more closely. Staring's only really rude outside.

I hunkered up against the wall and hugged myself, half-wishing that I'd kept the helmet on – but a helmet without a bike will attract attention anyway. Better to look like the runaway kid I was, homeless and hungry and not quite brave enough to beg.

She came out soon enough, with two tall covered beakers. I'd forgotten to tell her I only like my coffee straight and black. "What did you get me?"

"White chocolate mochacino."

"What's that?"

"Exactly. You're too conservative, you need to splash out more."

"I don't have the money to splash out."

"No, but I do. I'm going to educate you, it's my project. Broaden your horizons. Even if you never have another blancochocomochacino, you should at least try it once."

I could hope to hate it; then it wouldn't be a temptation hereafter. As I'd been hoping for coffee, expecting coffee and – now that she'd brought the subject up – desperately needing coffee, hating it shouldn't be too hard. I wanted caffeine, not sweetness and froth.

Actually, that was a definition of what I usually got from Desi: the deep, dark, intense hit of the pure bean, and no sweetness and froth at all. I felt let down, in incalculable ways.

"Can you carry it for me?"

"It, or you. Not both, without a third hand. What's your preference?"

She had noticed, then. I straightened as best I could, and said, "Carry the coffee. I'll carry me. Where are we going?"

"Not far. There's a little park in Soho..."

There is; and I suppose it wasn't far, except that day, when it really was too far for me. I had to beg a halt halfway. Desi surveyed me critically, set the coffees down on a handy wall, propped me up against a pillar-box and said, "Wait there."

Again, I did as instructed, if only because I couldn't manage moving. Desi disappeared into the crowds at a swift jog; when she came back this time, she was carrying a paper bag with a pharmacist's green cross on it.

"Okay: mega-painkillers, in combinations that are probably illegal and certainly unwise. You can have those once I've got you sitting down. 'Til then, roll up your – no, you can't, can you? Pity: it was a nice shirt.".

And then she gripped my shirt at the shoulder and ripped the sleeve away, using her body to mask us just a little from the street. People would see, but likely most of them wouldn't be sure quite what it was that they were seeing.

Desi worked the sleeve out from between the stone hand's grip and me – surprisingly patiently, I thought, for her. It took a fair amount of my skin and blood with it, but I'd lost those a while back, fighting to get free.

The hand's grip was a fraction looser once the shirt was gone, but really only a fraction: not enough to make a difference, to give me wriggle-room.

Desi took a spray-can out of her bag, and shook it hard.

"What's that?"

"Magic. Just to kill the pain for now, to get you walking. This needs cleaning up and dressing properly, but not yet."

The spray was bitingly chill against my skin, worse on raw flesh where the skin was gone. By the time I'd stopped gasping, though, the whole arm had stopped hurting. It was properly numb now, sheer dead weight – and heavier even than it ought to be, with that hand attached – but I wasn't complaining.

"They use it in sports," she said, "to keep people playing through an injury. How does it feel?"

"Magic." I gave her own word back to her. "And yes, I've seen football on telly too. I just didn't realise you could get it over the counter."

"Oh, you probably can't. I charmed them."

Which meant she'd hit some poor unsuspecting pharmacist with her Aspect, and rules, laws, had almost certainly been broken.

I still wasn't complaining. I could walk without a jarring agony at every step; I could follow Desi through the streets and back lanes to her little park; I could subside – carefully! – onto the grass, find a way to rest my arm on my lap that was barely uncomfortable at all, and then one-handedly swallow the pills that Desi doled out for me.

And wash them down, of course, with sweet, warm froth. Sweet, warm, milky, chocolaty froth that did still have a coffee edge to it after all, that frankly and reluctantly I thought I could so easily acquire a taste for, if it weren't so very much a luxury I couldn't afford...

That was the best of the day, that moment of stillness, of sweet relief.

Maybe that's what Desi was watching for; maybe that's why she chose that exact moment to hit me with the gimlet eye, the sneering lip, the snarling voice.

"Now. I was about to say, I believe..."

"You were, yes. Could we take it as read? Please?"

"I suppose. If you want to take *all* the fun out of the day. I'll just skip the abuse and get on to the questions, then."

"Trade you. Question for question."

"Fair enough. I go first, though."

"Fine."

"What the hell did you think you were *doing*, blundering off on your own like that?"

"If that's rhetorical, it counts as abuse."

"It's not rhetorical. Seriously, Jay. What was this all about?"

"It was about talking to someone who dealt with Fay, who packed up her stuff, who might have ripped off her stuff, or might have some clue who she hung around with in the last days she was there."

"Well, but I could've –"

"Talking to them *without* you there, without having to wonder if you're suddenly going to drag me away before I've even got started; without even telling you, in case you tried to stop me going in the first place. Sorry, Desi, but you've not been exactly helpful so far. You asked me to play detective, and you've spent all your time since snatching the pieces away."

"Apart from saving your life a couple of times, I think you mean."

"Well. There is that, yes. Thank you."

"You're welcome. So who – ?"

"Uh-uh. Turn and turn about; I get a question now. Thank you for the rescue, but how the hell did you get there so fast?"

"I followed your texts."

"Not that quickly. You couldn't have." I'd sent her two, one from the train and then again from the house, my secret weapon, the message keyed up on the phone in my pocket and my finger on 'Send'. All I needed to do was press it, and I had – just – managed that. *Help!* it had said, and the address. I'd figured that would about cover the situation, whatever it was that happened inside. If it went wrong.

Which it did, and she'd come, but too fast. If she'd followed me to London the moment she got my first message, she couldn't have been there by the time I sent the second; she couldn't conceivably have covered the rest of the distance and found her way through London to an unknown address without breaking all the traffic laws and the laws of physics too. Not even a daemon had gifts of transportation; not even a chrome-bright Hog could fly.

I glowered accusingly. She shrugged and said, "I had a tip-off, okay? I was halfway to London before you told me you were coming."

"A tip-off? From who?" *How?* would have been an equally good question, as I'd told no one but the man who ambushed me.

"My question now. Who was it in that house, what did you learn before they nabbed you, and how come they'd left you like that?"

"That's three questions, that's cheating; fitting them all into one breath doesn't make them one question."

"Give me three answers to one question, then; that way we'll be even. Tell me everything."

I grinned at her. "That's not a question."

"Jay..."

"All right, don't get scary." Maybe it was the pills cutting in, a chemical cocktail in my blood; maybe it was just the relief from pain, but I was starting to feel light-headed. "I went to see the janitor from that house where Fay was living. I thought he was the janitor, it said so on the door. Gave his number. So I phoned it, and arranged to meet him. Where you found me." Now that I was talking, I was on a roll, I didn't want to stop. I guess that's how confession works, in church or in prison, same difference. Make a breach in the wall – with pain, with fear, with drugs, I'd had them all today – and watch it all come flooding out.

I wasted all that question-earning credit and did indeed tell her everything, in one long spiel. And thanked her for the rescue so many more times I was starting to sound like one of those drunks who sits on the stairs and tells you you're their best friend, over and over. Definitely the drugs, then, I could blame them – but right now I needed to get over them, get back on track...

"Desi."

"Yes, Jay?"

"Who tipped you off, where I was going?"

"Oh. Yes. Look..."

She took out her phone, called up a text and showed it to me:

FOLLOW J TO CHIZZICK NOW – SIBYL

"By the time you sent the cry for help, I was already in the area. But – does this mean who I think it means?"

"I think it'd have to. There's only one Sibyl. Besides, how else would she know?"

And besides, we were sitting right there in Soho; and our phones chimed with an eerie split-second malevolence, and we gazed at each other in wild surmise before we looked.

The same message for each of us, of course:

COME ON DOWN – SIBYL

CHAPTER TEN

NEITHER ONE OF us had been there before, but we both knew the address. Some places are just iconic.

In one of Soho's side-streets is a door with no brass plaque, no name or number, no letterbox. No doorbell. You know it, or you don't. It's just a door. It opens if it chooses to. If it does, then chances are it opens on a staircase, leading down. Rumour says that sometimes, for some people, that's not true. I wouldn't know. For us, that day, Sibyl said *come on down* and so we did.

Behind this door is Salomon's place, and you're welcome to it. If you can find it, if you can afford the price.

Salomon himself sits in a cubby at the foot of the stairs. He doesn't vet the incomers; if you've got that far, if the door let you by, then you're entitled to be there. Thus far, at least: at the foot of the stairs, one step short of entry.

If you get to make that extra step – well, that's up to Salomon, or else it's up to you. If you're slick, if you're lawyered-up, if you're a Power or a millionaire, it'll cost you. Maybe money, maybe pride, maybe something that counts for more. He's an expert assessor, what people are prepared to pay. He had his start in blackmail, and this is much the same.

If you say *no*, if the price is too great or you're too mean to pay it, that's fine. Turn around, climb the stairs, goodbye. Don't come back. Don't ever try to come back; the door won't open for you, or if it does – well, that's rumour again. Let's not go there.

Kids, the broken-hearted, the down on their luck: Sal's been known to pass them in for pennies, for promises, for free. He has a fondness for victims. Years of experience in making them and breaking them, I guess it leaves you with a taste.

Do I need to say I'd never been here, never been near, never even thought about coming before this? If I do, you haven't been paying attention.

Desi might have been a regular, for all I knew. She said not, but there was nothing so far to stop her lying. That I hadn't caught her at it, that might simply be a measure of my own naïvety. I did know that she was holding out on me, trying to keep things hidden. Lies of omission, lies of commission: there's only a couple of letters' difference.

She knew the street, she found the door. It might have taken me a minute longer, but no more than that. Icons pull at you, like the drag of an eager tide.

Salomon's draws you down.

Under the street, it's a whole other world. I've lived on the street and above it, I've lived high on the hill; this was something else entirely.

* * *

THREE WHITENED STEPS between a curve of railings, leading us up to the door. It was black, glistening in the sun. We climbed the steps, and it swung open for us.

I looked, of course I did, to see if I could spot a camera, a mechanism, a daemon behind the door.

Nothing.

The door conveniently closed itself behind us, as if to prove it had nothing to hide.

"Smug," Desi said.

"Uh-huh."

I was the opposite of smug, nervous and uncertain, doubly so now that our exit was cut off. I wouldn't fancy even Desi's chances of kicking a way out through that door.

You could hardly call it a hall, this space where we were standing. A landing, perhaps: ochre walls with embossed wallpaper, ancient brown lino on the floor, an umbrella stand and coat-hooks. Nothing more.

The lino ran on down the stairs: cracked and peeling, broken back to the canvas where too many feet had caught on it too often. One bare lightbulb above our heads lit the drop; down there, it was all shadow. Desi and I looked at each other, and I felt her crank her Aspect up another notch. Like tucking her arms through the sleeves, where before she'd only worn it flung across her shoulders.

I did keep thinking of it like a coat. Next thing I knew, she'd be buttoning it up, or maybe reaching into the pockets.

But this was Salomon's; if there was security anywhere in London, neutral territory, it was here. Trouble wasn't let in through the door.

No worries, then.

Right.

My arm was hurting again, despite the magic spray and all the floaty drugs. I hugged it against my chest, and supported the heavy stone hand as best I could, and still every step woke bright fire all up and down the arm, hot lead pooling in my elbow.

I'm not outstandingly strong, except in one hand; I'm not brave at all, although I have endless experience of doing things that scare me. If there's one thing I am good at, it's endurance. I didn't so much as whimper. If Desi wanted to diagnose pain, she'd have to do it from the back of my neck and how I carried my shoulders; she'd get no more from me.

Nor would this man waiting for us behind a hatch at the stairs' foot. He blinked at me in the half-dark; I nodded back, didn't introduce myself or Desi. If rumour had it right, he'd know us both already.

I'd lived all my life with stories about Salomon, so I had a firm picture of him in my mind's eye: squat and bald and toad-like, lurking in his shadows and knowing everyone, knowing too much. Swallowing information like a toad swallows flies, to make a jewelled nugget in his head.

It was wrong, of course, as such pictures always are. The facts held, the metaphor might hold, but he didn't look anything like a toad. He was neat and silvery, in flowing hair and flowing beard and in his voice also, as he greeted me by name.

I flinched, he smiled. I'd just put down the first instalment on my entry-price.

"No one will trouble you here," he said.

"I've heard that. Unh, we're here by invitation..."

"On the guest-list, you mean? With the band? I'm sorry" – and his hands gestured across the counter, which was conspicuously bare – "no such list exists."

No one got in for nothing, he meant, unless he chose it so.

"I mean, Sibyl told us to come."

"Ah now, but that's not the same thing, is it? This isn't Sibyl's place, it's Salomon's." The two were inseparable by all reports, indistinguishable in the public – no, the private, the very private eye. Sibyl played at Salomon's, and that was that. But yes, it was his place, that too. If she had no rights of invitation, we were dependent on his generosity or our own resources.

"Of course. And it's a privilege to meet you. Desi's with me," I added firmly, though she was hanging a couple of steps behind, increasingly reluctant.

He twitched an eyebrow and tutted, and I gathered that wouldn't work either. Whatever price he levied, we would have to pay it separately.

He was playing with us, I thought, in his cravat and his perfect suit and his comfortable embonpoint.

"That's a very fine amulet you wear," he said, although it was only a crude clay plaque on a leather thong.

Had I sweated before, in the stone man's grip? I sweated now, suddenly and unexpectedly. The stairwell light was far above, behind us; the only light down here was his own, in his cubby, and his eyes glittered with it. I was dizzy and chill, and very much afraid.

"No," I said. "Not that. Nothing's worth that. I'll leave."

And find gods-knew-what waiting for me up above, his eyes suggested. Who but they could know, where that door would open to?

But then he laughed – yes, definitely, playing with us – and said, "Don't worry, lad. I wouldn't ask that much, unless I had more to offer. You will leave us with less than you bring; that's all that matters here. You're welcome."

His hand made a little gesture to underline it, and there was light and music – as there always had been, I understood, only that I hadn't been able to reach it before this. Now it lay just a step away, through the open doorway; and I stood still, and gazed at him, and said, "I'm with Desi."

Again that smile, less playful now. "As you wish."

He turned to her, and waited patiently until she stepped down off the last stair and came to the counter; and he said, "Des*dae*mona. That's a little… fey, isn't it?"

Her Aspect? Pulled on and belted tight, buttoned all the way and the collar turned up high. Whatever she'd had in the pockets was in her hands. Metaphorically speaking. In fact her hands were empty and she'd never looked more defeated. She stood there like a refugee trying to face down a tank: utterly exposed and utterly defeated, armed only with this bitter and hopeless courage.

And he saw that, of course, as clearly as I did; and that was what he wanted, or a part of it, because his smile was suddenly broader as he said, "I hear you're driving a fine motorbike these days. A Harley-Davidson, isn't it?"

That was it: all he said, all he needed to say. I had it half in mind, halfway to my lips to say *no* again, to take her up and out onto the street, not to let her do that on my behalf; and remembered just in time that the world really didn't revolve entirely around me. We'd both had that message from Sibyl. She was here in her own right, and I had no voice in what she paid or didn't pay.

If she didn't, I'd be beside her on the slow walk up and out. That was my choice, but this was hers.

It was hers, and she made it. She reached into her pocket and produced the keys for the Harley, laid them on the counter before him. The quiet care with which she did it said more than she'd like, I thought, about how much she loved that bike.

At least it's not the boat – but even I wasn't quite crass enough to say that, although she might have guessed what I was thinking, if she'd lifted her head for a moment to look at me.

Salomon slid the keys into a tray – a tray full of keys, it was, and how many of these transactions had he been through, how many people's dreams did he have saved up as collateral? – and gestured, and I saw the moment when Desi became aware of the doorway, the draw of the music, the promised light of comfort.

She still hesitated one moment longer, before she stepped forward, slid her hand through my good elbow and steered me inside.

YOU'D THINK IT was a jazz club, the way it was laid out.

Perhaps it was, perhaps it is, in every way that really doesn't matter.

These might have been the cellars at one time, to one or more – surely, more – of those houses up above. Alternatively, Salomon's might exist in a different space entirely, a separate dimension at right angles to every one of ours.

Whatever: picture a series of smaller rooms knocked through to make one large and massively irregular space broken by pillars of brick, by whole walls left standing apparently at random, by clutters of unmatched furniture, by beer crates and wine boxes in towering stacks. Lights are scattered and curiously placed – and yet, despite the heavy shadows and impossible angles, everywhere in that chaotic space has a clear sight of the stage.

Stage, did I call it? Well, everyone does. In fact it's half a dozen salvaged fire doors, laid over a foundation of more beer crates. It stands right at the centre of the room, the heart of the club, but even so the sightlines shouldn't be so good. They just are: because that's what it's all about, your visit here, this is why you've come.

You may think you're here for the drink, for the craic, for the company. You might have arranged to meet up with this group or that individual. You might tell yourself and Salomon and anyone who'll listen that you only want to sit in a corner and nurse a glass of sorrows for a while.

You're not fooling anyone. Nobody would pay Salomon's prices for anything they could find elsewhere. What brings you here is the lure of the extraordinary. That's not in the setting, though it bends light and space and physical laws to be there; and it's not in the clientele, though in here you meet people – in the loosest possible definition – on terms that do not apply outside.

No. What's truly extraordinary at Salomon's is in the floorshow, on the stage. Eventually.

AS DESI AND I made our way in, there was a three-piece – double bass, clarinet and snare drum – playing something loose and easy. Desi did have a lot of music on the boat, and much of that was jazz, but if she recognised this she wasn't saying. She wasn't talking at all, in fact. But then, neither was I. There was a bleakly dangerous set to her face, and I didn't fancy breaking through the silence, for fear of what might be brewing underneath.

We negotiated an awkward path between close-set tables, into a corner that lacked any light of its own. There was enough spillover from wall-lights and distant overheads to help us find our way, but precious little to spare: nowhere near enough, I hoped, to show our faces to other customers, once we were settled in the furthest, darkest shadow.

Not that other customers were much of a worry yet. Hard to be sure in so much gloom – and I was being unreasonable again; I wanted a spotlight on them all – but there couldn't have been more than a dozen in, so early.

They sat in twos and threes, scattered throughout the space, heads together in quiet, plotting, or sprawled at ease on softer chairs with half an eye on the house band, half an eye on each other. They all looked more or less human, so that still left one eye to spare for us; I watched them warily, and didn't see anyone conspicuously watching back.

More or less human can be deceptive, of course, in more ways than one. Vampires look more or less human, even when they smile. Werewolves ditto, ninety per cent of the time. Daemons, always.

Desi had left her Aspect at the door, deliberately or otherwise. Otherwise, I was willing to bet: she looked stripped without it, bereft, as though she'd lost far more than her Hog. It seemed like *lèse majesté* to be feeling sorry for her – for Desi, of all people! – but you can't always help what you feel.

There was a loom in the half-light, a shadow approaching: Salomon, unexpectedly light on his feet, ghosting between the tables with a bottle, a corkscrew, three large glasses in his large hands.

"You'll take a drink with me, I hope?"

Desi eyed him dubiously. "Is this where you sting us again, with the bar prices?"

He chuckled, entirely in comfort with himself. "No, no. Once you're in, you're in. Didn't I make that clear? You can drink 'til dawn if you want to, smoke yourselves kipper-coloured, whatever you fancy. Other intoxicants are available: just ask one of the boys. The membership fee is the only cost at Salomon's, and one time pays for all. You're in for life, and welcome so. Which is why" – a pop, and a rich rising smell of cedar and Christmas pudding – "I trust you'll have a drink with me."

"Well. I suppose I'm not driving anymore."

"Indeed." I caught a glimpse of the bottle's label as he poured: not to read it, only to register how old, how tattered, how expensive it looked. And the wine looked old, and expensive. Red like garnets, dark at the heart, fading tawny at the edges. "I might have charged you more, you know. A lot more."

"I know." And she worked her shoulders as though she, too, thought of her Aspect as a coat, and missed the weight of it, wished she hadn't checked it at the door. And then she turned that into a shrug, and said, "Oh, hell, it's only money."

She wasn't convincing. Even I wasn't convinced, and I'd have liked to believe her.

Salomon said, "No. Not that. If that were true, I wouldn't have been interested. Money I have." And he passed us each a glass. Long-stemmed heavy crystal, they sang of cost, though I was willing to bet the wine was costlier.

"Bikes you have," Desi snarled, losing it at last, "looks like you've got a trayful."

"Ah, but this one's yours, and that's what's

important. To you. Money isn't personal. I think you'll find that membership here is cheap at the price."

"Maybe I will." Although she was the one who needed convincing now. "Not for Jay, though," she went on. "I don't know what you did to him, but he's really hurting."

"Yes. That's none of my doing – well, except that I have made this a place where truth matters, because it matters to me. The truth of his arm, the real damage, is rising, and your drugs can't mask it. You brought him to the right place."

"I didn't bring him for this!"

"No – but again, truth asserts itself here. See..."

He reached across the table and unfolded my arms for me; just as well, because I don't think I could have done it by myself.

I didn't scream, but that's the best that can be said for me. I am damn sure I whimpered, and Desi says I swore also.

With my left arm laid flat, even in that half-light we could all see just how much damage was coming through. It was swollen badly, above the elbow and below; the skin was tight and streaky, and the lightest pressure hurt. No bones broken, but soft-tissue damage, oh yes. All my soft tissues, as damaged as they come.

Laying it out flat like that, with his big hand on my wrist to hold it steady – yup. That hurt.

The black stone hand had tightened its grip, of course, now that my arm was swollen. I came closer to that scream, when Salomon reached to touch it.

He gripped the stone hand and my elbow together with soft strong fingers, where the softness did not at all mitigate the strength, nor the hurt it caused. Then he took a pen from an inside pocket and began to scribble on the flattish stump of the hand, where Desi had sawn it from the stone man.

The pen wrote in silver ink. I suppose that was just as well, to have it show up on black stone. I still thought it was an affectation.

I had to stretch and squint, just for a glimpse of what he was writing. That one glimpse was enough; Salomon seemed to be writing in the same language that I'd watched trek from man to boy, under the skin of both.

I thought I'd not ask, I really didn't want to know. He wrote and sat back, recapped his pen and put it away, gazed down at the hand with a smug contentment.

After a minute, I saw what he was waiting for: how colour – no, pallor – crept in against the black of it; how resistance ebbed into resilience, into mutability; how that which had been stone came back to flesh again.

How its fingers flexed a little and opened a little of their own accord, even before Desi reached over and peeled them one by one away from my elbow.

She still had to lift my arm and lay it down again, out of the dead thing's grip. I couldn't do it. I was still, entirely, hurting. It felt a cleaner hurt already, though, without that foul hand's clinging.

"You see?" Salomon said. "Truth rises. I had to remind this what it was; now it remembers."

So then I did have to ask after all. "What was it, that you wrote there?"

"Oh, letters out of the old earth, dark times; one of the hell-tongues, we call them now. You'd know, if you had stayed longer."

"What will you..."

"...do with this now?" He surveyed it carefully,

found it not to be bleeding from its raw red stump, and wrapped it loosely in a handkerchief of silk. "Salt it down, perhaps, as a membership fee. Or pickle it. Or mummify it. It'll be no use to its previous attachment; he's not coming back to claim it."

Those marching words were migratory, he meant, moving on and ever on. Poor Billy.

Salomon finished his glass, stood up, and slipped his new souvenir into a pocket so well cut it hardly bulged at all. He bowed a little to each of us and said, "Enjoy your evening, and come back whenever you care to. This is a place of safety now, for both of you; you have paid the price I asked, and you stand under my protection."

Which was not to say that we would not meet those that pursued us, right here in this room; that was understood.

Desi would be all right anyway, she was the pursuer. She chased down what enemies she could, and raced others in the hunt for her sister. And rescued me as a side-issue, seemingly.

I was grateful; I touched my glass to hers, to say so.

She looked at me quizzically. "What?"

"Oh, nothing. Just, here's to us."

That made her frown for a moment. "Do you want more drugs?"

"I don't think there's any point, is there? As long as we're here? The pain's still going to come bubbling out from under, however much I swallow. It's easier anyway, since he took the, the…"

A gesture finished something else I couldn't say. I was lying, in any case. It wasn't better and it might be worse, on a scale of one to eleven. Blood, I supposed, oozing back into all those crushed tissues around the bone. I still felt happier about it. It did hurt and it was going to hurt some more, but at least it had a chance to heal now.

Also, I had wine. Second day running, and it was only mid-afternoon. I should probably have asked for something soft, but my resistance was shot. I told myself it was medicinal, and just this once, and so forth.

Also, it was one of the most astonishing things I've ever put in my mouth. Deep and rich and complex, more flavours than I could distinguish but all of them resonant like bells together, making my mouth ring. It probably wasn't quite worth a motorbike in and of itself, but there were probably people in the fine-wine world who'd pay that much for a bottle.

I wanted to have a proper look at the label, it seemed only respectful; but one hand was out of commission and the other had a glass in it, and the name would mean nothing to me anyway. Nor would it be useful hereafter; I didn't seriously think I'd be drinking any more of this. Even if it was the house wine. I didn't expect to come back. Word would get around, that I'd been here; there'd be a watch kept, in case I came back. Didn't matter how safe Salomon's was, in and of itself. He couldn't guarantee the street above.

"Hey." Desi nudged me gently. "Drink it, don't spill it. This is special."

"Eh?" I was drinking it. Sipping, even. Just a sniff of this filled my head.

She nodded down at the table-top, where dark liquid had pooled in the crook of my elbow.

"Not my spill. Maybe the bottle dribbled...?"

But I'd seen Salomon pour, and no, it hadn't dribbled –

Oh.

"Um, I think I must be leaking."

"Oh, shit. Come on, then, let's get somewhere we can see to patch you up."

That same awkward edging between tables, then, this time trying not to get blood smeared all over. I could feel it trickling down my forearm, and I didn't even have a sleeve left to blot it with.

The other thing I could feel was eyes watching me. A shaven-headed boy blundering back and forth with a striking girl for company, here in this most exclusive of clubs, we were always going to attract attention. And Salomon could protest the safety of these walls as much as he liked – and I did believe him, I had to, truth rises – but I was never ever going to be safe.

Everybody dies.

Everybody who doesn't die first has to have their eighteenth birthday. Sooner or later. I couldn't put it off for ever. This might be a good place for a party, invite my family in. If Salomon would let them pass the door, of course, there's always that. They'd need to pay.

I wondered what my parents would be willing to part with, for the occasion.

And decided I still didn't want to find out. I might be scared and in pain but I wasn't depressed enough for that, I was completely not ready yet...

"Can I help?"

I doubt it. Honestly, I do.

But he was a nice young man, not much older than me and dressed in black, and he wasn't talking about my parents or my birthday party. He'd intercepted us, that was all, with that professional concern that people have when you're taken ill on their patch.

Aspect or no Aspect, it was Desi that he looked to.

She said, "Which way are the toilets, please? It's not much, but Jay's bleeding..."

"This way."

Not far, through the murk and the sudden pools of light: one of those freestanding walls turned out to be a screen, behind which was the bathroom door. Just the one. The guy ushered us through into a room of high wooden cubicles and heavy Victorian sanitary ware, big mirrors spotted with age. No urinal. I was briefly startled by the concept of a unisex toilet, even in such a very private club; but then, it did have to be unispecies too. If the person in the next cubicle could as easily be a revenant as an immortal, it probably doesn't make that much difference whether they're a man or a woman.

No strip-lights, no halogen spots, but it was definitely brighter in here; it needed to be, for the man who was standing at one of the wash-basins, plucking his eyebrows in the mirror. He glanced around at the three of us, dropped his tweezers into a capacious make-up bag and said, "What have you got there, Ronan?"

"Not sure yet. It's a bit of a mess really, blood all over." The young man had taken charge, it seemed, or Desi had ceded it to him. He steered me to the basins and peered critically at my arm.

"Well, get it cleaned up, and let's see."

Was that the young man ceding charge in his turn, to this older guy? Seemingly so. He did as he was told, at least, running cold water down my arm and reaching for paper towels. I was the only one who didn't have a voice, apparently. That was fine with me. I'd been looking after myself so long, it was a luxury to have anyone else do it for me.

The bite of chill water was welcome; Ronan's

hands were firm but gentle, cleaning blood and muck away to show us all the damage.

A stone hand's grip is mighty. Livid black and purple bands had risen up – like truth, I supposed – to show where every separate finger went. Ripped skin and raw flesh were testament to underlying damage, to show how hard I'd struggled and how futile it had been. I was proud of that. It felt like the banner of my life, its whole story, endeavour and futility written on my skin.

A wad of soaked towels stopped the worst of the bleeding. It did hurt, firm pressure on an elbow that had been crushed too hard already, but again I was glad to feel it.

Being so close to him and intimately physical already, it felt natural to turn my head into Ronan's shoulder when the pain really built, when I started feeling dizzy with it.

Which is how come I spotted the sticking-plaster on his neck. The two little sticking-plasters, rather: round ones, about three fingers apart...

I couldn't help it, I jerked away. He startled in his turn, and between the two of us the wad slipped, my elbow twisted, I shrieked.

"What?"

That was Desi, instantly there. Protectiveness was second nature to her, and I could envy Fay; I could wish Desi were my own big sister, looking for me in a world turned bad.

"Sorry," I said, "I just, I hadn't expected –"

"Expected what?" That was Ronan: fair question, but he knew already. His cheeks were fiery. I thought he was lucky to have blood enough to blush with.

Truth rises. "You've been fed from. By a vampire."

"Yes. Mr Salomon gives us shelter here."

"Us?"

"All Sal's boys." That was the older man, behind me. "They're not all bitten, but they've all had trouble with immortals, one way or another. Sal needs staff, they need somewhere safe; it works well. And he loves his little charity, playing Mr Bountiful. Doesn't he, Ronan?"

Ronan looked away, and I wondered if he was even younger than I'd thought. "He's very kind."

"Kind. Oh, yes. He is that."

"Well, he is."

I suspected that Salomon was kind within boundaries, when it suited him to be so. Where those particular boundaries lay, and what was encompassed within them – well, it was none of my business. My elbow hurt.

EVENTUALLY RONAN PEELED the pad away, Desi came to look, the other guy nodded briefly. "Give it a few days, you won't feel a thing. Ronan, be a love and run out for sticking-plasters, would you? Analgesic cream would be a good idea, too."

"We've got a spray," Desi said.

"But drugs don't work in here," I added, suddenly uncertain. It sounded strange said aloud, even in this unlikeliest of clubs.

"No, they don't, but you'll want it later. Go on, Ronan, shoo. Ask Sal for cash."

Ronan slipped away. Desi said, "Don't you keep a first aid box down here?"

"Yes, of course, and it'll be out of plasters. Those boys go through them like, like telephone minutes; they're always cutting themselves, or fighting. Or getting bitten. Cigarettes and plasters, we're perpetually running out. Oh, and food, of course."

"Oh. Do you *do* food? For customers?"

"Members. Yes, we do. Once you've got him all stuck up, just go back to your table. I'll tell the kitchens to feed you. You'll get burger and chips, most likely; that's about all the boys know how to cook. It's the club burger, though, Sal's own recipe. I think he had it from his mother, and it's been through God knows how many generations since, in an accelerated kind of way. The old boys teach the new boys. I'll see you two later."

And then he was gone, leaving his make-up bag on the shelf beside the basins.

Desi blinked at me, and said, "Was that – ?"

"I guess so. Who else?"

She nodded. Then, "You should've asked..."

"Or you should. Or neither of us should, which is what we did. What we both chose to do. I don't know. How do you tell, what's best?"

She shrugged. "You do what you do, and learn after. If you're lucky. Hold still, you're seeping again..."

RONAN CAME BACK, with plasters and cream, as promised. He and Desi patched me up, and we went back to our table; and one thing I learned that night, great wine makes good burgers taste like fillet steak.

Of course, it's always possible that they were fillet steak. I couldn't tell; it had been a long, long time since I'd had the chance to be fussy about my food. My parents had tried to train a palate into me, but I'd lost that, deliberately or by the way. Even so: I really hadn't been feeling hungry – more sick from the pain, and dizzy from the whole day – and yet the smell of them made me nibble on mine, and that first nibble led to a bite, and it was gone soon enough that I half thought about asking for another.

Chips were good, too. With ketchup. It didn't look like a ketchup sort of place – everything here was coordinated, like his suit, to suit Salomon, and he was certainly not a ketchup kind of man – but ketchup there was, in its own little dish, and even that was the best I'd ever tasted.

Burgers and wine, and the bottle was empty and yes, my arm was mellowing, and so was I. Pain kept me sober, but wine took the edges off. Other drugs might not work; alcohol was still allowed to weave its magic. Truth rises, and *in vino veritas*.

Ronan came over, to see how we were doing. I asked if we could have more wine.

He looked at the bottle, and grinned. "Not that. Mr Salomon's private store, that is."

"Damn." But I'd been fairly certain. Even a motorbike doesn't buy life membership in that kind of cellar. "Bottle of the house red, then?"

"Surely."

"Can we keep the glasses?" That was Desi, rolling hers around her palm for the sheer pleasure of it.

Another of those friendly grins. "We'll search you on the way out. Those are Mr Salomon's as well."

But we had licence to drink from them tonight; and the wine he brought stood up to them determinedly. So we drank, and listened to the music, and listened to each other in between. No more awkward questions, though. For now, we were both content to talk.

I told her what I carried in the bag, and why. *How To Outshriek a Banshee and Other Tales*, by me. A boy's life on the street, and the best way to survive it. How I started to rescue those who were even more lost than myself. Only for the reward money, of course, I was clear about that.

Of course, she said. In return, she told me something about a daemon's life in service. *How To Be A Mercenary Whore*, by her. Down towards the end of the second bottle she was remarkably forthright about it. She still wouldn't give a name to her master – and I wouldn't ask: see above, no more awkward questions – but this was why her term of service had been so strikingly short, she said. Because of what she'd done for him.

Fighting or fucking or both, nothing so unusual in that – but to find a teenager up for it and apt for it, a teenage girl, that was rare. A teenager prepared to lose the fight if necessary, if that was what it took to get the man – or the woman – into bed, when she was doing it all under orders, for a cause not her own? Rarer still. Looking at Desi now, seeing how solid, how confident, how grounded she seemed, I wondered how in the world she could have been so broken, to sign up for such a life. She must have despised herself, and I couldn't imagine why.

And couldn't ask, of course, that was a pact tonight. So I listened to her tales of bravado and told her mine, for all the world like two old soldiers in their cups after the war is over. And we were both of us telling true, because truth rises in Salomon's; and at the same time we were both of us lying through our teeth, because the war wasn't over, it was out there waiting for us and we both knew it. And were afraid of it, or at least I was, and I wasn't so sure about her anymore; I thought there were cracks in the shell of hard competence she showed to me and the world beyond. I thought her real face was starting to show through.

If so, this was the place for it. Truth rises. And the inescapable truth of the evening, that rose too. We weren't here for the drinking, nor the music; we weren't even here for the talk. We were waiting, nothing more than that.

TIME PASSED. My arm hurt. People came.

Not a crowd, I don't suppose Salomon's ever filled up; his door policy would make sure of that. There would always be seats and quiet corners, opportunities. People came here to deal, as much as anything; where else could you trust what your opposite number said?

In the end, though, people came here for Sibyl; and, in the end, on she came.

THE BAND WAS protean, like good bands can be. It had lost its clarinet and gained a guitar, had a fiddle for a while but put it down somewhere, picked up a sax and a trumpet. Now it blew itself to a climax, and then to a hush.

Into that silence stepped Salomon, walking light-footed through the shadows, as though he had a spotlight on him all the way. For sure he had the attention of his audience.

He stepped up onto a corner of the stage and spread his arms, not to hush the room but to embrace its hush, the courtesy of its attention. "You all know me, and you all know why we're here. This place bears my name, because I made it; but I made it happen for one purpose and one purpose only, and here she is. Ladies and gentlemen, appearing uniquely at Salomon's, I give you – the one and only Sibyl!"

No showman, he said it almost with a sense of irony. It was true none the less, and yes, this was what we were here for.

The drummer struck a roll, and the whole band broke into a tune that even I could recognise, 'My Favourite Things,' from *The Sound of Music*. They played with the melody like a jazz riff, tossing it from one instrument to another and back again with that ritual ease that comes from long practice, from ritual; and at last, just as all the instruments hung together on a back-beat, that moment before they had to break and roll again, in came the voice.

The words were new, but the words were nothing: a pastiche, a joke. The voice, though – the voice was the real thing, tobacco soaked in gin, rubbed raw by experience and gifted with loss.

Boys in blue denim with black leather boots on;
Boys in the city with sharp city suits on;
A boy who wears bracelets and gold signet-rings:
These are a few of my favourite things.

There must be speakers somewhere, everywhere, built into every shadowy corner; that voice was omnipresent, filling the space with an insidious whisper of lust bracketed by hope on the one hand and the anticipation of pain on the other.

Boys with blonde hair that's all curly and bubbly;
Boys in the morning, unshaven and stubbly;
A boy in the bathroom who splashes and sings:
These are a few of my favourite things.

I may have brains, but I don't often get the chance to use them. It had taken me this long to understand what she was doing with the words: that this was a parody of a pastiche, a mockery of the thing she did herself, and yet done – and so, necessarily, done – exquisitely well.

And then I saw her.

Someone who understood her had laid down those pools of light, those bars of shadow; as Salomon had said, this whole place had been built for this, her moment.

There were more words to the song and she sang them as she came, but I paid them no attention. All my focus, everybody's focus, was on her. She might as well have walked in total silence, all we wanted to do was watch.

What do I do, to describe her? I could run amok with words, a berserker in language, bleeding and battering myself all unheeded; I could run out of words entirely and build her out of absences, those things my words can't say; I could run away and leave her there, leave you with nothing, no grip on what she was.

She was, of course, the man we'd met in the bathroom. That was understood. I *hope* that was understood...?

She'd been tall before; she was maybe seven foot tall in her platinum beehive wig with her heels underneath her. She walked as though she'd been built to be that high. She had that native sway to her, that cruel balance that just throws taunts at gravity. You could call it grace, perhaps, but that overlooks its edge, makes it seem more generous than it is. I speak as someone short by nature, of course, and you can murmur all you like about envy – but we're in Salomon's here, and truth rises.

She wore a brilliant tiara in that shimmering hair, and nothing beneath it disappointed. Her dress was like threaded water, a million translucent beads that played with light to show you nothing but themselves; however it had been made – not cut, not woven, I didn't know the word, or else I didn't know the craft – it had been made so artfully that it could slash down to her waist and still seem to leave her with a cleavage. To the right it swept the floor, despite her glittering hi-rise stilettos; to the left it opened at her hip and fell away to show all the long smooth magnificence of that leg.

She wore a tattoo on her ankle. I only saw it for a moment as she stepped up onto the stage, but I was fairly sure; not a butterfly, no. That was a moth.

On stage, for a moment there, the lights found nothing but her face. It should have been a mask, the make-up disguising the man, but it never was. That was hers, and perhaps the truest face here, not a secret to be hidden. Not like the rest of us.

She gazed about the club, she gazed at us; and despite the dark corners she was looking into, it was impossible to deceive that gaze. She saw whatever there was to see, which was us.

She found someone, I don't know who, man or woman, it was impossible to tell in the gloom; she sang, directly to them.

The band couldn't have known before she started, what the song would be. There was no running order, that was inherent to what was happening here. They were good, though; they picked it up, almost from the first note. If they hadn't, if they'd lagged, if they'd failed her altogether, it still wouldn't have mattered. She could have sung the entire number *a cappella*. This was Salomon's, and she was Sibyl: every note was true.

But the band was right there with her, rehearsed

and witty, or else intimately familiar with the material and hence witty, or else simply astonishingly good. She sang 'Stand By Your Man,' and whether she'd aimed it at a man or a woman, a Power or a pedestrian, a wiccan or a wannabe, we all knew there was something there besides the platitudes. This was a message, a truth, a seeing.

This was why people came; presumably, this was why we were here. Because she'd asked us, because she had something to say.

Something to sing.

People didn't talk much, outside of Salomon's, about what went on in here. How Sibyl told her truths. If you couldn't get in, if you weren't willing to pay the price, you really didn't need to know.

Now we did know. This was the potency of cheap music made manifest, fortune-telling through the popular song. Ironic use of the popular song, I wanted to say, but how could I know? I didn't understand the message.

Until she looked at me, until she sang to me.

Ironic or not, everything she did was very self-aware. This was no mystic in a trance, some Power speaking through her; wherever her sight came from, she knew what it meant. She chose this, as a way to pass it on.

She chose to look at me and slam from the country sobs and the power ballads and the rock-chick classics, straight into a spiritual. God, she had range, and her voice could contain it all; perhaps because she mocked it all, or else because she believed it all. I didn't feel qualified to say.

She looked at me and the band held its breath, the room held its breath and so did I. Desi's hand closed over the fingers of my good hand, my stupid hand, my right. That was fine, I didn't want to drink right now; I think I might have spilled. There was a tremble in me that I couldn't quite control.

Weeell...

The single long note, long word, the teasing drawn-out promise of a preacher, revelation, truth to come.

Well, I...

And perhaps the band knew where she was going with this, or perhaps they only knew the style, the key, the mood of it; but there was a clash of cymbals, there were slow chords building on her breath, supporting her voice, drawing her on to the moment where she threw herself headlong into the song, because by then there was simply nowhere else to go.

Well, I looked over Jordan and what did I see
Comin' for to carry me home?

Desi's hand was crushingly tight. It was her own strength, necessarily, nothing of her Aspect here; it wasn't enough. Nothing she had to give me could have been enough that night.

There was a band of angels comin' after me
Comin' for to carry me home.

You could say that, I supposed. Except that they were none of them angels and I really truly didn't want to go.

More than the obvious, though, this was truthsaying: bitter and potent, stripping away all dreams and fancies, laying out the bones of what there was. Cold, hard, irrefutable. When she said *comin'*, she meant it. She could see. She had said so.

SO THAT WAS me, then. Finished. Done.

I freed my hand from Desi's, only to rub the cold sweat off my scalp, the sting of it out of my eyes. I took a gulp of wine, and reached blindly back for her hand again: not for my comfort, but for hers now. We'd both of us been summoned here. Her turn must surely come.

Not immediately, though. Sibyl turned away from us and crooned to a stranger, some song about a matelot, I didn't know it. I guess he did, though; he spilled his whisky, half a bottleful all over his table and his friend. Salomon's boys moved in quickly to clean up and calm down, to bring another bottle and offer a change of clothes. Sibyl kept on singing, just scatting quietly to herself until the room was ready again. I wondered if she was a doomsayer rather than a soothsayer, if all her visions were grim.

She sang to someone else, and someone else again. Desi was fidgety at my side; my arm was hurting even through the cold leaden feeling that Sibyl had left me with, that weighed in my belly and bones and brain all together, that earwormed my thoughts like a song – of course like a song, like *that* song – playing round and round in my head, over and over.

At last Sibyl did come back to us, to Desi; and there was that momentary hush where no one knew what was coming, where she had to sing a line into the silence before the band could pick it up; and she did that, she sang –

At first I was afraid, I was petrified...

– and then everyone knew, and even I could have joined in if it had been anything like a singalong, and I reached across the table to trap Desi's hand and couldn't do it, couldn't find it, because it wasn't there.

Because Desi was on her feet in that same instant, and heading directly for the door. Not blundering, not clumsy with distress, just absolute: she was leaving, and if there were chairs, tables, people in her way, that was just too bad for them.

Lucky she didn't have her Aspect on her; I thought she might have walked through walls, just as heedlessly.

CHAPTER ELEVEN

I FOLLOWED HER out, of course. Far more awkwardly, banging my elbow as I went, getting halfway and then having to clatter back for my bag, chasing after her again, feeling the whole club stare at my back.

All except Sibyl, at least. She was crooning, while the band held her place with a riff. Whether she'd finish the song when we were gone, whether she'd move straight on to something, someone else – who knew?

By the time I made the door, Desi was up the stairs and gone. I shrugged a hasty apology to Salomon in his cubby; he waved a hand, *don't worry about it, happens all the time.* Perhaps it did. Perhaps people were always doing this, running out in pursuit of the furious or the terrified or the tearful.

The street door stood wide for me, and it opened onto the proper street, and I could see Desi's back as she ploughed along the pavement. This was Soho after dark, it shouldn't have been that easy to spot her in the crowds, it probably shouldn't have been possible at all; but she must have recovered her Aspect somewhere on the stairs. She left a wake.

So I chased her, though the pounding of my feet woke every nerve in my arm from fingertip to shoulder. People who had already dived out of her way pulled each other back again to keep the hell out of mine, and God alone knows what I must have looked like. Bald kid running crazy, hugging himself as he went...

"Desi, wait! Wait up...!"

"What for?"

She hurled that at me just as I caught up, hard enough to bring me to a standstill for a moment, so that I had to skip on after her again. Which hurt, again.

"For me. Please? I can't keep up, I can't *go* this fast..."

She did slow down at that, but only so as to pierce me with a glower, and, "I'd be going a fuck of a lot *faster* if I still had my *bike.*"

And you wouldn't be on the back of it, seemed to be the subtext there. That hurt too, in a wholly different way. "Oh, what? That's not my fault, you can't blame me for –"

"Jordan," she snarled, "everything about today is your fault. Everything last night, too. I've had twenty-four hours of crap, thanks to you, and I just don't want any more of it right now. Is that clear?"

Oh, it was. It was entirely clear. And entirely unfair, but this was not the time to say so. Nor the time to ask just what that song had meant to her, why she was so utterly frightened.

She'd have liked me to hack back at her, I think. I didn't do that, but I gave her everything else she wanted. Space, privacy, solitude. I stood there and gestured helplessly, and then could only watch her as she stormed away.

There was a wall handy, so I went and leaned against it for a while, till the worst of the shaking had stopped. Then, awkwardly one-handed, I fumbled my bag open and felt for drugs. Pills, and spray: I dry-swallowed more of the one than I should have done, and squirted the other liberally all around the edges of the plaster patchwork on my elbow.

Yup, drugs were working again. The arm numbed up quickly. The pity was that the alcohol still wasn't cutting in. I'd have liked to be drunk.

Instead I was adrift, abandoned and in pain, in the heart of London where I most feared to be. With a vision freshly planted in my brain, *a band of angels comin' after me*. I'd always known they were out there, looking; Sibyl said they were closing in. Close.

It takes two hands and good eyes to work an A-Z. I couldn't do it with one hand helpless and my sight clouded. I could function well enough to ask directions, though, without being beaten up, sprayed with mace, run away from or arrested. Good.

I asked, and people pointed me towards Paddington station. Desi might want shot of me, or she might not; once she'd walked off that terror-temper, she might recognise that it wasn't really me she wanted to fight with, nor me she was trying to leave behind.

Either way, I still had a ticket back to Henley. And the rest of my stuff was still on her boat there, whether or not there was any welcome left for me. I had half a mind to abandon it and just move on, where neither she nor anyone could find me; but I no longer believed in that safety-of-the-road illusion, if I ever really had. I did believe wholeheartedly in Sibyl. I thought they'd find me now, wherever I went.

Besides, there was Desi. It wasn't her Aspect which held her like a dark vision behind my eyes. No, it was the girl herself, with all her history, all her mysteries, her tales half-told and her vanished sister. She could send me away – maybe, if she tried really, really hard – but I couldn't walk. I couldn't.

To PADDINGTON, THEN, without getting too much lost or turned about; and before I was halfway there, I knew that she was trailing me.

Well, of course she was. She had to get back too, that boat was the only home she had. Without the bike, she was dependent on trains, as I was; and she wouldn't want to run into me *en route*, proud Desi who had left me stranded and gone her high way off.

What else would she do, then, but follow warily from a distance? And what else could I do, but make it easy for her? I found my way to the station, I found the platform, found the train; went all the way to the front and took a seat without ever looking behind me.

I didn't need to look. I felt her at my back, I knew the moment when she boarded. This was a dance, and I had to keep it up now all the way to the boat, I had to keep at least one veil between us.

It was harder where we had to change, from the main line to the little branch that ran through to Henley. We avoided each other magnificently on the platform; thankfully the train had two coaches, so I could board one and she the other.

Where we had to disembark, there was only the one narrow exit from the station. Hard to avoid each other there, but I felt her hanging back, so I hurried forward. And knew when she tucked in behind, and didn't so much as glance sideways for a shop-window reflection as I made my way down to the river.

Along the towpath in the gathered dark, and she was still behind me. Then the boat, with the bike's gangplank left down to show how hurriedly she'd raced away this morning; I climbed aboard and hauled that in one-handed to show willing, not to rub her face in her loss.

For a little while I waited up on deck there, but she was gone, I couldn't sense her watching. Fair enough; how could she come now, like a silent confession that she had been on the same train all the way? She'd find a pub, have a drink, wait an hour.

She'd locked up, but I knew where to find the spare key. Lord, was it only this morning she showed me...? I could just retrieve my bag and go. Now that I was here, though – well, all that stuff that we'd left on deck to dry, that was all still up there. The sofabed mattress was still damp, so I left that, but everything else I carried below. Slow, careful trips, with my head little more use than my bad hand, light and dizzy from the pills. But I did at least think to put the lights on, so that she'd know I was still there; and I did turn the heating up to finish drying out the corners of the cabin, where that river-smell still fractionally lingered.

Then I thought it all looked too much like a stage-set, the two of us here late at night and just the one bed made up and me waiting to negotiate whether or not I could stay. She'd jump to the wrong conclusions, think I'd put the whole cabin together just to force that particular card.

So I went back on top and dragged the second mattress down anyway. It had taken two fit people to haul it up into the sunshine; on my own and handicapped, it was one of those tasks that leave you close to tears with helpless, exhausted frustration, where your mind can see absolutely what needs doing and your body just can't achieve it.

Still, I achieved it in the end. And made up the sofabed with sheet and pillows and duvet, and no one would have guessed to look at it, just how damp it was.

I'd slept in sodden woods before this, I'd slept out in the rain; I'd slept in wet clothes times without number. I could sleep in a damp bed. If I woke up sneezing – well, I have caught an everlasting cold. It wasn't going to matter, soon enough.

I left all the portholes open – except the one we'd lost to the undine, just a hole now, which Desi had sealed over with roofing felt. With heat and air, with luck, she wouldn't sniff the dampness out.

Of course, I was still setting the stage. She might react against that altogether, she might just tell me to leave. I collected my toothbrush from the head, slid it into a pocket of my rucksack. There. Packed and ready.

"Going somewhere?"

It should have been Desi, it really should. I'd left the doors open for her – her own boat: how could I shut her out? – and I'd been listening for her booted feet on the towpath, waiting for the boat to rock as she jumped aboard.

None of that, not a sound from the bank nor a shiver in the timbers: only the whisper of a step on the companionway coming down and then that voice, which was dry and cold and not her voice at all.

I'd been turning already, looking over my shoulder

to welcome her and assess the degree of my own welcome. Now I turned altogether to face this most unwelcome stranger, feeling the rush of useless adrenalin, *fight or flight*, but I was not good at fighting at the best of times, my only effective weapon was out of commission and he was standing between me and the only exit. I might have pulled a circus-dog trick and dived clean through the roofing-felt porthole into the river, but I didn't fancy my chances.

Nor, immediately, could I see any reason to try it. I didn't know this man; I didn't have any obvious reason to fear him, except that he was here all unannounced.

And making rather an obvious point of standing by the companionway, that too. He could still have been a friend of Desi's, with licence to come and go, but I didn't really believe that. Even before he smiled.

When he did – and really it wasn't so much a smile, more a sort of gloat-with-teeth – I caught the waft of his breath on the dank air even before I saw that fine and sharp array.

Oh, right. Vampire. Not a friend, then. Once that had sunk in, it took only a moment longer to recognise him. I may be slow to start, but I catch up quick.

"Actually, yes. I was just leaving. If you'd like to come along...?"

He shook his head in an idle pantomime. "Sorry, no. I think I'll stay. I think we should both stay; I'm expecting someone else."

Me too. I thought he was not being too sensible, standing so close to the companionway. I was sure he wanted vengeance, but – well, he'd seen Desi in her wrath, he knew what she could do. If he thought he could stand against her, I thought he was wrong.

Perhaps he hoped to surprise her. For sure his

attention was shifting constantly, from me to the steps and the open hatch, and back to me again.

Aloud – indeed, loudly – I said, "You're the vamp from Headrest, aren't you? Your happy seaside hostel? The one we chased away." The only one that got out alive. Head honcho, king-pin, probably the bright spark behind the whole idea. He'd come quite close to killing me that night; his wasn't a face I was inclined to forget.

Hurtfully, that sentiment was clearly not mutual. I swear he blinked, though that may have been a learned response, a joke, *this is how we express silent surprise.* Certainly he raised his eyebrows, and took a moment before he said, "Ah. Of course, it was you. A girl, a daemon-girl, and you. I heard you were with a girl tonight. Well, well."

He looked pleased, in that way that you do when a happy coincidence drops bounty in your lap. My heart plunged double-deep. He hadn't come here for Desi, but I'd just given her away; but *he didn't come here for Desi* meant he didn't come here for revenge. Which meant that he came for me.

I heard you were with a girl tonight. At a guess, it was Ronan who had said it. Ronan with the vampire-bite on his neck. We knew that this particular vamp liked to feed more than once from the same dish. That didn't mean he had to hold his victims by force, as he had in the hostel. Vampires famously draw people to them time and again. In the club, Ronan was under Salomon's protection, we could assume that hold wouldn't work; but Sibyl had sent him out for medical supplies.

Sibyl had sent him, Sibyl who saw futures. Salomon had let him go, Salomon who must have known the truth.

So Ronan slipped out of that protection and under the influence again; Ronan who had just been cleaning and treating and plastering up my arm, who could not have failed to notice the extra finger on my hand and the white stubble fuzzing up my head. With that news fresh and true, knowing how very much I was wanted elsewhere, of course he'd phone his vampire master, earn himself some credit. Maybe he was even saving up his credits in hopes of being turned, a made man, to bite as he had been bitten. People do do that. People are odd.

Anyway, he phones: "Master, master, I've found him, I've found Jordan..."

And Master comes to see for himself, in the street above, no need to go clubbing tonight. It wasn't Desi I'd felt behind me, all the way home. Desi might be anywhere; the one clarity was that she wasn't here. No rescue to be looked for, coming down the companionway.

On the other hand, my unwelcome guest was most definitely waiting for someone.

Ronan had phoned him; he'd followed me back here, and then phoned in his turn –

PHONED WHOM?

Whom do you phone, when you've found the Boy Most Wanted of all the boys that are out there on the street, on the run?

I hadn't realised that dread could be quite such a heaviness. Once on the move, I suppose it gives you momentum, keeps you moving; once stopped, once trapped, it's leaden and binding. I wanted very earnestly to sit down, but the sofabed was, oh, paces away, several paces, too far.

We waited, then, the two of us, vampire and boy who'd be a man, a dead man any day now; and yes, there were footsteps on the path. And yes, the boat rocked a little, as someone jumped confidently aboard.

Footsteps overhead, slow and measured.

Feet on the companionway, black Italian boots under crisp Italian jeans – I'm good at fashion, I get to read a lot of magazines – and I still couldn't guess who it was, who the vampire had called out this night.

Not until he was all the way down, and I blinked, startled, at a face I didn't recognise – indeed, I was astonished to find myself insulted, that they would send a stranger to fetch me back – and saw beneath it a face that had once been more familiar than my own. A face I'd seen, kissed, punched, laughed at, spat at, all day and half the night, when it was smaller. Younger.

And he stood there – almost in reaching-distance for the first time in uncounted years, almost close enough to be kissed, punched, spat at, any choice except the laughing now – and he was a young man now where he'd been a child before. And he had a smile to make the angels sing out of sheer nervousness, and the darkest hair the night could conceivably imagine, and eyes just as dark to go with, soul-black eyes; and he smiled that smile at me, and he said, "Hey, bro. How's things?"

His voice had a little catch in it, which I guessed the girls would find sexy as hell, if it was girls he went for. The scar across his throat wasn't too brutally obtrusive, but even so, a cut that deep – yes, that ought to catch a little at your words.

Actually, I guessed the girls – and the boys, too – would find pretty much everything about him sexy

as hell. He was well-made as well as well-dressed, a
fine fit figure of young manhood. And that darkest
of dark hair fell back in a tumble to his neck, those
well-deep, well-black eyes were bright and wide
and full of laughter, and that scar only added to the
interest, the danger, the wicked edge of the man.

I suppose, when you're a Prince of Hell, you're
entitled to a wicked edge.

I do believe I was jealous. For a moment, that first
fleeting contact, when I saw how my little brother
had grown up.

Then I said, "Asher. I wish I could say it's good to
see you."

"I get that a lot." He smiled, looked around,
perched himself on a corner of the kitchen worktop.
Briefly, something in the way he moved reminded
me of Desi – until I realised that it wasn't actually
in the way he moved, it was in the way I watched
him moving. The monkey enthralled by the snake.
Except that Desi had to put her Aspect on, to claim
this total focus. Asher wasn't putting anything on. It
was natural to him, this air of being the wolf in the
sheepfold, of knowing damn well that all the sheep
were paying him the closest of attention.

Which was quite a change from the grubby little
boy I'd grown up with, who could only command
attention by virtue of who his father was.

I'd run away, and he'd had his adolescence in my
absence – but that didn't cover the change, couldn't
begin to embrace it.

The scar on his throat, though, that was more
than enough. A mark of belonging, it was also a sign
of promotion, of investiture. He could never actually
be Number One Son, but he could step up into my
place and position. Apparently.

Which being true, "Ash," I said, "what do you *want?*"

"I want you to come back with me."

"What for?" He wanted to be displaced, he was saying; he wanted to come second again, to live in his brother's shadow. He walked in here like a demigod, one who had earned and deserved his inherited place – and he wanted to make way for this scrawny, craven creature who had rejected and denied that place, run away from what was properly his own?

"It's what everyone wants, Jordan. Just come home."

It wasn't what *I* wanted. I was seriously reconsidering that dive through the roofing felt, one last desperate bid for survival. I wasn't sure if I could swim one-armed, and I was very aware of a weir not so very far downstream; better to try and fail, though, better to drown and die in chill waters and stay dead, sweep downstream to the sea in one last bitter bid to be free. Sooner that, any day, than follow my brother to the blade and the bleeding and the cold resurrection.

Maybe I showed some of that on my face. Maybe I glanced inadvertently towards the patched-up porthole. That, or Ash and I still had a remnant of fraternal telepathy, left over from the days we shared a bedroom, lived in each other's pockets and knew what wickedness the other would be thinking before he'd even had a chance to think it.

At any rate, Ash jerked his head with all a rich kid's confidence, the boss's son giving orders, never a moment's anxiety that the other guy was vastly older and vastly more experienced. And he was right, of course. The vampire went, admittedly not meekly, and crossed the cabin to stand right in front of that vulnerable patch, between me and any last brief hope of freedom.

Ash said, "What's the matter with your arm?"

"Oh – someone crushed my elbow." Someone who was really part of the hunt for Fay, I thought, not the hunt for me: just an opportunist. Like the vampire here, and his little friend Ronan. And Sibyl *knew*, that was what got me; Sibyl must have known... "It'll heal."

"Of course it will. We can *fix* that. Soon as we get home." His puzzled smile said that this and all my mortal woes could have been fixed long since, if I'd only stayed around. Telepathic we might have been, or the next best thing, but my brother had never understood me.

I used to think that was because he was younger, but evidently not. He was significantly older than me now, and just as baffled.

"Lucky me." I hugged my arm again, although it really wasn't hurting now, I was feeling no pain: only a dizzy detachment that was half drugs and half fear settling in for the long haul, all the way home from here.

"Jordan." He said my name and waited, patient as the night, until I looked up at him. "I have missed you, you know. We all have."

"I do know that. I worked it out. How many years is it now, I've been ducking the bounty hunters my parents sent after me?"

"If they put a price on your head," he said softly, "it's only because they value that head so highly."

"Yeah, right. High enough to cut it half away, if I give them the chance. If you do. How valued did you feel, when my mother opened your throat for you?"

"A lot. But even then, I knew I was just a substitute. I'm a placeholder, no more than that." He fingered his scar and said, "This really should be yours." And said it as though it was a badge of merit, a heraldic achievement: something to be ultimately desired. As though I should be the envious elder brother, seeing his junior displace him.

Perhaps I had been, for that little moment when he first walked in. Seeing him in all his power and beauty, all his grace: who wouldn't be envious of physical perfection married to eternal youth and unfathomable charisma, marred only by the kinky, sinister slash of that scar and the echo of it in the husky scratch of his voice?

My own long-stretched-out youth was something other, a pause in the eternal clock, a desperate clinging-on against the mainspring urge. He had his scar and I my amulet, and there wasn't much question which one would outlast the other.

"No, thanks," I said. "You keep it."

"Well, I will now, they can't take it away from me – but you can still claim your share. Your *birthright*, Jordan." As though something deep and true and honourable were betrayed by my holding out, as though our family stood for anything more than greed and heedlessness and hurt.

"I don't *want* it," I snarled back, hating the disappointment in his voice, that sense of his big brother letting him down when it most mattered. Futile and despairing, I wanted to lash out at him, I wanted sibling rivalry, a fight I couldn't win, something, anything to stop myself going tamely into this everlasting defeat –

– AND THEN ALL of that was forgotten in a moment, as my head snapped around and so did his, our attention riveted elsewhere.

The vampire was slower, maybe because we turned in his direction, and he must briefly have thought we were both of us staring at him.

He felt it too, but less immediately. He turned more slowly, confusedly, towards the ripped steel hole in the hull where the porthole used to be.

Just in time to meet the arm that punched straight in through the roofing felt, curled around his neck and pulled his head out through the hole.

I suppose we could have grabbed his legs, Ash and I, and tried to yank him back inside. But vampires are strong and fast, he could make a fair effort at it himself; indeed he did, bracing hands and feet against the inner hull and heaving monumentally.

There wasn't much we could have usefully added to that. Not much that I could add, at least, with one dead arm and strictly mortal strength in the other. Asher, now – well, if Ash pulled too hard, he could probably pull the vamp's head right off. And he knew it; and besides, he was intrigued, amused, deeply curious. He'd felt her impact, as I had, the moment she switched it on. Even so, I didn't think he'd know just who or what she was. I was sure that he was mad keen to find out.

And in the meantime, not feeling at all threatened, no. Why would he? Might as well invite an oak to fear a willow-wand, the river to flinch from the rain.

He likely wasn't too anxious for the vampire, either. Vampires are strong and fast, and as immortal as anyone: which means 'immortal until someone kills you,' always, for everyone.

We watched his struggles from inside, but they were misleading. Outside was where the action was, and all we could really do was listen.

First there was his voice, rising, cursing; becoming

incoherent, thinning, stretching into a high whine, a sort of static Doppler effect.

Then there were the sounds that his body made: sounds of strain, creaks and snapping. Sounds of damage done.

Then there was a wet, tearing sort of noise, like meat being ripped apart; and at last a surprisingly gentle popping, nothing so loud as a champagne cork, and the vampire fell back into the boat.

Uh, most of him fell back into the boat. All vampires are corpses, I guess, by a strict definition; but this was a headless corpse, definitely an ex-vampire.

One more noise from outside, a very solid splash, as it might have been something heavy being discarded into the river.

The boat rocked, and there were firm, determined bootsteps heading across the deck.

Asher twitched an eyebrow at me, in a kind of pleased anticipation. If he could sense my anxiety – and yes, I'm sure he could – no doubt that just added a little extra frisson.

He was clearly a young man who enjoyed his life, my brother. I was glad that one of us could.

Desi came down the companionway swift and easy. I wanted to shriek at her to be careful, but she didn't give me time; she stood there, almost in arm's reach of my brother, and cocked her head on one side and said, "Hullo. Who's this?"

"My little brother. Ash."

"Oh, cool. I didn't know you had a brother."

Which had to be a lie, surely, she knew so much about me. Besides, I was a rumour and a mystery, but Ash was almost the definition of the *jeunesse dorée*, a celebrity in his own right.

Willing to play along, though. He said, "Half-brother, to be fair. I had another mother."

Half-brother, half-breed: it had been a source of constant friction when we were kids. He accused himself, and I defended him.

Now as then, apparently. I said, "Brother, in everything that matters. We grew up together, Desi."

"Until you stopped growing up. I get it."

"That's right. I used to be the elder, but I'm younger than that now."

"You're not much alike, to look at."

Well, no. White hair, six fingers: these things don't run in families. They're freak by-blows, the random consequence of having two immortal parents. Asher only had the one.

Besides, I'd been hungry for a long time, while he lived off the fat of the land. It makes a difference.

Desi shrugged cheerfully and said, "Jay, help me get rid of that" – a jerk of her head towards the body in the corner – "before it rots down and stinks out the boat."

I only had token help to offer, one-handedly. Even that token was unnecessary, though, as she slung the body over her shoulder and carried it very easily by herself.

Even so, I followed her dutifully up the companionway and out onto the deck. I could feel Asher's sardonic gaze on me all the way.

Up top, Desi sent the body to follow its head, sliding it over the side and into the deep of the river. Then, straightening up:

"So," she said, "that's the notorious Asher, is it? So how come I ended up with you?"

And then she tutted, because I guess some expressions show, even in the dark, and hissed, "Oh, for God's sake! *Jo*-king, okay? *Both* sides of what I said. The Playboy of the Overworld? I wouldn't tell that conceited toady that his jackboots were on fire. And I have not, in any sense, ended up with you. Nor you with me. This is not the end of anything."

"It is, though. Where can I go from here? If he's conceited" – and he was, of course, that really does run in the family – "it's for a reason. I can't escape Ash, now he's found me."

"You could try," she said. "Go on, make a dash for it. Downriver, look," and she pointed over the side, to where a rowing-boat was tied up at the bows. "You take the skiff, and I'll delay him down below. By the time he gets out here, you'll be well gone."

"Desi, don't even think it. All you've got is daemon-strength. He's – well, he's what he is." A Prince of Hell, what I should have been. "You couldn't hold him up for a moment, he'd rip your Aspect from you without blinking –"

"– and then he'd linger over the rest of me, take his time, for the sheer arrogant pleasure of it. Trust me, I know the type. You'd have plenty of time to get away."

She might even be right, except for the two fatal flaws in her argument: that she didn't understand my brother as well as she thought she did, and she didn't understand me at all, if she thought for a moment that I'd let her test him out.

I shook my head, and looked back over the side to where a slow, rank bubbling showed how the vampire's body was decaying already in the dark waters. "Is that where you came from, that little boat? I haven't seen that before."

"It's not mine. I saw the lights from way back, and I saw your Asher come aboard: just a silhouette, but he obviously wasn't you, so I thought I'd better find out what was occurring before I came waltzing in. I borrowed the skiff upstream" – meaning that she'd helped herself, I gathered – "and let the current bring me down. I heard your voices, then I saw the vamp through a porthole. I wasn't having that creature on my boat."

So she'd slammed her Aspect on, which was what Ash and I had sensed instanter and the vampire a little more slowly, a moment too late. She'd snatched him sight unseen, which is a good trick if you can do it, tugged his head out and – well, tugged it off. And then dialled her Aspect back down to idle and walked casually in on us, two scions of one of the greater Powers having a face-off.

She was a fool to herself, and I adored her for it.

And I still had to go back down and face my own particular music, and I couldn't bear to do it any less well than she had, but even so I would rather she wasn't watching. "Desi, you could... just go away for an hour, you know? Let me and Ash do what we have to do, you don't have to witness..."

"You mean you don't trust me, not to interfere," she said cheerfully. "Quite right, too. You think I'm seriously going to let him just walk off with you? You're my main man, you're the one who's going to find Fay for me. I need you more than he does."

"It's not him that wants me, he's only the messenger." *And he could still crush you without a second thought.*

"Then let him go back empty-handed and make his apologies as best he can. He's a charmer, he'll worm his way out of it."

"You know he's not going to do that. He's got no reason to."

"Then we'll give him one. You can't just give up, Jay. Not after all this time."

"Of course I can. Why not? They were always going to catch up with me eventually." And Sibyl had warned me, hadn't she? Warned me and still let it happen, or made it happen, or helped, or...

"So okay, they've caught up. Okay, he's on a mission, and we can't beat him up and disappear." Although from the sound of it, she regretted not having the chance to try. Daemons can be idiots, sometimes; all that wham-bam goes to their heads, they get to think they're invulnerable. Until someone teaches them they're not.

"No, we can't. He's my brother."

"He's – oh, never mind. No violence, I said so. I get it. But we can still try to talk him out of it. He's your kid brother, isn't he supposed to listen to you?"

"He used to. Once." Too many years since, listening to my parents. In my absence. He'd outgrown me, any way you cared to take that.

"Well, then. Go talk to him again. I need to wash my hands, after handling that, that..." An expressive wave of the hand, towards the river. "That. Ugh, I do hate vamps. I feel slimy all over."

"Um, Desi? The bad news?"

"What?"

"You are, a bit." The body had started sliming up during that brief portage, slung over her shoulder. "Don't reach to find it, but you've got something nasty in your hair."

Her hand went up, despite my injunction; I caught it just in time. Firm but gentle, shy but determined.

"Seriously, don't. You'll just get it on your fingers too. Sorry, but you really need a shower."

A scowl that wasn't truly meant for me, I was

confident of that; a quirky smile, that surely was. "There aren't many boys who could tell me that and expect to live, after. You might be the only one. But then, you're probably the only one who'd think to apologise first. My kill, my hair; not obviously your fault. Okay, I need a shower. Bugger, it'll be cold, too..."

"No. I turned the water on, along with the heating."

"Did you? Saint. Angel. All the better, then. I'll disappear into the head, you have a heart-to-heart with your brother, try to wear him down. Then I'll come out all pink and moist, and seduce him."

After a moment, she punched me. Quite hard.

"Metaphorically speaking, moron. Okay?"

"It's a waste of effort, Desi."

Harder.

"I said, *okay*?"

"Yes, okay, okay! Stop hitting me..."

I still thought that by the time she came out of the shower, we'd be gone. My bag was packed, I was ready to go; what did we have to wait for?

ASHER HAD BEEN prowling down below, while he waited – in perfect confidence – for us to finish our conspiring and come back to him. He'd found Desi's store of wine, and something in it that he was at least prepared to drink.

He was playing the gentleman tonight, because he could: because it amused him, and because he knew that we knew he could just have opened the bottle and helped himself and we would have shrugged and said nothing because that's what a Prince of Hell does, when he mingles with mortals. He amuses himself.

So he'd waited, simply for the amusement of it; and greeted Desi as we came back with her bottle in one hand, her corkscrew in the other, a raised eyebrow and an enquiring tilt to his head.

"Oh – please do," she said. "Of course, help yourself. Whatever you fancy. My dog is a tennis player."

"Excuse me?" The eyebrow climbed rather higher.

"*Mi barca es su barca* – oh, never mind. Bad joke, among the boat-owning sorority. I'm going to have a shower. You two boys entertain each other, will you?"

She vanished into the head; Asher grinned at me wolfishly, and popped the cork. "So – Jordan got himself a girlfriend, did he?"

"What? No! No, nothing like it..."

"What, then? Bodyguard? C'mon, bro, she's a daemon. Cute, I grant you, but still only a daemon. What did you think, she could save your throat from the knife?"

"No, Ash. I never once thought that. And no, she's not my bodyguard. She's not coming near my body." Not a word of where she'd been already. If I had anything left that I could usefully do in this life, I could protect Desi. Try to. If she'd cooperate. "She asked me to help find her sister, that's all. I said I'd try."

"Ah, right. My brother, the good Samaritan. We've heard the rumours, how you help the lost go home. Kind of ironic, don't you think? In the circumstances?"

"I was never lost, Ash. I just left. I walked away."

"I know it. I was the one you left behind." He let that sink in, and then he smiled. "Oh, don't look so guilt-struck. I'm sure you are, but you really don't need to be. That's what happens, people go away. Mostly, they come back. Sooner or later. And then I got to go through this" – with a sideswipe at his throat that made me shudder just from the implication of it – "and it's not so bad, Jay. Can I call you Jay? I like that. Really, it's not."

"She's not your mother."

"No, she's not. My mother's dead. Yours makes a bloody good substitute. And yes, she cut my throat; yes, she drained all the blood out of me, and made me as I am. And the blade was just as sharp, birth-mother or not, and it still hurt like hell. Is that what you're scared of, the pain?"

"No," I said wearily. "It's not the pain. I've been hurt." I was hurting now, and too proud to swallow pills in front of him.

"So what, then? What's worth all this running away?"

"What's worth it? Not being like you, that's worth it." I said that, snarled it, just to see him shaken; and then regretted it, of course, the curse of being human, and hurried to justify myself. "Not being a lord of the overworld, not being a demigod among mortals. Still giving a damn who gets hurt, still wanting to help the lost find a way home. That's what I mean, that's worth it. Everything you've got, Ash – all that power, strength, cruelty, immortality, carelessness, the whole package – that's what I'm running away from. That's what I don't want. You're untouchable, and I do quite like to be touched."

I waited for the smirk, *oh, so do I*, and the inevitable glance at the forward bulkhead, behind which Desi was audibly scouring. Instead he nodded, filled two glasses, passed one to me and said, "Fair enough, then. Let's have a toast. To Mordecai."

"I'm sorry, I don't – who's Mordecai?"

"The one who brought us together, after all this

time. You just gave him a burial at sea. Eventually, when he gets there. He'd have hated that."

"Oh – right." The vampire. They might not need coffins full of the sweet earth of home, but they did notoriously hate too much water. "Uh, sorry, Ash" – and there I went again, apologising for what was not my fault, barely even my business – "was he a friend of yours?"

"A *friend*? C'mon, Jay, you've just been telling me that I don't give a fuck about anyone."

"Well, vampires are immortal –"

"Not noticeably –"

"All right, immortal until someone kills them. That's true of everyone. It's even true of you."

"Oh, yeah. It surely is." And he gazed down at himself with an air of deep satisfaction, *bring it on, what is there in this world that I can't survive?*

And I had to laugh, and I wanted to throw something at him, only nothing presented itself in time; so instead, I flung a desperate idea at his smug self-satisfied immortal head. "Ash, will you give me a leave of absence?"

"Will I what?"

"You've found me, you've caught me. That's an absolute; I can't run again. If I give you, oh, my parole, if I swear to come back when I'm done, will you let me go just a little while longer? I signed on to help Desi find her sister; and we've got close, but we're not there yet. And she needs me, truly, she can't do it without me. Just let me finish this one job. I swear, once it's done, I'll come and meet you, wherever you say."

"It's not me you have to meet," he said. "And I can't say yes to that, you know I can't. Do you want me to go back and say 'Actually I did find him, I had him there and then I let him go'?"

"Just for a little while, Ash. Let me save Fay's life. It's the fucking *Cathars* after her, and you know what that means."

He did know. He went quiet for a moment; then, "What did she do?"

So I told him, and he said, "Jesus. How are you going to save her life? Even if you do find her?"

"I've got an idea," but I didn't tell him what.

He said, "Are you going to tell me what?"

"No."

"Because it's dangerous, right? Dangerous to you?"

"The Cathars are dangerous to everyone."

This, now, this was a dangerous game on its own. I was trying to play my family, which always carries risks. But we never have got on well with the Cathars.

After a little more thinking-time, Asher said, "Hold on."

He took out his mobile and made a call. Listened, spoke. At one point, he held it out to me. I shook my head frantically, and backed away; he rolled his eyes heavenward, spoke again, flipped it shut and put it away.

And said, quite gently, "They're not the monsters you make them out to be. You know that. They're worried for you."

Yeah, right. They were my parents, and they wanted to slit my throat and watch me bleed out.

"You could have talked to them."

"No," I said fervently. "No, truly, I couldn't." I'd been running from them more years than I wanted to count; how could I conceivably put all that behind me, and have a conversation? On my brother's telephone?

"Well, Mum would have liked to talk to you."

She wasn't technically his mother, but she might as well have been; they suited each other profoundly. "What did she say?"

"She said yes. You can finish what you've got to do." I felt a surge of relief, a wash of astonishment; they both vanished when he went on, "And I can stay to watch you. Watch over you."

BY THE TIME Desi came out of the shower, in a long bathrobe with her hair all tied up in a towel, we were into the second bottle and I was reconciled, more or less. Even to the prospect of sharing a bed with my brother. We hadn't done that since he was a little kid, when he used to sneak in under my duvet for comfort or for late-night whispering or just to see what I was reading under there. Thankfully, by the time I graduated to dodgy magazines, my parents had finally accepted that we didn't need to share a room to make us bond like brothers; we did that anyway, by nature.

When I left, I bequeathed him all my porn. It was my only witty moment, in the whole grand gesture of the thing. Probably the last thing he needed was a pile of magazines almost impossibly hard to hide; but I was nearly eighteen, he was fifteen, it's a brother's duty to pass these things down the line...

DESI FOUND us sprawled on the floor midway between the two beds, the bottle handy between us. She fetched a glass and poured herself a splash, no more; and sat on her bed and listened, said little, barely anything until she said, "Well, I'm going to bed now. Jay, are you coming, or do you want to sit up with your brother?"

And then, "Mind that arm, stupid! Here..." And she reached down to grip, pulled me easily to my feet and all but carried me, all but needed to against the fuzz of alcohol and the strains of the day and the bewildering enchantment of her. And then I had trouble with my shirt, so she undressed me and rolled me into her bed, all under the delighted gaze of my brother. And slipped herself naked under the covers to join me, entirely heedless except for asking him to turn out the lights when he was ready, oh, and to close all the portholes too, stop any stray undines oozing in...

And it was just a little while later, drifting sleepward in her warmth, my hand found where her hair was still damp and I almost choked on the effort of swallowing laughter; and I could hear the frown in her voice as she murmured, "What?" and I couldn't tell her so I just hugged myself a little closer and fell into the long dark wondering just how long it was since my brother had slept in a damp, damp bed...

CHAPTER TWELVE

LONELY'S OKAY, TRULY, until it goes away.

It's a retrospective sorrow; you never really know how bad it was back there until it's over, until you're safely tangled up in that slew of other troubles that we call company.

Everything about Desi was a revelation, but it wasn't all about Aspect and indomitability. Quite a lot of it was simply to do with her being a girl, and willing to share: her body, her bedspace, her time. Normal things that a boy my age should be taking for granted, that I'd hardly ever taken at all.

SEX IS GREAT, better than great, but that goes away too. You can't keep it up forever.

Some mornings, you can't get started.

Some mornings, you wake up and your brother's in the room; and then it doesn't matter that the girl's right there, warm and solid and laughing quietly at you, teasing, tangling. The thing's just impossible, and there's nothing you can do except lie there and wait for the want to go away –

– AND IT FEELS wonderful, that's my point. Waking up is better than going to bed, when you can do it in company after long years of doing it all alone. When you realise, suddenly and irrevocably, just how lonely it is that you've been, and today you're not.

Tomorrow's something else, a whole different issue, but the world is suddenly a place to inhabit here and now, to live in the moment and think not at all about the future.

It's those little moments of intimacy, the glances and touches, the discovery that sex doesn't go away just because you're not doing it right now. It's lingering all around you, all the time, it's in her breath and the toss of her head, the sound of her voice, the touch of her fingers even when she's actually touching something else entirely.

I loved the way she sprawled across me for her watch, to check the time in the strengthening daylight. I loved the way she forgot completely to be careful of my elbow, and her knee came down on it hard, so I had to muffle my yelp against her shoulder; and then she was all apology and pulling back and finding gentler ways to nestle, but she couldn't ask how the arm was without touching it, stroking, and I loved that too. It's a world of touch, in bed in the half-light of a waking morning; talking's a second language, a clumsy translation.

*   *   *

WE DID GET up, eventually, necessarily. No arguments over who got to pee first; I did the gentlemanly thing, let her go, only in order to have that crucial five minutes in the bed by myself, to recover my dignity before my brother saw.

Desi came back complaining about the fug, opening portholes, saying she hadn't realised how damp the cabin still was. Asher lay propped up on one elbow, watching without comment; when I borrowed her bathrobe to scuttle through to the head, I felt his sardonic smile aimed at me all the way.

IT WAS STILL good, that whole being-with-people thing. Better than good, it was wonderful. Despite what was hanging over me, what was hanging over Desi. Nothing hung over Ash, as far as I knew; as far as I could tell, he didn't even have a hangover, although evidence said he'd drunk another bottle on his own last night, as well as reading through half the ship's library. I wasn't sure that he really needed to sleep at all. Maybe he'd only gone to bed to show willing. Damply willing, in this instance.

At least I didn't need to worry that he'd catch cold.

It was like a slow Sunday morning, three young people doing what came to hand because there was no urgency, no pressure to do anything else. For once in my life, no worries, no looking over my shoulder; being caught is a great reliever of stress. And no danger, no threat from anyone else. We two weren't much on our own, maybe, just a daemon and a freak, but we had Asher with us now. All by himself, Asher was the big battalions.

We drifted around the boat, taking turns in the shower and setting the cabin straight. Desi insisted on helping me in the head, because I couldn't conceivably manage one-handed. It was for Asher's benefit more than mine, patently, like her taking me casually to bed last night: a stamp of ownership, perhaps, or at least of interest. I wasn't complaining.

Ash enlisted my help to put the sofabed to rights, though I could clearly be small use except for knowing how it worked. I pulled the bedding off to show him, and found it all quite dry, as was the mattress beneath. He either had water-repelling properties, or else he slept hot, my brother.

Prince of Hell, and all that...

Oh, that's nonsense, all that hellfire stuff, pits and screaming and demons with pitchfork tails. Even so, there was something in my brother's veins that was not his native blood, and that bed was surprisingly dry. I wondered, and couldn't ask; he knew I was wondering, knew I couldn't ask, and had a particularly aggravating smugness about him as he folded bed neatly into sofa with nothing left over except a stray brother holding bedclothes. Frustratedly.

Families can famously drive you to a killing frenzy. I remembered dozens of times I'd wanted to throttle Ash when we were kids; and right there, right then I wanted to hug him, wanted to confess to being happy that he'd caught me at last. Glad that it was him.

Didn't do that, of course. It was just some kind of accelerated Stockholm syndrome, the captive embracing his jailer; he was still going to hand me over to my parents, who were still going to watch me bleed out. I was still scared shitless.

Just, I was happy. Right there, right then: folding bedclothes with my brother, while Desi sang out of tune in the shower and voices floated in on the sunlight, people idling along the towpath or working sculls on the river.

"Is THAT IT, then?"

"What?"

"Around your neck."

"Oh – yes. That's it."

"Relax, little brother. Big brother. Bro. I'm not going to take it off you, I'm just curious. Can I see?"

Damn right, he wasn't going to take it off me. Well, not without a struggle, which I'd lose in a moment. Less than a whole moment, probably. I would still struggle, though. It's the human thing to do.

"Seriously, Jay..."

"My name's Jordan."

"She calls you Jay."

"I know she does. That's the point. You call me Jordan."

"All right, bro. You prickle if you want to. But I won't hurt your magic juju, I promise. I only want to look."

I stood there wordless, which he took for consent. My plaque, my talisman on its thong: it was proof against wear and water, guaranteed to be ever-new, ever-fresh, as unaging as I was myself. The thong was just a thong and needed replacing as and when – I did that canny, threading the new one on and tying it around my neck before ever I took off the old – but the plaque itself would have lasted me far longer than this, as long as I could stay ahead of my family.

Asher could have broken it in a moment. He just didn't need to. He had me now, he had my promise and my parole, and for some reason he thought he could trust that.

For some reason, I thought I could trust him. I stood still, and he cupped my talisman in his fingers and looked at it, and smiled.

"Actually, that's rather neat," he said. "Simple, clear and effective. Who did you get to do this?"

I trusted him, but not that far. I shook my head, still wordless. Anyone prepared to make an artefact that worked against my parents' interests was entitled to my silence, what little protection I could offer.

I hoped I'd still think so, after my mother had invested me into the family business.

The plaque looks like a Nordic rune, except that it isn't in any of the futharks. (I told you, I've spent way too much time in libraries. Futharks are the runic alphabets, and yes, I can read them.)

Draw a figure-of-eight, only with straight lines and sharp angles. You can do it with four strokes, yes? Top, bottom, two diagonals intersecting at the midpoint. Good. Put a dot in the middle of the upper segment.

There. That's my talisman, my charm. That's what kept me young, poised for ever one day short of my eighteenth birthday: that design, drawn in clay. It's not a figure of eight with a dot in it, it's a stylised hourglass with one grain of sand remaining. Poised for ever, one moment short of the fall.

It's 11.59 on the clock of the world, and the clock is standing still.

Asher held it between his fingers, and let it go on standing. He dropped the amulet back against my throat and said, "I'll buy you something else, when you're ready. Something fabulous, you'll love it. We're going to have fun, bro. I promise."

I nodded, and didn't try to hide the shudder.

*   *   *

IT WASN'T SUNDAY, but it might as well have been. I think we all joined in an unspoken conspiracy, to make it as easy as we could. Maybe we all knew we were only displacing, finding ways to delay the evil moment. I knew I was. But it felt good, it made me happy. I wasn't going to break that.

Unhurried wash-and-brush-up, then, for both boat and persons; and then we looked at each other, and more or less simultaneously said, "Breakfast?"

To which we all, more or less simultaneously, said *yes*.

For someone who had such a profound and affectionate relationship with food, Desi didn't have much aboard that you'd want to eat. Either she wasn't here much – well, she hadn't been, I knew that: she'd been hunting me – or she just didn't cook. Or both.

"I want bacon," Ash said plaintively. "And eggs. And sausages, and mushrooms."

"And toast," I added. "Butter. Marmalade."

"Black pudding," he said.

"Danish pastries. Croissants. Jam."

"Hash browns. More bacon. Scrambled eggs."

"You've had eggs already."

"Those were fried. And besides, I haven't had eggs. That's my point. I haven't had anything. I'm *hungry...*"

"We can go out," Desi said, "there's any number of places to eat."

"Nah," Asher said, "let's shop, and eat here. It's more comfortable, and we can talk. I'll pay." He produced a fat wallet that yielded twenty-pound notes without any observable pressure.

Desi held her hand out and took them in a rather magnificent gesture of contemptuous surrender. I

admired her hugely for that – but then, I admired
her for everything.

When Asher said, "Let's shop," he obviously
meant, "Let's *you* shop." The Golden Boy had done
enough, his attitude suggested, as he sprawled on
the sofa. I flung a cushion at him, which he caught
neatly and tucked beneath his head; then I said, "I'll
come with you, Desi. Carry your bags."

She snorted. "Fat lot of use you'd be, one-handed."

"Stay," Golden Boy dictated with an airy wave.
"We'll have a fraternal heart-to-heart. And coffee."

"Thanks," I said, "but I'm shopping. Find yourself
another book to read; we may be some time."

Just for a moment, his eyes narrowed as he gazed at
us. I don't know if he really thought we might run off
together, or if he just liked the effect. Then he shrugged
and nodded, graciously granting his consent.

I think Desi did actually snarl. I thought she might
hurl his money back in his face, throw us both off
her boat. But I grabbed her hand and positively
towed her out of there, and she came.

"Your brother's *insufferable*."

"Of course he is. Why do you think I ran away
from home?"

"Idiot. I know why: you couldn't take the heat.
But was he always like this?"

"Not when we were kids, no – but then, he used
to be younger than me. He's had everything that was
coming to him, spoiled younger son, all of that, and
then everything that was coming to me too, heaped
on top. He's been the heir and the spare, both
together – and actually, what I've seen so far, I don't
think he's turned out too badly. Considering." He

was letting me have this last run, rescue one more lost girl, even if I was on a leash; he was giving me time to catch my breath after the long, long chase, giving up his own time to bring me in quietly where he might have dragged me screaming.

"He's a playboy."

"Of course he is, and he does it rather well. Don't you think?"

She had a very expressive snort, and I wanted to hug her. Girlfriend or boss notwithstanding. If I'd stayed at home, I'd have had all the same opportunities and endless encouragement to run along and play with the world, bend it or break it as I chose. Instead I'd run away to become the narrow, uncertain person that I am – and Desi seemed to prefer this person to that, me to my brother. That was reward enough for all the years of hiding.

I said, "You didn't ever meet Jacey, when your sister was going out with him?"

"No," she said flatly, steering towards a market out in the street. "No, I never did."

"Me neither – but I have heard the stories."

"Like how he goes around getting innocents pregnant and then setting his fucking family on to hunt them?"

"Not that, no, I'd never heard that one." That was rare, from any angle. "But – well, picture Ash out on the town" – trashing nightclubs and breaking hearts, it really wasn't hard – "and I'm pretty sure you're seeing Jacey too." They'd probably done it together, or at least been in the same clubs on the same nights, partying with the same crowd, long weekends in the same grand houses. Longstanding family rivalries would stop them being friends.

"Maybe that's why he raises all my hackles, because I look at him and Jacey's what I see."

"Maybe so – and maybe that's a truer picture than we know. We could hope so. Okay, Jacey's a Cathar, but that doesn't make him evil. I'm not evil, nor is Asher, and look at our heritage."

"That's the heritage you ran away from, because you're not evil. Asher stayed."

"That's my point. He stayed, and he's not evil. Maybe Jacey isn't evil either. Fay did fall in love with him, after all..."

She shrugged, a gesture as magnificently eloquent as her snort; even with her Aspect set at zero, she still carried a native intensity. Everything was still focused, determined, potent. Even when she was casual, she was *emphatically* casual.

"Girls have been falling in love with bastards since the worlds began," she said. "Evil's sexy, you know that."

"Sure – but sexy isn't always evil. Look at Ash."

"You keep saying that. I've had one evening and a morning to look at Ash, and I don't like what I see."

"You don't want to like it. You still let him sleep on your boat overnight, and you've left him there unchaperoned this morning. Who else would you do that for?"

"Well, he's your brother..."

"...And you've just been trying to tell me that counts for nothing. I think you're right. I think you trust him because of who he is, not because of who I am."

"Oh, and who's that, then? Who is this Asher?"

"He's a young man with charm and charisma and way too much money, with very powerful parents and a history of indulgence at his back, all of which has given him an overdose of self-confidence which you, Desdaemona, are reacting very badly to, because it rubs up all antagonistically against your own – but he's still the guy who crashed uncomplainingly in a damp bed, and folded it all away nice and neat this morning." *And negotiated my licence to stay and help you find your sister before I die,* but that was a bit heavy for this conversation, so I let it stand unspoken. She knew.

"Oh, and that's your definition of not-evil? Putting stuff away when he's done with it?"

"It's one of my definitions of a nice guy, maybe."

That snort again. "Nazis were big on being neat and tidy."

"Hah," I said. "You lose."

"What?"

"First person to introduce the Nazis loses the argument. It's an internet thing. Look up Godwin's Law on Wikipedia."

"We are not," she said, "on the internet; we are doing real live shopping in the real live street. And I notice he didn't come with us."

"Yes, I noticed that too. If you stopped trying to think the worst of him, you might decide that was an act of generosity on his part, to let us have a chance to talk. I'm fairly sure my parents said not to let me out of his sight, but here we are. Trusted. That's another of my definitions."

Her silences could be as intense, as eloquent as her noises; more so, maybe, as they weren't so common. We bought eggs and bacon and sausages in a smart little deli, and she didn't say a word. As we moved away, though:

"You're too soft on him, that's all it is. Because he's your kid brother."

"Used to be. And no, I'm not. This is the guy I've been running from all this time, remember, because I know exactly what he is and what he wants; he's my parents' emissary, and they all want to see me dead. He scares me shitless."

"But?"

"But. Exactly. He's caught me and he's been kind, he's been – well, brotherly. Concerned. Not evil. That's what I'm *saying*, Desi. That's all I'm saying, I don't want to set myself up as an advocate for what I hate, that whole immortal schtick – but if Ash can accept it, absorb it, live it so thoroughly and still come out as okay as he is, then maybe Jacey can too. If you don't want to give him the benefit of the doubt, you could at least let Fay have it instead. Stop being her big sister for a moment, and give the girl some credit. Maybe she picked a good one."

She was silent; then she shrugged and said, "Makes no difference. He's still a Cathar. And your brother's not so okay, you're just naïve. What I can't work out is, however did you live so long? How did you stay ahead of him all this time, as gullible as you are...?"

And then, *mirabile dictu*, she took my hand and held it, just for a moment, some unequivocal statement, because Desi absolutely did not do equivocation. Then she passed the carrier bag from her hand into mine, and closed my fingers around it.

"Manage that?"

"Yes. Of course I can manage that."

"Good. No point bringing you, else. After breakfast, I want a look at that arm of yours. And yes, that does mean taking the plasters off. I let you wimp out in the shower, but only because the light's so bad in there and there isn't really room to play doctors. If you struggle, I'll get your brother to hold you still. I bet he's good at that. I bet he'd *enjoy* it..."

*   *   *

WE SHOPPED MORE, for cheese and fancy breads and spreads. We spent as much of Asher's money as we could, without cheating; no way three people could eat everything we bought – even when they were all three of them hungry young adults, and two were male, one was a daemon and one a demigod – but everything we bought could legitimately be eaten for breakfast. We thought that was fair.

And so back to the boat, where we found Ash swabbing the decks with a fine piratical leer. Truly: Golden Boy was mopping the foredeck hard, to shift the dry mud and tyre marks left by the absent Harley. That was still a raw wound for Desi. Whether Ash had picked up on it, I couldn't say. She wouldn't talk about it, nor about the song that Sibyl sang her.

I kept thinking about it, and I didn't like the way my thoughts were tending.

What I did like, I liked my brother. Just then, that morning, I liked him very much indeed. He'd even laid out the gangplank for us; with the awkwardness of bulging bags to manage, that made a difference. So we walked up onto a wet and gleaming deck, and he fussed around our feet with his mop to keep it so, which made even Desi smile.

Then he tracked us downstairs and helped with the unpacking, making happy noises over some of our choices and threatening to quarrel severely with us over others – "*Tangerine* marmalade? What the fuck?" – and then he lit the stove and started to cook breakfast.

Chased us out of the galley completely, he did; gave us coffee and told us to read the papers. I said it wasn't Sunday and he said to make believe.

So we ended up on the sofa, once Desi had stripped and studied my elbow, approved its mending and strapped it up again. Its colours were spectacular, Gothic blues and purples and blacks on tight and swollen skin, with scabs like dark ramparts in a landscape of war. In honesty, though, it didn't hurt half so much this morning. I swallowed drugs on principle, but I probably didn't really need them. Even so, when she kicked her boots off and swung her legs up onto my lap, I was at pains to point out that I couldn't manage a foot-rub. Not that day.

"Jam yesterday," she sighed, "and jam tomorrow..."

"I'll rub your feet for you," Ash called over. "I'm a specialist. Women have melted."

"Damn," I said. "I believe him."

"Me, too." And then she tipped her head back on the cushion, to focus on him upside-down, and said, "Shut up and fry, rich boy."

He grinned. "Can't hurry a good sausage. If I buy you a new bike, do I get to rub your feet for you?"

"I'll buy my own bike, thanks. When I'm ready. And I'll pick my own masseur." Her foot nudged at my thigh lightly, pointedly.

"Oh, be like that. I'll just cater to the inner woman. Not that the outer woman's going to get much from him." He wafted a mean spatula in my direction. "You'd be better off cuddling the ship's cat, by the look of him this morning."

"The ship hasn't got a cat."

"I'll *buy* it a bloody cat..."

AND SO ON, bantering until that late, late breakfast. It was as if someone had told him he still needed to win Desi's trust; so he made an extravagant play for her heart instead, with a cheerful insincerity that won smiles even from her reluctance. It also won me more open displays of affection than I had come to expect. I knew they were just tools from her armoury, rebuffs to him, but I drank them up anyway, fresh in from the desert, thirsty and unashamed.

I guess breakfast had turned into brunch, at least, by the time we carried trayfuls up on deck and further up, onto the wheelhouse roof to eat. Early lunch, even. No matter.

What mattered more, everything that had been put off till now was suddenly there, between us, demanding attention at least as greedily as the plates and mugs and bowls were. Around mouthfuls, then, and disregarding trips down and back again for refills, extras, what we hadn't had hands enough to carry first time up:

"What shall we do today, then?"

"With what's left of the day, you mean?"

"Yes. That."

"Go find Fay. Obviously." That was all that was left for me, and I thought we could probably fit it into a day.

"Be a neat trick if you can do it." Her words might be casual, but her voice was not.

"I'm sorry. Look for Fay, I should have said. And what I think, we have to go back to London. There's something about that house. Sorry, Ash, I know you're not up to speed on all of this – but the Cathars wouldn't waste effort watching it, just on the off-chance that she might turn up. Not to the point of double cover, having a shapeshifter right there and the janitor on call. Or whatever that creature was, that was living in the janitor..."

"A lithiad?" Desi suggested.

"No. Not that. You can't just – never mind. Just be careful around anyone with tattoo writing all over 'em, whether or not it moves. Even so, I think we need to go after little Billy."

"Who's little Billy?" Asher asked, blandly curious.

"He's the one the tattoo writing crawled onto. The janitor it crawled off from, it left him a lump of rock... Oh, look. We'll *tell* you, all right? On the way."

"Hang on," Desi said. "You haven't convinced me yet. Why do we need to go after this boy Billy?"

"Because he was the janitor's sidekick; he may know something, why the Cathars were so watchful on that house, what Fay left that she might have come back for, where it is now... Any of that. All of it. Something else. *Something*. Desi, he's the only lead we've got."

That was thin, and I knew it. My only advantage was that she had nothing better to offer, and there was a great need on us to be visibly doing something.

"Um. Didn't you say that he went off to find the Green Man?"

"That's right."

"Who he will have brought back to fetch you, and instead found – well, a pile of rubble. And no you. If Puffing Billy is still extant, if the Green Man didn't just pull his head off" – a beat, an instant of pure telepathic certainty, where she and we were all thinking the exact same thing, *like she did to Mordecai, just last night* – "then chances are they'll be together, hunting for you. Do you really want to go anywhere near the Green Man?"

Are you insane? was the subtext there.

"Rather not, thanks – but if it happens, it happens."

"*Jordan...!*"

When she used my name, it was deliberate. Even now I'd been caught.

I shrugged as casually as I could manage, as far as my body would allow the lie. "What? You're forgetting, we've got Asher now. He's got me. What's the big deal?"

"Jay, when did you get to be so reckless with people's lives? It doesn't suit you."

"It wouldn't, no – but I'm not. Desi, I'm sorry, were you not introduced? This is *Asher*. Son of my father. Prince of Hell. With all that that implies. Trust me, the Green Man is not going to meddle with Ash. Nor, hopefully, with any of us."

"Hopefully?" Fair enough, she was the one most at risk. Would have been. In truth it didn't matter, because no, I wasn't going to lead them anywhere near the Green Man; but they didn't know that, and I couldn't tell them. This was a sting operation, I was setting them up, and I didn't dare let them get a whiff of it.

"Absolutely," I said. "I misspoke, I meant absolutely. We'll be fine. Ash'll look after you. Fay too, if we find her."

"He comes at you," Ash said, fixing her with a fine and noble stare, "at either of you, only through my dead body."

"Asher," she retorted, "your body is dead already."

"Only in the most technical sense. It's warm, it's friendly. See" – and he seized her wrist, held her palm to his chest – "I've even got a heartbeat."

"Jay, is he faking that?"

"Honestly? I've no idea." I wouldn't put it past him, if he needed to calm the anxieties of some pretty young thing he wanted to bed.

"How can you say so?" he protested. "Desi, it beats for you."

"I think that's what I said. If you had a heart you'd

keep it to yourself, like regular people do. But, Jay – assuming this Billy has anything useful to tell us, and assuming that he'd tell us anything anyway, with that lithiad under his skin; and assuming you can get him safely somewhere on his own to ask him, and even assuming that he's not hanging on to the Green Man's coat-tails; assuming all of that and whatever else you have to, to make this worth all the risks, which I don't think it is, by the way – how are you going to find him in the first place? One boy, last seen running off in the direction we most don't want to follow?"

"Oh – yes, I've got an idea about that. Ash, lend us your cellphone."

"*My* phone?"

"Please."

"What for?"

"I want access to your address book. Obviously."

"Brother of mine, there are girls out there – yes, and boys, too – who would kill just to have my number, let alone access to my address book. But you won't find the Green Man there, if you were thinking of calling him and asking for Billy."

"Not that. I don't think the Green Man carries a phone. But – well, you're in touch with pretty much all the people I've been running away from, and now I need to talk to some of them."

"All right. But phone home, while you're at it. Talk to your mother. Or at least talk to Dad, if you can't face her. They're on speed-dial. And, Jordan, you know what? They might even *help*..."

"Yeah, right."

"Never can tell."

"Ash, one absolute, okay? I am *not* going to ask my parents for help," any more than I would ask him except in this dishonest way, the loan of his phone.

What I did, I did myself: alone and treacherous and hopeful.

ONE THING ABOUT playboy princes, they do have a lot of contacts. I don't say friends, necessarily, but these young bloods: they don't have to work, they've got no one to hide from, their lives are their social lives. One long giddy whirl.

So I found the number that I needed, walked off down the towpath and used my own phone – just in case, so no one could check on Ash's to find out who I'd been calling – to have the conversation I was seeking. Difficult, but not long; and ultimately positive. I'd been right about one thing, or at least I thought so.

BACK TO THE wheelhouse roof, then, where Desi and Ash were being snarky with each other in a desultory manner. Not meanly, just finding a way to relate in my absence.

"Sorted," I said.

"Congratulations," Asher said. "Sorted what, and where, and why?"

"We're meeting Billy this afternoon. He's agreed to talk to us."

"Why so?"

"Oh, I said he could have the negotiable contents of your wallet. I couldn't say how much is in there, but he was willing to risk it, on the nod."

For a moment, Asher just looked at me, son of his father; in other circumstances, I might have quailed. As it was, what did I have to lose? *Except my life, except my life, except my life,* and that was lost already. Mortgaged to my word, if I had nerve enough to meet it.

Then he grinned, and nodded. It was only money, after all. He had more.

Desi was suspicious, and rightly so.

"Meeting him where?"

"Neutral territory."

"Where's that, then?"

"Back at Salomon's."

"Jay, no. *No!* I won't go."

"Yes, you will." *Sibyl says so.* "Seriously, hon, it's neutral for everybody. Where better? He can talk, and whatever they are, those tattoos can't touch him and neither can you. Salomon's is the ultimate in safe ground."

"I don't want –"

"I know you don't. But Sibyl won't be there, she's going out: a presentiment of unwelcome, she said. Salomon says he'll close the place, he'll be there just for us. It's a win-win situation, Desi."

She looked at me like she knew I was lying, but I thought that was just Desi being cynical about win-win situations. I hoped.

All she said – eventually, after making me really wait, the best revenge she could manage – was, "How are we going to get there?"

"Train, I guess." *In the absence of a bike...*

"I," said Asher, "have a car."

Well, of course he did; but I knew him well enough already. "Will it take three?"

"At a pinch," he said. And, "Bags I do the pinching."

HIS CAR WAS a low, louche sporty number, soft top and a hard stare, the kind that gets stared back at in the street. I knew it would be. He had his profile to sustain.

Of course it was only meant for two: what was he, a bus? He'd come here to collect me, that was all: private taxi service, man to man, fetching his brother home. This was an unplanned diversion, and we'd simply have to make shift.

Which meant I had to sit on Desi's knee, apparently, rather than she on mine. I muttered that I could take her weight, no problem, but that earned me nothing. Nothing good.

So there was a sideways folding, a degree of awkward but not unpleasant squishing and wriggling, the odd pointed remark and one proddy finger, and eventually we found a way where we could be mutually uncomfortable but in a fairly good way, all in all.

The seatbelt was impossible, but Ash wasn't the kind of guy who'd have an accident. He drove with a flashy confidence and an unerring, unnerving skill: swift and loud and heedless, knowing just how good the car was and just how fast his reflexes were. I wasn't anxious in the least, my head was doing a Sibyl, dwelling in the future –

I just walked in to find you here with that sad look upon your face

– and angsting entirely about how it would all fall out, until we hit the open road outside Henley and just suddenly the world fell in upon us.

Or not the world, perhaps, but something physical and brutal, dangerous to cars.

By definition, then, dangerous to humans also.

Me, I was still human to the core. With my arm out of action, I wasn't even human-plus.

Desi plus Aspect: human double-plus.

And then there was Asher.

Two out of three ain't bad. We should have been *formidable*.

What can you do, though, what can you *do* when the wind gets up?

IT STARTED WITH a twitch, an abrupt jerk that sent the car half over into the opposite lane. Desi's arms tightened around me, as though she'd pulled her Aspect around both of us at once. Ash corrected, no harm done except to his pride, because he suddenly didn't seem like such a good driver after all.

"What was that?"

"I don't know. Thought I'd lost a tyre for a moment, but this car would tell me. Nothing on the dash, no warning signs, just –"

Just the same thing happening again, a wicked slew across the road, throwing us right under the noses of oncoming traffic. This time, no question of Asher's being responsible, or irresponsible in his flash motor; we'd all felt the sideways shove, like a hammerblow against the kerbside door. It was Ash's speed and competence that saved us, whipping the low bonnet back to our side of the road and skidding the tail after, through a blizzard of brake-squealing and car horns.

Any normal person, caught up in a near-accident of that magnitude, scraping your way out of it by the thickness of the metallic paintwork on your pride and joy – well, you'd stop, wouldn't you? You'd pull over. Your heart would be pounding, your hands too sweaty to hold the wheel, your legs tremulous in the footwell. You'd need a minute to get out of the car, walk up and down, look back along the road and try to figure out what the hell happened, maybe go down to talk to the guys you nearly just slammed into, who'd be doing the exact same thing a hundred metres thataway...

Asher accelerated.

I didn't suppose for a moment that his heart was pounding or his hands sweating, his knees trembling at all. Even so:

"Ash, slow down. What's happening?"

"We're being attacked."

"Who by? I can't see –"

"Me neither, but they broadsided us back there. Maybe we can leave them behind..."

Maybe not. Another buffet hit us from the rear, just as we approached a corner. As near as anything, it slammed us off the road and into a ditch. Again it was Asher's reflexes that kept us the right way up and moving. The car behind wasn't so lucky; the driver did well to avoid us as we veered across the highway, but she still ended up in a hedge.

"Get off the road," Desi urged. "At least we don't have to take other people with us."

"Agreed. Soon as –"

The chance came just then: an open gateway our side of the road, a garden centre, glimpses of greenhouse roofs and brick. Ash slowed not at all, just slammed on the handbrake and wrenched the wheel around; the car left the road sideways and fishtailed a couple of times before he had it straight and speedy.

Car parking on the left, garden centre on the right. People, inevitably, coming and going between the two: people with trolleys, people with armloads of plants, people with kids. The kids were the worst of it, standing in the middle of the road, staring at this doom that thundered down upon them, parents barely snatching them away in time...

I expect Ash would have found a way to avoid them, if he'd had to. I do expect so. But he trusted the parents to snatch, seemingly. He didn't even blast the horn; the roar of the engine – and, yes, the screaming – were warning enough, that here came a crew of morons gunning their car down a private road at a stupidly dangerous speed.

Lucky it wasn't Sunday; the distant reaches of the car park were empty, which gave us space enough to spin the car around and sit there, revving and ready.

Ready for what, we didn't know. What could slam a car about, with a punch like a force nine gale?

We waited, watched; felt nothing, saw nothing. Well, nothing that mattered: only a security guard from the garden centre heading officiously in our direction, with a couple of managerial suits hurrying after.

I felt amazingly vulnerable, sitting squashed up there on Desi's knee. Whoever it was out there, I wanted to meet them on my own two feet.

When I reached for the door-handle, though, she slapped my wrist away. "Don't be stupid, Jay."

"Better out than in." It's the runner's instinct, I suppose: don't let yourself be caught in a trap, always have a way out. In the car I was helpless.

"No. Better in, with Ash behind the wheel. 'Til we know what's coming. Here it comes."

Here it came, indeed. Or here they came, rather, three dark shapes like coherent shadow, shadow-wings, sketches of crow: out of the sky they came, tumbling and swooping over the glittering glass slopes of the greenhouse roofs, screams trailing in their wake as the glass shattered beneath them like windows in a hurricane of wind.

Wind they were, daughters of wind, storm made solid. It must have been terrible below, shards like shrapnel drawing blood, taking eyes out, wrecking lives. And that was incidental, not what they were here for. They were here for us.

"Harpies," Asher said, and even he sounded depressed about it.

Thing is, you say *harpies* and everyone thinks Harryhausen, bird-women snatching an old man's lunch.

Ray Harryhausen is a great man, but what he doesn't know about harpies would fill encyclopaedias.

Harpies: meant to be daughters of Typhon and Echidna, like so many of the Greek monsters. Treat it as metaphor, treat it as true: it makes no difference. They are what they are, daughters of the wind. They give shape to the air; they are the gale, folded into a fist.

And yes, sometimes they are women with the wings and legs of birds. Why not? Sometimes they are birds, with the heads and breasts of women. Or the other way around. They are what they choose to be, making and remaking their form from moment to moment, as the whim takes them; they are what they are, which is vicious, deadly, casually destructive.

They came at us, for reasons that we could not fathom; and on the way they flattened those poor foolish men who'd been coming at us on their own account. Flattened and stripped them, the way an explosion will strip the clothes from a body; flattened and stripped and excoriated them, flensed them, ripped skin and fat and flesh away in a bloody and heedless exultation.

And came on at us; and yes, I was glad to be in the car. Sorry and appalled for those who were not, who had no hope of shelter; guilty for having brought this down on them; doubly eager to be away.

We had fetched this horror here. We could at least lead it somewhere else.

I had less hope of actually leaving it behind. Not even Asher could outdrive the wind, not even his wheels would be fast enough.

I don't suppose he'd have agreed with me for a moment. He sat gunning the engine and glancing this way and that, picking a route; then he slammed the car into gear.

It leaped forward, guttural and aggressive, its own expression of power, fixed and focused, to set against the harpies' chaotic mutability.

We didn't even make it out of the car park.

Ash's car was a low roadhugger of a beast, but one of the harpies went lower. She swooped towards us like a squall of rain, colourless and speedy, hard to see through but harder to see, an impression of God's thumb-smudge in the air.

We hit her at speed, full-on. For a moment it was like driving into storm, and then for a moment it wasn't, it was like nothing at all, because she wasn't there.

She was underneath us, and when the wind's beneath your wheels, slamming up into your chassis – well, that's when a car can lose the road.

At that speed, with that much grunt behind us, we nearly flew.

The nose lifted, Ash swore; Desi had already clamped the two of us within her Aspect. I felt both helpless and protected, awed almost, no time to be afraid –

* * *

– AND THEN THE soft roof tore apart just by my head, and then I was afraid. I might have screamed. The car seemed to hang in the air and a great dark claw hacked in at us, wind made solid, iron-grey and iron-hard.

It met Desi's hand, daemon-fast and daemon-hard: claw met flesh and bone, wind met Aspect, harpy met human-plus, all the pluses that Desi had contrived to earn or learn in her years of service.

In that brief, endless moment, it seemed like the whole carful of us dangled from the harpy's wings, from Desi's grip on its claw, while the two of them wrestled unfairly for supremacy.

The harpy had all the advantages, or I thought so, and I found time enough to be overwhelmingly afraid for Desi.

In the end, though – at the end of that single snip of time, one frame cut out of the reel – it was the harpy that screamed.

Mind you, they do that anyway. I could hear their voices all around us, airless screeches like a hacksaw blade on a fiddle's highest string. But this was different, ragged and twisting; and then the claw was gone from Desi's grasp, gone from the car, snatched away or else just melted into air.

And then, of course, we were falling.

Falling and rising again, toppling and spinning wildly, tossed about by harpies one to another before they let us crash to ground.

We fell sideways, onto the driver's side, Asher's; we fell and rolled, over and over before the car groaned and fell back, done with rolling. Done with moving altogether.

No seatbelts and no solid roof, but the car had roll-bars, presumably because Ash thought they were sexy. Turns out they're useful too, when a car is rolling. Even better, I'd had Desi and her strength wrapped around me as we tumbled; it seemed like nothing could harm me, nothing but her could even touch me. My arm ached profoundly where she was crushing it against my ribs, but I only realised that afterwards.

Not immediately after, even then. First came the rolling, the sense of being wrapped in an unburstable bubble; then came the stillness, the silence, the sudden hush of the world. Even the harpies were quiet, unless shock had rendered me deaf.

For half a breath, while my mind was still spinning dizzily, I waited for the *whumpf!* of the petrol tank's explosion. That's what happens, I know this. I've seen the movies. There's a car smash and then there's a *whumpf!* as it all goes up in flames.

Asher's car was maybe smart as well as flashy, maybe it had devices and desires built into it, not to let it do that.

At any rate, half a breath, no exploding, not a flame to fret over. Then suddenly I was free, and there was a great wrenching and tearing of metal all around me – and that wasn't the harpies ripping their way in, that was Desi and Ash, simultaneously ripping our way out. Roll-bars that had barely dented through all that crash-and-tumble were snapped, plucked out, tossed aside.

I'd been all but tossed aside myself, or it felt that way, with Desi just erupting all around me. I lay sprawled half in the footwell, all tangled up among those legs of hers; then she was stooping, dragging me up, pretty much throwing me out of the wreckage. Maybe she too was waiting for the *whumpf!*

At any rate, she jumped out pretty smartly behind me, hooked an arm around my ribs and started me running. We looked back as we ran; I can't speak with confidence for her, but as for me, I was looking first for Ash, then for the *whumpf!* then for the harpies. Definitely in that order.

In that order, then:

Ash leaped clean over the car's wreck to join us. From a standing start. *Prince of Hell*, I thought; and absurdly did also think that would have been an Olympic record right there, if Princes of Hell qualify for the Olympics. My guess is that they don't. What on earth would they do about a blood test?

The *whumpf!* just didn't happen. Slow of me, I suppose. Smart car or otherwise, no Prince of Hell was going to be troubled by a little chemical fire. I guess petrol wouldn't dare explode around Ash, without his explicit consent.

The harpies – well, they might have been celebrating too soon. I don't know if harpies actually have a happy dance, but that's what it looked like. I could just see them, like three dust-devils, swirls of smoke high up and cavorting together.

We could see them; they could see us. That's the way it works.

Unfortunately, at least one of them did happen to be looking.

So there was a cry from way up, that sounded like frustrated rage to me; and the three of them came plunging down like raptors. They did suddenly look like raptors, full harpy plumage, women's faces, streaming hair and I even thought I could see a suggestion of bare breasts.

So there were they, coming; and here were we, running. Even Asher, Prince of Hell: even he wasn't too proud to sprint for it, in the face of what we'd seen them do to folks caught out in the open. I didn't *think* they could strip Ash or even Desi to the bone, but I really didn't want to see my faith tested. Besides, I was damn sure they could do what they liked to me, even despite Desi's arm around me and her Aspect flung over like a cloak. Three of them: one each to distract the other two, left one free and clear on me.

So no, we ran. Not to the garden centre: that offered no kind of shelter, only a panic of people who hadn't deserved what we'd done to them already. We couldn't conceivably bring more of the same down on their heads.

Beyond the centre, though, behind its service-road lay a close-planted wood of conifers. You looked at that – just the way we were looking at it, desperately, already on the run – and you couldn't avoid the word 'wind-break.'

In honesty, I didn't feel like I was doing that much running. Oh, my legs moved, and I kicked at any ground I came into contact with. But Desi was bounding, and half-carrying me, and our leaps were all out of synch with each other's, and hers won. So I sort of flew the distance, with my immortal brother on the one side of me and my adored daemon boss on the other; and we did – just – make it to the treeline ahead of the coming harpy-strike.

To the treeline and through the fence, just straight through, leaving wire mesh curling and steaming behind us; and we were in among the trees as the harpies hurtled to ground, and they tried to barrel their way in behind us.

One of the things about being effectively disembodied, building your self out of what air or dust or water comes to hand, you really do need clear open space to work in. They came at those trees and weren't fluid enough or fast enough to slide between them, the way a normal human would. They wanted to do the air thing, the water thing, and flow round both sides simultaneously; but they'd taken on too much physicality to do that, so they slammed full-force into the trunks of the trees they were trying to encompass.

It didn't do them any harm, and it splintered the trees. The first few trees. But, yes: wind-break, that's the word. It broke them up, scattered their coherence. They could have chewed up the whole damn forest, but it would take them time, they had to pull themselves together – in a curiously literal way – after every broken tree, and meantime we were getting further and further away.

They knew it, too. After too short a time – they were depressingly bright, as well as powerfully ferocious – we heard them circling overhead, trying to spot us through the greenery rather than chase us all through the wood.

One good thing, perhaps: they weren't bright enough to circle in silence. Like Stukas with their deliberate sirens, I guess harpies have had a lifetime – a long, long lifetime – of inducing fear with their screaming. Maybe they just don't know how to stop. So we heard them, and ducked down into roots and hollows, and weren't seen.

At last they drifted off, passing entirely out of hearing. And slowly, on foot, still a little wary of the skies, we made our way through woods and across open country only when we had to, back to Henleytown, the river and the boat.

CHAPTER THIRTEEN

ALREADY WE WERE too late to take a train into London and make our appointment. I called back to rearrange. Same time tomorrow; we could do that. I apologised, I reassured. I mentioned the little problem that we'd had, which evoked a sudden swearing from the other end, and assurances that we would not be bothered again. Which was interesting.

Ash was still seething. I couldn't quite work out whether he was more upset over the affront to his dignity or his car. Once we were out of close cover he'd done more stalking than walking, and he was pacing still, up and down the length of the cabin, answering questions in harsh phrases like a crocodile snapping after fish.

It amused Desi enormously, which I'm fairly sure he knew. He could hardly have missed it. She tossed him so many little queries – what should we eat tonight, should we go out or get takeaway, would he like a clean pair of jeans because she was sure she had something in his size? – someone a lot slower than Ash would surely have understood that she was doing it just to watch him snap.

That was one reason I'd slipped up on deck to make my call. I didn't enjoy watching her goad him, I didn't see the pleasure in it, and I particularly didn't want to be there if he lost patience and lashed back.

Even so, I was still impressed by the man my brother had become. He might have been raging, breaking things apart, smashing up the cabin; he might have been doing the same to Desi. I'd known Powers that would, without a second thought, after such a humiliation. He might just have abandoned us and gone off in pursuit of private vengeance. Instead he was keeping a brake on his temper, even if the cable was tight and straining; when I left them he was still answering Desi's little questions, even. His voice might be a rasp on a steel edge, but at least he was using it.

Using it up, by definition. I had phoned and had my answer; I was still lingering, wondering when I'd find the nerve to duck down below and test the water, when he made it unnecessary. He came up to join me, with a tight smile and, "Keeping out of the way, bro?"

"Well out, thanks. I'm sorry, Ash, she's –"

"She's going shopping," she said tartly at my back, where I'd been focused on Asher and simply hadn't heard her come up the companionway behind us. "Anything you fancy?"

"Actually, yes." I gave her a smile, and a list: bread, mustard, ham. Pork pies. Crisps. Chocolate biscuits. Beer, wine, whisky. "And whatever anyone else fancies, of course. But I think those are the basics."

They were both staring at me, Ash with just a hint of his humour returning. Good, I'd been trying for that.

Desi was just flummoxed. "What, are you planning a picnic?"

"Sort of. An all-nighter, at any rate, and I think we might get hungry. Can I explain later? After you've shopped?"

"No. I like to know what I'm shopping for. Explain now."

"We still have to go to London," I said. "For tomorrow, but we have to get there. No car now, and the train is a little too easy to watch, and to interrupt."

"So what are you suggesting?"

"This is a boat, I presume it's riverworthy, and this river will take us all the way. Not fast, and there'll be locks to go through; but we've got all night and all morning if we need it. They don't, uh, lock the locks at night, do they?"

"No. The lock-keepers go off duty, but we can still work the gates." The smile on her face said she didn't get to cruise around much, in this beloved boat of hers. "I'm up for it, if you boys are."

"Ash?"

"Desi's the skipper. Her boat, her shout."

"That'll be a yes, then." She was pleased, which pleased me unduly. I was achingly conscious of having cost both of these people something they treasured, while the only price I'd paid so far was in bruises. And now here I was proposing that Desi should toss her other beloved transport, her own home, into the same unreliable pot of fortune, for uncertain ends and no guaranteed benefit at all.

What made it worse, I was lying to her; but I could push that thought aside, indeed I had to, cloak it in the black dark at the back of my mind. I wasn't sure about Desi, but Ash's mindreading was still impressive. I might be confident that he wouldn't object, even that he'd help me if necessary – but it is possible to be both confident and wrong. I've done it, time and again.

DESI TOOK MORE of Ash's money – on principle, I think, rather than because she needed it – and went shopping, for her own idea of munchies fit for an all-night cruise. She was muttering darkly about apples and energy bars as she left.

She left us with instructions, how to set the boat up, to make it fit for cruising. I went dutifully below to pack things away; Ash stayed in the wheelhouse, playing with the engine. Warming her up, he called it. Between the two of them – one possessive and one avaricious – I guessed I wouldn't need to learn my own way around the controls.

Half an hour later Desi was back, with bulging bags and an organising gleam in her eye. Five minutes to stow the shopping; five minutes for her to run checks on the engine, all of which Ash had done already; then she sent us off to the mooring-ropes at bow and stern. We cast off on her order, and were away.

I DON'T KNOW how fast a Dutch barge with a well-maintained engine can go, if you slam her throttle down hard and let her rip. Five miles an hour is the legal rate on the river: no slamming, no ripping allowed. And then there are the locks. I'd had no idea how many there were, nor how long it takes to pass through them, especially in daylight when there's a lock-keeper on duty and a queue you have to join, nice and mannerly.

It made for an idle, easy end to a day that had started much the same. Even I couldn't keep up my levels of anxiety, once I was sure there weren't going to be more harpies coming out of the clear sky. There was sunshine, there was the slow chug of the diesel and the slow drift of the landscape, banks and trees and people sliding backwards, out of my sight and away. I was on the foredeck, sprawled in a lounger with duties at the locks but none otherwise. Desi and Ash were in the wheelhouse together, and I might have been jealous of either one of them – but no. Couldn't be bothered, really.

THE RIVER WENT by, nothing but the odd cloud shaded the sun, nothing stirred the water more malevolently than the odd duck dabbling for weed. Once I thought I saw a water-vole swimming for the bank, but it probably wasn't. Not Ratty, more likely a regular rat.

At any rate, no undines, no harpies. No one who didn't love us, bar the odd surly lock-keeper and a fisherman or two who just hated every boat on principle.

Towards twilight, Desi came forward to bring me a glass of wine. She perched on the rail where I could look at her without moving my head, which was considerate.

"Don't tell me, let me guess: my little brother is in seventh heaven among your wheels and gauges, and he's taken over so completely, he just left you feeling redundant?"

"She's still my boat," said her captain. Firmly. "And I'd say sixth heaven, no higher than that. He's a tad frustrated, not being able to slam on the speed. This is not the time to attract the inspectors' attention. I thought I could probably trust him, though, not to hit the bank or swamp any families out punting. The kayakers and racing eights can look after themselves, they're a vicious crew. As is mine."

"Not me," I said. "I'm just a passenger. With a bad arm. Even my good bit's bad."

"Have you been taking your drugs?"

"Yup. Fully floaty, ma'am." Which was another good reason for just lying here.

"Good. Don't overdo it, but keep yourself topped up. And if the locks are too much for you, just say..."

"Desi. I can jump off and loop a rope around a bollard, honest I can. I can even hold on to it. It only needs one hand, you know."

"So I've heard." I snorted, she grinned; then she went away and came back with hot water, dressings, antiseptic ointment.

"Let's have a look, then."

"I said it's all *right*..."

"...And I've just noticed the way you're holding it, and you're lying to me, sunshine. C'mon. Show."

So WE DID all that, we went through the arguments about how it was all still swollen and black and needed an X-ray but we couldn't afford the time, and how I'd promise to see to it immediately we were finished except that immediately we were finished would be the time Ash took me off to see my parents and I really wouldn't need an X-ray after that, so why worry?

And she scowled and fussed and patched it up one more time, with lots of numbing spray and her fingers gentler than her words were. Then she filled my glass again and told me to stay still, leave the next lock alone, captain's orders.

* * *

THE LOCK CAME, and I just sat there and watched it happen: watched my brother jumping on and off with the bow-rope in hand, listened to Desi in the wheelhouse calling orders.

He was okay, my brother. I decided.

LATER, AFTER DARK, I did try to make myself useful, carrying a plate of munchies up from the galley. Desi still had her captain's hat on, all boss tonight; one look, and she tried to send me to bed.

"Jay, you're exhausted, you're in pain, you're drugged up and dizzy with it; you need to rest. Sleep, if you can. We don't need you on deck."

"I know that," I said, and maybe the bitterness came out despite myself. "I know damn well you don't *need* me. Oh, except to find Fay, of course, let's not forget that. But not needed on voyage, no. I *know*. But this was my idea, this is my plan, and I'm not going to just disappear and leave the two of you to, to, to do whatever it is you would do, all night on an adventure by yourselves."

"Jay, for crying out loud – are you *jealous?*"

"D'you know, Desi, I do believe he is? Perhaps we should be flattered."

"Of course I'm jealous," I cried. Yup, out loud. Confessing to myself, over all my own denials. "Do you have any idea how bloody dull my life's been, all these years? Going for a walk is about the most dangerous thing I've done for I can't remember how long. Mostly I hide up in cafés, in bedsits, in libraries. And here we are, it's a bright moonlit night and we're going to sneak downriver all the way, all through the dark – and you want me to go to *bed*...? This is the closest I've been to fun since –"

"Oh, thanks," Desi said. "Thanks a lot. Well, fine. If you –"

"Desi," Ash said firmly, speaking over the top of both of us, "as it happens, I can manage the boat perfectly well single-handed. There's a long spell to the next lock, and I do know how to work them by myself. Why don't you *take* my remarkably dim brother to bed, and *keep* him there, by whatever means necessary? I'll wake you when I need a break. I'll wake you both. There's no point all three of us staying up all night anyway."

He was probably right, though I was still sure they'd have done just that without a second thought, if it had just been the two of them. As it was – well, Desi took me in an armlock, steered me to the companionway and pretty much kicked me downstairs.

And then not so much helped me undress as stripped me, tender with my arm and rough with the rest of me; and kissed me more or less the same way, tender-but-rough; and shed her own clothes in some mysterious unknowable fashion that may have been daemon but was probably just girl, and then there we were in bed together.

And I said, "Asher –"

And she said, "– isn't coming down here. He'd better not, he's got my boat in his charge."

"But, but, he's right above our heads..."

"Yup. Do you want to holler, or shall I?"

"No! *No*...!"

"All right, hush then. Let's see how quiet we can be. I'll go gentle with you."

She meant, with my arm. I think she did.

I'm sure she did.

*　　*　　*

WHEN I WOKE, it was because she was leaving me.

Not left, not gone altogether: just pulling her clothes on quietly, trying to sneak away.

I said, "Oy."

She said, "Hey. How are you feeling?"

"Abandoned." But that was pathetic; so, quickly, "No, I'm fine. Do you have to – ?"

"Yes," she said, all captain. "This is still my boat. I do have to. You don't. Stay there, go back to sleep."

"Don't need to," I said. "Seriously. Dizzy all gone, arm not hurting." *You're my drug of choice.* "You go. I'll bring you up a cup of tea."

"That'd be nice. Thanks. Don't forget one for your brother."

So I PLAYED cabin-boy, three mugs of tea with their proper tot of rum, one necessarily gripped in my dead hand as I carried them up, praying urgently not to slip or fall, not to spill, at least where anyone could see me.

And made it up the companionway – barely – and so into the wheelhouse, where I was all insouciance. "How're we doing?"

"No problems," Ash said, taking a mug, grinning at me. Grinning before he sniffed it, for reasons that had nothing whatsoever to do with tots of rum. "How are you doing?"

I ignored him, magnificently I thought, and checked with Desi where we were. We weren't exactly alone on the water, but conspicuous, yes. Chugging down midstream, with lights burning fore and aft as well as in the wheelhouse, it felt like the opposite of sneaking, more blatant than discreet. If anyone was looking on the river, we would surely not be hard to find.

I said this. Desi said, "That was always true; it always has been true, of rivers. Once you're on the water, there's nowhere much else you can go. But there's a whole cascade of logic they have to go through, before they can come after us. First, they have to figure out that we went back to Henley after the car crash. That's not certain; Asher's a big lad in a temper, he's got influence, he could just call for back-up and have us whisked away."

"Yeah. I could. Remind me, why didn't I do that?"

"Because you're a big lad in a temper, and half of you hopes that they do come back and find us. Obviously. You want a fight."

"Well. Maybe, yeah."

Half of him, perhaps. The other half would cheerfully avoid the fight, but still didn't want to surrender anything to higher authority. He had undertaken to support Desi and me in our search for Fay, and then to deliver me up to my parents, as per my promise; pride would leave him very reluctant to yell for help now.

"Then," Desi went on, counting off on her fingers, "if they do figure that we went back to Henley, they've still got to work out where we are now. They'll be fairly sure that Ash and I weren't hurt in the crash, but they can't be sure about you; they may spend some time checking hospitals. If they figure we'd still head out of town, then our first likely move would be the train, so they have to cover that. Or there's hire cars or taxis, or just staying in the town. Hopefully they'll work their way through all of those, before they start looking at the river. It's hardly the most obvious way to go."

"It's pretty obvious," Ash said, "if they know you've got a boat."

"Maybe they don't. It was your car they hit, it's you they know to look for; they may not have figured me out at all. And if they have – well, there are plenty of other boats on the water." If there were regulations about being out at night, we weren't the only people flouting them. Add in the numbers that were moored up, all along both banks and crowded into marinas, we could hide among them like one book in a library. With the lights off. As it happened we weren't doing that, but searchers weren't to know.

After the second time we nearly hit a boat out on open water with its own lights off, Desi suggested that she'd find a forward look-out really useful. I went willingly enough. It's good to be useful, I've never minded being alone, and while that prickle of jealousy hadn't gone away – Desi and Ash together in there, me out here on my own – it was something to be hugged close, to be welcomed. At least I had someone to be jealous about, someone to be jealous of. It had been a long time, since either of those was true.

It was cold on the water, though, at the dog-end of the season. Chill and darkness worked against me, as did the lighted windows in moored boats and riverside housing as we passed. I felt isolated and bereft, on the verge of losing the last sweet thing I had, my one boast, my life. This was the backlash of loneliness. The mortal version at least had a certain terminus; you could only be lonely for a lifetime. In an immortal body, it could last forever. A boy could be stranded like this, in the prow of something strong and unstoppable, eternally alone, eternally aware...

He could be pathetic and self-pitying, and aware of that too, and equally unable to change it.

* * *

"HEY. MY TURN to play skivvy; I brought you tea. *Tee mit Rum*. I figured you could use the warming-up."

"Oh – thanks, Ash."

"Welcome. Mind if I join you?"

"No, sure. Four eyes are better than two. If Desi doesn't want the company."

"I don't think Desi knows what to do with the company. You could give it a try, but she seems very... self-absorbed."

"Not to mention self-sufficient, and self-aware. Tell me about it."

"Nah, you tell me. My brother and the daemon, that's got to be a story."

It was, but not one ready for the telling. I told him other stories instead, stories about being on the run, while he countered with stories about hunting me down. Putting the two together, place by place, I think we were both surprised how close we'd been to each other sometimes. Just as well we didn't know at the time; I'd have been so scared, he'd have been so frustrated...

TIME PASSED, LIKE the water beneath the hull: slow and dark and secret, intimate, soft-spoken. We didn't talk about the big stuff, my parents, my future. We talked about ourselves, which I suppose means we talked about each other. I was rediscovering my brother, and finding that I liked the process as much as I liked the man, which meant vastly more than I'd been prepared for.

At last he stood, he stretched; he said, "That's another lock, up ahead. I'll work the gates, then spell Desi at the wheel, give the two of you some time to be out here. Maybe she won't be so focused, when she's not actually driving the boat..."

"Desi's always focused," I said, and then cut myself off sharply, before that long easy hour of talk could lure me into an indiscretion.

He heard it anyway, unspoken; his teeth flashed brightly in the night and he said, "Just that sometimes she turns that focus onto you, right? Nothing else for her to focus on, up here. Jordan, you're *blushing*."

I was. It was utterly unfair that he could see it; his eyes must do something inhuman in the dark.

Well, of course they did. Everything about him was inhuman, what my parents had made of him. Prince of Hell. *Junior* Prince, just a placeholder, until they regained possession of the heir apparent and could install him in Asher's stead. Uniquely powerful, uniquely privileged: the playboy of the overworld.

Just one more river to cross.

DESI BROUGHT THE boat in towards the bank – not too close, nowhere near close enough for me, if I'd been making the leap – and I felt the deck rock as Ash sprang ashore. My all-too-human eyes saw him land neatly on the towpath and then run swiftly ahead, out of sight. The lock was a distant glow. Desi kicked the engine down to a bare tick-over; by the time we got there, Ash had cranked up the paddles, filled the lock and opened the gates for us to motor straight in.

Moving barely faster than the current, just enough push from the engine to steer us away from the weir and into the narrow delta of the lock, it felt as though we ghosted those last metres, as though we were finally being as discreet as good sense dictated.

Ash closed the gates behind us. Then he came walking forward to open the paddles ahead, empty the lock and let us out onto the river one more time.

He never made it that far.

Something hit him from the shadows, something dark and shadowy itself, a vague impression of arms and trunk and head: humanoid, apelike, somewhere between the two. Whatever it was, it hammered into my brother hard enough that even mighty Asher was knocked off-kilter.

Without the boat riding so high, he'd have been thrown straight down into dark, deep water. As it was, he slammed into the hull, and I wasn't quite sure he hadn't dented it. Certainly he hit with force enough to nudge us away from the lockside, to open up a gap.

Anyone else would have fallen into that crushing danger between the boat and the lock wall. Not Ash. Even as he struck, he was reaching one arm up and feeling for the rail.

Feeling for it, finding it, swinging himself over in an extraordinary one-handed feat of acrobatics. In a gym display, in a circus even, it would have left you with a sense of breathless wonder, that any mortal flesh-and-bone body could do such a thing.

But of course he wasn't mortal any more. Which being true, what he did was spectacular but really not astonishing, just another graphic demonstration of that truth.

What astonished me more was what had attacked him. It launched itself at him again just as he did that one-armed hoist-and-twist manoeuvre, so that it struck the hull full force, just as he had.

Dutch barges are hulled with solid steel, and again I wondered if the boat hadn't buckled under the impact.

That creature might have all of Asher's power, all his savagery and more; it lacked any of his grace and swift thinking. No recovery, no athletic miracle. It plunged, rather, into the waters of the lock. And Desi was at the helm, with the engine and the tiller both to work with; and that creature had attacked Ash and worse, it had attacked the boat. You don't spend time as a daemon without developing your ruthless streak.

Not so much a streak in Desi's case, more a full-blown sociopathic condition. The boat came back hard towards the wall, until the rope fenders fore and aft were all that saved her paintwork. I was leaning over the rail, trying to see into that narrow gap. It was dark down there, but there was turbulence that was nothing to do with us, and I did think that I maybe heard a crunching sound, as it might have been bone caught between brick and steel.

Then we drifted off again, just a little way; and there was movement in the water, and where I was looking for a body's helpless rise, what I actually saw was a hand strike up from below. One, and then another; they seized the concrete lip of the lock, and the creature hauled itself out.

Ramming into Ash, it had just been speed and shadow, vaguely man-shaped but somehow wrong. My mind had logged it as apelike, hominid, not-quite-human.

And then it had been down into the water, it had been caught between boat and wall, and I'd seriously expected it not to rise again.

And now here it was, and what came up into the light was a man, the thing entire: human all the way down, from the trimmed hair and shaven chin to the smartly polished shoes.

Except that the body was broken now, badly broken, I could see the breaks. It couldn't stand straight, and when it did stand there were bits that hung wrongly, and something in the abdomen bulged out where it ought not to be bulging.

IT NEVER HAD moved the way a regular man does, comfortable inside his own skin and knowing his own limits. That was what had deceived me. It hadn't moved like a man, and it had been way too strong. What mortal man could hammer Asher over? But some kind of infestation, a spirit of another kind taking possession of a man's body: it would move that body like a puppet-master, awkwardly at one remove; and it would use and misuse that body brutally, utterly unconcerned about damage done.

And, broken as it might be, such a spirit would bring it back and back again. We might need to dismember it altogether, before any of us could be confident that it wasn't coming back one more time.

No matter, I was sure that Ash could do that. Given what it had just done to him, I was equally sure that he'd be willing. Nay, eager.

So there I was, watching in fascination, not worrying in the least; and so I saw the second man come out of the shadows behind the lock-keeper's house.

And the third.

They walked calmly out into the light, an absolute expression of threat; and I still thought that their confidence was misplaced, because I had a daemon and a Prince of Hell aboard with me here, and I figured the two of them were worth any three out there. With room to spare.

A fourth man, and a fifth. Okay...

And then Desi's voice came yelling down to us, and a moment later she emerged from the wheelhouse. She'd left the engine ticking over in neutral, which she never ever did in a lock because you have to keep the boat clear of the gates – she'd said – or you can end up with a bent rudder at best, a flooded boat at worst. But she left the wheel now, and came out on deck to join us; and the reason for that was on the other side of the lock, where another four men were emerging from shadow, walking unconcernedly into the light.

Nine of them. And I wasn't worth a toss, fighting-wise, even against a normal human man. Against one of these – men who took no account of any harm, men who would break themselves to pulp in pursuit of breaking their opponent – I wouldn't even make a placeholder, fit to hold him up until the real fighters came around.

Nine of them.

Nine is a potent number, which magic keeps coming back to. There might be, oh, any number of reasons for nine men out there to oppose us. But – well, nine of them. Nine men. And that thing about possession, the certainty that what we were facing here was not the original possessors of those bodies, but some spirit or spirits animating them...

Nine Men's Morris.

These days it's a game of strategy, that's as much as anyone knows, who isn't tapped into the overworld. Also, 'Morris' only ever makes people smile, contemptuously or otherwise: visions of beery, bearded men in white, dancing in troops with bells and handkerchiefs and sticks.

Every source of light casts its own shadow. Morris is not, it never has been anything to laugh at.

A Morris side, yes, they hop and jig to jaunty

tunes – but even that is a parody of truth. You see these men jerk to a dictated choreography, and never wonder why.

I thought that this was why; I thought I was looking at it, right there at the lockside.

Both sides, locking us in.

NINE MEN'S MORRIS isn't a spirit, or a creature, or a personification. It's a skill, a tool for the talented; I suppose you could say it's a spell, if you wanted people to misunderstand you deeply.

For those who have the craft of it, they can borrow a man's body and impel him to their will. More bodies than one: I suppose any number in the end, as many as you have the strength to control. The tradition is strong, though, and it tends to work in threes. Three Men's, Six Men's, Nine Men's Morris – and three times three is very strong indeed, they multiply each other.

Whoever it was out there hunting us, who had tracked us down and picked us out and ambushed us here where the river narrowed to a slot, where they could come at us from dry land and both sides at once, they were strong enough to handle the full nine. And apparently to hurl those men to destruction against us, which is never easy. You can possess a body and overwhelm its mind altogether, but it still has instincts of self-preservation. Overriding those takes more than power, it needs a Power.

And okay, we had one of our own, and a daemon to back him up; but I looked at the nine of them, and the three of us – the broken three, two plus one, where to be honest I was really pretty much of a minus – and I wasn't confident.

Desi's voice called down to me, "You just keep out of the way, Jay, we'll handle this," and that of course did wonders for my confidence. Especially as it was clearly nonsense anyway: how could I keep out of the way? There were nine of them, and they weren't going to line up neatly to take their turn with Desi or with Ash, one at a time for each.

Stand by to repel boarders. There was a long boathook up on the foredeck, for fending off other river traffic, or else for pulling it close. I couched that under my good arm like a lance, and stood by.

For a moment, one of those brief instances that seem to hang like smoke in the sky, none of us moved, on board or on the locksides. Even the boat was motionless in the water, not drifting, not rocking now.

Which I suppose only shows how brief that moment really was, because I don't believe the laws of Newtonian physics were truly suspended. Conservation of energy is still something good to hang your hat on.

What Newton made of the overworld, I don't think that's recorded. He must have run into it, surely, a man with his interests. Maybe that's what led him into alchemy in the end, an encounter with some Power that defied everything he understood to be true about the world. A man who has seen the strength and potency of the immortals – well, such a man might well believe in the Philosopher's Stone, when he's seen what seemingly ordinary flesh and bone can do.

Ordinary flesh and bone was what we faced now, but it was animated by something truly extraordinary. Not knowing who or what that was just made everything harder, and it was hard enough to start with.

If there was a signal, I didn't see or hear it. What need a signal, though, when the same intelligence is driving the whole team? It waited, I like to think, until that pure moment of suspense had passed; and then it flung its men at us, all of them together.

I'd been sure that it would.

They leaped the gap, less graceful than Asher, less efficient but just as effective; we suddenly had nine men clinging to the rail, swarming over.

I had two of them all to myself, almost certainly more than I could manage. It was stupid to let myself be distracted, to worry about the others. I did, though; of course I did. Ash and Desi, how not? One was my brother, my hunter, my nemesis. He had been big in my past, and he would likely be bigger in my future. The other – well, not my girlfriend, we knew that, we had said so. Not really my boss anymore; certainly my fascination, my adored. The one I couldn't take my eyes off, even with two Morris-men bearing down on me.

I saw Ash actually help one man over the side, lift him on board, purely so that he could twist the guy's head around before he threw him back again. Eww.

Desi had two to cope with at once, and she did it old-school, the way that teachers used to: gripping their heads, one in each hand, and then slamming those two skulls together. Except that teachers never did it with daemon-force, or at least I hope not. Both those skulls came up broken, brutally dished; and then, like Ash, she hurled both men back across the rail and turned to look for more.

Actually, to be fair to myself, it was only half an eye I kept on them. I wasn't quite as distractible as I make out, not with my own life balanced on the razor's edge. While the men were still hauling themselves over the rail, I swung my boathook horizontally, pivoting on my heel like a hammer-thrower, feeling the centrifugal whip as I smashed the hook end hard into one man's face.

Physics, again; good old Newton. I could never have pushed or punched him hard enough to knock him loose, not with my good hand gone bad on me. Acting at the other end of a lever, though, I caught him such a crack that I felt bones crunching. More importantly, I saw him lose his grip and fall; I heard his splash.

Meantime, the other man was over the rail on the other side of the boat. No hope of sending him to a watery communion with his companion, and I daren't let him close with me; with one arm out of action, I'd be the one who went over the side if it came to wrestling. I settled that boathook under my arm, trained it on him like a lance, and charged.

They may be daemon-strong, these Morris-men, they may be daemon-fast when their possessor hurls them forward, but that's all blunt-instrument work. They're not so good at the subtle stuff, apparently. Like swaying out of the way when someone jousts with them. I learned this in the doing.

The great brass double hook slammed him in the solar plexus, right where a regular man would have been paralysed, breathless, helpless. I guess Morris-men don't worry too much about breathing, any more than they – or their masters – worry about broken bones or torn organs. He didn't fold up, the way he should have done.

At least he didn't just stand there and take it, though. This was a night for physics in action, even if biology was letting us down. Whether it was the simple force of my strike that lifted him off his feet, or whether he took a step back and tripped over the winch directly behind him, I don't know; but he went sprawling across the deck in an inelegant slide that brought him to Ash's feet.

Who kicked him in the ribs, hard enough to break a few of them, before he slid onwards, under the rail and into the water.

Easy to think that this was easy, but none of us was stupid enough to do that. Just then, though, I'm fairly sure that both Desi and Ash were still thinking it was possible. Hell, they'd dealt with and disposed of half the trouble headed their way, without breaking a sweat. Not that either of them did sweat, but they could probably still hang on to the metaphor. And I was willing to bet that each of them had been keeping half an eye on me, for entirely separate reasons, and they'd seen me handle two out of nine on my own. Feeble, human, damaged me: which being true, what was there to worry about?

What there was, of course, were the remaining Morris-men, plus the first ones coming back again, sodden, and damaged in all manner of visually unappealing ways that didn't seem to impede their determined progress. My own first victim sported an eye hanging out of its socket, where my swinging pole-arm had shattered his cheekbone and orb together.

It was someone else's determination that drove them. That made it worse, when the wet ones clambered back aboard: seeing how much they were hurt already and knowing that they weren't going to stop, nothing was going to stop them so long as they had legs to carry them and arms to clutch. It was like fighting zombies, too stupid to know that they're dead – except that with these people, we knew that they weren't dead. Whether they hurt, whether they were afraid or in pain or conscious at all, I didn't have a clue. If they got their bodies back after the Morris, after the possessor withdrew – well, then I was pretty sure they'd all be dead. Already so, or very soon thereafter.

Or we would, of course. That was always an option.

Early triumphs boost overconfident heroes: that ought to be a mnemonic, but actually it's just an observation. They were cocky, Desi and Ash, which laid them right open to being overwhelmed. The Morris-men came at them three and four at once; I watched Ash disappear altogether under the simple weight of bodies, while Desi was grabbed – deliberately, I thought – by one man on every separate arm and leg.

That worried me. There still had to be a reason for this, and now I thought I was seeing it. They were happy to swamp Asher, happy just to keep me at a distance; they had other plans for Desi. Their controlling entity did, rather. Intent was stamped absolutely into every one of those men. She struggled mightily, but they had weight and strength beyond their mortal allowance: I'd seen her kick through a solid Victorian brick wall, but I wasn't seeing her break free of them. I wanted to help, I went to help – but then there was a dripping man between us, him with his eye dangling down his cheek. I don't suppose he was feeling vengeful; I don't believe he was feeling at all. I hoped he wasn't.

I swung my boathook at him, low and hard – and he put a hand out to catch it in mid-swing. That should have broken his hand, and perhaps it did, but if so it made no difference.

It felt like I'd slammed the boathook into concrete. The impact bruised my hand and jarred my whole body, so that my bad arm burned with the shock. I cried out, I think; and then again as the boathook was dragged from my grasp and I simply couldn't keep a hold on it.

The man tossed it over the side and took one step, two steps towards me.

I've never been the suicidal type, or I'd have killed myself long since. I had wondered, though, often and often, how hard I'd fight to stay alive, if a quick, clean and permanent death was on offer. As against the one my parents would bring me to, slow and filthy and peculiarly temporary.

Now I knew. Either I had more survival instinct than I'd guessed, or things had changed in these last days. I'd found reasons to stay alive, perhaps, even just for that extra day or two.

I glanced past the Morris-man, and saw only a heap of struggling bodies where Asher ought to be, and – yes, no help from Desi either, she was being carried over the rail and onto the lockside. Squirming and kicking, and helpless nonetheless.

Where were my mighty immortals, just when I most needed them to be mighty?

The man had nearly reached me now, and I couldn't see any alternative.

I jumped for it.

One arm on the rail and I vaulted over, down onto the lockside. And landed badly, but solidly, on concrete. And there was the boat, riding hull-high in the full lock, and there was the Morris-man above me, barely reaching the point of looking over; and right in front of me, yup, there was the torn roofing felt, taped over the gaping steel where that seductive undine had ripped out a porthole. Was that only two nights ago? Felt like ancient history already.

Felt like an opportunity; I didn't even need to tear the felt. I dived straight in through that porthole.

Well, I *say* 'dived.' Don't picture an athletic spear of motion, and a rolling recovery across the floor of the cabin. More like a graceless scramble, legs kicking futilely in mid-air while my hands groped for the deck, while my mind dreaded hands snatching my ankles and slowly pulling me back...

Didn't happen. I dragged my legs inside and fell into an awkward tumble in the corner; and for a second I wanted to stay just there, huddled and alone, while all those terrible truths acted themselves out overhead, part of someone else's story, nothing to do with mine. This was my story, running and hiding, as it always had been...

The world hung that way, suspended, while I faced my own craven dishonesty. Faced it, and faced it down. And then I moved, and the world moved, and I had to chase to catch up with it.

It was my mind more than my body that had to do the chasing. Desi was up there, out there, being carried off; I was down here, in here, and I needed help. Somehow, I needed to help her.

Up on my feet, then, and casting about desperately: beds, table, nothing any use. Damn it, Desi, why don't you keep a few dramatic weapons down here?

Because she was a weapon, of course, sufficient unto herself; she never thought she'd need anything more.

Kitchen units. That was better. Frying-pan, for the classic comic strike-to-the-head? No – this was no laughing matter, and besides, I wasn't at all sure that their heads held anything that mattered. In their hands was all that I cared about, my Desi, being carried away...

Knives. She might not cook much, but she had

good knives. Of course she did; everything she had was good. Except me, perhaps. I was being tested here and not standing up too well. Still. Knives.

Smart Japanese knives, in a shiny metal block. Little knives – sharp as fuck, but too delicate, too dainty for this. Big knives, just as sharp. I snatched up a knife – then saw something else, hanging from a hook on the wall. Dropped the knife at random, and lifted down the meat cleaver in its place.

I'd seen butchers use these, to hack their way through bones; I'd seen Chinese cooks use them for everything, those times I'd been clearing tables and washing up in exchange for a dinner and a place to sleep. I couldn't imagine what Desi would use hers for, but it was here and it was lethal, edge and weight together.

And she was in their hands, and I really did need to hurry.

UP THE COMPANIONWAY, then, at a rate of knots.

Here's Ash – presumably – under this heap of Morris-men, which may be all they're meant to do, hold him down until the others are safely away with Desi. Still not good; I want him up and fighting – no, I want him up and *winning*. In a position to help Desi. What's a brother for, if not to help when my beloved needs it?

Besides – well, Prince of Hell and all. What was he doing, being overcome by a handful of mortal men? I'd thought him bigger than that...

All right. Not being fair. *Nine Men's Morris – three times three completes it.* There was something exponential about the numbers: because there were nine of them, each of these men multiplied the others, so that two of them working together became more than twice the trouble. And so on, and Ash had four of them on top of him, and I couldn't even do the sums to work out how massively hard that would be to resist.

I didn't have Desi's super-strength, to pull a man's head from his shoulders. What I did have, I had a blade in my hand, a honed and heavy Chinese chopper; and the nearest of the Morris-men, the one on top of the heap, he was giving all his attention to keeping Ash underneath them.

It was hard, knowing that he was just a man at heart, at the core of him. He hadn't asked for this, for any of it; he didn't deserve it. Maybe the mind controlling him could withdraw and leave him whole and unharmed, if it weren't for me. I didn't know. All I knew was, I needed to save my brother before I could go on and save Desi, which meant –

WHICH MEANT THIS: that I swung that chopper with all the pent-up energy I had, all the nerves and terror and distress. One-handed, wrong-handed, but even so – I saw the nape of his neck and I drove that blade at it, as hard and fast as I could.

There's a reason why my Chinese-restaurant friends only ever let me wash up. Desi doesn't cook much, though she has all the equipment; me, I never really had the chance to cook at all. I have no kitchen skills. Not with the cooking, not with the spicing, and most definitely not with the chopping.

It isn't easy, hacking your way through a man's neck.

Even if it were just meat on a slab, it wouldn't be easy. Butchers make it look straightforward but they've had years of practice.

Even if it were a regular human who was guaranteed to lie still once the spinal cord was severed, to stay dead once I'd got through the jugular and the carotids and the windpipe – well, it still wouldn't be easy, would it? But this was a Morris-man and I didn't know, maybe none of that would be true. Maybe I could cut his head off and the body would still come at me, clutching...

I didn't know, but I had the opportunity to find out. And I had the advantage of a good blade, and the extra spur of Desi's voice suddenly crying out, alone and abandoned, abducted and suddenly afraid.

So I hacked, with everything I had. The good blade cut deep into flesh and bone, but didn't sever anything; and then the man was rising up from the writhing pile of his mates, and even that was a plus, it gave Ash less to deal with. Maybe he could handle three, where he couldn't handle four.

But meantime the one man was coming for me, spraying blood from his neck; and there was still one stray on the foredeck, turning now towards me. I swung the chopper and connected again, sinking it deep into his throat. I jerked the blade free, and now he was losing blood and air together, and some motor control too; one leg seemed to give under him, so that he dropped onto his knees before me. His hands were still reaching, though, grabbing at me, and I think I was yelling myself as I skipped out of their clutches and swung one more time, clamping my left hand around my right and never mind the pain in that arm, I needed the extra purchase and the power because this had to end, I had to end it now...

So the blade drove down and this time, yes, I caught his neck just right, between one vertebra and the next, so it severed the spinal cord completely and bit half through the muscles too.

Which answered some of the questions I'd had, because however much the possessing mind may goad and drive the Morris-men, past the limits of pain and injury and fear, apparently even that can't drive them when they're dead. I hadn't cut his head off, but I'd hewed through everything that mattered. In other words, I'd killed him; and he lay sprawled and messy on the deck there, and then there were eight.

Which was the point, because we weren't playing Nine Men's Morris any more, we weren't facing three times three.

And there was a sudden eruption from beneath the struggling pile of bodies, and that would be Asher, rising.

I left him to it, and ran; ducked under the snatching arms of the man from the foredeck, vaulted over the rail again, landed in a sprawl again, kicked myself up and ran again, to where those other four had carried Desi past the keeper's house and out onto the road already.

When there weren't nine to multiply each other, I didn't think the four left on board could control Ash. On the other hand, four was still just about enough to handle Desi, though they were having more trouble with it now. I guess that's the difference between a daemon and a true immortal, or at least one way to measure it. An Aspect is magnificent, but it's still only a coat, a skin of strength. If you'd cut Ash open – if you could, if he'd stood still and let you do it – he'd have said 'Power' all the way through.

Just because you're dealing with one aspect of the supernatural, it doesn't mean that everything else has to match. There was a very mundane van waiting for the Morris-men in the lay-by. One man to drive, presumably, while the others sat on Desi in the back. I wouldn't have fancied their chances in the traffic, but I didn't intend to let them take that chance.

I caught them up on the road, and this time there was no dithering, no doubts. I saw Desi's face, and even through the ferocious concentration of her Aspect, I could see how terrified she was. It was startling to see; I even thought there was a plea there – *help me!* – when her eyes found mine.

One more time, then, I swung the heavy chopper. And maybe it was the result of even that little practice, that I'd learned how much effort the blade needed against bone; or maybe it was the result of that single glance, the realisation that now she really did need me.

Whatever. I swung, and connected, and followed through. The blade struck a Morris-man's wrist, where he was gripping Desi's arm.

Struck and bit and carried on, severed his hand altogether.

He didn't scream, didn't even grunt. It didn't matter. Necessarily, he'd let go, and Desi had an arm free. Neither of us needed to speak, or to blunder on, wondering what was best to do next. I just turned the chopper in my hand and slapped the handle firmly into her palm. Her fingers closed around it, and then – well, pity the poor Morris-men. It wasn't their fault; someone else was telling them to hold on, forcing them to do it, when by rights they should have been running.

She took her cue from me, which was sort of heartwarming. Her turn to swing: left-handed and awkward, with minimal room, while three men struggled to constrain her, and she still made it an act of grace. Grace and speed together: she used the chopper so fast and to such furiously good effect that the third man lost his hand before the first was entirely done with dropping her.

So she fell, pretty much straight downwards. It should have been flat onto her back and all the wind knocked out of her, except that she was Desi, and being Desi, she managed somehow to fold her feet beneath her, and to arch her back and kick herself up to vertical, so that she was upright before I'd finished wincing for her.

She stood and looked around at the four men, all bleeding heavily from the stumps of their wrists, weakening visibly but still trying to come back at her, still utterly possessed; and then she shrugged, grabbed my hand and hauled me away.

"Ash," she said. "Let's go help."

Oh, she would have loved that, the chance to rescue my struggling brother. I'd done what I could already, though, and apparently that was enough. We found Asher breaking the spine of his last assailant, across the boat's rail.

"Oy!" Desi cried, trying for insouciant outrage. "Mind my boat!"

"Sorry. Next time I'll use my knee." Ash flung the body ashore, then reached down a hand to help us aboard. He was matching her mood, both of them playing the heedless devil-may-care heroes at the end of an adventure, as though they were entirely unruffled by what just happened. One or the other, I might just have believed, but the two together just overdid it. I'd seen how Ash was lost and helpless, outnumbered and outgunned; I'd seen how Desi had been panicking in the Morris-men's grip, utterly unable to break free.

I smiled inwardly, took Ash's hand and let his strength draw me up, while Desi vaulted casually and unaided over the rail.

"Is that it, then?" Desi asked.

"I guess that's it. Get them one at a time, they're not such a problem. I've killed, uh, four, I think..."

"I got one!"

"...And the other four have lost at least one hand each, and they're not coming back, so..."

So there was an unexpected sound of engines, a sudden procession of cars coming down the quiet of the lock road. They drew up in order, doors opened and slammed in unison, a parade of men came marching down to the water.

Three times three. Nine Men's Morris. Randomly drawn, I guess, from the traffic on the bypass: the first nine men that the controlling mind could snare.

Asher swore, briefly and potently. Desi hefted the chopper in her hand and looked thoughtful.

Me, I was panicking utterly, though I did try not to show it. For those two even to hesitate told far more truth than their effortful quipping; they knew how close they'd come to losing that last encounter.

"We just need to kill one," Desi said, and even that sounded uncertain.

And there were more cars, more men. Twelve Men's Morris? Or just reserves to be held back against deaths in the ranks of nine, to provide instant substitutes?

I didn't know, and I didn't find out that night. Asher straightened, glared with magnificence at all of us, allies and approaching Morris-men indiscriminately, marched to the front of the boat and did his Prince of Hell thing.

More specifically, his Prince of Hell Running Away thing.

To be exact, he stood in the bows and transferred that dreadful glower to the waters we rode in on and the gates that held us back.

It's one of the things that happens, when you spend too much time hanging out with immortals: they're so casually astonishing, they don't think twice about the little feats of strength or speed or whatever that leave the rest of us gaping, so you tend to forget that these really are little feats. They're the wrapping, not the gift.

Plus, of course, I'd had days and days with Desi, and that really was the limit of what she could do with her Aspect, strength and speed and nothing more.

Right now, Ash unwrapped himself, and reminded us what more it meant, to be a true immortal.

No thunderstrike, no lightning. He didn't need to be flash.

He didn't noticeably *do* anything, in fact. He just stood stiff and proud and furious, like a figurehead. If he spoke, I didn't hear it; I don't think he gestured at all. His eyes held all the humiliated rage he needed, I suppose.

Anyway, he broke the gates apart.

LOCK GATES ARE of hernia-inducing heaviness, due to the sheer mass of water they have to hold back. Basically, of course, they're dams, and they're constructed and engineered on the same principles. The weight of water holds them closed, and the weight of their own massive timbers holds them together.

In a phrase, then: very, very hard to break.

Asher didn't just break their hinges, their joints and fittings, to send them tossing away in great baulks on the floodwaters of their unleashing. Maybe he even stopped to think about that, to understand just how deadly dangerous those baulks would be to anyone in a boat or on the bank downstream of here. Maybe.

At any rate, he splintered those gates. I have no idea how, but they disintegrated all in a moment.

Which left a large lockful of river water hanging unsupported, with us riding on its back.

For one more of those timeless moments, it did seem to hang there, and so did we, while the Morris-men came on closer.

And then, of course, Newtonian physics one more time: gravity did its thing, and the whole lockful plunged forward, on and down, one giant wave with the boat like an involuntary surfer on its back and us – well, Desi and me – hanging on wildly to each other and to anything else that seemed more solid, that could be hugged at the same time. Stanchions and such.

As running away goes – and remember, you're talking to an expert here – it was pretty spectacular.

We left the Morris-men standing, their possessor – I hoped – staring, agape, astounded.

One lock-load of water, in a whole river's-worth: it's not so much. You empty that much into the lower river every time you use it. Not all at once, though, that's the point. There's the slow push, and there's the punch: they transfer the same amount of energy, and they do vastly different damage.

Like the ruin after the Dambusters' raid in World War II, the damage we did that night on the river could probably be cleared up in fairly short order, a few days' work except for the lock itself, which would be a major task to repair. But – like the Dambusters' raid again – the devastation was extreme to look at. Doubly so to watch it happening in real time, on either side of us while we rode the middle of the river.

Whatever way you look at it, we were lucky to survive that initial plunge. After that, either we went on being lucky, or else the boat was remarkably sound, or else Ash was still working in his statuesque pose in the bows there, keeping us safe and centred. I know which one I favour, of those choices.

At any rate, we watched by moonlight as that great wave of water burst the river's banks, flinging moored boats to either side as it went. Some smashed into trees, or concrete abutments; some were swamped; some were simply stranded, high and dry as the waters hurried on. Some of those boats, by the laws of averages, must have been occupied. If people were hurt, we didn't have the time to see. We were just swept onward, and somehow – Asher-how, I think – we clung to the back of the wave and the centre of the channel, even where it swept around bends. Nobody was steering, or trying to steer; nobody but Ash was in control, until at last the fury of the waters ebbed a little beneath us, to the point where Desi felt safe to let go of the boat and me.

"You hold on," she said, transferring my grip onto a handy rail, "and stay there, in case your stupid brother has any more bright ideas."

"Hey, not so stupid. He did get us away from there."

"He did break the lock, and every boat below it, and... Well. Not so stupid, maybe. Just so very *boy*..."

And she went into the wheelhouse, to see if the boat would answer to the tiller.

I think Asher must have felt it, that first tentative enquiry; I think he slacked off whatever it was that he was doing, slowly, until both he and Desi were sure she had control.

Even I felt it when the engine bit against the water, when we got our motive power from the propeller rather than the flood. So did he; that was when he turned and came back to join me amidships.

"If you ever," he said, "*ever* tell *anyone* that you saw me run away –"

"– twice," I pointed out, "on the same day –"

"– then I will scrag you, little brother. I will do all those same things to you that I was doing to that bloody crew back there, until it seemed advisable to make a hurried exit."

"That's *big* brother to you, Asher," and he'd have to be quick. A few short days he had, to bully me at whim. After that – after he'd handed me over to my parents' tender ministrations – we'd stand on a more equal footing. He might still be physically the larger, since years of bad diet and hunger had stunted my growth, but I was the elder and the heir. And both my parents were Powers. This wasn't a zero-sum game, but it might even be that some of what he had would come to me, that he would be diminished by my enlargement.

Which I guess he knew. Better than I did, probably; he'd know what was his by right, and what was only borrowed.

Also, he was feeling better. That hell-ride – say we rode a shiver, down the river's spine – had eaten his adrenalin and cooled his temper. When you're a man, it's always good to break things. And to watch, as other things are scattered and broken all around you. And to get soaking wet, of course, which he was.

"There's a change of clothes in my bag," I said. "If you want them."

"Oh – no, don't worry. I don't suppose they'd fit." He ran a hand down his own sleeve, and steam rose from it; he grinned through that, and tried to look demonic. And then gave it up, in favour of a serious moment. "Who was it, though? Someone strong, to find us and set an ambush and keep it coming that way."

"Someone who wasn't interested in us," I said. "Someone who only wanted Desi." And she knew; she'd been terrified. I couldn't shift that image from my head, her wild panic as they carried her away. She'd been a mercenary and a whore – I thought – for her master, and yet there was still something out there that could scare her past all bearing. "I think we should ask her."

So we went into the wheelhouse, where she was not at all in the mood for talking: fiercely concentrating on the river, driving the boat through all the chaotic eddies and swirls of a dying, dissipating flood, falling back on itself.

"There's another lock coming up," she said, "and we need to be through before the river police get here, because they'll close it off for safety reasons, before they start trying to figure out what just happened. Ash, I want you up ahead opening the gates, please. Anyone they find on this stretch of the river is still going to be here tomorrow. There shouldn't be any damage to the gates, but if there is – oh, I don't know. Do your thing. Hold them together somehow."

"Uh-huh. Aye-aye, cap'n. And if I meet more Morris-men?"

"Deal with them."

She was bleak, determined, unhelpful. He grimaced at the back of her head, gave me a glance that I could read as I chose, and departed to make another of his fabulous, impossible leaps ashore.

Desi didn't noticeably soften, in his absence. Her back stayed just as rigid, her attention just as focused, both just as deliberately turned away from me.

I wasn't having that. I went to stand behind her – irritatingly close, if she was in a snappy mood;

unignorably close, whatever mood she was in –
and rested my hands on her hips, my chin on her
shoulder. She was wet too, I suppose we all were,
her damp hair hung against my cheek. I supposed I
could grow my own again now, if I wanted to.

Mummy's *good* little white-haired boy...

"Hey."

"Hey what?"

"You all right?"

"Yes." And then a pause, and a sigh, and, "Yeah. I
will be." She sort of nestled back against me, losing
at least a little of that stiffness; her head turned, her
cheek pressed against mine through that veil of hair.
"Thanks."

"Save the thanks for after the inquisition." That
put the steel back into her, as I'd been afraid it might,
but I did have to ask. "Who was that, back there?"

"Morris. Didn't you get it?"

"Yes, I did. I don't mean those poor buggers, they
were just random victims, caught up because they
were nearby. I mean, who was behind them? Who
wants you that badly?"

"Cathars, I suppose," she said. "Because they
think I can lead them to Fay."

"Not if they snatch you, you can't. If they follow
you, follow us, then maybe – but we haven't found
her yet. Doesn't make much sense to grab you first,
does it?"

"I don't know, Jay. What do I know? Who else
would be after me?"

It was a good question. They both were. I thought
one was rhetorical, but not the one she wanted me
to think was.

I didn't press her, though. Well, I did, but only physically. She said, "How are you doing, how's that arm?"

"So-so."

"Uh-huh. Remind me to tie you to the bed when this is over. It's the only way you're going to get better."

I made the obligatory innuendo-noises while I suppressed a shudder, the private certainty that when this was over, the last thing I'd be granted was time to let my arm recover, under her curious notions of nursing or otherwise.

Then her eye skewered mine, from the distance of about an inch, and she said, "Jay, are you standing on *tiptoe?*"

"Uh, no. Not quite. Stretching a bit, maybe."

"Well, stop it. Come round here."

So I went round to the side of her, where she could steer one-handed and snuggle with the other; and I found that while tall girls' shoulders are interesting to peer over, they are better by far for resting your head against.

I also discovered that she had lied entirely to my brother; the next lock was better than a mile ahead, and now that she'd knocked the engine back to near-idle in the last dying swirls of the flood, it was going to take us a long time to reach him.

CHAPTER FOURTEEN

MORNING FOUND US moored just above Teddington Lock, where the Thames turns tidal.

We might have gone on through, no reason not; we could have sailed – no, I'm sorry, dieseled – all the way to the Embankment and been a short hop and a scuttle from our goal. But Desi said that finding anywhere to tie up legally in central London was the devil's own work, and she wouldn't risk a ticket. Besides, whoever it was that chased us, they knew now that we were on the water. Far the wisest course was to get off the water, then, before we met whatever next they'd planned to intercept us. We'd been lucky twice – or, as Desi would have it, we'd been strong and smart twice, strong to fight them off and smart to run away; she kept saying that in Ash's hearing, allegedly to boost his ego but actually I thought to puncture it – and we surely couldn't count on a third time.

So we left the boat securely and lawfully moored, and a bus took us to a Tube station and the Tube took us to Leicester Square, and there we were in the heart of Soho, a very short walk from Salomon's.

I was nervous all the way, bus and Tube and walking. Asher was bold, aggressive, arrogant, himself; Desi was the opposite of herself, increasingly anxious, constantly wanting to turn back, suddenly utterly unconvinced by any reason I offered for going through with this meeting. If it had just been the two of us, I think I would have lost her. Ash's being with us gave me the leverage to keep her close: she wouldn't let him see her chicken out.

Besides – boss or not – I was holding her hand all the way. My bad hand, my best hand, with the extra finger curled tight around hers. She couldn't slip free, against that grip; she couldn't pull away without costing me pain and extra damage, which she wouldn't do. Girlfriend or not.

The door opened for us and down we went, into the hollow gloom of a closed club. Salomon met us at the foot of the stairs: not in his booth this time, but standing and looking anxious on his own account, the reluctant intermediary. Which seemed odd, when his club was so widely known as neutral and honest territory; he must host difficult meetings all the time. Just not like this, I supposed, in the barren wasteland of a morning with no customers, no staff on hand, no support.

Ash had all the blatant ease of a regular, but Salomon hadn't been expecting him, and said so.

"Really? Did Sibyl not say?"

"Sibyl's not here."

That hushed my brother. Sibyl was always here, she was the point and purpose of this place, the total focus. Where else would she be – and why would she have left?

Perhaps I should have warned him, warned them both.

Salomon said, "I sent the lads away, as well. Just us today. What can I get you?"

Coffee was the general consensus: lots of coffee. We settled in an alcove which had a sight-line to the empty stage – of course! – but none to the door; he brought us a tall, stout cafetière with little cups, and warned us to go careful. He'd made it espresso-strong, he said, because we looked like we'd been up all night and we'd need to be sharp today.

Desi looked at him sharply enough as he said it. It was true, though, we all felt that. Sibyl might have gone away, but this was still a place for truth-speaking. Whether that just came with the package or was Salomon's own gift, or a residue from Sibyl's, I don't think any of us knew. It was a fact to be dealt with, to be exploited, and that was enough.

It was also a conversation-killer. It lay on the table with the coffee, strong and dark and inescapable, always at the forefront of our minds. There could be no pretending here. That absolute understanding, that if you risk a question you are going to receive an honest answer to it: well, it may sound ideal – especially if you're doing a little private-eye work, looking for a missing person, say – but once you start thinking, it just becomes a stifle to the tongue. Especially when you're with people who matter, and you all know that this won't last, there's an irredeemable end coming. Some truths, you just don't want them to rise.

So we drank hot bitter coffee, black as it came, and we didn't talk much. Desultorily about what had been, nothing about what was to come. No questions, no speculation. Asher told a few stories about our childhood, which I couldn't deny. It was an open invitation to retaliate, to keep the ball batting between us; it might even have been worth it, just to keep that superficial smile on Desi's face. She did have lovely superfices. But I was scared even to go there, so far into the past. My parents lived there, and I'd been avoiding them so long, I was all out of the habit of visiting.

Toast followed the coffee, bless Salomon; it came with a second pot. Toast and butter, honey, marmalade.

Even so, despite the distractions, Desi was getting more and more restive, and I more and more anxious; any moment now she was going to ask, "Why are we here, again?" more or less in those words, and it would be mortally hard to tell her anything but the truth. And then, of course, it would be mortally hard to keep her in her seat, in the building, in my life at all. What brief lifetime there was left to me.

Not enough to waste on self-pity. I just worried and stressed instead, until – thankfully, and how weird did that feel, to be grateful that betrayal would go ahead, not be forestalled, not fail? – there were footsteps on the stairs, voices in the doorway, one slow solo entrance.

Where we were sitting, she couldn't see who came. That was deliberate; I'd picked this particular alcove and manoeuvred her into sitting right in the corner, Ash on one side and me on the other, with the table entirely blocking her in.

Actually, none of us could see who came, until he was right there. I didn't need to see, of course; I knew. Asher, I think, had guessed. For once in her life, Desi was slow, so slow. Maybe she did work it out in those last seconds, from the sound of his footsteps. She didn't look up until he was right there, standing over us.

I'm not sure that any of us were watching him as he came. Must have been an odd experience, to approach a tableful of people and be utterly ignored, when you're so used to being the centre of the world. I was watching Desi, though, and so I think was Asher.

At last, she lifted her head. She saw him.

Did I think the universe had paused before, those pregnant moments in the lock?

This was a world of difference, a different world. This *hurt*. All of her pain, all of her fear thickened the air around us, froze whatever it is that keeps time spinning, threw grit in all the gears. We sat there, caught like bees in amber, fit for a million years of nothing.

He had to be the one who moved. We couldn't shift a muscle, not even I, who'd been most ready for this. I was her creature, more now than ever. I had betrayed her utterly, and her total helplessness destroyed me.

A day late and a dollar short, she reached for her Aspect, and of course it wasn't there. She'd checked it at the door. No superpowers manifest in Salomon's, except what's bred in the bone. What you have is what you are, is all you can bring in with you. Truth rises.

Truth pulled back a chair, the one we'd left there specially, and sat down at the table. Me on one side, Asher on the other, Desi directly across.

None of us said anything, at first. Salomon came over with a tray and cleared the table swiftly. Being careful of his crockery, perhaps, protective of his cafetière.

He didn't need to worry. There were only two people at that table capable of wreaking mayhem, and they were being good boys. Perfect gentlemen. Guarantors of each other's good behaviour, perhaps, if only because they so much didn't like each other.

It was easier, though, with the clutter gone. Nothing for Desi to hide behind, nothing for her to focus on or fidget with. Only her hands, flat on the table, trembling, his fingers beating a silent rhythm on the edge.

It occurred to me that he was as nervous as anyone, though not at all flat-out scared like she was. I thought that was a good sign. I hoped so. I needed something urgently, to suggest that maybe after all I had done the right thing here.

Amazingly, it was Desi who spoke first. She found her courage somewhere, found her voice; lifted her head again and spoke to him.

Said, "Hullo, Jacey."

He said, "Hullo, Fay."

WHICH WAS THE moment that I knew I was right. Before then, I'd had suspicions that had grown slowly into certainties, but you can be certain sure of something and still be wrong.

As witness: after a long, slow time she turned her head, nothing more to say to Jacey now. She looked at Asher and then she looked at me, and nodded with an utter, bitter certainty.

"That's it, isn't it? You worked a deal out, you and your brother. You sell me to the Cathars, the Cathars give your parents whatever, I don't know what, doesn't matter, something, and that buys your freedom for you. They let you live, the way you're so determined to."

So determined that I'd sell her life in exchange for mine, apparently. That was how she saw me.

Never mind. She was scared, and maybe she had reason. She surely thought so. I was hoping she was wrong about that too, but all I had was hope. Well, hope and promises, but they're not worth much to an immortal.

Except in Salomon's, of course. Truth rises.

I didn't try to defend myself. Nor did my brother fling himself between us to save me from the lash of her scorn.

It was Jacey who denied her.

"No," he said. "No deal. Jordan phoned me, to ask if I wanted to see you. Just that, nothing more. No conditions."

Truth rises, but truth couldn't save me. The truth was that I'd betrayed her. Never mind why, the fact of it was absolute, irredeemable.

She said, "That's great. So, what, Jay, did you do it for the simple achievement of the thing? The ultimate in tracking down runaway girls?"

"You came to me," I reminded her drearily, almost depressed to find that I was going to defend myself anyway, where I knew there was no defence she could listen to. "You asked me to find Fay. So I have."

"I wanted you to *fail!*"

You're not supposed to be able to hiss a line that doesn't hold a sibilant. She could do it. Of course she could; she could do anything, except what she most desperately wanted to do, hide and stay hidden. For a daemon's long lifetime.

In a daemon's long lifetime.

I said, "I know. It was your final test, wasn't it? I knew more about hiding from immortals than anyone else on the planet. If you could find me and fool me, if I couldn't work out what you'd done, then maybe you could feel safe."

Truth rises, but sometimes it comes up slowly. I managed to squeeze that out before it tripped me. She'd been fooling herself, though, if she really thought that. You never do feel safe, never ever. She'd have spent a long, long lifetime looking over her shoulder, waiting for the world to catch her up.

Jacey said, "What did you do, Fay? Jordan didn't say, where you'd hidden or how you'd managed it so long."

Did he think this was long, these few years she'd been running from him? He was young, genuinely young, not just eternally youthful. He had a lot to learn.

She said, "Don't call me Fay. Fay's dead. Call me Desi." And then, when he just shrugged in bewilderment, she sighed – overdoing it, I thought, in her desolation – and said, "You tell him, Jay, why don't you? You were smart enough to work it out, all by yourself. You explain."

"I had an advantage," I said. "I didn't meet you here."

All Jacey was seeing, of course, was an attractive girl, a girl he'd once loved, who'd changed not much more than her hairstyle. There wasn't anything more to see, here in Salomon's. Everything else got left at the door.

Which was why he was gazing between us with that *I-don't-get-it* look; which was why Asher was bursting to tell him what she'd done; which was why I had to jump in quickly. She was right, it was mine to tell if she wouldn't.

"She turned daemon," I said simply. "Sold herself to a master – and don't ask me who, she hasn't said – and disappeared that way, into a new name and a few years' service. It's no wonder you couldn't find her. Fay

– well, she's not dead, exactly, but she really doesn't exist anymore. Outside here, at least." Fay had done what Desi told me, she'd run away; only she'd done it in the most complete way possible, into a whole new persona. "You can't see it now, of course." I'd picked the one place where he would still see the girl he'd known, where truth would bring Fay bubbling up out of Desi. "But even without her Aspect on, Desi – Desdaemona – is someone else altogether." Built of sheer nerve, for one thing, where Fay was built of nervousness. She'd sat there in the seafront café, our first meeting, and calmly shown me a photograph of herself, knowing that I'd only see a sisterly resemblance.

Jacey was having trouble, clearly, seeing the Fay he knew as a daemon. Trying to see some trace of the daemon, I suppose, in this girl he faced, but he couldn't do it; all he'd find there were old hurts and fresh fears. Still, he took it on board, or made the effort, at least: applauded the smartness of the move with a soft whistle, then said, "All right, never mind who" – meaning *I'll find out, some other way* – "but what did he have you do for him?" Like me, he was immediately and obviously puzzled by how brief her service must have been; like me, he was anxious about what she might have sacrificed in exchange for time. Unlike me, he was dangerous, and sounded it.

She just shook her head, meaning *I don't want to tell you* and *it's none of your business,* both in the same convenient gesture. Also, perhaps, *what does it matter now?* I knew that feeling too well, the despair that slams down on you after a long run is finally brought to a halt.

His fingers were still for a moment; then, "Well, all right, then. Let it go." *For the moment.* "You are free now, though?"

"Oh, yes. Entirely free. Unprotected. You don't need to worry about that."

From the look on his face, that wasn't exactly what Jacey had been worried about. But she wasn't seeing that, she wasn't looking.

His voice was remarkably gentle in the circumstances, even if his language wasn't. "For Christ's sake, Fay –"

"Desi."

"Desi. Whatever. What do you think I'm going to do, drag you off and feed you to my family?"

That was, of course, exactly what Asher intended to do with me. It didn't matter now. I was watching Desi lift her head.

"Yes. Yes, of course I – You mean you're not?"

"No. I'm not." Truth isn't just black and white, even in Salomon's, it can be many-textured; this one came layered with hurt that she could even think such a thing, let alone believe it so utterly. And of course that hurt was completely genuine, it couldn't be anything else. And if I couldn't miss it, then she who knew him so much better, she who had loved him, she must have felt it like a slap in the face. With a barbed glove.

She did flinch, and then colour. Which only underscored how pale she'd been before, how very frightened of him. And of course he saw that too, if I did; and again it meant more to him, it cut deeper.

She still wasn't prepared to take him on faith, she wanted more reassurance than his plain word. She wanted understanding, and could only come there by way of pain. "I've been hiding, running from you for years..."

"Not from me."

"*Yes*, from you! Oh, maybe it was your so-charming parents and your cousins and your aunts who were actually keen to kill me – nice and slowly, while they watched and commented and took pains to explain it all, how wicked I was and how presumptuous, and just how much it was all going to cost me – but you were the one I was most scared of. You were the one I *loved*, and you would just have stood back and let them do it. Wouldn't you?"

"I couldn't stop them, once you'd run away. You don't know – or, no, scrub that. You *do* know what they're like. They're a juggernaut, they'd just roll straight over me."

It was strange, hearing the burning-bright playboy confess himself so helpless; almost as strange as seeing my blazing Desi so reduced, physically and emotionally, actually helpless. We were no help to her, Ash and I.

"And what," she asked, "if I'd stayed, how would you have stopped them? Stood in the doorway and said *no, you can't have her, she's mine*? If you'd done that in the first place, Jay –"

Whoo. That must be what she'd called him, when they were close; and she'd transferred the name to me wholesale, and she stumbled over it now as she found it in her mouth, her eyes moved from him to me and back to him again and I wasn't sure what any of that meant, the transfer or the stumble.

No matter. It meant nothing to him. He said, "If you hadn't run away, I wouldn't have needed to. You'd have been with me, we'd have learned that you were pregnant, *together*, and everything would've been different. My family would have welcomed you..."

"As a brood cow, you mean? I wasn't good enough to be your lover, but to be mother of the next generation, I might do? Lucky me. I think I prefer their honesty, when they drove me away." Nothing about whether she would have preferred to stay with him, to have his child, to be his family. Likely she didn't know anymore. Too much had happened, between that possibility and this reality.

"Anyway," she went on, shuddering against the memories, unless it was against visions of her future, "it's too late for that now. And they're still a juggernaut, and I don't think you've grown big enough to defy them. You say you're not going to hand me over, but..."

"But you could be wrong about me," he said, gently, firmly. "It could be that I have grown, that I can stand up to them now, draw a line in the sand, say it's over. Jordan thinks so, anyway; that's why he phoned me."

That's why she looked at me, why her eyes called me *traitor*, while her mouth scorned to talk to me at all.

I said, "You can't run for ever, Desi."

"That from you? Jordan?"

My name, in her mouth: a snare, a capture. A cold weight of rock.

One more river to cross.

"That, from me. Yes." *I know how this works, and it's all about inevitability. You get scared, you can't face what's coming, so you run. Of course you do. And then you can't stop running, you need someone to stop you; and, in the end, someone always does.* A glance past her, to Asher; he was watching me with a cool, contented smile on his face. Pleased, fraternal, affectionate; self-satisfied, and satisfied with me. Big brother, back in the fold. No, back in the pack: immortals have always been predators. I wasn't immortal yet, but that was coming. All I had to do now was die.

That scar on his throat. Even in the shadows of the club, it seemed to flare. A summons, a promise.

Inevitability.

"They'll kill me."

"No." That was Jacey, positive, reaching over the table for her hand.

She gave it him, with my other name as a gift alongside. She gave it to him; she took it away from me. The price you pay for treachery. "They will, Jay."

"If I'd thought that, I wouldn't have come. I'd have told Jordan to keep you hidden. Sure, if they found you now, if the Green Man just walked in and took you, they'd do it without thinking – but that's the point, they only need to think, and they'll see it's pointless to hurt you. Worse, it's harmful. I can tell them, they'll listen to me now. I'm not a kid anymore."

Which is the universal cry of kids everywhere, of course, and it didn't persuade Desi. She snorted. Ash grinned.

So did Jacey, reluctantly. "All right. It's true, though. I can make them listen, and I can make them call off the dogs. Cancel the bounty, tell the world you're safe, you're under my protection, hallowed ground. I can do that, Fay. Desi. You can be Fay again, if you want to."

You can be my Fay again, he seemed to be saying, or his fingers did, linking with hers right there in front of me.

She didn't pull away, but she wasn't going to take his word for it. Not unsupported. "How?"

"Because I'm their golden boy, son and heir, I have the keys of the kingdom – and I'll hand them back and walk away, if they don't give you a free and public pardon."

"I don't understand."

"I'll change my name, Fay. Desi." That time it was deliberate, to make the point. "Everybody's doing it."

That was immense, it was terrible. It had been my idea, my suggestion, but I couldn't claim the credit. I couldn't claim anything from her now: the price you pay.

She shook her head, bewildered. *Daemon or not, she's only mortal – this isn't native to her, she can't feel the weight of it. You'll have to convince her, Jacey. I can't do it. I can't say a word.* All I could do was worry, and wait for them to feel the same urgency that sweated my palms suddenly. Truth rises, and sometimes it comes up cold. I knew he wanted me – or the bounty that came with me, the high credit of pleasing my parents – but I hadn't known that the Green Man was after Desi too. Bounty is bounty, I guess, and the Cathars too are people worth the pleasing.

"I'll leave the family," Jacey said. "Not be a Cathar any more, not be their son. Leave them barren, without an heir. We can do that, it comes with the territory. If you can't die of natural causes, you have to be able to walk away."

Not run, of course. Running was different, frowned on, illegitimate – and you couldn't walk until you came of age, and you had to do it in public, in the presence of your parents. That was the trap, the catch-22 that had me pinned just where I was, one day shy of my majority. The moment that calendar clicked over, they would have me, wherever I was; and the moment they had me, it was too late for me to save myself. They would hang me by my heels and drain all the blood from my veins, replace it with something hot and hungry, make me – well, into another Asher.

I kept trying to tell myself it wouldn't be so bad. Right now I couldn't even hear myself say it; there was a surge and suck in my ears, a rising tide of tension. *Nine coaches waiting – hurry, hurry...*

Jacey didn't tell her the cost of leaving. There's always a price; in this case, he'd be handing in his immortality. That was the trade-off: leave the family, and leave the overworld. Be human.

So long as he meant it, though, he knew it was a price he'd never have to pay. That was the paradox, the inverse of catch-22, the virtuous circle. If his parents believed him, they'd capitulate at once. They could not bear to lose him, it was an impossibility, unthinkable.

Win-win, then. For everybody concerned, except me. I betrayed her to save her, and all she could see was the betrayal.

Betrayal and Jacey across the table, the boy she'd been driven away from, the boy she'd hidden from, the boy she hadn't seen since she loved him. The boy who was sitting there promising to renounce his family for her sake, waving his grand romantic gesture under her nose, saving her life.

Did he want her back, and would she go? I couldn't tell, I couldn't guess, nobody could ask.

I was barely aware that it was a question. There were two things happening at once here: the great reconciliation and rescue scene, that they really needed to get done and over with, because I was coming over all Sibylline and terrified. Something was building, something was coming and I could feel it, sense it, taste it. I even thought I could give it a name.

There had been the harpies, and they were only outrunners. There had been the Nine Men's Morris, and that was just a precursor, a herald for the main event.

If the Green Man just walks in, Jacey had said, and I thought he'd had a Sibyl moment of his own, a precognition all unknowing.

I was right.

IT WAS MY own fault, of course. I'd thought I was only betraying Desi in order to save her; in fact, I'd betrayed her and all of us.

The Green Man wanted Desi, Fay, to hand her to the Cathars. The Green Man thought that Jacey was most likely to pick up word of her, one way or another; he also thought that Jacey might not share that word. For one reason or another. So the Green Man put a tap on Jacey's phone. Technical or magical, whichever. He'd been listening in when I called. He heard us negotiating, learned where I was and who I was with. Sent the harpies first to intercept us, but they lost us in the trees. Once he'd figured out our next move, he gathered his Nine Men's Morris, laid his ambush and tried to take us on the river, but we rode away on the flood.

Now – well, now he came himself, in his own person.

The Green Man just walked in.

CHAPTER FIFTEEN

EVERYTHING YOU THINK you know about the Green Man is true, but none of it is right.

Perhaps I should have said that the other way around.

Most people see him first in church, but of course they don't know what they're looking at. Just a face cut into the granite of the wall, or carved and painted to embellish a wooden roof-boss: a man's head surrounded by a wreath of leaves, or perhaps his beard is made of leaves, or even his whole face is. Or else he has his mouth open and there are branches springing out of it, bearing fruit and flowers. Or those branches spring from every orifice of his face, eyes and ears, nostrils too.

You'd think a runaway lad might spend a lot of his time sheltering in churches. Not me. I knew he'd come after me, he's always liked the hunt. I don't know that he can use those faces, all those representations of himself to spy from – but I don't know that he can't. I could never be comfortable under the carved cold gaze of the one I was most in fear of, most hiding from.

So that's him, that's where he's most embedded, and not just in England, either. You'll find him in banks and temples from New York to Nepal. Again, perhaps I should have said that the other way around; it's more likely the way he travelled, out of the east.

Hunting all the time, leaving a trail behind him.

Death and rebirth is what they say. He's a symbol of the endless cycle, John Barleycorn, a personification of the seasons in all their terror and glory. That's why he dances with the Morris-men – yes, Morris again, I was truly slow there – as Jack-o'-the-Green; why he's Robin Goodfellow in the pastures and fields and Robin Hood in the greenwood, except that of course he *is* the greenwood too, every tree and leaf of it; why he is both Gawain and the Green Knight, monster and mentor to an aspect of himself. The Celts called him Viridios, the Muslims al-Khidr. It's all the same. None of these are names, they're only ever descriptions, and they all say the same thing. He's the Green Man. Nothing to add, because no words will do it.

You'd think he'd be a creature of the countryside, needing sun and rain and soil, uncomfortable among the works of man. You'd be wrong. His roots go deep, and the shallow scratches of human enterprise trouble him not at all. He is the green of mould and moss, the eerie glow of luminescence in the sewers, as much as he is the fresh grass-green of the meadow or the deep shadow-green of the forest floor.

He walked into Salomon's like a punter, like a regular, except that he didn't pay a price at the door.

How he'd got in from the street, why the top door

would ever have let him by, that I don't know. But the door was wood, necessarily older than whatever injunctions had been cast upon it, and wood maybe remembers the days of its growth; his roots go deep.

He came down the steps, and Salomon must have intercepted him at the foot.

By now, we all knew he was coming. Desi was magnificent, magnetic when she had her Aspect on, she could draw my attention through solid brick walls; the Green Man would have drawn it through the steel door of a bank vault, through the concrete of a buried bunker.

Where we were sitting, we couldn't see the doorway. We didn't know how Salomon tried to stop him, or what he did in response.

We heard Salomon's scream, that was all.

And then the footsteps, coming in.

By then we were all of us on our feet and moving, out of that cramped alcove and into the more open spaces of the club. Shadows lay over shadows, nothing was clear to be seen, but we could look, at least. We could meet him standing up.

Not on level terms, never that. Not even the immortals among us could come close to such a claim. Eye to eye, though. That was something.

I felt Desi trying to snap her Aspect on around her, for whatever good that would do. Trying and failing, of course. She couldn't even make a fight of it. She'd hate that.

No more could I make a fight of it. It wasn't accident that the other two pushed themselves ahead of us, and it wasn't accident that I let them do it. If anyone here could stop the Green Man, daunt him or turn him aside, it would be my brother or Jacey, or the two of them working together.

If they *could* work together. Jacey would bargain for Desi's life and freedom; Ash would bargain for mine. If bargaining failed and it came to fighting – well, who knew? Maybe they'd just fight each other.

Maybe not. I'd already surrendered to Ash, and through him to my parents. I wasn't running any more. There wouldn't be a bounty for the Green Man, if he brought me in. He should know that by now, so it would be for Desi that he came. For Desi that he'd hunted us through the night. And all our beautiful subtle planning, how to save her: that would all go to waste if he dragged her off to the Cathars now, before Jacey could work his blackmail.

Two princes of the kingdom stood against him, if they chose to stand shoulder-to-shoulder. I didn't think they'd be enough.

Nor did Desi. She was trembling, at my side. I reached out my hand – my good bad hand, my left – and locked it loosely around her wrist. There would be pain, but there would be persistence. She couldn't pull free of that grip, without her Aspect. She couldn't plunge forward and sacrifice herself in some heroic, despairing gesture, simply give herself to him. Nor could even the Green Man break that grip of mine without breaking me entirely, physically, hacking off my hand. Short of that – and I thought he would stop short of that – if he took her, he took both of us together.

He might do that, of course. Heedless of whether it would please our respective families or enrage them, he might do it anyway, for the simple love of the chase, the capture, the victims fetched home. His was the wild magic, untamed, chaotic.

He didn't look it. He walked into the club neat, spruce, shorter than I'd looked for and slender as a birch. Clean-shaven: that was a surprise. Smartly dressed, in a suit that was more grey than green, although his tie was brighter. I'd have called it blood-green, if that made sense. Just then, just there, it seemed to.

He stood in shadow and looked at us, and his eyes were sparks in the darkness. His voice was as I'd imagined it, unimaginable, compounded of all the slow, slurred sounds of the greenwood: creaking branches and falling leaves, roots digging into black soil, cracking rock. Rain, streams. Bogs and black water, where black roots come to drink.

All of that, and more. There was ice in him, and sap, and that sunshine that works only on the skin of things and never reaches the heartwood.

He said, "I have been looking for you. For two of you."

"And you are too late," Asher said, just as Jacey said, "And you can have neither one of them."

And they did, they stood shoulder to shoulder between him and us; and I don't know if they surprised each other more than they surprised themselves, but they sure as hell surprised me.

Desi was beyond all this, away, lost already; tugging at my hand, trying for release. She wanted to go to him, just to spare the rest of us, sure that she was doomed already. That's what I'd been most afraid of, why I'd got her in that gentle wristlock.

Asher said, "Jordan is with me now, and coming home."

Jacey said, "Fay is with me now, and I will speak to my parents on her behalf. Thank you for your efforts, these last years, but we do not need you now."

I don't know if they truly imagined for a moment that he could be dismissed so easily. If they did, they were due a disappointment. I'd have liked to be cynical, to feel that it would be good for them, two golden boys used to getting everything they demanded, everything their fancy or their whim dictated; to let them learn that some things actually were not so easily obtained.

But no, for crying out loud, let them not learn that lesson on our bodies...

I thought they would have to. Certainly the Green Man intended to teach it them. He said, "I will take them now," as though the boys had said nothing at all; and there was the first hint of his true nature – or the second, perhaps, because that voice disguised nothing at all – but it was like the flash of a leaf turning out of shadow into sun, a brief glimmer of something barely seen, like a fish catching the light where it rose through the murk of a stream. It was cold and wet and dangerous, beyond the pale, outside this city world – or rather he had brought it in with him to the city, and it was here, and entirely to be feared.

And then there was a voice behind him, that surprised him as much as it did the rest of us, I think, or perhaps a little more. Because he knew already what he had done to Salomon. And yet there was Salomon, bloody and pretty much bowed, actually, but *there* nonetheless, and saying *no*.

Saying, "No. Not from here. Anywhere else, it lies between you and them and those who seek them, although I think the lads are right, that you are too late to seize them now. But this is my place, and it is common ground, neutral territory by long agreement and sworn word. You *know* this..."

Of course he did; which was why I knew what he would say in return, before he said it.

"That is not my agreement; I swore no such word."

And he was the wild magic, owing fealty to no one Power, living on bounty, what passing credit he could earn by satisfying passing hungers. And sometimes, often, acting entirely for himself, to satisfy his own. I was no more safe than Desi here, and only fooling myself one more time by thinking so. He had sought me, he wanted me, I was his for the taking.

"It was sworn on your behalf, by those who are your masters." That was Salomon again, incredibly, stupidly coming back at him, and coming into the light now, coming where we could see what damage he had taken already, in trying to deny the Green Man entrance.

There was blood, yes, and damage worse than bleeding. He held himself hunched over, and one leg dragged, and the trail he left on the floor was only a signifier of how badly he was hurt inside. His voice carried the same message, a desperate wheezing thing, built of pain.

"No one masters me." It was hard to be clear in the shadows, the way they seemed to shift as the Green Man moved, but I thought his face was shifting too. The fringe of dark beneath his chin had more solidity to it, as though it wasn't just absence of light down there, as though something was growing at last where I'd really expected him to sport a beard. At the same time I thought his skin was darkening and peeling, hanging more loosely than skin ever ought. At first it seemed scaly, like a snake's, and I thought he was shedding it.

"The Powers That Be may choose to let you run free in the world – but that is their choice, and not yours. In here, even *they* choose to bow their heads to the commons, and do no harm."

Salomon's place was needful, he was saying, for more reasons than to give his little gift somewhere to stand, with Sibyl's on show beside it. And he was right, we could hear it; but the Green Man feels other, older bindings than we petty mammals can detect. Those weren't scales on his face, they were too textured for that. I could see veins, all the form and structure of leaves emerging. And that beneath his chin, that was growing to encompass his head: not a beard, no. That was a wreath, writhing twigs that came black and dead but sprouted buds and leaves as we watched.

He had meant to do this, or he had not. He was susceptible after all to Salomon's truth, rising like sap in him, driving him into his heart's form, stripping away his cod humanity as it had stripped away Desi's cod immortality. Or he was not. I couldn't tell.

Salomon had probably never needed to throw anyone out of his club before. He had doors to pre-empt the unworthy, fees to discourage the uncommitted, a searing honesty to discomfort the unwelcome. Between them, those must have been enough. But he laid hands on the Green Man, to cast him forth, and we could all tell how bad an idea that was, even before he started screaming.

It was foresight that he lacked, I guess, without Sibyl there to sing it for him. Wise Sibyl had run away, not to have to watch this.

It wasn't only the Green Man's skin that had been changing. That silky shimmering greeny-grey suit had tightened and stretched so that it was like a skin itself now, like smooth bark beneath a crown of leaves. That was what Salomon seized hold of, one arm above and below the elbow, as though he thought – tree or demigod, it made no difference – he could simply walk the Green Man out of here.

Tree or demigod, the Green Man wasn't moving. I almost looked at his feet, to see if he'd cast roots through the club's hard floor into London clay or bedrock underneath. Almost. I was just a moment too late to do it.

Instead, my eyes were snared by that grip of Salomon's, because what he gripped suddenly looked nothing like bark, any more than it did a suit. More like a bed of reaching worms. It erupted into a mass of pale, groping tendrils that twined themselves about Salomon's fingers and wrists/. And he screamed, and I couldn't see why until I saw more of those tendrils – like a cutting's new rootlets, I thought – bursting through the skin on the back of his hands, dark-dyed and glistening wet.

He couldn't break free. We saw him try, but those slender rootings snared him like wires, threaded through and through his flesh.

Jacey muttered something utterly profane, and took a step forward – and was stopped not by Desi's cry, though she did cry out to stop him; not by Ash's hand on his own sleeve, though Ash did reach out to stay him; not even by my urgent wishing, though I did most urgently wish for him to stand still. Rather, he was stopped by the same thing that had stopped us all.

Not the expression on the Green Man's face, because the Green Man had no face left worth the mention, certainly not enough to express anything.

There are snakes that dislocate their jaws, in order to swallow their prey. Their whole head stretches into an obscene glove-puppet parody of snakehood, that same way that their body distorts around the form of what they've eaten.

This was worse. His mouth hinged open, yes, and whiplike shoots surged out, already budding even as they roiled through the air, and already he'd lost any hint of false humanity, so what came next shouldn't have mattered. Only it did, because we had seen him in his mock-human form, we'd *spoken* to him, just moments earlier, and now fresh shoots emerged from his eyes, from his ears, from his nose. As though he had been a hollow man all this time, eaten out by serpents. I've seen caterpillars on TV, eating and growing and seemingly healthy until they suddenly erupt with wasp-maggots that have hatched inside their bodies and consumed them altogether from inside. This was like that, only worse again.

Worse for us, just watching. Worst for Salomon, when those sharp writhing shoots pierced his body, one after another.

He kicked and threshed, lifted entirely off his feet by their strength. And then one by one they withdrew, and the last of them flicked like a whip to send him hurtling through the air and crashing into a corner.

Desi moaned and went after him, pulling free at last because I couldn't hold her. I was torn, dithering, useless, taking a step after her and then a step back towards the boys, where they were still trying to face down the Green Man, knowing full well that he stood between us and the only exit.

And then she shrieked, and that decided me, to the point where there was no need to make any decision at all; I was beside her in moments.

And staring, useless again, infected with the same horror that had caught her. The day before – no, an hour before, after this night just gone – I'd have said that nothing in the world could make Desi shriek that way. Now I was looking at it, and if I'd had any breath to spare I might have shrieked myself.

Salomon was… sprouting.

Not dead, either. Not yet. There was a glitter in his eyes, something beyond agony, beyond terror: something close to truth, I suppose. He could hardly escape the revelations of his own gift. He must know exactly what was happening to him.

What was happening to him? Like the wasps that lay their eggs in caterpillars, those shoots had left seeds or sprouts inside his flesh, and they were growing. Heedlessly, mindlessly destructive, they broke out of the darkness of his wounds, into the dim shadows of the club, forming leaves and groping for light, in a fast-forward horrorshow.

We assumed the roots that tapped back, into Salomon's flesh and blood and bone.

No. We didn't assume anything, we didn't need to. We could see the truth in him. He was still alive, this was still his place. His rules applied.

I took Desi by the shoulder and turned her away, before she could think to try plucking out those seedlings. She shuddered against me, and came with.

Of course, turning her away from Salomon, I had no choice but to turn her towards the Green Man. There was nowhere else to go. Still, she was Desi again; she'd sooner face what she had to fear. Running away was Fay's trick, not her own.

Truth rises. She lifted her chin and found him where he stood, beyond the boys. I confess, I was slower.

Jacey glanced back at us. "Is he going to be okay?"

"No," Desi said flatly.

That brought a grunt from Jacey, a hiss from Asher. Everything was tighter suddenly, no more fencing. No more neutral ground. The club had lost its sanction.

If the Green Man could still speak, I didn't see how. His mouth was so entirely full of tendrils, shoots, call them what you will. Whips. They flourished from him, like so many serpents, so many tongues; they twined with each other, and with those that sprouted from his eyes and elsewhere. He was monstrous, appalling, vastly larger too than he'd been when he walked in – or else he was beyond scale, perhaps, beyond anything in that room, beyond comparison.

Except that he stood in that room with a Cathar and a Prince of Hell, and I thought that actually either of those would stand comparison with him, young though they were against his age.

He seemed not to care, not to heed them at all. We were what he'd come for, Desi and myself, and he meant to take us now.

Like whips, those long shoots of his uncoiled over and around the boys where they tried to make a wall. Like whips, they reached for us, snapping in the air, snapping at us.

I did that thing you do, when you've been all the way through terror and come out the other side, when you've done the despairing already, when you've given yourself up for lost. I did the hero thing, pushed Desi back – and how often had I been able to do that, even with my good hand, moving her at my insistence? – so that it was my body now that stood between him and her.

It was my body, then, that those whips flailed around, that they caught and seized and began to haul towards him. He didn't care; he wanted both of us, and he might as well take me first. I was dead anyway, given up for dead, promised to my parents. If he took me, I was no worse off, and there was still a chance that Desi might be able to get away, although I couldn't see it.

They clung to me, those whips, those shoots; and

I felt – well, what? All greened out. Sucked in to the slow rhythms of the sap as it rose, slower than truth but more revealing, peeling, digging to the core of me. Finding everything that was weak and craven, mocking as it seized –

– AND THEN SUDDENLY his grasp was broken, unexpectedly, appallingly, a brutal ripping-out; and I screamed, and my eyes washed clear of the green and there was Desi, rending like a mad thing, grabbing each of those tendrils and snapping them savagely while their broken ends fell away from me and their broken stumps flailed uselessly and recoiled, all the way back to the mouth or the eyes of the Green Man.

It took me a moment to catch up, but soon enough, I did understand.

Salomon had died. Whatever there was growing in that shadowy corner, it was him no longer, it only fed on him.

Which meant that Salomon's rules – here in what had been his place, common ground, where everything was equal – no longer applied. We'd lost that tang of truth, of originals, of what lay at the heart of us.

Which meant, in short, that Fay was unequivocally Desi again, and Desi had her Aspect back.

And was using it wildly, exultantly, and for a moment even the Green Man didn't have an answer to her.

Which gave the boys time to come up with an answer of sorts, to him. In truth, I suppose they hadn't just been standing there trying to make a physical shield between us, or trying to intimidate him – *him!* – with all their second-hand reputation, whatever the family names were worth. They must have been desperately thinking, maybe muttering to each other, what to try against him: this? or that?

Where we stood, though, it seemed like Desi bought them just that little moment of time, and they seized it. Or Jacey did, at least, securing his place in the roster, justifying every liberty he'd ever taken in the name of the Cathars.

Actually, I think he was just plain angry. He'd come here a playboy on an errand of mercy, to make things right for a girl he'd loved. He'd been spied on, compromised, betrayed, by a Power effectively working for his parents. He was young, he was strong, freshly come into his own proper strength; he'd never had any reason to train or restrain his temper, and he didn't find one now.

Instead, he just let fly.

Everything I've said about the Cathars as a family has been negative thus far. Yes? Cruel, arbitrary, greedy: the mafia of magic. To some extent – to a large extent – that's true of us all; the overworld is a hierarchy of blood and exploitation. It earns its name. The Cathars have no monopoly, only an epitome: they do it very well.

Jacey took a step forward, and where he stepped – no, just ahead of where he stepped, the floor ripped itself up and threw itself away.

It wasn't exactly a sprung-wood ballroom dance-floor, but Salomon must have paid a lot to have that floor laid in. Great boards of weathered oak: they lifted, tore and splintered, to show the concrete base that they'd been laid on.

That shattered in its turn, at a glance from his young lordship, the scion of an upstart clan. Shattered and rose like truth, pitching and tossing as though on a turbulent sea; some of those chunks of concrete were hurled up and out to either side, but most sank into what they churned among, a dark dank subsoil that bubbled up out of the pit that Jacey had wrenched open.

The smell of it was rank, like pond-life dragged up to the surface; and it lay between us and the Green Man like a bar, a ditch, a prohibition; and he laughed – he did, I heard it, some grim and frothy expression of a deathly glee – as he stepped forward into it.

And it curled around his feet, and made shift to climb his legs as though it had a life of its own, that tide-tossed earth, that mock-Gaia; and I don't think any of us had any doubts that at the same time he was sinking roots deep, deep into it, to tap into strength that was native to him and inaccessible to us and what in the world had Jacey been thinking, had he been thinking at all...?

AND THEN ASHER opened a gateway into Hell.

WHEN WE SAY that a Prince has the keys to the kingdom – well, we're not exactly joking. Latchkey kids, old-style: you reach your majority, you're assumed to be an adult, you get a housekey of your very own.

Those men, those smart boys who really didn't like each other very much at all: they must have worked this out between them, in not very much time on not very much information, a wing and a prayer and a hissing conversation, half glances and telepathy and trust.

It's never so far, between Hell and here. The two worlds are really quite cosy together, so far opposite that you only need to turn all the way around to find them side by side.

So: the monstrous, mind-shaking, inaudible noise of the great gates slamming back; a vanishing of shadows, as we stood abruptly in the hard light of Hell, all under the heat and weight of it; I wasn't the only one who yelled, though I'm damn sure Desi would deny it. Ash just threw his head back and howled, a wolf come home.

The Green Man screamed.

He threw his head back too, but not at all in the same way. It was an agony in him, a stiffening like a live body fallen into boiling water, except that the pain was all internal. There was a scorch and a scour to the air, but that was nothing; even my skin could tolerate that, even my shaved pink head could take it for a while, and he had bark to stand against it.

But he had his roots plunged deep; and while, yes, we were still in Salomon's in one sense, in one world, this was Hell too. His roots were buried in ash and rot, hot searing soils, and he was drinking what came oozing through them.

He was burning from the inside, a deathly corrosive acid in his veins. And he screamed, and his arms reached upward and his head turned the same way and all his free shoots writhed like knotted snakes about each other, and he'd never looked more like a tree if trees could be in torment.

I suppose, *in extremis*, you reach for what relief you can. Never mind the cost to yourself, to anyone. A drowning man drowns others, in his struggles towards land. Immortals, Powers, they're not so different.

Poisoned and panicking, the Green Man did the only thing that he could see, the only sure way to haul himself out of Hell.

All those whippy shoots came flying, but not for me this time and not for Desi. We were past that now, past bounty and benefit and betrayal.

All his shoots, all his strength, curled around my brother Asher. And some of them punctured him in the eyes and mouth, in the flesh; and whether they left their deadly little seeds there I don't know, we never learned, because it couldn't matter.

Other shoots coiled like cables around his neck and body, and they gave us no time to think, to understand, to respond.

They simply pulled him apart.

CHAPTER SIXTEEN

SOMETIMES YOU CAN only win by losing.

Dead already, Asher died again, and we fell out of Hell and its gates rocked monumentally shut behind us. And then it didn't need Jacey to hurl himself in a savage fury at the Green Man, inheritor of all his family's gifts, pureblood immortal giving everything he had. He did that, but it wasn't necessary.

Desi would have done the same, except that I had that rock-solid, agonising grip on her wrist again, and she wasn't going anywhere without me. Even with her Aspect on, full force, she couldn't break that grip. Drag me after, yes, she could do that; but then she couldn't fight. It only took a pace or two for her to understand that.

Besides, she wasn't needed either. Her rage, her vengeance, they were as redundant as Jacey's.

The Green Man knew what he had on his hands now, something hotter, darker, more precious than blood. He'd killed my father's son, my brother, and killed him for real, killed him dead. All Hell would be in mourning. And then – well, then the hounds of Hell would come hunting.

Had I thought myself sought, sought hard all these years? Did Desi fancy that she'd been looked for, urgently? All that running, that life of hiding from a brutal death, was nothing – a playground squabble, children screaming for each other in a game of hide-and-seek – next to what lay before the Green Man now.

He was gone, before Jacey could even reach him: gone with a wrench and a flurry of falling leaves, dragging himself out of the earth and into some semblance of human form that he could run in, trailing a moaning, shrieking cry of pain and loss as thin and hurt and as little human as himself.

Not even the gods might know what door he'd find at the top of the stairs, opening into what world: only that there would be no shelter there for him.

Jacey moved to follow nonetheless, hot in the hunt. Desi called him back, though, before he'd crossed that pit of broken earth, and – to my astonishment – he came.

WHICH LEFT THE three of us staring at each other in the half-dark, not a word, not a movement to share between us, only that fixity of purpose, not to look at what the Green Man had made of my brother.

IN THE END, of course, one of us had to do it.

In the end, of course, I couldn't let it be anyone but me.

* * *

I WENT TO him and, well, I gathered him together. Too much harm done here for even my parents to mend, but even so, they had to be told. I had to tell them.

I borrowed his mobile, one more time. Top of the speed-dial list, one button, our father.

"ASHER. YES."

"Uh, no, Dad. Not Ash."

A beat: then, *"Jordan?"*

"Yes, Dad."

"Goodness. How long has it been? You don't sound a day older."

"Don't. Don't joke."

Again, that beat, that brief silence while he caught up. Too bad; he'd probably prepared the funnies, ages back, in hopes of getting the chance to use them. No matter. He shrugged them off. "Jordan, has something happened?"

"Yes."

"To Asher?"

"I – yes," *but only because he stepped in to save us. Me.*

"Tell me."

"I can't. I'm sorry. Just, just come, will you? You and Mum together. We're at Salomon's. Ash is, Ash is here..."

AND THEN I hung up; and then I left his phone carefully beside my brother, not to have any of those handy, tempting numbers with me anymore; and then I left.

* * *

I JUST LEFT, up the stairs and out. Left Jacey, left Desi.
Left Ash.

It's what I do, what I've always done: I run away.

THE DOOR AT the top was just a door, hanging open,
broken-hinged. The street outside was just a street.
You'd think nothing had happened, except that the
door was bust.

DESI CAUGHT UP with me, halfway down the street.

For a while she just kept pace, shuttered and
protective behind the shield of her Aspect.

Then she said, "Where are you going?"

I shrugged. "Away."

"I thought you promised, at the end of this, you'd
go back to your family?"

"I promised Ash. He's dead." A voice in my head
said, *He always was dead*, but I managed to ignore it.

"So you're just going to let your parents find you
both gone, when they get here?"

"Desi. You know what they'll do to me."

"Yes."

"Do you want me to just sit and wait?"

A pause, a moment; then, "No. No, of course not."

Which was all either of us could find to say, about
any of that. After a while, I dug up a question, just
to break that impossible silence: "What did you do
with Jacey?"

"I left him. Obviously." Which led to a deal more
walking, before she said, "Jay?"

"What?"

"Do you want to come back with me?"

"Yes," I said, emphatically. "Yes, I do. Yes, please."

I THOUGHT SHE meant to go back to the boat, but I was wrong. Again.

It took me a while even to notice. I suppose I was just walking because walking was what was there to do, being with Desi because she let me do that too, and it took away any need to think. She could think for the pair of us.

Eventually, though, it sank in that we'd walked too far and in the wrong direction.

"Desi?"

"Mmm?"

"Where are you taking me?" She had her arm through mine by then, deliberately steering.

"You'll see, when we get there. Trust me."

WHAT ELSE WAS I going to do? I trusted her, I went with her. Paddington station, train; Twyford, another train. Henley.

By the time we got there, of course, it wasn't a surprise. The line didn't go anywhere else. That didn't mean I understood it, until she took me by the hand and led me down to the river, along the towpath, to the cottage where she moored her boat.

By the time we reached it, she had keys in hand, ready to let us in.

"I thought..."

"What?" There was a spark of amusement in her eyes, despite all the tensions and horrors of the day. "What did you think?"

Suddenly, I wasn't sure. That the cottage belonged

to her former master, probably, and all she had was permission to use the mooring. That could still be true, of course. She might have keys to the house, but no permission to use it.

I shook my head. "Never mind."

We were here; it was a roof, shelter. Somewhere to be. Tonight, that was enough.

OUTSIDE, IT WAS a Victorian cottage: small windows, pitched slate roof, porch above the door. Inside, it was a thoroughly contemporary, luxury riverside home. We walked on bleached wood floors, climbed an open spiral staircase to where a broad bed lay beckoning.

"I don't know about you," Desi said, "but what I reckon, a good hot shower and a nap would be best right now," and her hands were not so much leaving the question open as shoving it aside, already at work on my buttons, stripping me with a gentle swiftness that left me no decisions to make. I didn't even need to cooperate. "We can eat later, if we're hungry." If I ever wanted to eat again. Right now, it seemed unlikely: appetite was a forgotten thing, left behind somewhere on the other side of the river.

She was still steering: into the wet-room and under the shower, a blast of scalding water and strong hands working gel into my suddenly shivering skin. I ought at least to respond, to reply in kind, but I couldn't; both my hands were helpless suddenly, although only the one of them was hurting.

It didn't seem to matter. I was washed and dried, and so somehow was she; and we were walking back to that bed, and she was making me swallow pills before she let me lie down on it. And then there was softness and firmness together, and that was the bed;

and there was softness and firmness together, and that was Desi wrapping her arms around me, and I don't know if she was using her Aspect at all, it really made no difference because there was nowhere else in the world I wanted to be, and I knew I couldn't stay.

NUMBNESS AND PAIN. They both wore off, and there were tears and sleep at last, possibly even in that order.

AND LATER THERE was food, there was a bottle of wine that turned into a bottle of whisky, and I'm not sure how any of that happened, because I don't believe either one of us left the bed.

THERE WAS TALKING too, eventually, soft voices in the darkness; and I don't remember much but I do know I was quite insistent that I couldn't stay.

"They thought they had me and they've lost me again, and this time Asher too. Desi, they can't take that. This time they'll really come after me. The Green Man'll be nothing, next to who they'll set on my trail. I can't have you anywhere near me now. You're too close already, they'll be after you too. I'm sorry, but you do need to disappear again, and you can't do it with me. Two people are always easier to find."

"Don't worry about me," she said easily. "Tonight, don't worry about anything. Worry's for the morning. I'll set you on your road, with everything you need; and honestly, I'll be fine. You just lie back now – whoops! don't spill the whisky – and let everything go, this whole day, just let it go. Come the morning, we'll be fine..."

* * *

COME THE MORNING, I was anything but fine. Desi was brisk and efficient, though, just what I needed. She had me out of bed and back in the wet-room, this time neck-deep in frothy perfumed water, lying at full stretch in her slipper bath.

She said, "Sit up, make room. I'll shave your head for you, this one last time. You're all white velvet, and you won't like that."

She seemed to, running her fingers lightly over my scalp in a gesture of loss, of regret. Then her blade followed her touch, that clean, incisive edge leaving me smooth, reduced, anonymous again. Fit to run.

Then she climbed out of the tub and dried herself off quickly, while I wallowed, heat and comfort and sorrow sapping me of any will to move. I watched her instead until she left, waited until she came back, fully dressed, with the cut-throat razor still in her hand.

She sat on the edge of the bath and I felt her fingers one more time, sliding over the watered-silk smoothness of my shaven head. Then I felt the steel chill of her razor, sliding down the nape of my neck – and then one thing more, a sudden parting, a loss immeasurable.

Her hand moved to catch the amulet at my throat, before it could slip under the bubbles, under the water; she snatched it away with the thong that she'd cut, while I was still gaping up at her, still trying to understand.

She said, "Happy birthday, Jay," and kissed the top of my head there, where she'd shaved it. Then, "You can't run forever," my own words handed back to me by the girl I'd betrayed, as she walked to the door with my only protection like a trophy in her hand. "You don't want to live like that; and I've seen it now, and I don't want you to either. And you said yourself, it'll be worse, now that they've lost Ash. I can't let you do that. Or put them through it, either. They're your parents, and they've lost one son. You're all they've got now, and they need you. Be good to them." And she stepped out, and closed the door behind her.

I HEARD HER footsteps on the stairs, going down; and stayed where I was, because there was just nowhere else to go now.

The next thing I heard was two sets of footsteps coming up. One was light and dry, my father; the other slower and more measured, heavier, my mother come to claim me.